Praise for *The Law of Dreams*

"Peter Behrens is a highly gifted conjurer; the past he evokes is as mythic as it is historic, as seductive as it is nightmarishly, gorgeously real."
—HEIDI JULAVITS, author of *The Effect of Living Backwards*

"[*The Law of Dreams* is] not only sprawling, cinematic, exquisitely detailed, exactingly researched, and keenly felt, it's also a powerful work of excavation that achieves what historical fiction often can't—credibility, along with a sense of the transportive."
—Boston *Phoenix*

"This book is a beautifully written, poetically inspired tale of heroism, love, yes and sex, and the triumph of the human spirit over murderous greed. It's a long road that Behrens makes shorter with many a surprising turn. *The Law of Dreams* is one great book."
—MALACHY MCCOURT, author of *A Monk Swimming*

"Behrens has fashioned a beautiful idiom for his book, studded with slippery archaisms and mournful, musical refrains."
—*Newsday*

"Blending excruciating detail with the hopefulness of beauty, *The Law of Dreams* is a novel of struggle and fulfillment; of trust and the hollowness of betrayal. From a mountaintop in Ireland to the beckoning promise of America there are scenes that will remain, forever, imprinted upon the reader's mind. Peter Behrens is a tremendously talented writer."
—ALISTAIR MACLEOD, author of *No Great Mischief*

"I've been lost in the world of this book since page two. The story is beautifully made. The writing is stunning, like nothing you've read before except itself."
—BETH GUTCHEON, author of *More Than You Know*

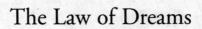

The Law of Dreams

THE LAW OF
DREAMS

A Novel

PETER BEHRENS

RANDOM HOUSE TRADE PAPERBACKS

New York

The author thanks the Blue Mountain Colony, the Canada Council for the Arts, the MacDowell Colony, the Ucross Foundation, the Virginia Center for Creative Arts, and Yaddo for their generous support. He also thanks Anne McClintock, without whose help this book would not have been written, and Sarah Burnes, who never gives up. *Beannacht.*

2007 Random House Trade Paperback Edition

Published in the United States by Random House Trade Paperbacks, an imprint of The Random House Publishing Group, a division of Random House, Inc., New York.

RANDOM HOUSE TRADE PAPERBACKS and colophon are trademarks of Random House, Inc.
READER'S CIRCLE and colophon are trademarks of Random House, Inc.

Originally published in hardcover in the United States by Steerforth Press in 2006.

ISBN 978-0-8129-7800-1

LIBRARY OF CONGRESS CATALOGING-IN-PUBLICATION DATA

Behrens, Peter, 1954—
The law of dreams : a novel / Peter Behrens.
         p.   cm.
ISBN 978-0-8129-7800-1
1. Ireland — History — Famine, 1845–1852 — Fiction.
2. Immigrants — New England — Fiction. I. Title.

PR9199.3.B3769L39 2007
813'.54—dc22   2007004343

Printed in the United States of America

www.thereaderscircle.com

246897531

For Basha Burwell

Again, traveler, you have come a long way led by that star.
But the kingdom of the wish is at the other end of the night.
May you fare well, compañero; let us journey together joyfully,
Living on catastrophe, eating the pure light.

Thomas McGrath, "Epitaph"

Éist le fuaim na habhainn, mar gheobhiadh tú bradán.
If you want to catch a salmon, listen to the river.

Prologue

The Irish Farmer, Perplexed

ALONG THE SCARIFF ROAD, heading northeast toward home, Farmer Carmichael rides his old red mare Sally through the wreck of Ireland. The cabins are roofless, abandoned. He encounters an ejected family at a crossroads and hands the woman a penny, for which she blesses him, while her children stare and her man, a hulk, squats on the grassy verge, head sunk between his knees.

Saddle creaking, still four miles from his farm, Carmichael rides along a straight, well-made highway, the pressure of changing weather popping in his ears and the old mare between his legs, solid and alive.

Owen Carmichael is a lean but well-proportioned man. All his parts fit together admirably. He wears a straw hat tied under his chin with a ribbon, a black coat weathered purple, and boots that once belonged to his father. His town clothes are in a snug bundle behind his saddle. Looking up, he sees clouds skirl the sky, but along the road the air is mild, with a slight breeze out of the west, and he has not been rained upon since he started this morning. He often watches the sky. It provides a vision of cleanliness, of possibility, of eternal peace.

Sensing a flicker in the mare's pace, he lowers his gaze. Studying ahead, he sees a pile of rags humped in the middle of the road.

The mare gets the stink first, begins to flare and whinny, then Carmichael sniffs death, sour and flagrant on the light wind.

He gives her rein and nips her with his heels, pushing the mare into a steady, purposeful canter. He steers her wide around the pile of flapping rags. There is a white forearm stiff upright and a fist and a crow perched boldly on the fist. More birds are hopping furtively in the grassy ditch . . . if he had a whip he would take a crack at them . . .

Upwind, the stench evaporates. Carmichael halts the mare, swings down. Clutching reins in one hand, he bends to pick up a stone. He takes aim and fires at the crow but the missile flies past its target, clatters on the metaled road. The bird hesitates then beats up into the air, cawing lazily, circling the corpse, and Carmichael.

Depressed, anxious, he remounts and continues homeward.

He has been to Ennis to see the agent who manages the affairs of his landlord, the sixth earl. Remembering the interview causes Carmichael's back to stiffen. He hates it all — the pettifogged transaction of legal business, the rites of tenantry, the paying of rent, the dead smell of ink.

He himself is a man for the country, for the scent of a field and the promising sky. He has the hands for the red mare, a strong-willed creature. He paid too much for her, twenty-five pounds, but it was long ago, and he has forgiven himself the debt.

He had been glad to get clear of Ennis, those awful streets pimpled with beggars. Wild men and listless women sheltered beneath every stable overhang, the women clutching infants that looked raw, fresh-peeled.

The fifth earl's sudden death, in Italy, of cholera, had revealed encumbrance and disarray, legacy of a profligate life. Now the affairs of the infant heir are being reorganized on extreme businesslike principles.

"Meat not corn. Beef and mutton is what does pay," the agent had explained. "That mountainy portion of yours — sheep will do nicely up there."

Flocks of sheep and herds of Scotch cattle were being imported.

"I have sixteen tenant families living up there," Carmichael protested.

"Too many. Can't be work for all of them."

"There isn't," Carmichael admitted.

"Get rid of 'em," the agent said briskly. "Ejection. That portion ought to be grazed. You'll have to graze, indeed, if you expect to meet your rent. Whatever sort of arrangement you have with them, it gives no right, no tenancy. You don't require the hands but two or three weeks in the year. You can get hands at wages and not have them settle. You'll have to move them off."

Carmichael has spent his life watching, coaxing mountainy people, and he knows them. The peasants are peaceful, in fact sluggish, if only they have their patch, their snug cabin, their turf fire. They breed like rabbits and content themselves with very little, but if you touch their land, attempt to turn them out, they get frantic and wild.

"If I throw them off they'll starve."

"And if there's blight they will starve anyway, sir! The only difference being, you shall starve with 'em, for you'll be paying the poor rates on every blessed head! No, no, rid yourself of the encumbrance. There's a military in this country, thank the Lord. If you've whiteboy troubles we'll set a pack of soldiers on them. Sheep, not people, is what you want to fatten. Mutton is worth hard money. Mutton is wanted, mutton is short. Of Irishmen there's an exceeding surplus."

A brass clock ticked on the mantelpiece. The ashes of yesterday's fire had not been swept from the grate. The agent had previously begged Carmichael's pardon to eat his dinner of bread and cheese. Crumbs of wheat bread on his desk. Waxy yellow cube of cheese.

Soldiers were no good. No protection on a lonely farm.

"Whoever ejects them — people like them, mountain people, cabin people — stands to get himself killed," Carmichael heard himself saying.

Was he afraid? Fear had always been his goad, a spur. He'd always thrown himself passionately at what he feared most.

"Oh dear," the agent drawled. "I was assuming you would be eager to incorporate the mountain to your —"

"It's shoulder bog," Carmichael said sharply. "Good for nothing but mountain men and their potatoes."

It wasn't fear, no. He wasn't afraid of whiteboys and outrages. It was a sense of hopelessness he felt. There were too many of them. He had always been too generous, granting too many conacre arrangements as his father had before him. Now there were dozens of wild people living up there toward Cappaghabaun, dug into the mountainy portions of the farm that they'd overrun. They'd woven themselves into his land like thistle.

"Sheep," the agent said. "Scotch cattle and sheep."

"I can't get 'em off." Carmichael heard the weakness in his own voice and it disgusted him. It reminded him of his own tenants, their various cadging pleas.

"Is there blight in your country?" the agent asked. "I heard there was. Is my information correct?"

"On the mountain they haven't lifted a crop yet. So it's too early to tell."

"But there is blight around Scariff, yes? Lands along the river, yes? Leaves standing black?"

"Yes." He'd seen it that morning.

"Then they will suffer it on the mountain," the agent declared with satisfaction. "There ain't no dodging. Without the praties, if they linger, they will starve. I tell you, one way or another you will be clear of those people. Overpopulation, sir, is the curse of this country."

And it is the truth.

ANOTHER MILE closer to home, and Carmichael finds himself riding alongside a turnip field. There is not a man in sight, but females in cloaks and little naked children are scattered across the flat field like a flock of seabirds blown off-course by the wind.

Owen Carmichael tries to fix his vision upon the straight, well-made highway. He tightens his knees and nudges the mare a little quicker. He will certainly be home in time for his dinner. Afterward he will inspect his early cornfields to determine if the crop is ripe for cutting.

Women close by the road straighten up from their scavenging to stare.

He has no cash and cannot meet the poor rates on paupers breeding like rabbits and overrunning his farm. No, he cannot possibly.

Ejection, ejection.

The agent's voice, flat as paper. "Any investment, Mr. Carmichael, must show a decent rate of return."

A woman calls out in a language Owen Carmichael has heard all his life but does not understand. Instead of ignoring her, he makes the mistake of turning his head, and instantly there are a dozen or more paupers closing in on the road, a tide of females with gray mud on their legs, holding up naked children screaming with hunger.

* * *

THAT EVENING, inspecting his field of ripening wheat, plucking a stalk and pressing the grains out onto his palm, he tastes one on his tongue. Cracks it between his teeth.

Then opens his hand.

Light and dry the pale grains are, wholly ripe, practically weightless.

In a second, the casual wind has swept them away.

PART I

The Mountain and the Farm

IRELAND, 1846

Eating Pain

HE WOULD SLIP FROM THE CABIN before the rest of them were awake
and come down the mountain, hoping to catch a glimpse of her. With his dog,
he'd course the slick, foggy slope, then down along the river and across
Carmichael's meadows. Feet brushing cold wet silver grass. Slipping the straw
rope off the fanatic dog, freeing her to nose under hedges, at dry burrows, her
tail swinging.

Approaching the farm, they'd pass Carmichael's rich black mountain of
manure and the stone haggard, crowded with hay.

The Carmichael farmyard was flanked by stone walls six feet high, built to
withstand — built for war. The only entrance an iron gate.

The yard was paved with blue stone. He had always distrusted the alien firmness of the stone on his heels. And the gaunt, whitewashed farmhouse eyeing
him so bitterly: the whitewashed face of disregard.

He had always felt deficient here. He had tried convincing himself he did not
but why else the constant self-argument, the tingle of thoughts inside his head
rising up like doves off a perch, fluttering and billing, all confusion?

He would come hoping to catch a glimpse of Phoebe Carmichael in the steel
light of morning, milk pail in her hand.

His old playmate. He had known her all his life, as he knew everyone.

Seeing him waiting at the gate, she'd offer him a drink.

— *You wouldn't get it any fresher.*

— *No, miss.*

He loved Phoebe's narrow pink feet on the blue stones. Her bare forearms, and the clean fabric of her gown and apron.

She was the only female of the Carmichaels. Her mother a consumptive, dead at twenty-nine and buried in the yard of the Presbyterian church at Mountshannon.

Setting the pail down on the cobbles, Phoebe took a blue china cup from a pocket of her apron and handed it to him.

Dipping the cup then raising it to his lips, he'd pause before tasting the milk.

— *Try some yourself, miss?*

— *No I will not, Fergus. But you go ahead.*

The milk scent sweet and cloudy. He'd drink in two swallows, warm and thick with fat, coating his teeth.

— *Thank you, miss.*

— *You're welcome.*

And every night he'd lie awake, in the cabin on the mountain, listening to his parents breathe. Phoebe became an ember in his mind, burning down through his thoughts, glowing. Could she feel what he felt? Did she lie awake in her father's house, thrilled with trouble, wishing for a tug on the warm red line connecting them?

HE HAD always lived on the mountain, his people tenants of Carmichael.

Farmer Carmichael who kept a red mare. Name of Sally. He'd purchased her for a hunter in a time when the strong farmers of the district had a fad for hunting and shared the expense of a pack of hounds.

Red, with a black mane. Not tall, but deep-chested, strong. Plenty of heart.

The first Carmichael in the country had been a bloody soldier. Protestants, English speakers, the Carmichaels held the farm as lease-holding tenants of the earl of Liskerry, the great landlord, *tiarna mór*. No one had ever seen *tiarna mór* himself, said to hold ground all over the country and live in Rome. Carmichael's subtenants lived in cabins on the mountain, each family with their cabin, their pig, their allotment of potato ground. In exchange the cabin people owed the farmer a certain measure of labor. Working in Carmichael's fields at harvest-time, they often would catch themselves staring at red Sally in the little pasture where she grazed. Some of them hated the big mare, and others felt a pride of connection. Telling themselves that Carmichael's Sally surely was the finest bounder in the country.

So sexual and easy, her ramblings in that little field.

Fergus relished the red mare. He used to creep into Carmichael's stable, climb into Sally's stall, and settle himself on her back. No one had ever caught him there. The stable — infused with scents of old hay, neat's-foot oil, corn — felt safe. It was warmer, drier, than any cabin on the mountain. He'd sit aboard the mare an hour or two, legs splayed out, fingers combing out her stiff mane.

He was fifteen before he attempted to ride her. Until then he hadn't felt the need of mastering anyone. Climbing aboard in secret — that had been enough. Then one afternoon, lying on the grass, head resting on one elbow, watching the lovely mare graze — her lips pulled back, blue gums and yellow teeth crop-ping grass blades — he suddenly felt that he must get aboard her and ride.

The feeling came on him suddenly, like a hunger pang.

He sat up and looked around, wary.

There was no one in sight. It was midsummer. A lull between hay cuts. The meadows were empty, silver sun rippling across.

He got up and approached the mare softly. At first she shied, but each time he renewed his steady discourse in Irish, speaking calmly, and at his fourth approach she let him catch hold, twisting his fingers in her mane, laying his cheek against her neck, smelling the sun's heat there.

He led her to the stone wall, climbed the wall, and swung a leg across. When he kicked lightly with his heels the mare ambled on the grass, pausing to sniff at a butterfly twitching through the poppies.

They slowly perambulated the little pasture. When Fergus knotted his fin-gers tighter in her mane and bunched with his knees, Sally broke into gorgeous canter.

He found it difficult to stay firmly seated, and began springing higher with every stride. Catching a sideways glimpse of Farmer Carmichael standing at the gate, Fergus lost his concentration. Relaxing his grip, he was pitched off her back, landing hard on hands and knees, stunned.

The mare shook herself, stopped, bent to munch. Looking up, Fergus saw Carmichael striding across the field toward him. The farmer wore an old black swallowtail coat, muddy boots, and a straw hat tied under his chin with a scrap of purple ribbon. He carried a blackthorn stick.

Wary of a beating, Fergus stood up hastily, looking around for a rock to defend himself with.

The mare rubbed her feet on the grass.

"The knees!" the farmer shouted. "She'll want a good strong grip! Comes from the knees!"

He had a brown, chiseled face. The inflexible lips of the English. Phoebe, his daughter, had the same lips. She liked to play-bite.

"Use your hands gentle, but keep your knees firmly. She will carry you like a cloud if you have the right hands and strong at the knees." He peered at Fergus. "You're Mike O'Brien's boy, yes? Grandson of old Feeny?"

Fergus nodded.

There was silence troubled only by curlews sputtering over, winging sharply toward the byre. Carmichael reached out and caught his mare, grabbing a fistful of her mane. Sally sniffed at his pockets, and the farmer dropped his stick in the grass.

"Let's see you aboard."

Fergus hesitated, unsure. At the same time angry. It was impossible to be around a farmer for very long and not feel the ancestral glow of tedious, unilluminating anger.

"Come, boy!" The farmer interlaced his fingers, making a footstep, insisting. "Quickly now!"

Better to be up above the farmer, looking down. Fergus stepped into Carmichael's hands and was instantly thrown up across Sally's warm back.

"Hold her steady, boy." Carmichael circled around, eyeing them keenly. "You're sitting like a plowboy. Straight back! Don't slump!"

Fergus let go of the mane and thrust his shoulders back.

"Don't use hands at all," the farmer instructed. "Only knees. Come now. At a walk. Step her along. There it is. There it is."

For half an hour Fergus walked then jogged the mare around the little field while Farmer Carmichael criticized his seat and called out instructions. "Feel her muscles working. Feel them slide, feel them knit. You'll never sit properly until you know your horse down to the bones. Loosen up and keep loose. Your knees are your voice with her. Your hands come later."

AS HE walked home that afternoon, up the mountain, four young men — one a cousin — stopped him on the path. Before a blow had been struck, while the cousin was still boiling up insults, calling Carmichael's mare *a sorry lump of leather*; *a bag of goat bones*; *a mustard fuck*, Fergus lowered his head and ran at him, butting him in the chest and knocking him down. Seizing a stick, he held off the others until his cousin stood up, grunting like a bull. Fergus threw away the stick and ran. They gave chase, screaming like a pack of hounds, and one of them finally brought him down with a brute shove that sent him sprawling.

He lay with nose pushed into the decaying leaves, his cousin's knee pressing in the small of his back.

"That girl's a goat-boned whore," the cousin whispered in his ear, giving his arm a twist. "Say it, Fergus. The little cunt Phoebe, your sweetheart, is nothing but a goat-boned whore."

But he would not. He never could bring himself to give in. He would eat his pain.

His cousin wrenched the arm back another inch so the joint was grinding on the rim of its socket.

Eating pain. It was a kind of food. Made you dizzy.

He was aware of the young men's raucous laughter. Sunlight splitting though the oaks. Moldy leaves scratching his eyebrow. Scent of turf.

Phoebe would smell like cold water or honey, or the black turf. When a turf bank was sliced open, the strongest, purest fragrance was available only if you got down on your knees, put your nose very close, and breathed it in. He always felt compelled to do so and the scent always spun him — clobbered his chest, strove at his heart so he felt his heart as a muscle working. Other turf cutters — men and boys kicking at their spades, constantly relighting their pipes — laughed at him kneeling on the ground, inhaling, losing himself. No one else felt such a need — or if they did, they stifled it.

He could barely hear the taunts. They seemed as distant as the crying of hawks on afternoons when he lay upon his back in the rough of some mountain pasture and listened to their hunting remarks, watching them floating on cushions of pure heat.

Phoebe Carmichael, neat and clean.

He let out a sigh, and his cousin must have realized the hopelessness of the situation, because he released the hostage arm and stood up quickly, kicking Fergus hard on the hip then stumbling away up the mountain with his companions.

Three barefoot boys howling a rebel song.

You could eat pain and come out alive. It was a silent meal. You could eat pain, even find a relish. You ate unhurried. You made certain to taste every bite. You could eat pain; it wouldn't kill you.

Mi an Ocrais

LATE SUMMER BEFORE the new potatoes were lifted was *mi an ocrais*, hungry month, when his father returned home to work on Carmichael's harvest.

The only season of the year his parents were reunited. His mother was red-eyed and weary in those few blazing weeks, before her man left once more. Together they drank *poitín*, which she would not touch the rest of the year. Everyone on the mountain was famished then — teeth glaring, eyes bright in sunburned faces.

His mother and father had gone off together just before Carmichael's harvest began, leaving Fergus to feed his little sisters on Indian meal porridge. When they returned, three days later, he knew from their sun-flayed appearance, from the grass in their hair and the scratches on his father's face, that they had been roaming, engaging, sleeping on grass, drinking *poitín*, living on butter and birds' eggs.

His mother caught him looking at her and must have sensed his anger and confusion. "Life burns hot, Fergus. Too hot."

He resented such willfulness, their capacity to abandon every responsibility, including their children.

"You think I'm a robber," his father, Mícheál, told him.

They had been standing in Carmichael's best field of wheat, *the rosy field*, whetting their blades. People on the mountain had names for each corner of Carmichael's farm. Their language knew that land like a bee knows a flower.

Fergus's mother insisted that the rosy field had been red once in flowers.
Mícheál said, "In blood."

The rosy field. The black field. The field of the altar. Carmichaels did not use
the names, perhaps were unaware they existed.

Mícheál could whet a blade like no one else could. Whet to pure sharpness,
to an edge like a spoken word, barely there. And he cut and mowed faster and
cleaner than anyone else could on the farm.

"You are a grim fellow. You look at me like I've stolen something," Mícheál
said, testing the hone by scaling his thumbnail and peeling back the thinnest
film of tissue.

They owned nothing, certainly not the harvest tools. The iron blades and
wooden handles belonged to the farmer, to Carmichael.

Little girls scampered like mice over the wheat stubble, gathering stalks in
armfuls and setting them down in stand-up sheaves. Women forked the stand-
ups into an oxcart driven by Phoebe's brother Saul.

Mícheál was still the strongest hand for harvest, but Fergus would surpass
him eventually. Not this year. Next year, perhaps. Insects cackled as they worked
through the crop, feeling the sun's stare on the back of their necks. Friction of
grain dust made red the creases inside their elbows.

When Farmer Carmichael came out to see how the cut progressed, he spoke
to Mícheál in English, and Fergus felt the grit of that language washing over
him, scraping and stimulating; the language that poured out of Phoebe's
mouth. Wanting to feel closer to her, he kept fitting his thoughts in English as
he worked up and down the rows alongside Mícheál and the others, swinging
and cutting, swinging and cutting, though English words — or none he knew
— didn't suit such work. Not really.

After the harvest was made, Mícheál would leave them again. Going for the
north, traveling with a gang of barn builders, wall builders, going up into
Ulster, sometimes so far as Scotland, and not returning before the next August,
when he'd show up at harvest once more. Mícheál rarely spoke of his life on the
roads, but Fergus had imagined it anyway: new barns and fresh walls. Stone
towns and salmon rivers. Fat fields of horses grazing.

In another week or two Mícheál would be leaving.

"You're no good," Fergus said when they stopped at the end of another row and were sharpening again. "You're never here. I can't call you my father. You're no good for us."

Mícheál shook his head. "You're such a farmer. You're too stuck to that ground of yours."

"Someone has to be."

HIS GROUND.

Carmichael dispensed potato ground in patches, annual arrangements, and no one ever had the same patch twice; but Fergus always felt his ground was his. Once he had his crop in, the patch belonged to him, and he'd kill or die for it.

He could raise enough potatoes on a quarter acre of well-dug beds to keep his mother and sisters through the year — nearly. In those last, blazing weeks of late summer, just before the new crop was lifted, they had to survive on yellow meal — but his potatoes yielded at least ten months of perfect nourishment. The only tool needed to cultivate them was a spade to open the lazy-beds and turn and chop the soil a little. No plow, no horse. To his regret he could not keep a horse on mountain grass. A horse would not stand it, and any plow would burst between the rocks.

Each spring he spaded his beds and laid the sets. Summer they came up in green stems and beautiful, viney flowers. The pig was kept on potato scraps and sold to pay the annual rent — they never tasted the meat. He himself consumed five pounds of potatoes every day, steamed, boiled, or mashed. Over the winter, his mother might make a *kitchen*, using salt and a few herrings, but usually it was potatoes plain, and he never tired of that food.

Potatoes were not *made* or *cut*, like the farmer's hay or corn; they were *lifted*, joyfully, the surprise of the world.

Phytophthora infestans

THE LAST NIGHT OF CARMICHAEL's harvest they burned off the straw and the farmer fed his cabin people a supper — ham and butter, wheat bread and apples — on the side of his best meadow, under oaks, wind ringing through their branches. It was dark before the tenants started back up the mountain. Fergus walked ahead of his parents, who were carrying the little girls, asleep. The night was warm.

They had passed the first cluster of cabins when he first caught the stink of putrefaction, physical and wild, rolling down the mountain path with all the violence of a loose cartwheel or a drunk with a club. "What is that terrible stink, my God?" his mother cried. "They've been tearing the graves!"

Unbaptized infants were buried under stones so dogs could not get at them. The piles of stones were sometimes shifted from one grave to another too early, and the dead left unprotected — but this wasn't that smell. It was too large.

Men and women galloped past him on the path, snorting like ponies, but Fergus made himself keep to a steady pace.

There had been blight in the district the year before, but restricted to lands along the river. They had not suffered blight on the mountain. And his plot, this year, was good sharp limestone ground, well drained, the safest. Farmer Carmichael did not like his cabin people planting any plot of ground more than one season, fearing they would grow too attached to it and forget that it was his land, not their own.

Through the darkness, Fergus could see people reaching their plots, falling on their knees, and scrabbling at the soil with their fingertips. Unable to restrain himself any longer, he broke into a run with Mícheál galloping after him, carrying in his arms one of the little girls, howling with delight.

Reaching his plot, Fergus immediately saw that his plants, healthy and green that morning, were withered and black. Falling on his knees, he pulled one up, then another and another. The potatoes clinging to the roots were shriveled and wet. He dug up every plant in the row and the potatoes were nothing, purple balls of poison, and he heard neighbors' screams floating in the dark.

Tumbling

TEN WEEKS LATER his people were the only ones left upon the mountain.

All the other cabin tenants had accepted the quit fee Farmer Carmichael offered and had gone to the workhouse to submit themselves. Or had gone on the roads, begging. Or were trying the public works: breaking rocks at sixpence a day, living under hedges and in scalps and burrows dug in along the edges of public roads. Narrow and grassy, those road verges — *Ireland's long meadow* — were the only lands in the country, apparently, that didn't quite belong to one farmer or another.

Anyway, the neighbors and relations had disappeared. Weakened by hunger and black fever, they'd been easily removed, like shavings swept off a table.

The abandoned cabins were being torched. The farmer and his two sons — black Abner and sandy Saul — were lighting the roofs of straw and turf using oily, smelly torches. Then they knocked down the walls one by one, swinging a thick timber ram with an iron head. The cabins were reduced to rubble left in ungainly humps. Some of it the Carmichael boys picked over, chipped, cleaned, and left aside to be built into the farm's future — fresh walls, footings, new chimneys.

Fergus watched Phoebe's brothers knock down a dozen cabins. Sometimes he worked with them in exchange for food. A wheat roll with butter slapped on. Piece of cold mutton. Cheese. An apple.

They called it *tumbling.*

* * *

ONLY HIS father, Mícheál, who had been traveling all his life, refused to quit the mountain. Farmer Carmichael rode up to the cabin and offered more money and still he refused.

Fergus sat on a stool outside the cabin watching the farmer aboard his red mare confront Mícheál, leaning on a stick.

"Do you know, Mick, you are trying me very hard, indeed you are. Don't think I don't con what you are trying by starving yourselves. You hope to exploit a Christian conscience by having your own family suffer needlessly."

"I only know what the roads are like, master."

"You can't stay here."

"We can't leave, master. You know yourself what will become of us if we quit."

Mícheál said the word *master* like it was something you'd throw out with dirty water. Carmichael sat up straighter and Fergus noticed the old-fashioned bell gun, with its flared brass barrel, strapped awkwardly to his saddle.

There had been outrages on the other estates in the district. Landlords' agents had been attacked and beaten by whiteboy gangs.

All Carmichaels believed the land belonged to them. Fergus remembered Phoebe long ago, when they were eight or nine — playmates — insisting that her father held the farm after her grandfather who held it after his father who held it after his, who had defended it against the warrior tribes with painted faces, wild cattle, wicked paganry.

Not the story he knew, but it was a story.

"And what exactly is the wicked paganry, Pheeb?"

"Oh they muck about," nine-year-old Phoebe had airily replied.

"Muck about how?"

Both of them fascinated by crime, cruelty, disaster, mishaps, freaks of nature, curses, evil eyes, poison cooks, and all aspects of evil and degeneracy.

"Terrible devices. Cut your mizzle off and pickle it. Make a soup of your ears. The priests sang like sheep. They'd roast a book in the fire, use the ashes for salt. Steal babies. There are still pagans alive in the hills."

"Are there?"

"Oh yes."

"Never have I seen them."

"You must know how to look. Rebels and swingboys, whiteboys. *Goffers*" — her word for people they didn't know, though they knew almost everyone. "Boys with bloody hands."

Mizzle had been their word for prick in those days, when they were small; his had been the frequent object of curiosity. And language too, in those days, had been most thrilling — exercising, strenuous; a net you threw to capture what you didn't know.

Tenants spoke English in Carmichael's neat fields along the river and anywhere there ran a good road. The same men and women would speak Irish on the mountain, on the rough, or when handling cattle.

"You've no right to stay." Carmichael sat neatly on the mare — back straight, heels forward — his face a brown map of impatience. "Don't put me in a position, Mick. I've been more than fair."

Mícheál leaned deeper on his stick. "Here we are, and here we'll stay."

"There are the dragoons, you know, at Portumna — I suppose I could have you taken up and sentenced for trespass. How should your wife and children manage then? Don't make me come up here again, I warn you, Mick. Two pounds — that is the last offer you'll have, and it makes my hair turn to pay you so much."

Mícheál gave a slight shake of his head. Carmichael grunted impatiently and wheeled his mare. Fergus watched as horse and rider began deftly picking their way down the mountain.

Mícheál said, "What do you say, Fergus? Is your father in the right?"

"There'll be nothing left to eat soon."

"It's the same everywhere, though. Your mother and the girls wouldn't survive the roads."

"So you want us to stay. What for?"

"I can't give in to that fellow," Mícheál said. "I just can't. Perhaps I ought to but I cannot. It isn't in me, somehow. After I'm dead, you must do what you must."

Biting at the Grave

A WEEK AFTER CARMICHAEL'S VISIT, Fergus awakened one morning with a bitter taste of iron and salts on his tongue. He shared the sleeping loft with his two younger sisters who had started losing the hair on their heads while a black fur — hunger fur — sprouted on their foreheads and cheeks and the backs of their hands.

It was difficult to fall asleep, and more difficult to awaken. He felt thick and dull. Raising arms to pull on a shirt was an effort. When he went outside, his piss was mustard yellow, fizzing and foaming before sinking slowly in the ground. He hadn't noticed any hair falling out, perhaps on account of the bites he'd earned tumbling with the Carmichael boys, but he hadn't strength for tumbling now. Anyway the farmer had discovered what his sons were doing and forbidden them passing along any food.

None of the others was awake when he started down the mountain with his dog. Coursing for badger. Past the wrecks of cabins in little hamlets. Humps of rubble, the stink of moldy thatch. Where were those people now?

Badger was good meat, fried up and salty. It had been a wet night, but now the sun was driving light into the sky. Nosing the old holes and burrows, the dog found no trace, nothing that interested her. They worked the slope and finally came down along the river, coursing the bank for a while looking for the otter burrows, finding none. He had never heard of anyone eating otter. Finally he slipped the rope on her and crossed Carmichael's meadow, moving closer to the farm.

In the old days, the farm dogs — *weezers*, Phoebe called them — used to come running at strangers or tenants approaching the yard. Pink tongues out, paws slashing the stones, barking and howling at intruders.

Carmichael had gotten rid of the mastiffs the year before, after one of them had attacked Phoebe and bit her on the heel.

She had shot the dogs herself, after her father placed his gun in her hands.

Approaching the farm slowly, peering through the gate, he saw no sign of her though the kitchen chimney was smoking. He coursed the dog up along the road for a while then turned and walked by the farm again. This time as he passed the gate she was hurrying across the farmyard, steel pail in her hand.

He didn't call out, didn't step into the yard, but she saw him and came over. Her feet in slippers now that it was winter. Thick cowhide pampoots. Fresh linen apron.

"You'll try a taste of milk, Fergus?"

"Yes."

"You couldn't get it any fresher."

"No, miss."

Their ritual played out. Setting the steel pail down on the cobblestones, she took a cup from her apron and handed it to him.

"Try a taste yourself, miss?"

"I will not. But you go ahead."

The sweet fat taste of cow's milk.

"Thank you, miss."

Instead of taking the cup back, she looked him up and down, hands on her hips. "Does he treat you fair, do you think?"

"Who?"

"My father, who else?"

"He's a stiff old goner. Likes his way."

"That's what he says of your father, more or less."

"It's not true." Though perhaps it was. But his father's stubbornness wasn't driving people to their deaths. Or perhaps it was.

"What will happen to you?" she asked.

He shook his head.

"Listen to me. Two pounds, Fergus, that's more than fair. You'd better take it and take your mother and the little girls. You've never had near so much before. What do you see from selling a pig? — very little I expect. Take the fee, and go for Ennis or Limerick, you can surely find something there. Your father is biting at the grave to shame us, but it's himself that's shamed. Think of your poor mother and the girls. You know this is the truth."

"Can't leave."

"Don't say so. Of course you can. You must. Your father left every year, didn't he?"

"He always came back. If we leave now, we'll never come back."

"I believe," she said slowly, "you had better take the going-away *shee*" — using their old private word for money. "Tell your old fellow he must. He won't squeeze any more from Father, and if he don't quit —"

"Dagger the money. It isn't money, it never was."

Taking the blue china cup from his hands, Phoebe reached down to pick up the milk pail.

Phoebe Carmichael had always been perfect as far as he was concerned. Distinct mind like a polished ax. The two of them, babies in baskets left under swaying trees, alongside a meadow. Wind sweeping through high grass with a sound like bedsheets tearing.

It's funny when you're dying and never have been with a girl.

He watched her backing away, then turning, fleeing from him across the paved farmyard. Fleeing slowly, lugging the steel pail with both hands.

He watched her disappear into the farmhouse with its glass windows and slate roof gleaming in the fresh wet of the morning.

He turned, started back up the mountain. There seemed nowhere else to go. He felt extremely lonely. It seemed as if Phoebe had been his last hold on life. Later that morning on the upper slopes his hungry dog caught a scent and ran off howling, and he never did see her again.

THEY ATE sparrows, songbirds. His mother pleaded with his father to quit, but he would not. He had been leaving all his life and now he wouldn't.

Exactly why, Fergus could not say. A feeling in the blood. Perhaps he shared it. Perhaps they had something in common after all.

They finished what was left of the yellow meal and lasted another two weeks on stirabout, mostly water, with wild herbs and nettles boiled soft. They gradually lost the strength needed to snare and trap small game and spent more of each day in bed.

Carmichael kept away. Fergus did not go down to the farm again or see Phoebe. He was just strong enough to tend the fire, feeding it little parcels of turf. His father had stopped speaking. Then his mother. They lay glassy-eyed in their bed.

They saw no dragoons. The little girls lay in the loft mewing like cats. Their bed straw grew filthy, and Fergus hadn't strength to change it. One afternoon he spent hours — or maybe it was just a few moments — watching a spider scuttle in and out of the fire.

WITH A little water, dying will last a long time.

It was black fever in the end. Typhus.

The first sign a raging headache. He understood what it meant. While it was still possible to think more or less clearly he made himself smoor the fire, carefully, so it would burn as long as possible. If it went out, there was no possibility of lighting it again. Then he climbed into the sleeping loft, lay down on the straw, slept and dreamed. He could always stir up Phoebe in his dreams. In his dreams that girl came up out of herself with enthusiasm deep and furious. It was her gift.

Ejection

HE AWOKE TO THE SCENT of a soldier.

Grease, gunpowder. The polish applied to brass.

Pungent and complex, the scent filtered into his brain and startled his stomach, which drenched itself with acid that rose, scorching his throat, and made him cough. The cough blew him awake.

His eyelids were glued with crust, and it hurt tearing them open. He lay on a pallet in the sleeping loft of the cabin, his two sisters beside him. His skin felt stiff, but the sores on his arms and legs appeared to be healing. The air was hazy with smoke from the fire he had smoored hours, or days, earlier, just before giving himself up to the fever.

Peering down from the loft, he could see the soldier standing just inside the door.

Fergus sat up suddenly, and the soldier yelped in fear and started backing out. The tip of his bayonet caught the cowhide flap in the doorway and he cursed, jerked it free, and disappeared.

Fergus looked at his sisters lying beside him on the straw.

The dead were always powerfully still, a fixity that could never be mimed.

One summer, following cattle up on the booley, the mountain pasture, he had spent much of an afternoon staring at a dead fox, entranced by something he could not name. Dead shapes had a passion.

Living on milk, charlock, and yellow meal, a herd saw no one for weeks, and the solitude up there had been tangible and exciting; the world presented itself like a fresh thing. Wandering bracken slopes and shoulder bogs, he had observed the rippling mountain ranges the way a bird might view them, lumps of emptiness swallowed whole, July sunshine rifling patterns of light on the hills.

He heard a horse scuffling outside, and men's voices.

The smoke inside the cabin was laced with the woody aroma of typhus. Peering from the loft, he could see his parents in their bed near the fire, but he could not tell if they were alive or dead. He shut his eyes.

He was alive himself. Certainly, he was.

Crawling to the ladder, he eased down the rungs and approached their bed, where they lay in filth. He studied his father's face. Bone knobs glistening under waxy yellow skin. The eyes suddenly snapped open, violet and sensitive, like hungry birds, starlings.

"Soldiers outside," Fergus whispered. "What shall I do?"

The eyes flapped shut.

"What shall I do?" he repeated. His mother raised her head and looked about the cabin wildly. "Water," she whispered, then her head fell back upon the straw.

He stared at the doorway. Had he really seen a soldier? Was it just a fever dream? Perhaps the world was dead.

He should go outside, see for himself.

Walk outside. That is what you do in dreams. The law of dreams is, keep moving.

Soldiers

"THAT'S ONE!" Farmer Carmichael cried. "What of the others?"

The soldier who had been inside the cabin was bent over, vomiting on the snow. Straightening, he wiped his mouth on his sleeve. "All dead," he gasped.

"Quite sure?" called an officer mounted on a beautiful limber horse.

"Dead as rabbits."

"I warned O'Brien he must quit." Carmichael spoke loudly. "I did warn him there'd be nothing for him if he stayed."

"Better have a look yourself," the officer said.

The farmer approached the cabin, the icy puddles crackling under his heels. Pushing Fergus aside, he slipped through the leather curtain and went inside. Smoke leaked out from the doorway, curdling in the bright air.

Stung by daylight, eyes aching, Fergus buried his face in his hands.

A few moments later Carmichael, coughing, emerged from the cabin. Seizing Fergus's shoulders, the farmer shook him roughly. "Two pounds the fellow was offered!" Carmichael shouted to the officer. "Desperate, morose, wild fellow! All his life worthless! Always on the roads!"

"Well, he was a strong hand at harvest, though, he was," Abner Carmichael said softly.

"Do you suppose I enjoy this work?" the farmer cried.

Fergus's attention was concentrated on a biscuit that one of the soldiers was munching. Seeing him staring, the soldier broke it and held out half. Twisting free of Carmichael, Fergus stumbled toward the soldier and grabbed the chunk, but when he tried to bite into it, it was too hard, and his gums were too tender. He began licking to soften it, then broke off a small piece and put it in his mouth, sucking.

He turned around just in time to see Carmichael's two sons touch the cabin roof with their torches. There was a thin layer of snow, but the scraws of turf underneath had a ferocious appetite to burn. The horse whickered at the flow of red sparks, and Fergus felt the officer staring at him. Something in the officer's face — pity, disgust — pierced his stupor. He gave a howl and barged toward the cabin, but Saul and Abner intercepted him easily. "Let her burn now." Abner's kind, moony face closed on his. "It's all for the best, Fergus. There's no life in it."

He was unable to resist another nibble at the biscuit. Thinking he had surrendered, Abner and Saul released him. He instantly broke from them, dashing for the cabin door. He heard the officer shout but got inside before anyone could catch him. Strings of fire drooped from the roof. Embers stung his neck. He tried to reach the ladder for the loft but couldn't find it in the smoke. Burning scraws of turf were falling everywhere. His parents' bed was ablaze — he saw their arms lifting up, flames shooting between his father's legs. Fergus tried dragging him from the bed while the fire pecked his hands fiercely. His father's clothes were alight, his eyes were open, wide and white; his mouth was open, a hole. A burning scraw of turf dropped onto Fergus's neck. He let go of his father and wriggled and danced trying to shake the fire off himself. Now it was so hot he felt himself breathing fire. The smoke clawed at his eyes and he couldn't see. Blind and wheezing and scratched by fire, his body stumbled for the doorway. The moment he was outside, someone knocked him down then threw a horse blanket over him to smother his burning clothes.

Shrouded under the rough wool he lay thinking this was death — this was how it felt. A weird remove. A sense of distance, and vivid pain stinging in the hands.

Death smelled strongly of horse.

Then Abner Carmichael snatched the blanket away, pulled him to his feet, and wrapped the blanket about his shoulders. "There you are, old man, there you are."

The soldier who had offered the biscuit was facing the cabin, holding out his palms to feel the heat. The officer had dismounted and was standing with his back to the fire, adjusting girth straps on his horse.

Saul and his father stood holding the iron-tipped ram, ready to tumble the walls.

Fergus watched the roof crumbling as it burned. In a few moments it collapsed entirely, and the cabin was a white cup holding nothing but flame.

Succor?

HE STUMBLED DOWN the path after the men, clutching the horse blanket, unsure if he was their prisoner. They ignored him; perhaps they were ashamed. They had biscuit, so he followed.

As they came into the farmyard he looked about for Phoebe but saw no sign of her. Carmichael, his two sons, and the officer disappeared inside the house. The soldiers headed for the stable. Clutching his blanket, ignored, Fergus finally stumbled after them.

Where was Phoebe while her men were tumbling? What kept her busy? Where did she hide?

In the stable, the soldiers stacked muskets, unbuckled their white cross-straps, and shrugged off their knapsacks and ammunition boxes. The sergeant handed him a biscuit, then allowed him a swallow of fiery *poitin* from a clay jar.

The old mare, disturbed by the presence of strangers, was fussing in her stall.

The soldiers settled down to filling and lighting their clay pipes. They continued to ignore him as if he were a ghost and they could not see him. Perhaps he *was* in a dream. Or perhaps he was a ghost; perhaps he was dead already. How would you know if you were dead? He finished the biscuit quickly and licked the crumbs from his hands. The old mare would know.

Approaching her stall, he started whispering to her, then stroking her nose. It seemed to settle her, so he must be alive still. Her warm, sweet breath clouded his face. He felt tears dribbling down his cheeks. Climbing one side of the stall, he settled himself aboard her, legs astride. Leaning forward, letting his arms fall down either side, he lay on her neck, absorbing her heat.

"Fergus? Is Fergus here?"

Startled, he looked up and saw Phoebe at the stable door.

"Miss, if that is the name," the sergeant said, pointing at Fergus. "The creature found in the paddywhack."

He gripped the mare with his knees, knotting fingers in her mane as Phoebe approached.

"Come with me, Fergus."

"I'm sick, I'm dazzled."

"I'll give you something to eat."

"They are all dead, the cabin is tumbled, no one is buried, they are burned."

Phoebe was looking at him blankly.

This is the way it is in dreams. You speak and cannot be heard.

Then he realized he was speaking Irish, which the Carmichaels did not have, not even Phoebe. He sat on the mare, dumb, staring at her.

"Come inside, it's all right," she said. "I promise."

Something inside him gave way and he started weeping.

Reaching up, Phoebe touched his leg. "Oh don't you, Fergus! Can you eat, do you think? Come inside, I'll give you a cup of broth and some of our bread." She touched his hand.

"You be careful of that wild creature, miss," the sergeant warned.

SHE CROSSED the farmyard, and he stumbled after her. She had nothing to say. Her clean clothes; her brown hair smelling of light. She knew she was going to live a long time, marry a farmer's son, have sons of her own. Fergus was going to die soon, and that was the difference between them. When they came to the kitchen door she pushed it open then took his elbow, pulling him inside. The door boomed shut behind him. He was standing on warm flags in the farmhouse kitchen, a large room with low beams and a tin-plated range throwing heat that smashed into his chest painfully, as though the last thing he'd been keeping safe had been broken into.

Your soul lived in your chest, did it not.

The fish-faced officer looked up from the table, where he and Phoebe's brothers had been eating ham and cheese on toast and drinking porter. Farmer Carmichael who had been scribbling on a scrap of paper looked up, surprise on his face, sour as cheese.

"What do you suppose you are doing, Pheeb?" her brother Saul demanded.

"He must be fed. Look at him!"

"They were fever cases up there, Pheeb. He wants keeping outside, or we'll catch it."

"I shall give him something to eat first."

The tin-plated range was throwing wild heat. Fergus, light-headed, could feel himself starting to sway. If he fell down now he knew he would die here on the kitchen floor, in front of them.

Phoebe looked around and saw him stagger. "Fergus, sit down. Look at you, boy. Oh look at you." She guided him to a three-legged stool and pushed him until he sat down.

"It was their choice to stay, it was," her brother Saul was saying.

"Well, whatever it was, it's done now," said Phoebe. "Listen up, old Fergus, sweetheart. We must put some nourish in you. They are going to take you away, you see. Abner is taking you in the cart. You'll need a little strength, won't you?"

He was powerless. All he could do to hurt them was die in their kitchen, and he wasn't ready to die.

There was a red ham in a pan on top of the range. Stropping a knife, Phoebe briskly cut off a slice, sawed two cuts of wheat bread, and gave him the food. He took it and could feel the salt swelling up his lips as he chewed.

Carmichael at the table was back at writing, steel nib scratching the paper.

"They'll have to admit him to Scariff workhouse," Carmichael said to the officer. "I pay the poor rates after all, and they're a burden. He'll be cared for, they'll feed him."

Crouching on the stool, Fergus ate furtively from his hands, feeling heat exploding off the range and soaking into him like something dangerous.

"There, you see, you'll be all right," Phoebe said. "I'll come to visit you."

He watched her carry more bread and butter to the men at table and refill their noggins from the jug of porter. The room was quiet except for the click of the fire and the scrape of knives on plates and the slap of liquid pouring. He knew she was lying. It stung her to have to look at him; she wanted him away, perhaps more than any of them did.

Fergus wolfed his food. She was feeding him up for the road.

Abner Carmichael went out to harness the donkey to the cart while Fergus continued to eat his bread and ham like it was dream, like it was his old life he was consuming. He could hear Phoebe's other brother, Saul, laughing hoarsely at some joke the officer made.

Phoebe, making up a little parcel of food, kept her back to Fergus.

The food had warmed him up inside, and his brain was moving. When Abner came into the house saying the cart was ready, Fergus understood this was ejection. They were ejecting him. The Carmichaels had won.

Phoebe stood in front of a window, with light pouring through her hair. She was smiling as she made some remark to the officer then took a dainty sip of porter from a cup.

You look at a girl, and see she isn't your girl, and understand she never will be no matter how much you want her. You grasp that, finally. Awareness pierces the chest like a spike being driven in. The world doesn't belong to you. Perhaps you belong to the world, but that's another matter.

Still, when it came time to go, he didn't go easy — he felt he owed his father, Mícheál, that much. He grabbed an iron pan off the stovetop and pitched it at Saul's head and grasped a hot stove handle and threw it at Abner and was trying to seize one of the kitchen knives when Saul and the officer knocked him down and held him on the floor writhing while Abner wrapped up his ankles and wrists with yellow twine.

"Hold steady, boy, we don't wish to harm you now. Hold steady."

Such lies, he thought.

Phoebe was nowhere in his field of vision as he was hung over Abner's shoulder like a trussed boar. Perhaps she had left the room. Perhaps she ran upstairs, threw herself on her bed, and covered her ears with pillows so she wouldn't hear his protests as Abner was lugging him from the house. Perhaps she lay very still the way her mother, trying to avoid another rack of coughing, had kept perfectly still on her deathbed, like an animal hopelessly caught in the jaws of another, larger, animal.

He was weeping, shouting *You're not my girl! You're not my girl!* as he was carried out, and it was Irish anyway, and none of them would understand.

Abner laid him in the cart very gently then climbed in over him. Taking up the reins, Abner clicked his tongue and the donkey started off, iron shoes clicking across the cobbles then out through the iron gate. And that was the end of the old life, dream life, Phoebe life, life of the mountain.

PART II

Bog Boy

IRELAND, NOVEMBER 1846

Workhouse

AFTER A WHILE ABNER STOPPED the cart and unbound him, and he sat with his legs dangling from the back as they continued along the road. He could smell the lard that greased the wheel hubs.

The company of soldiers following on foot.

With every jolt from the road, his legs flew up, kicking. He considered jumping down, scrambling over the nearest wall, fleeing across the field. Finding his way back up the mountain. Perhaps the soldiers would shoot, but he doubted it. Perhaps they would chase him. But probably soldiers would not like leaving the dry road to muddy their boots. Which they must clean and rub constantly, he'd heard, or be constantly beaten.

What did soldiers care for a tenant on the loose? It wouldn't mean any more to them than a hare. Probably less. Not worth a scramble. Not worth a bullet. Abner had untied him, after all, and might stand to let him go. He had strength to get himself over the nearest wall, but probably not much farther. He knew that if he lay down in a field he'd stop breathing. And he didn't wish to die there, with magpies pecking at his eyes.

So he stayed on the cart.

Abner passed him his fuming pipe. Fergus held the warm clay bowl in his paws and puffed and watched the company of soldiers veering off at the crossroads.

A dab of wild scarlet moving into the glen, disappearing.

Sunlight beckoned, then rain swept in.

The pipe went out as they were crossing a bog that was split with precisely cut trenches where the turf had been excised, and Abner had nothing to light it with. The donkey trotted on, passing isolated cabins and potato plots where leaves and stalks lay smashed on the ground.

Mother and father, dead. Sisters, dead. You feel very light: floating. Not much attaching you to the world it seems.

Cramps, in the belly, stiff with gas.

Entering Scariff, the road became a street lined with ruined cabins. He had visited the town every year, come to the fair to sell the pig, and it had always seemed exciting — threatening, hurrying — but now it was dead.

Roofs burned out, one after another. Abandoned cabins stared at one another across the road.

Scariff stank of the moldy thatch that was left, too wet to burn.

Beggars standing outside the iron gate of the workhouse were cawing like crows as Abner drew up the cart.

"Now, Fergus, it's the Poor Law Union, you know. The workhouse."

Fergus unwilling to open his mouth.

You guard what you have when it's nothing.

Emptiness, silence.

"Very good establishment they say it is, and you must do as they tell you." Abner was pulling him off the back of the cart. "They'll feed you and take care of you, never fear."

The other son, Saul, had always had a jeering tendency, but Abner was usually kind, and good at working cattle. Cattle could not be worked by anyone who hated them or feared them or did not comprehend their sensitivity.

You could have been cattle, or a horse. Or a rabbit. Fox, badger. Anything that lived on the mountain. A stone, a piece of turf, white root of a mustard plant.

The beggars outside, some clutching children, were hoping to be admitted to the workhouse, but they cleared the way respectfully for the farmer's son to approach the iron gate.

There was a porter's lodge just inside. The workhouse itself was a handsome stone building with a courtyard. Fergus felt Abner's grip on his arm holding him down; otherwise he might flutter into the sky, like a moth.

Where was his mind? If he were a plant growing on the mountain, or a stone too large to be shifted —

"Keeper!" Abner shouted through the bars. "Keeper!"

A bonfire was crackling in the courtyard, inmates herding around it, attempting to warm their hands.

A uniformed keeper stuck his head out a window in the little gate lodge, and the beggars standing in the street began screaming "Soup! Soup!" while holding up howling children.

"Go away!" the keeper shouted.

"Open up, you!" Abner's voice was firm. "My father's a ratepayer, and this poor fellow is ours."

Abner thrust a scrap of paper between the bars. "Here is the ticket all made out. Now come, you, and let him in."

The keeper's head withdrew and the little window banged shut. A moment later the lodge door opened and the keeper came out, buttoning up his blue coat. "You don't expect me to greet every pauper in the country, do you?"

"I don't expect nothing but your duty. Now let us in."

"You must hold off these ragged pigs."

"Hold them off yourself, it's not my concern."

"Let me see your ticket." The keeper glanced at it, then shoved it in his pocket and started unlocking the gate. The beggars were wailing and pressing, trying to get inside. The keeper opened the gate just enough for Abner to push Fergus through, then banged it shut, catching the wrist of a beggar, who began screeching like a cat.

"Do as they tell you now, *an mhic*," Abner was saying between the iron bars. "Good luck to you. God bless you, dear."

He was on the point of opening his mouth and pleading with Abner to take him back, to take him home, but something stopped him, and he remembered his father's silence. He watched the farmer's son climb aboard the donkey cart, crack his whip lightly, and start driving away.

Go, you hasty fucker. I'll get you.

"Look smart, boy." The keeper gave him a shove, pushing him toward the bonfire. "Here is the warden coming — Mr. Conachree. Strip off your clothes now, they go in the fire."

A small official was beetling across the yard, followed by an orange youth lugging a pail in each hand. Ignoring them, Fergus turned to stare at the fire.

Everything red, warping, and changing.

Water cascaded over his head. While he was still gasping and sputtering the keeper and the orange boy seized and pinioned him, peeled off his rags, and threw them in the fire. Then they held him while the official began clipping his hair with sheep shears.

Looking down at the flagstones, Fergus watched snips of his hair twitching with lice.

"Hold still or Warden might slip and snip off your ear," the orange boy warned.

He could feel the tears but fought them back. Humiliated, trying to hold on to some string of himself, he attempted to withdraw inside himself.

Are you just that voice inside?

Frightened, cagey. A rabbit dashing for a hole. Heart beating fast and hard.

Shearing done, the warden dropped the clippers into the pail of strong-smelling fluid and left without a word, walking across the yard and disappearing inside the building.

Fergus stood naked, shorn, gasping and shivering. The orange boy was pulling on a pair of leather gloves. "Close your eyes, man. This goo stings very wicked." Dipping his gloved hands into the pail, he began vigorously rubbing Fergus's scalp. The acrid solvent stung at cuts and welts, made his eyes tear.

He felt like a badger, trapped, killed, peeled.

The orange boy gave one last violent knead then pulled off the gloves. "There, that'll do you I reckon."

He would remember his shearing as the end of everything, therefore a beginning as well. A kind of birth, in sheep dip. He knew himself then — skin and soul and nothing else. He would not forget.

Digging into a sack, the orange boy dropped some clothes at his feet. "Put on your jacket, fresh fish. We dress like gentlemen here."

Schoolroom

Fresh fish was what you were called until they had gotten used to you.

Paupers were fed in the yard, where the steam of soup was stunning, and he lingered over the kettle until the warden screamed at him to take his noggin right fast and move along, move along.

A hundred men and boys slept on straw pallets in the male paupers' sleeping hall. He fell asleep instantly but awoke in blackness in the middle of the night, with strangers lying flat as the dead, and the fire too far off to give any light or heat. He had wet himself, and the sour stink of piss on straw reminded him of Carmichael's stable and the red mare in her stall. Carmichael calling out instructions as Fergus trotted her around and around the little pasture.

Use your knees! Straight back! Don't slump like a plowboy!

He struggled to stay awake, afraid of the night, the breathing of strangers, afraid to sleep, afraid of death, but his eyelids were heavy, his face had no strength, and soon enough he was gone.

AT DAWN the paupers arose obediently at the clanging of a bell. He followed the others outside, passing six fever cases writhing on the floor. They trooped out to the yard, where snow had fallen overnight, greasing the stones, and an iron kettle was seething over a fire.

Breakfast was a thin porridge of yellow meal. Paupers ate in silence, standing about in the snow, using their fingers to scoop the gruel. After they had finished eating, boys began launching snowballs over the walls.

The orange boy was packing a snowball in his hands when he suddenly wheeled, cocked his right arm, and took aim at Fergus.

Feeling reckless, without any edges, Fergus said, "Throw it."

Yes, then I'll murder you, so. Yes I will.

The boy hesitated, then spun around and heaved the snowball over the wall.

If you'd thrown it at me, I'd have taken off your head. I would have. Yes. Somehow.

"Know what that is there, fresh fish?" The boy was pointing to scaffolding on the gable end of the building.

"I don't."

The scaffolding supported a wooden slide made from yellow planks. The slide sloped from the second-story gable window to a pit dug in the ground.

"Up there is black room for fever cases. They push the dead ones out the window, and they tumble down into the pit. Have you had fever yourself?"

"I have."

"Only once?"

"Yes."

"You'll get the relapse, then. I am Murty Larry O'Sullivan. I can sniff the ones to live and ones to die."

"Which am I?"

But Warden Conachree came out on the steps, shaking a bell, the sound banging across the stone yard, and Fergus followed Murty into one of the ranks hastily forming.

Paupers stood coughing and scratching while the little warden wandered up and down the ranks, peering into their faces.

"Scouting for fever cases, the wee rogue," Murty Larry said softly. "The overseers prefer paupers dead — it's cheaper. They pay Warden sixpence for each one buried."

They filed into a long, gloomy hall with rows of benches facing each other down either side, and daylight filtering through broken windows high in the roof. Murty Larry pointed out a fat woman wearing a cloak, sitting on a stool near the fire. "Mam Shingle, our schoolmistress, the old whore. Her and Warden are robbing the Union blind. They say he's bought a farm. Did you like that porridge they fed us?"

"Trash, I thought it was."

"Cheap old dust! Workhouse has gone to Hell. In the old days I approved of the grub. Why, we used to have mutton every Saturday — it did me nicely."

He knew something of the ABCs, not enough to read or write easily. An old Waterloo hero gave lessons in one cabin or another on the mountain, costing a penny and a turf for the fire. He'd had the turf but rarely the penny.

Mam Shingle lit her pipe and took a few puffs. The benches gradually filled with paupers of all ages, some carrying children in their arms. Instead of drilling them in ABCs, Mam Shingle began singing, in a high, quavering voice, a song about white horse and a battle. She sang in Irish. Her accent was unfamiliar, and he could not make out half the words. Murty Larry was already dozing, chin on his chest, and many others appeared to be asleep. Fergus turned up the collar of his jacket. The fire was too small and far off to deliver any warmth. Smoke curdled through the room, until all he had in his head was its powerful gassy flavor.

The old witch was still singing, but another song — he couldn't make out a word. Perhaps it was the *uilecan*, a funeral cry.

Perhaps it was.

Slumped forward, or resting their heads on one another's shoulders, most of the paupers seemed asleep. Knocked out by the lazy, heavy smoke clogging around the benches.

Not knowing the words — were there words? — he began to sing with the old poison cook. Keening, an animal sound. Wind through trees. Rise and fall.

Sensing a fluttering overhead, he looked up and saw a pigeon flapping around the beams. He stopped singing. More birds were fluttering in through broken windows, high in the ceiling.

"There you are, your honor," Murty Larry said, abruptly coming awake and digging Fergus sharply with his elbow. "Pigeon pie for supper? I don't think so."

Many of the paupers, Fergus saw, had come into the schoolroom with their pockets stuffed with stones. Standing up on the benches, they began to fire at the birds. Stones rained on the floor and he joined a scramble of men and boys scavenging ammunition while Mam Shingle waddled up the aisle hitting out with a cattle quirt. The paupers ignored her, screaming in frustration as sleek, plump pigeons began to escape, plummeting out the windows.

Only Murty Larry sat still on the bench, arms crossed, looking grave.

The last bird had escaped. Frustration feeding rage, the paupers began firing stones at one another. The air sang with stones, and a young man in front of them suddenly spun around, hands cupping one eye, blood leaking between fingers.

Fergus watched the scarlet dripping, feeling cold and remote, careless.

"Get down or it'll happen to you!"

Grabbing him by the wrist, Murty Larry pulled him to the floor, where they were shielded by benches and bodies.

"Faction fight! Mountain tribe against the fishermen! No one ever kills a bird! I don't like excitement myself. It encourages fever."

On the mountain there had been faction fights, brawls — one set of poor relations against another. No one ever fought the farmer, but against one another they were busy.

Murty Larry and Fergus huddled on the floor while the stones whizzed. Phoebe was suddenly in his mind.

I would cut you with a stone. I would kill you.

When Mr. Conachree entered the hall, shouting for order, he was met with a flurry of stones and fled with Mam Shingle. Gangs of boys began raiding back and forth across the hall.

Suddenly a pair of hands seized him, hauling him to his feet. Before he could put up his fists, a yellow-haired stranger with a face like a knot of wood had punched him in the lips.

The hot, salt taste of his own blood was immediately stimulating and he began to punch and kick in a flurry. The taste of fury, almost joy. The stranger tripped over a bench and fell on his back and Murty Larry, scrambling across the bench, kicked the stranger briskly while he lay on the floor, three kicks to his yellow head. Then Murty grabbed Fergus's hand and began guiding him through the tumult of fighting, steering toward the thick doors.

"I tell you, fresh fish," Murty said, "workhouse ain't no place to obtain an education."

The door when they reached it was locked so they sat down on the stones with their backs against the wood. The stranger's unexpected attack had left him breathless. After a while his blood began to cool but his knuckles were stinging. He looked at them. They were raw, smeared with blood.

The fury in the hall was quickly spent. Exhausted paupers lay shivering on the benches and floor. Soon the hall was quiet except for the groaning of the injured.

From the other side of the door, they heard Mr. Conachree shouting that fever would burn the wickedness out of them! And meanwhile they should have no rations! And the door to stay locked!

Exhausted paupers pounded on the door, screaming defiance. They wept.

"These janglers, these herds!" Murty Larry was scornful. "They've stirred up bad air with their hassling."

Fergus looked at Murty. He was trembling and his face seemed dark.

"Were you hit by a missile?" Fergus asked.

Murty shook his head so violently spit flew from his mouth. "Not hit, no! Something inside! My head hurts something awful. It does. Like birds a-pecking at my eyes."

These were unmistakable signs of fever.

"It won't get me! You'll help me, won't you?"

Help you? How? You have the curious journey before you.

"Promise you won't let them take me to the black room!"

"Yes," Fergus agreed. "All right."

Murty Larry

ALL DAY HE REMAINED SITTING with his back against the locked door, trying to pay as little attention as possible to the others caught in the same trap. He tried thinking of Phoebe in her blue dress. She was alive, but he'd not see her again. Hard to believe.

Hard to believe in the mountain, that the place still existed, or ever had.

Murty Larry, feeling stronger, wanted to talk. He said he had been wheel boy for a wagon builder who'd emigrated for Ohio.

"I said he must take me with him, only he didn't think so. Said he had his own mouths to feed, and there wasn't enough to spare for my passage."

"What did you do then?"

"He left me a shilling and a pair of tongs. I spent the shilling on porter and sold the tongs in exchange for a spoileen — I was that hungry. I went to the holy well and tried to fish some coppers, Fergus, only I couldn't. Tried to steal a boat and go for the holy island where there is rabbits, only some women stopped me. Fished for a while — some days — by the lake, only couldn't catch nothing. Still, only one salmon is all you need.

"I went a-hunting birds, trying to bang 'em with rocks. Did you ever try to kill a bird so? It's not easy. I squeezed milk off a cow, I did. Got some yellow meal. The potatoes are gone. I was plucking turnips when they caught me and put me in here. Now it's very hard getting in, they say. If I get out of here, I'm going for Ohio."

"How do you go there? Where is it?"

"I don't know. Perhaps I'll fly." Murty laughed weakly. "Now no more *craic*. Leave me be. I can tell there's a lick of fever coming on, and I must buckle down and fight it off. Black room won't get me."

MURTY MOANED and sweated all night while Fergus stayed awake, his back against the thick door. The workhouse was no refuge. If they stayed in it they'd die. All of them must end up in the black room. Promise or no promise.

The only safety he could imagine was up the high pastures, on the booley, where as a young herd he had followed cattle week after midsummer week, grazing animals from one grassy brow to another.

But winter up there so high was wild and empty.

Phoebe's bare feet on blue stones.

Perhaps she would do for him.

Steal rations. Keep him fed.

Easy to think so.

But would she? She'd turned him off. She was one of them.

Forget what you know and don't know.

Invent the world to stay in it.

WHEN THE door finally swung open at dawn, there were four fever cases writhing on the benches, two lying dead on the floor.

"I am weak this morning, fresh fish. And feeling so quiet." Murty Larry spoke in a whisper. His eyes blinking behind pink slits.

He helped Murty out to the yard where the little warden was standing close by the fire trying to warm himself while a keeper served out the porridge. The air smelled of smoke and snow.

While he ate his ration, Fergus watched Warden Conachree. The little man looked like a rabbit with his pink chin and white flecks of beard. Swaddled in his coat he kept shuffling closer to the heart of the fire, inch by inch — it seemed Warden Conachree couldn't get enough of heat. The toes of his boots, Fergus noticed, were dusty with fine gray ash. His rabbit face was flushed, and he was shivering. As Fergus watched, the little man unbuttoned his gorgeous coat and held it open to the blaze. His teeth were hammering.

Chills were a sign of fever. You didn't feel warm until you were blazing.

Fergus studied the florid, gasping little warden. His breeches were nice yellow whipcord, fresh and new. Beautiful coat and boots and —

You're no one's keeper now.

Paupers were crowding around the fire like cattle in a storm, the stink of their bodies unfurling in the violent warmth. Fergus saw Murty Larry was staring stupidly at his ration.

"Eat it, man, you'll feel stronger."

The orange boy's weakness and helplessness were somehow provoking fresh strength in Fergus, which he could hear in his own voice. He felt harder, more fixed.

The warden's face was sweating white drops like an onion.

"Shall I?" Murty sounded listless.

"You will, sure."

The warden suddenly dropped onto his knees where he wavered, then toppled, falling forward into the heart of the fire.

For a few seconds no one moved. Frays of cloth caught light instantly, flaring. You could smell the burn. His cheek, his neck, sizzling on the coals. Frying meat.

Grabbing the little man's spindly legs, Fergus started dragging him out of the fire, out of the ash, then turned him over gently on the snowy pavement stones. He was snorting and muttering — alive, but insensible. His pink face steaming. Ashes and bits of char stuck to his flesh.

"Fever case! Black room for him, the old gouger!" Kneeling, Murty Larry began to rifle through the warden's pockets. "Devil old man, sour guts, what do you suppose? Will you burn in Hell now?"

Fergus watched Murty work through the warden's pockets. The keeper who had been serving out the ration made no move to stop the orange boy.

Digging up a handkerchief, an apple, a twig of tobacco, and two pennies, Murty stood up stuffing the goods in his pockets. "As good as fresh meat, an apple is." He began polishing it on his sleeve, then looked at Fergus and grinned. "An apple, Fergus, is all I need to lick the fever. It's a gift of God."

Two paupers with sticks were trying to fish Conachree's hat from the fire.

As Murty Larry ate the apple, two keepers came up with a carpet, and Fergus watched the warden rolled up inside, and heard his muffled screams as they carried him away.

Finishing the apple, Murty tossed the stem on the fire. "He's for the black room, isn't he, Fergus?"

"I reckon."

"Well, he deserves it, don't he. He has stolen our rations, the old pecker, and sold 'em. I'd like that coat he had on his back, I'd have that, I would."

Murty began to snuffle and weep.

"What is it?" Fergus said.

"God watch over me, Fergus. I shouldn't have took his apple, should I?"

"He won't be needing it."

"No, but it's feverish, ain't it? You mustn't touch a body's goods what has the fever. No, no. It's all a poison. Oh my. Do you think I'll catch it?"

Murty was a fever case now, what did it matter what he touched or ate?

"Who knows?"

"Do I look nice, Fergus? I don't look ill, do I?"

Murty Larry's skin was straining dark, which was fever.

"You don't."

WITH the warden in the black room, many of the keepers deserted, slipping through the main gate, carrying off sacks of Indian meal. Mam Shingle refused to hold schoolroom. Girls and women were set to picking oakum, and boys were left out in the yard with the men. A few began swinging hammers and breaking rocks, trying to stay warm, but there were not enough hammers to go around, and most of them lay down on the pavement, too weak to make any effort.

Fergus cruised around the yard, keeping close to the wall. The morning's ration, however thin, had nourished him. He felt strong. Climbing onto a pile of broken rocks, he stared over the roofs of the town, thinking of roads, the magic of roads, which had given his father a kind of hard joy and shape.

Time to burst out. No life in this place, only dying.

"No, it's getting very close," Murty whispered. He had scrambled up on the rock pile beside Fergus.

"What is?"

"Winter. You're looking flashy, captain. What are you thinking?"

"To get away."

"There isn't any getting away, not from here."

"There must be. If we stay we'll die. Look at them."

Paupers lay about the yard, soft as gutted trout.

Of course there was a way out; he had only to find it. He'd go back to the farm and bark at them. Go up the mountain and scream for the dead.

Or forget them all, and go for Ohio.

But he couldn't stay in this place, no.

Climbing down off the rock pile, he strode up to the main gate. There were no beggars clustered outside trying to claim entry to the workhouse — either they'd abandoned the fantasy of rations and shelter, or the snow had driven them off. Or perhaps everyone else in the world was dead.

Grasping the bars, he rattled the gate, then looked back at the gatekeeper's lodge. No smoke in the chimney, no sign of life. Perhaps the gatekeeper had deserted with the others.

If he could get into the lodge, he might find the key. He went to try the door. Finding it locked, he shook it.

"Get away!" the gatekeeper's voice roared from inside.

Returning to the gate, Fergus tried to squeeze between the iron bars, but they were set too close. He tried climbing. No one paid any notice as he writhed, grasped, and struggled on the bars. But the gate was too high, the iron too slippery. He gave up. Limping around the yard, he studied the walls closely. The blocks of dressed limestone were fitted too neatly to give purchase for toes and fingers in the cracks.

Calling Murty Larry over, Fergus made the orange boy stand in a corner then tried climbing onto his shoulders to see if he could reach the top of the wall and pull himself up, but Murty wasn't strong enough to bear the weight, and quickly crumpled to his knees, sobbing.

"It ain't no good, Fergus, I ain't got the iron for it, my bones all soft now. Why do you fluster me? Help me up, help me up or I'll stay here, I'll stick to the stones I will, I'll lie here like a splatter of sick. That's all I am."

"You don't want to give it up, do you? You don't want to die."

"I don't care so much anymore."

"If you could stand on my shoulders, perhaps you might reach the top of the wall."

"She's too high, too high, Fergus! You never shall conquer her! Such hard walls ain't made for climbing but to keep us in. Oh, I would fashion wheels in Limerick town. If I got out of here, I would so." Murty Larry was snuffling again. "They are going to carry me off to the black room, Fergus, I know it."

Fergus left him and kept cruising along the walls. Running hands over blocks of seamless, smoothly fitted stone. Promising himself he would not die here, but find a way out.

LATER he brought Murty a noggin of soup and stood watching over him so no one would steal it.

"I don't want it, Fergus. I haven't the stomach for it."

"Drink it, man, that's your life in there."

Murty sighed. Dipping two fingers, he licked soup. "Jesus, but the gunk tastes awful."

"It isn't good, but it's better than nothing."

"When did you last eat a potato, Fergus?"

"Don't remember."

"I'd take a yellow lumper, big as a fist. We used to eat 'em by the basket, sometimes with a relish of herrings. Smash her in a bowl with a stirrup of milk. Butter on top." Murty Larry dipped and licked his fingers again. "I shan't die tonight, captain, shall I?"

You might. You have a look.

"If I goes in the pit, you must cover me up. Don't let me lie there in the sky, captain, but cover me up, and make sure my eyes is shut."

No one welcomes death, those nearest the most reluctant.

Dragoons

HE EXPERIENCED A SERIES of beast dreams. Wolves with fishes on their backs. Speaking badgers. Carmichael's red mare laughing at him, through a hole in the stable.

He swam to consciousness like a fish in a cold hole, rising sluggishly to the light. He lay for some minutes before realizing there was daylight outside.

Carmichaels — the dispossessors, they had everything now.

The bell had not sounded.

Others were stirring. He got up quickly, and went outside where it was snowing — the stony yard was covered with pure white stuff. No footprints yet. The fire unlit. He hurried to try the gates, but they were locked. The gate-keeper's lodge was deserted.

Emerging from the sleeping halls, paupers stood about the yard, rangy and nervous as cattle in changing weather.

There was no one in Mam Shingle's room. No sacks of meal in the store-room. The last keepers had fled during the night, taking all rations.

Fergus saw Murty Larry pacing up and down by the iron gate. They had been abandoned by Mam Shingle and all the other keepers, who had fled and locked the gate behind them, deserting with the keys.

Murty looked wilder then ever, pacing by the gate. Some spirit in the orange boy was strong enough to keep him on his feet. Even if it was only fear of the black room.

A fox in a trap would bite off its own leg to get away.

A female pauper clanged the warden's handbell for a long time as though the sound itself might summon rations. In pewter light Fergus climbed the rock pile and stared out across the walls at the snowy roofs of the town.

You might set for rabbits nicely, in such snow. See the tracks neat.

He could scrounge lumber off the black room slide, find nails and tools, build himself a ladder, and get over the wall that way.

Hearing a squeak, he looked up and saw the gable window of the black room swinging open. A body was being shoved out through the window, feet first, onto the wooden slide. It was the little beetle man, Warden Conachree.

Whoever was inside let go of the ankles, and the warden's corpse flew down the slide and tumbled soundlessly into the pit at the bottom.

A spade of powdered lime, flung from the window, clouded the air before it began to settle over the pit. The window closed.

Excited shouting at the gate caught his attention. Hurrying over, peering through the iron bars, he saw a company of dragoons mounted on black horses clattering and steaming in the road.

Paupers howled through the bars at the soldiers, begging for food. The dragoons were escorting a miller's cart piled with fat burlap sacks of Indian meal. An English officer was braying orders. Fergus watched two soldiers on horseback uncoil rope and throw two lines over the top of the gate, snagging the iron bars. They began spurring their black horses. The lines sung taut, the gate began to flex, and he heard the iron twisting, screeching on its hinges.

"No good, no good," Murty Larry groaned. "Them sojers want to crush us all."

The gate snapped off its hinges with a loud twang and clattered down on the pavement. Looking around, Fergus saw pauper women already fanning a fire. The miller's cart, driven by a frightened-looking boy, rumbled over the flattened gate and into the workhouse yard, dragoons crowding in behind, their massive horses creaking with gear and leather.

Murty Larry bowed low, sweeping his arm toward the open gateway and the snowy street outside, in a gesture of magnanimous invitation.

Fergus looked back at the fire where a dragoon was piercing sacks with his saber and pauper women were already sluicing yellow meal into the kettle. The inmates stood about anxiously like cattle waiting to be milked.

Looking through the opening in the walls he saw Murty Larry running away down the white street, already a dim figure in the mist, leaving black footprints on the snow.

The scent of the raw meal — sweet, dusty — was tempting.

You might stay, get yourself a ration.

The road, the road.

Red soldiers, famished inmates.

Rations might keep you alive, but they were all you'd ever get, and you wanted more.

Phoebe, Ohio, the mountain, a place to dream.

Stepping over the iron grillwork, he started away.

Lost

SNOW SCALPED THE HILLS surrounding the town. Murty Larry tried begging from a gentleman in a cloak, who ignored him, then from a couple of drunken soldiers who laughed and threw him a button.

Fergus was stiff, shy, no good at begging — he couldn't speak to strangers. One lady wearing spectacles shoved a tract in his hand then hurried on while Murty Larry shouted, "Give me something I can eat, you old whore!"

Grabbing the tract from Fergus, Murty pitched it in the gutter.

"Never mind, Fergus, never mind — pleading is not the game, not for us, it won't serve. People are too wicked here."

"We ought to get out of this town."

"Going where?"

He shrugged. "Back to the mountain."

"Mountain? I ain't going for no fucking mountain, captain. No, I am not. Starve like a crow on your old bonny mountain. Limerick, that's the place — look here, look at this old creature."

Peering through the gray curtain of snow falling, Fergus saw a beggar woman sitting up ahead in the road.

"We'll get that shawl off her," Murty Larry said.

"Her shawl?"

"Just watch me now."

As they were walking by the old woman Murty Larry reached down, grabbed a corner of the shawl, and tried pulling it off her.

"Thief! Thief!" Screeching, the woman hung on.

"Let go, you old wretch, let me have it!" When Murty kicked her in the side she let go of the shawl and Murty raced down the street, slipping and sliding on the snow, waving it like a banner.

Fergus stared at the old woman on her hands and knees, muttering and spitting, unable to stand up.

Feeling pity and not pity. A gauze-over-all feeling.

"Come on, come on!" Murty Larry screamed.

IN A livery stable behind a beer shop, they warmed themselves lying on horses' backs. "We shall go for Limerick. Find a wagon man in Limerick. You'll learn the wheel trade, Fergus. Only we must have shoes for the road."

They swallowed handfuls of oats soaked in water, then Murty Larry slid off his horse and started making slippers, tearing up the old woman's shawl, wrapping the cloth around their feet.

Wearing the wrappings they quit the stable, Murty Larry insisting he knew the way for Limerick. But after they had passed the beer shop twice, Fergus realized Murty could not even lead the way out of Scariff. The cloth binding their feet was already shredding and dissolving.

"This isn't going to work, man."

"Limerick's the mighty town," Murty insisted. "Lots of roads going there."

"I don't know why I'm following you — you don't know the way."

"Don't lose me, Fergus." Murty Larry began to weep. "I am getting awful fights in my head. Hurts so it's killing. My stomach hurts too."

Fever.

Start in one direction, keep going.

He started down a long street of wrecked cabins, resolved to follow it wherever it went.

"This ain't the way for Limerick!" Murty Larry protested. "This is the road for Hell." He kept falling behind but Fergus refused to slow down or turn around. In ten minutes they had reached the end of the town. For as far as he could see ahead the hedges along the road were lined with men, women, and children sitting under the branches or lying in holes and scrapes dug into the ground and covered with sticks and rags.

"Don't leave me, captain!" Murty Larry had stopped in the road. He was swaying, clutching his belly. "This isn't the way out of the world. I can't walk so hard, Fergus."

A heavy dray, the type called a *land carriage*, was coming up behind them, loaded with freight.

"It's a road," Fergus said. "We can't stay here or we'll be as bad off as the rest of them. We have to move along."

"Do you know where she goes? Is it Limerick?"

"It's a road, man, we'll follow it and see."

"This is worse . . . everything's worse . . . I want something sweet again," Murty moaned.

Four heavy gray horses were drawing the dray; he could hear the harness jingling. Fergus pulled Murty out of the road and watched the big wagon rumble past, loaded with stacks of newly built pine coffins and lids. The teamster was swaddled up against the cold.

Murty Larry sank down on his knees and began coughing and vomiting bloody dregs.

"Only don't leave me here, your honor," he whispered. "Only take me with you!"

Fergus looked at the dray disappearing down the road. "Come on then." Half carrying Murty, he struggled along the road after the dray.

The people under the hedges were already dying, rain was dissolving them, they would all be finished soon.

"My head is knocking, Fergus, I can't think."

The horses were plodding along steadily. Supporting Murty Larry, Fergus struggled to catch up to the back of the dray, but they were losing ground.

"Put me down, captain, put me down. You're killing me."

Murty Larry's legs were soft and would no longer support him. Fergus brought him to side of the road and let down gently on the frosty grass.

He stared after the dray, hearing the hubs squeaking and the harness jingle as the horses moved away under the moon.

He looked down at Murty Larry flopping on the grass, barking, his face dark. In a few hours the maroon fever sores would be blossoming on his chest. But he wouldn't live that long, not in the cold.

He looked at the dray, moving away from them.

You had to stay alive; every instinct told you. Stay in your life as long as you can. If only to see what would happen. Every breath told you to keep breathing.

Kneeling, he rifled Murty's pockets until he found the warden's coppers. Gripping them tight in his fist, he stood up and started running after the dray.

After catching up, he didn't try to climb in at first, but kept a few paces back, close enough to reach out and touch the tailboard with his fingertips.

The teamster in the driving seat didn't know he was there. The horses plodded on.

Light bled from the sky. Rain ceased and the sky blew clear. The road hardened with frost. There was no other traffic. Fergus stared at his feet, concentrating on the effort required to keep going. Finally when he knew he could walk no farther, he dragged himself aboard and wriggled in between stacks of empty coffins. He lay in a tight space, smelling pine pitch and glue and iron nails, and let the horses' footsteps lull him to sleep.

The Bog Boys

WHEN HE AWOKE THE DRAY was still moving and he had no sense of how far they had traveled. The moon had arisen. Looking back, he could see a patchwork of stone walls and fields falling away from either side of the road. The cold was thorough and sour. He could hear the teamster snoring. The wheels banged and thumped over the frozen road.

Suddenly a youthful voice called out, "Halt and stay! Halt and stay!"

Peering out between the coffins, Fergus saw a young man walking alongside the dray, holding up a pitchfork and addressing the teamster. "Lift your mitts, or we shall drill you quick."

Peering ahead, Fergus saw a soldier standing in the middle of the road, aiming a musket at the teamster.

"Hoppers aboard, Luke!" the soldier cried, seeing Fergus and shifting his aim.

"Don't shoot me, if you please," the teamster begged. "Swear before God, I haven't any money."

Small boys were dropping over the walls, grabbing the bridles, pulling the team to a halt.

"I'm a poor man, sir," the teamster was saying, "I've a dozen mouths to feed."

"Shut your trap, we'll kill you all soon as blather." The soldier swung his aim back to the teamster. "Shall I shoot him now, Luke?"

Luke, the leader, was dressed in layers of rags fused by weather. His breeches were torn off below the knee, and a clay pipe was jabbed in his hatband.

Stepping up onto a spoke, Luke studied Fergus. "Stand up."

He stood slowly, clenching the coppers in his fist.

Luke was small. Dark hair and a thin, white face.

Kill me. I wouldn't mind.

"What do you have there, in your hand?"

Fergus said nothing.

"What is it? Show me."

He opened his fist, displaying the two coins.

"Here, give them over." Luke reached out.

Instead, hating obedience, Fergus closed his fist and flung the coins hard and high out over the frozen fields, where they fell without a sound.

The hungrier you were the stronger you hated it.

"What is it?" The soldier sounded panicked. "We'll kill the fellow — what is it, Luke?"

Luke had turned to stare out over the fields. "Why'd you do that?" he said softly.

"Didn't wish to give them over."

"Tell this one he must give over his coat, Luke!" the young soldier cried, roughly poking at the teamster, who had sunk into his greatcoat. "Give it over, you beast, or I'll skin it off you."

"Come along, mister," Luke said, "you'd better give Shamie what he wants."

"And boots — I'll have them boots as well, you great fat pig. I'll have them boots or skin you."

The small boys had been boosting one another aboard the team. Suddenly a horse bucked and snorted, jolting the dray.

"Easy there, men, easy." Luke turned his attention back to the teamster. "Come now, mister, you must skin yourself, or Shamie'll do it for you."

With a groan the teamster stood up and began unbuttoning his greatcoat. As he handed it down, the straw that was padded inside for extra warmth fluttered down on the road.

"Now with them boots," the young soldier insisted.

The teamster sat down on his seat and began pulling off his boots while the soldier pulled on the greatcoat over his red jacket and cross-straps.

"I'll freeze to death," the teamster said, dropping the boots on the road. "Sure you can't take everything, boys?"

"We'll have those," said Luke, pointing at the teamster's red stockings, "and your shirt, if you please."

"And breeches!" said the young soldier. "And look smart about it!"

"Boys, boys, you don't want the death of a poor man on your conscience. I'm father to nine."

"Give him your shirt and breeches, or he will shoot you in the brains," Luke said. "Shamie, pass that here."

The young soldier had found a clay jar in the teamster's coat. He handed it over to Luke, who plucked out the stopper with his teeth, took a swallow, and coughed.

"How's that?" Shamie said eagerly. "Give it here, if you please, Luke, a taste of old stormy would do me nice."

Instead Luke offered Fergus the jar. "There you go, take a bite."

A horse screamed.

"Easy there, men, easy!" Luke cried. "Take your turns, fair is fair."

The children had nicked a vein on one of the horses — *houghing* — drawing blood, which they were licking.

The *poitín* tasted like smoke. Fergus coughed, spat, and thumped his chest, then handed the jar back down to Luke, who passed it to Shamie.

"Are you going to shoot us?" Fergus asked Luke.

"Have anything else worth robbing?"

"I haven't."

"Where have you come from?"

"The workhouse."

"Shamie! Shamie!" Luke called. "This fellow is out of the workhouse."

Luke looked at Fergus thoughtfully. "We were told they serve out rations — meat soup, three rounds a day. Is it true?"

"No. The soup had no meat. They have fever there."

"Do they?" Luke sounded disappointed. "Ah well, I was not believing there was any such place, anyhow. Meat soup — it was hard to credit."

"Alls I want," Shamie said, "is meat."

The teamster had pulled off his stockings and his linen shirt and was dropping them on the road. Flesh swelled from his breast in two pouches as he stood up and began unbuttoning his breeches. His belly was round and white. Stepping out of the breeches with a sob, he dropped them on the road. Shamie picked them up delicately on the tip of his muzzle.

"Leave him his drawers?" Shamie asked.

"Are you ribbonmen?" Fergus had heard of bands of ribbonmen, tenants displaced, roaming the country and taking vengeance on farmers and landlords.

"He must give them over," Luke told Shamie, sounding weary. "Ribbonmen? Perhaps."

"I'll perish!" the teamster cried.

Shamie stepped up and pressed his muzzle against the teamster's breast. "Shall I shoot you now, you pig? I could flay the bacon off you, you great damned bastard. Get up, get up, and give us over what we want! Get up!"

The teamster peeled off his drawers and hung them on the muzzle, then sat down on his driver's seat, hugging himself, shaking with cold.

"The hat," said Luke quietly, "don't neglect the hat, Shamie, it will serve you nicely."

Jumping up on a spoke, Shamie lifted the teamster's beaver hat from his head.

"Is he a soldier?" Fergus asked Luke.

"He was a soldier boy at one time, but no more — he's a good clean deserter." Luke was studying Fergus. "Where were you, before the workhouse?"

"Ejected."

"Your people, where are they?"

"Dead."

"All of them?"

"Yes."

"What's your name?" Luke asked.

Fergus was silent. It was all he had. Why give it up?

"Come, give it over." Luke smiled. "We won't spend it. You'll have it back."

He was about to say his name was Murty Larry when something stopped him — a sense of violation. "Fergus."

"Thieving and outlawing ain't so bad, Fergus. We killed a sheep once, and would do better if there were more of us. When was the last time you had mutton for your supper?"

"Luke!" Shamie was smirking and clowning, wearing the teamster's hat. He spun his soldier cap at Luke, who caught it.

"If you was ejected they won't have you back," Luke told Fergus. "They'll drive you to a ship and send you over the water. You'll never see your country again. No, come with us. We'll give you the oath, won't we, Shamie?"

"He's a damned grasshopper stealing rides. It's not for him to question."

"We are the Bog Boys, Fergus. You've heard of us, perhaps?"

"No."

"No matter." Luke sounded resigned. "Better that way, I suppose. We ain't done nothing mighty yet. Will you throw in with us or not?"

The teamster was wailing. Fergus tried to shut his ears.

"Here," Luke said, "there's nothing for it now. You won't find no soup at Limerick. We're living quite a gallant life. We'll take you to our home and offer you a meal — what is there to say to that?"

"Why him?" Shamie protested. "He's a spy perhaps."

"Come, Fergus. We'll be your sure ones."

No use resisting. Spurned, they'd kill him. Murderous boys.

And Phoebe, and the mountain — that was over, he didn't believe in it, not really. And Limerick was just a word, Ohio another word.

Can't live on words.

Jumping down off the dray, he stumbled and fell on his hands then stood up quickly, wary.

Luke smiled at him. The moon glowered across the fields, and the tormented horses snorted and whinnied.

"Stand away, men!" Luke called. "Tell the fellow he may go, Shamie."

Delicately picking up the reins on the tip of his muzzle, Shamie raised them until the teamster took them.

"You may go."

"I'll perish, I'll perish," the naked man moaned.

"Well, God bless you, mister," said Luke. "I am sorry for your trouble."

The small boys had scrambled onto the stone wall and perched along the top, clutching stone, knives, and sticks, faces smeared with horse blood.

The teamster flapped the reins and the horses pulled. Shamie pointed his musket in the air and discharged, the barrel spurting red just as the horses snapped the wheels from the freezing mud.

Standing in the road between Luke and the soldier, Fergus watched the dray lumbering away, the cargo of coffins banging and squeaking.

"We might have kept them horses," Shamie said. "A troop does well off horsemeat."

"Whoever heard of outlaws eating horses? Jesus, Shamie, you would curse a fellow with your glooms."

The younger ones were laughing, frisking, pitching stones out into the fields, but Fergus stood with Shamie and Luke, watching the dray as it moved farther and farther away, until he did not see it at all.

Meat

THE BOG BOYS FOLLOWED LUKE across unkempt pastures under the moon. Fergus had never crossed country so wide. There were scars where hedges had been burned and uprooted, leaving white fingers of dead root exposed. The boys chattered like birds. The youngest ones stumbled along half asleep.

Luke dropped back from the head of the column to walk beside Fergus. "We are glad to take you home with us."

"Where is that?"

"The bog, Fergus, the bog."

Luke called back to the soldier. "Shamie dear! You were very cool!"

"I didn't mind it, so. I was very little scared."

"Bold, you were. Thought you was going to kill the fucker."

"I'd have shot him had he tried any business. Shot your hopper as well."

Fergus heard wind tugging through gorse. The sky green with dawn.

"If you hadn't stopped me, Luke," the soldier went on, "I'd have shot the juice right out of him."

"Don't mind Shamie," Luke said. "He is nervous."

"Nervous but not shy!" the soldier called.

* * *

THEY CAME through an oak grove, branches stark against the moon, and searched for acorns, but these had all been gleaned.

They crossed rough, wet meadow, then a piece of limestone ground divided into plots and beds where the ruined, blackened potato plants had fused on the soil, the stink of rot lingering faintly like a scar. At dawn the sky was gray. Mist floated over the country.

Luke led the Bog Boys through a deserted *baile*, a collection of wrecked cabins. In silence, in single file, they passed the ruins. Fergus thought of his family.

No graves for them. Tumbled walls and heaps of rubble stinking of moldy straw.

A memory is a hole, it would swallow you.

Breathe calm, breathe calm. Never a night like this.

You have broke out of everything.

THE GROUND was softer, and he could smell the astringent bog smell. They passed banks that had been cut into, the turf excised. Luke was leading them along a trench where turf had been cut from a fragrant black seam of peat.

Light-headed from hunger, Fergus stared at his feet plodding along the spongy ground, brown water squeezing out with every step.

The sun arose and cut their faces as they were climbing out of a trench. The wind stiffened and the bog plain sprawled as far as he could see, dotted with limestone islands that were striped with lazy-beds, for raising potatoes.

No roads on the bog. The sun was bright, not warm.

Luke halted so abruptly that Fergus walked into him.

Luke was pointing downwind at a hare crouched in front of a trembling gorse bush.

Fergus looked about for a stone to throw but Shamie had already swung the musket off his shoulder. Taking a paper cartridge from his pouch, he ripped it open with his teeth, spilling a few grains of powder into the pan and dumping the rest down the barrel. The bullet rattled when he dropped it in, but the hare didn't move. After ramming the bullet softly, Shamie stuck his ramrod in the ground, brought the musket to his shoulder, took aim, and pulled the trigger.

The powder flashed. The shot cracked. White smoke wreathed the soldier.

Two Bog Boys went racing across the ground, yipping. Shamie lowered his weapon. "Meat for the kettle," he said casually, wiping powder from his lips.

One boy was holding up the hare by its ears.

"You're the great man, Shamie," Luke said warmly.

They were all awake now after their long night march, excited with hunger. Luke ordered two boys to hurry ahead to get a fire started. "Chop the nettles fine, and get a broth boiling, but not so hard it spits."

Luke led the way across the bog plain. After a while Fergus could smell smoke, then see a curl of smoke rising over the plain, but he didn't see the camp until they were upon it, because the Bog Boys were living below the level of the plain in a maze of trenches and cutbanks worked into the peat bog by generations of turf cutters.

Turnip tops and herbs were already seething in an iron kettle. Shamie sat on a lump of bog oak cleaning his musket while Luke skinned the hare with his fingers.

After warming humself by the fire Fergus climbed up out of the trench and walked across spongy heather and bracken on the flat plain of the bog. From a distance the Bog Boys' camp was quite hidden, except for the smoke rising.

Luke's head appeared. "Come, I'll show you your quarters."

He followed Luke along a trench lined with scalpeens made of mud and sticks. Each Bog Boy had his own scalpeen. The little shelters reminded him of swallows' nests.

"You might take this one next to mine, there's no one in it," Luke said, pointing. "That next is Shamie's. Good day to you, Mary," Luke said to a little girl who was kneeling in front of Shamie's scalpeen, picking lice from a piece of linen.

"I smell meat," she said. "Has Shamie killed us a sheep?"

"Only a hare, but a large one. Fergus, this is Mary Cooley. Fergus here has joined up with us."

"Well, I was hoping it was a sheep," the little girl said. "Mutton for spoileen."

A spoileen was a feast, a dish of meat eaten at a fair.

"No spoileen, but still a taste of meat, thanks to Shamie."

"I shall congratulate him." The little girl trotted off, heading for the fire.

Fergus crawled into his scalpeen. It smelled of earth inside. There was a pad of soft bracken to lie down upon. His feet stuck out the opening.

"What do you think?" Luke asked.

"It's a long way from the roads." He was exhausted and knew that if he shut his eyes, he would sleep and the stirabout would be eaten without him.

"Shamie hates roads. He says you never know when you might meet dragoons. Come on, rations ought to be ready enough now."

LUKE SERVED out the stirabout into their wooden noggins. The scent of simmering meat had drawn all the Bog Boys from their scalpeens. They ate with spoons and with their fingers. It was mostly a broth of wild herbs with a handful of yellow meal and a bit of butter, but the scraps of meat gave it beautiful flavor.

"That's a good kill, Shamie," said Luke. "All our honor to you."

"Our sergeant used to say a soldier's first duty is obedience, his second is to fire low."

"A beautiful shot it was, and a joy to go venturing with you. I look forward to another."

"I don't mind," said the deserter. "We might pick off another dray sometime, on a quiet road, safe at night. Perhaps the next will be carrying stores."

Afterward Luke, Shamie, and Fergus sat about the fire, smoking coltsfoot in clay pipes, Fergus enjoying the warmth of the pipe's bowl in his hand. The Bog Boys had crept back into their burrows, though it was the middle of the day. The little girl, Mary Cooley, lay with her head on Shamie's lap, her thumb in her mouth.

"You did well by us, Shamie," Luke said.

"You might have let us keep the hare for ourselves, Luke. There weren't enough for all. We are the leaders, after all."

"No, we must all feed together, same rations, one and all."

"Well, what did it amount to? Hardly a taste for anyone," Shamie grumbled. "A soldier gets meat every day."

"Do you wish you was soldiering still, Shamie dear?"

"A soldier has proper rations. Bully beef, mutton, and beer money besides. Clothes and boots and smalls. Wish I'd never left off the life."

"Shamie was tumbling cabins and chasing whiteboys," Luke told Fergus.

"Only he never caught any, but saw some cruel things. Then his regiment was marked for India. He heard it was Hell on the passage — half the soldiers dying of fever and getting dropped into the sea. So he bolted."

"I would still go back if I could," the soldier grumbled. "I'd go to India in a minute."

"No you wouldn't, dear."

"We had rations!"

"You've rations here."

"We had mutton! The farmers used to feed us! We'd stand guard as they was tumbling, and they'd present us whiskey and a sheep."

"If the dragoons capture you, they'll brand you, you said so yourself, and flog you. Two hundred lashes. You said yourself."

Shamie's face had gone white. He stared at Luke, mouth opening and shutting, with no words coming out.

"They flogged Shamie once," Luke told Fergus. "Very cruel."

"For parade," Shamie croaked.

"A fly buzzed his nose when the regiment was on parade. The colonel seen him swat it, and for that he was served twenty lashes."

"On the triangles," Shamie whispered. "Fetched me on the triangles, twenty lashes, and burst my back."

"Have you seen a flogging, Fergus? I had a friend, a gentleman, he painted such a picture of it, I can't get it out of my sight."

"It is the drum major whose duty it is, a flogging," Shamie said. "He cares for it. His name was O'Rourke."

"They have the soldiers shape up on parade," Luke said. "It is very gay and musical. They form a square, facing in. The drum beats while they march the prisoner in. They strip off his clothes. The drum major — O'Rourke — binds Shamie on a triangle made from pikes, so he is stretched out, so his toes barely touch the ground, and the officer reads the charge —"

"Twenty lashes they served me! Do you know what that tastes like?"

"Poor Shamie." Luke shook his head.

"After six, they have your back like jelly!"

"We won't let nothing happen to you, Shamie," Luke reassured. "You're safe. Don't think about it. We'll never let the dragoons near you."

Shamie began weeping. Mary Cooley awoke and sat up staring at him, still sucking her thumb.

Luke looked across the fire at Fergus. "He is very nervous, but he's getting better."

Looking into the redness of the fire, Fergus could see his parents in their flaming bed, limbs rising up.

Life burns hot.

What do you do with the dead?

Try to forget them?

Are you supposed to live backward or forward?

He stood up, feeling very heavy, like something was trying to pull him down into the ground. "Thanks for the feed."

"You mustn't thank us, Fergus, you're one of us now."

Luke

FERGUS SLEPT THE REST of the day and through the night.

In the morning when he crawled out of his scalp and came to the fire, he found Luke alone, stirring the kettle.

"No meat today. Turnip tops and nettles, Fergus. Wish we had a bit of yellow meal, to thicken. But this will do. Help yourself."

The stirabout tasted of grass.

"Will you come scouting today, Fergus?" Luke was holding out small hands to warm at the fire.

"If you like. Ourselves alone it must be," Fergus warned. "Not Shamie nor the others."

Perhaps they would find something. Perhaps a badger hole. If they met another dray, perhaps he'd hop aboard.

Luke tucked his hands into his armpits and smiled. "It does me good to look at you, Fergus."

Yes, he understood — he felt more alive, looking at Luke.

Strange that a companion's bright face might keep you going.

"We'll go out for the day, the pair of us. Show you the country. You are the man for the country. I've been waiting on a fellow like you."

* * *

SHAMIE AND the others protested at being left behind. "The Bog Boys must stay all together! What if dragoons come a-hunting for us, Luke? What then?"

"Fergus and I can slip around the country quite easily, and get the lay of the land, and scout what there is. And we're more likely to meet dragoons out there on the roads than here in the bog."

At the mention of dragoons on the road, Shamie's face went yellow and he went to lie down in his scalp.

The others stood disconsolate by the fire, waving sadly as Luke and Fergus set off across the bog plain.

Brown, astringent water squeezing from the turf stung his feet, and he hoped it was burning his sores clean. The workhouse jacket chafed his neck but cut the edge off the wind. They passed through the wrecked village again, Luke leading the way, then traversed one field after another, crossing empty roads, climbing stone walls.

"The little ones, all they think of is their mouths. Poor Shamie is no good. But you and me, Fergus, we'll organize beautifully."

"I don't feel so."

"You and me, together, we might have a bold notion, make a plan, and hold to it — don't you think so?"

"I don't know."

"Shamie, he lives very small. Perhaps he was never much of a soldier. You're the one, Fergus — I seen it in you right away. Now things will go much better for the Bog Boys."

THEY CAME upon an old horse, lying on its side, in an enclosed field where all the grass had been cropped. The horse's hide barely covered its bones. The knobs of joints had broken through and insects were working in the wounds.

Kneeling, Fergus touched the old horse's neck. The eye swiveled at him wildly.

Black lips drawn over yellow teeth.

"Nothing here for us," Luke said. "No meat left on him, poor old man."

Going to the nearest section of wall, Fergus started working loose a stone while Luke stayed with the horse, stroking its neck and singing a song about warriors and cattle.

Dislodging one grainy boulder from the wall, Fergus lugged it over. Luke stood back, still singing, his voice thin and clear. Fergus raised the stone and looked at the horse's wild eye before dropping it on the skull, which broke with a noise like ice snapping.

Luke sang one more verse, then walked away and climbed over the wall. Fergus looked down at the smashed head. The teeth. There was no blood he could see. No eye.

"Come away, Fergus."

The heavy soil in the next field clumped at their feet and accumulated; it was like wearing heavy, muddy boots. They began chasing each other, slipping and sliding in the mud, screaming with laughter.

A TURNIP field was being gleaned by a crowd of women and children pecking at the soil. After filling their pockets with turnip tops, Fergus and Luke kept striking across the fields, avoiding the roads.

They were crossing a field of oat stubble when he looked up and suddenly recognized the shape of the mountain in the distance. The country untangled itself in one shake, and he identified a distant line of trees, the pattern of his father's stonework in the field wall, even an iron gate, painted bright red.

They were on Carmichael's farm.

Overcome, he squatted down. Was Luke a *siog*, one of the spirits? Was this walking in a dream?

"What is it, Fergus?"

He brushed Luke's hand away and forced himself to stand, turning his back to the mountain and facing the wind with his eyes shut, feeling it blast and chisel his face. He could feel fever coming on, a relapse. If he gave in it would kill him.

Perhaps it was fever that had brought him back to die in front of the farmer.

He opened his eyes and grabbed Luke's wrist. "Where are you taking me?" he demanded. "Where are we going?"

"First to the river," Luke said, looking at him closely. "Are you sure you're all right?"

He hated thinking it was a spell that brought him back here.

*   *   *

THEY STOOD by the little river. He wanted to dare his fever, shock it, do something violent to break the dream, if he was in dreaming.

"What I have to show you is on the other side. We can go along to the bridge, but someone might see us, don't you think? So I reckon we had better swim it. Are you game? Can you do it?"

Yes, he wished to blast himself alive, or drown. The river would be cold and he wasn't much of a swimmer, though he usually could keep his head up. Turning his back to Luke, he undressed quickly, dropping his clothes on the grass.

He turned around, and saw Luke standing in the white body of a girl.

"There it is, there it is," Luke said softly.

Fergus was too tired to feel anything except bewilderment, as though an owl had spoken.

"Do you think you've seen a *siog?* Touch me if you don't believe your eyes."

White breasts and red nipples, curved belly, dark patch of sexual hair.

Her little cut.

He didn't move. Reaching out, Luke took his hand and held it to her breast, watching him.

"I'm no *siog*, Fergus. I'm the real."

Through the softness he could feel her heart beating.

"Are you torn down? Is it disgraceful to be following a girl?" She let go of his hand. "Shall you resign? Do you wish to go home now?"

He had no words.

"I've lived hard and wild as any, Fergus. I'm strong, and will be stronger."

Yes. As a girl, she already seemed more formidable, possessing power he hadn't recognized before. "Do the others know?"

"They do. Only I suppose some have forgotten. The little ones, all they think of is their mouths. And poor Shamie is no good. But we'll organize beautifully, you and me — I know we will. You are a good, stiff one."

"I don't feel so."

"It scares me to look at you," she said, "for I suppose I am as thin as you."

"Am I so thin?"

"You are, very. I could count your bones. I used to be plump, a little. But those days are gone."

Without another word, she waded in through the yellow rushes, gasping at the cold. Wading steadily deeper, she suddenly plunged, coming up a few seconds later, her dark hair slicked back like an otter, screaming and kicking. "Whoo, whoo! Fergus, it burns like Hell! It is very cold! Oh my dear!" She laughed and began splashing for the opposite bank.

He stepped in tentatively. The cold was numbing. The bottom was sloped and muddy and he wished he hadn't agreed to swim but couldn't let her go across alone, his pride wouldn't stand it. He tottered a few more steps and then, about to lose his balance, plunged headfirst into the shiny current. The shock was like a steel spade smacking his chest. It hurt to breathe; he felt his lungs withering with cold. She was already climbing up on the bank. He could see her white body against the grass. As the current tugged him downstream, he started thrashing. After swallowing mouthfuls of water, he felt his toes touching mud.

He waded out through more dead reeds, heart roaring, skin on fire. Luke was laughing, her skin covered in goose bumps. "I wish we had a fire, I would bake in the coals, and you would eat me."

"I wouldn't want to eat you."

She scraped her wet hair with her fingers, looking at him.

"Come," she said suddenly. "It's in here — in the willows."

He followed after her, pushing through a little thicket of willows and alders. There was a little leather boat, overturned on a couple of stumps.

"I've been considering the use of the thing."

Not much bigger than a kettle, the currach was made of a cowhide, stretched over a basket frame of hazel wands, the seams sewn and thickly tarred. A pair of leather paddles were tucked up inside.

Fergus was delighted by the discovery. "I think we must light the river."

"How do you mean?"

"The best fishing is at night. I'll make a lister. You'll see. We'll need torches and a net. It would be fine to catch a salmon, wouldn't it, Luke?"

Reaching out, she touched his ear with cold fingertips. "There may be a keeper with a gun. But I figured you was a waterman."

He didn't have much experience on the river. The little boat belonged to a poacher, perhaps one of his uncles — he had overheard talk of lighting the river. There was no paid keeper on this stretch. Carmichael and his sons did not pay much attention since the fish did not belong to them.

"We'll paddle back over to the other side and hide it there, then come back at night."

There was just room for the two of them to squeeze into the little boat. They each took a paddle and worked quickly back across. Concealing the currach in the trees, they quickly dressed. He watched her pulling on her breeches, tying them with string.

Sunlight warmed the scented grass. He was hungry.

"I know Shamie is a coward," Luke said, wrapping herself in her layers of gauzy old linen shirts, "which is why the Bog Boys have done so little, and lived so meager."

He followed her out of the trees and across the pasture where Carmichael usually kept his bull in winter, but the bull was gone and the grass was thick, tufted in bunches.

He missed her body after she was dressed. Nakedness was powerful, like a separate thing between them — a spell; a mysterious bird.

Whatever it was, clothes hid it.

"It is time we acted," Luke said.

"Fishing is good."

"I mean other actions as well, Fergus. I mean war."

Suddenly he felt sick and cold.

"You're not shy. I know you," she said happily.

He knew what she was going to say next.

"There is a farmer. Rides a red mare. They say he is very rich."

Vengeance

A STORM WAS BLOWING UP black as they came along the road to Carmichael's. It suddenly felt cold enough for a snow. He wanted to turn back but something kept him on the road. A spell had carried him here, after all; why resist? He walked in a daze, hardly hearing her.

"I have not raised it with Shamie, thinking we could not put it over, but now, with you and me captains, we can. I know we can. A gentleman I used to know in Limerick, a land agent, told me this here is the richest farm of the estate. They keep a year of food in a storehouse."

They were coming past the badger wood, crossing the bridge. He didn't want to go any farther, but couldn't seem to stop himself, or change anything. Something strong had carried him this far and he couldn't escape it now.

"What is it, Fergus? Is something wrong? You look very ill."

"I know these people."

She stopped, gripped his arm. "Do you know where they keep the food?"

"A little stone house in the yard — he keeps tools there and stores in a cellar underneath."

People on the mountain claimed the little stone hovel had been a holy church in the days when there had been saints in the country.

"Are there dogs?"

"There was but she hated them so he got rid of them."

"Who hated them?"

"Phoebe. Carmichael's daughter."

"Bless her. I hate dogs too. Here." She took off the soldier cap and placed it on Fergus's head. "Now you look like a ribbonman. What stores does he keep?"

"Corn. Apples."

"What else? Meat?"

"Meat if they have slaughtered. Butter."

"Butter!"

"He keeps it locked."

"There's ways to kill locks."

They came around the bend in the road, and there were the familiar iron gate and the gaunt farmhouse, blinking at him across the yard.

Luke pointed to a thick little stone building with slits instead of windows, standing between the house and stable. "Is that the stores?"

"It is."

Luke scanned the yard. "It's perfect. If we come at night, who'll stop us, if we are quiet enough? We can boost a little fellow inside, through them skinny windows. Only we must wait the night without any moon, move quiet. We're plenty of hands to carry off rations. A noggin of butter, that would be famous."

The kitchen door opened. Carmichael stepped out.

"God, don't let the fellow know you," Luke said under her breath.

"Nothing for you here!" the farmer shouted.

"Only looking for soup, mister!" cried Luke.

"We give charity at Scariff, not on the farm! The soup kitchen is at the church. Keep on the road to Scariff and you'll be fed."

"Thank you, sir!" Luke bowed.

"Off with you now," Carmichael called.

"WAS that him? The fellow that ejected you?"

He nodded.

As they crossed stripped fields, heading back to the bog, Luke began telling her story.

"My mother sold me to a farmer when I was small. I was a dairy girl, only last summer the farmer decided he would emigrate. I supposed they would take me with them, but he gave me four shillings instead and turned me on the road."

"What was your name when you were a girl?"

"What does it matter?" She stopped walking and glared at him.

"I didn't mean to sting you — I only wished to know your name."

"Luke! Luke is my name!"

"All right. I didn't mean to cut you, Luke. I'm sorry."

"All right then." She smiled at him and they resumed walking.

"What happened after they left you on the roads?"

"Oh, I aimed for Limerick. Where they had gone. I was thinking to get a passage to America. No notion what it cost — six shillings was as much money as I'd ever seen. As I was going along, I met a mob of little herds down off the Galtee Mountains. All their black cattle were being sold up, shipped to England, and the boys were thrown out on the roads like myself, only younger. They had no place to go, and the potatoes everywhere was coming up black so there was nothing to steal. We moved along the roads, keeping together, a band of us, me the eldest, though I was the girl."

She stopped again. "I tell you, Fergus, we were frightened of strange country, the little fellows especially, grabbing hold my hands and not letting go. You see 'em now, how bold they are, but not then. Some of them were born up in the booleys. They always lived wild."

"I was on the booley."

"Were you? Some of them were sold up very young for herds, sold to graziers. None of 'em knew a life beyond grass and sky, rain and cattle.

"Two or three of them caught the black fever and died along the road. We kept asking people, 'Is this road for Limerick?' We never seemed to get there. We walked for days and never found a town.

"I'll tell you the truth, Fergus — we were frightened of towns, that's why we didn't find it." She touched his arm. Her hand was clean from the river, small and white. She had left her hair loose. She was small. Her body was like a whittled stick. Her face was white, clear, and fine. Gray bright eyes. Full, pale lips and good teeth.

"But finally we did come into Limerick. I was still a girl then. I was nice enough, and there were gentlemen that fancied me, spoke to me on the street. At first I thought it was kindness I heard, but it wasn't.

"I did well, whoring in Limerick. Oh, I did nicely there. I wasn't any soft one — no. They liked me small and rough. I had a gentleman kept me, in a room above a beer shop. Wanted me all to himself. Guinea a week he paid — that's a pound and a shilling. Once, looking down out my window, I saw a whore being mauled in the street. Pair of wolfhounds snapping her to bits and wouldn't mind any shouting. I seen her afterward, all ripped to pieces."

Her voice was clear. Her skin glowed.

"No, no, Fergus, a town is wicked, I suppose. In Limerick sometimes, I was so whirled I had trouble remembering my name. I'd never known a room before, nor slept in a real bed. In Limerick my bed was better than mistress's at the farm — white linen, soft pillows, rugs. My fellow, my gentleman, I would see him regular. He would give me a shilling extra if I'd let him lick my feet, and I did, and a few other things, and he always handed it over."

"He paid a shilling to lick your feet?"

She nodded, grinning.

"I don't believe it."

"You haven't been in the whirl, Fergus. Men will pay for just about any-thing." She started walking away.

He started after her. "I didn't mean any insult."

"What you can or cannot believe, Fergus, don't change a thing. Perhaps your head's too small for the world. You can't fit much in."

"I'm sorry."

They walked in silence for a while, then — "Do you want to hear it as it was?"

"Yes. If you please."

"My gentleman would pay, and I would buy a ribbon or two, and Indian meal for the boys. For I had all the rations I required, and they were living in a stable in exchange for sweeping out the stalls, and begging and ranging for their food; and what they call in my country *snow gathering* — stealing clothes off hedges when they're set out to dry.

"One evening my gentleman did not come, and next day a friend of his told me he had caught fever and was dead. There was wild fever in Limerick. Country people were pouring in, crowding the quays, selling whatever they could, buying passages for Liverpool, for Quebec. I wasn't able to turn a living no more, there was so many girls for the trade. Then, one morning, in the stable, I came upon Shamie, with his little Mary Cooley, sleeping in the hayloft. He had cut loose of his regiment. Where he picked up the Mary I still don't know. Seeing that Brown Bess gun of his gave me the notion for shaping the boys into a band of ribbonmen, outlaws. Rebels.

"Because my gentleman always said there was plenty of food only it isn't in the towns, the strong farmers have it. The farmers are holding it for themselves and selling dear. Anyone could see the carts and wagons lined up on the quays in Limerick, stuffed with food — butter, honey, bacon — and the cattle and sheep, everything going onto the ships, sold away to England.

"Everyone who couldn't afford a passage was dying in Limerick that week, so I made up my mind we should all leave the town and go outlawing and find some of that food my old fellow was talking about. I organized the boys, and found rations for the road, and Shamie come along with his little Mary, wearing a cloak over his uniform, with one of the boys carrying his musket.

"Shamie hates the road. He don't have the outlaw heart. He is a coward. You can't live on boiled nettles forever." Stopping, she turned and looked back in the direction of the farm. "The food is there, Fergus. I know it is. You know it. Butter. Honey. A fletch of bacon. What right have they, those farmers? Who gave them the land? Vengeance is due, Fergus. That's why you've come among us."

Vengeance? Fergus looked back at the mountain. Considered from a distance, it seemed small enough. There was the sky he had lived under all his life. It was hard to believe that the mountain had contained his life and the lives of everyone he had known.

"Don't you think, after all they have done, Fergus, that they deserve to pay?"

"They won't give up anything. They'll fight."

"The Bog Boys would rather die in a fight than in a ditch, Fergus."

The Oath

THE BOG BOYS SPENT the next few days searching for birds' eggs and beating through the gorse, trying to flush another hare. To Fergus's surprise, Luke did not mention raiding the farm to any of the others, and Fergus did not raise the subject, grateful to let it lie, hoping Luke would forget it. He had found a wooden handle from a turf cutter's spade and was making a lister, a fish spear, honing the tip to a sharp point and notching teeth in the shaft.

While he worked on the lister, Luke gathered charlock and other herbs.

Shamie amused himself by placing shots very near the little boys beating the gorse, who screamed with laughter as the bullets snapped by them.

"He is a fool," Fergus said angrily to Luke.

"Don't mind him. Shamie is careful."

"He's wasting powder."

"Practice is good for him."

When Johnny Grace, one of the Bog Boys, flushed a hare, Shamie killed it on the run and they carried it back to camp in triumph, Johnny Grace walking at the head of the column with the dead hare on his back.

It was quickly peeled and cut up, the meat added to the stirabout. While the kettle simmered, Luke and Fergus sat puffing their pipes.

"It's time you had the oath," Luke said suddenly. She looked around at the others. "What do you say, men? Shall we oath Fergus in?"

"No, no — not yet," Shamie warned. "You watch that fellow, Luke — he's not one of us. Let him put some meat in the pot before you oath him."

"No, it's time," Luke decided. She stood up. "Give me your hand, Fergus."

The small boys gathered around eagerly, as if the oath had a scent that tantalized them. Licking their fingers, they stared wide-eyed from Luke to Fergus.

"Repeat after me," Luke began. "I swear to defend the queen —"

"I swear to defend the queen —"

"— and true religion lost at Reformation."

"— and true religion lost at Reformation."

"I am bound to rebellion for life and death."

"I am bound to rebellion for life and death."

"True blood for true blood, or the devil take my soul."

"True blood for true blood, or the devil take my soul."

"There you are," said Luke. She kissed Fergus on the cheek, then Shamie. The small boys began kissing one another. Mary Cooley stood next to Shamie, holding his hand while sucking her thumb.

The deserter had watched the oathing with a sour expression. Now Luke took Shamie's hand and Fergus's and pressed them together. "There we are, boys, all brothers now."

"Another mouth to eat what's ours," Shamie said.

"Don't be grim, Shamie."

While the scent of meat simmered from the kettle, Luke started telling the Bog Boys about the farm. "They will have hams as big as any of you — pink, with a reel of yellow fat. They will have turnips and apples in baskets. I like an apple with my meat. Mutton for spoileen. When was the last time any of you tasted spoileen?"

"Will there be butter?" Johnny Grace asked.

"There will be, yes, plenty." Luke knelt, placing a turf on the fire and blowing at the coals. When the flames were singing, she stood up, facing them. "There's no use being outlaws if we never engage."

Fergus had been hoping that she had forgotten about raiding Carmichaels', but now he saw the idea was on her like an animal, with a scent and a weight.

"Yellow meal?" Johnny asked.

"Yellow meal, sure. And oatmeal. A casket of tea —"

"Potatoes?" asked a small boy whom the others called Little Priest.

"Sure there will be potatoes. And a jar or two of herring — I love a herring with my spuds."

"Is there a plan?" Johnny Grace asked. "I should relish any action, but I'd follow you to Hell for a plan, Luke."

"Of course there's a plan. Fergus and I have worked it over, very military."

No. It wasn't true, there wasn't any plan, not that he knew about.

To Luke, he realized, a wish was the same as a plan.

"Will some of us be killed?" Johnny Grace demanded. "Will we hang if they catch us? Will they transport us? It's not that I mind much being killed. Only if I was to go down without tasting no spoileen nor other stuffs first, it would seem cruel."

"Hanging is cruel!" Shamie called out angrily.

They all looked up at the deserter sitting at the top of the trench, his legs dangling. He had laid the musket flat across his knees and was rubbing browning on the barrel. Mary Cooley was beside him.

"We all know you ain't the fellow for raiding, Shamie," Johnny Grace said, grinning at the others.

"Watch what you say!"

"We're tired of withering out here on account of your old womanhood."

"I'm the one with a price on his head! I'm the one they served twenty lashes!"

"The rest of us are keen," said Johnny Grace. "You've killed two coneys in sixteen days and that doesn't make you a chief. If Luke and the Fergus have a plan, then I'm for it. You can stay here eating grass."

"Quiet now, fellows!" said Luke. "Don't be tearing each other up."

"We want food, don't you?" Johnny Grace said. "We want potatoes, don't you?"

"Potatoes! Potatoes! Potatoes!" the Bog Boys began screaming at the deserter.

"Potatoes and spoileen," Johnny Grace said.

"Potatoes and spoileen! Potatoes and spoileen!" the Bog Boys howled. Johnny Grace grabbed the Little Priest by the hand and they began to dance, whirling and leaping about the fire. Others joined the frenzy and the dance gathered momentum, boys skipping around the fire, howling, and Fergus realized they were unable to stop. Something wild and hungry had been let loose. They'd dance until they were dead, unless he stopped it.

He broke into the circle, going for Johnny Grace, seizing him and throwing him down on the ground. The dance stopped as suddenly as it had started, and Fergus held Johnny down with a foot on his chest while he writhed and screamed.

Boys were collapsing around the fire, crawling on their hands and knees, panting and coughing like ruined horses.

"Boys, boys, this ain't no way to carry on!" Luke was near tears.

Fergus lifted his foot away, and the herd boy sat up, blubbing and snorting, chest heaving, rubbing his fists in his eyes.

"Why, if it goes on like this, men, it must be hopeless!" Luke told them. "You wouldn't see such wildness in any careful army."

"Eight herd boys? There's no army here!" Shamie cried. "If it came to exchange, they'd howl and run like Frenchmen."

Luke looked at the deserter. Her voice was calm. "Myself, I suppose I would as soon be shot, or hung, as die famished. But them with a price on their heads, why, I shall not hold it against them if they don't care to venture."

Shamie rubbed his musket barrel furiously.

"As for me." Luke pulled the soldier cap off her head and dropped it on the ground. Sliding two splinters of cow bone from her black hair, she shook it loose then ran her fingers through it. "You all remember I was born a girl. I shall die a girl if it comes to that. I'd rather die than live so mean as we have. Every fellow that feels the same, step forward now and give me his kiss."

No one moved, at first. Fergus could hear the click of the fire.

Then Johnny Grace got to his feet. He was frail, his face was yellow, he wore rags for trousers, and his withered arse cheeks were exposed as he walked around the fire to Luke, kissed her, then stood next to her and glared at the others.

One by one, Bog Boys arose and stepped around the fire to kiss Luke, until only Shamie, Mary Cooley, and Fergus were left.

"Come, the rest of you, don't stay out in the cold." Luke was looking straight at him across the fire.

"Carmichaels will fight."

"They have stolen the land and the food out of our mouths. We have the perfect right to help ourselves."

"Shamie's right, Luke. They're herd boys, not soldiers."

"Farmers are not soldiers either. The food belongs to us. We are only taking what belongs to us. If they try to stop us, it's blood for blood, Fergus. Vengeance — isn't that what you want? Give us your heart. You won't be sorry. You'll know you're alive."

Mary Cooley suddenly jumped down from her perch beside Shamie and raced around the fire to kiss Luke.

"Poxed little bitch!" Shamie screamed. "Traitor!"

Luke looked up at the soldier. "What about you, Shamie?"

"You're the ones wishing to hang! Not me!"

"But if you stay out alone, you'll die alone, Shamie."

"Perhaps, but I won't be flogged!"

"I'm talking the truth to you now. I can see death coming Shamie, clear as my hand."

Shamie broke into ugly sobs.

"You know it, Shamie dear. You don't want to be alone. Come down now. Join with us."

"Only I don't want flogging, Luke, I can't stand another flogging."

"There shall be no flogging. Come join us, Shamie dear."

The deserter jumped down and landed heavily, clutching the musket in both hands. He stood facing Luke across the fire. "Promise I won't be captured, Luke."

"Sure, I promise. Now give us your kiss."

Weeping, Shamie came around the fire and kissed Luke, who took his face in her hands. "You'll be true, I know." Then she looked across at Fergus. "What about you?"

Oath or no oath, he could still have walked away.

Perhaps they'd have tried stopping him. Perhaps not.

He didn't want to die alone, any more than did the soldier. That was why he stepped to the other side of the fire, and why he kissed Luke. That was why he became the last of the Bog Boys.

Lighting the River

WHILE THE BOG BOYS DOZED in their burrows, Fergus, Shamie, and Luke sat by the fire, smoking coltsfoot in clay pipes.

Luke thought they should attack the farm that very night. "We have the spirit now after a good meat feed. If we don't go now, we might dissolve."

But it was drizzling wet, and Shamie insisted they must wait for a dry night, with no moon.

"A good black night. If it's wet, I won't answer for her," he said, patting the musket lock, which he had covered with a piece of greasy cloth. "Wet ain't reliable firing. I ain't going into action in rain. A farmer will have his powder warm and dry. When a fellow shoots at me, I shall exchange, not run like a Frenchman."

"There it is," Luke agreed. "I defer to the military. You are right, Shamie. We shall wait until a night when it's dry and the moon is gone."

"Have you ever seen a Frenchman?" Fergus asked the soldier.

Shamie sneered.

"It's all talk, isn't it?" Fergus said. "All the soldiering you ever did was tumbling cabins —"

"I'm thinking of a fish," Luke interrupted. "Is your spear ready?"

Fergus looked at her. For days, he had been honing and sharpening the lister, twisting it slowly over a flame, carefully roasting the point, hardening it.

"Yes."

"Are you ready, man?"

He nodded.

"Good. Tonight," she said, "we light the river."

TREES OVERHUNG the river, bare branches creaking in the wind. Fergus and Luke squatted together in the currach. Bog Boys stood in the shallows holding line attached to the little boat as Fergus paddled out into the current, hands dipping in cold water with each pull. At the middle of the stream, the line sprung taut from the water, dripping, holding them against the current.

Luke held a pair of bog-wood torches, more glow than flame. Light danced on the black water. In such cold, the fish stayed deep.

He felt the river strumming the taut leather hide of the currach as the current slipped by her hull. Luke was pale with concern. He took one of the torches from her.

"Sweep the light, now, nice and slow," he instructed. "Keep it close to the water so they feel the light." Luke leaned out of the currach and waved her torch tentatively above the surface. "Yes, just like that, that is the business. Nice and steady."

Gripping the lister in his right hand, he leaned out and began sweeping his light over the water. The river dashed under them, endless action, smelling of wood and rain. The fragile currach hung steady in the stream. He stroked the torch back and forth.

He sensed the salmon's presence before he saw the flash of silver. The hairs on his neck prickled. He cocked his elbow, ready to lunge. Luke had seen it too; she froze. He heard his own breathing. He leaned out harder, risking an upset. He could no longer see the fish but it was still there, he felt the presence, and he kept stroking his light just above the water.

The fish came up sudden. He saw its eye glitter in the light and drove the spear and felt a terse shock of pleasure as it went in. The fish writhing, fighting. Afraid the current would drag it off the spear, he gripped the shaft in both hands and levered the salmon out of the river. Luke was screaming. Fergus held the spear high so the Bog Boys on shore could see the salmon flapping like a pennant, spraying them with silver water and blood.

They carried the fish back to the camp and he opened it with the bayonet then scooped the guts out with his hand. He wrapped the fish in wet leaves and placed it next to the coals to cook. The meat was orange and there was enough to feed them all.

Hunger (1)

HE WAS LYING IN HIS scalpeen thinking of his family when he felt something tickling his feet.

"Can I sleep with you, Fergus?"

It was Luke. Before he could answer, she had crawled into the scalpeen.

The shine of her eyes, in her bony little face.

"We ought to have a watch posted," he said peevishly. "Anyone could surprise us. You might have been the dragoons."

"I'll leave, if you want me to."

"They'll drag us out one night. You'll see."

"Do you want to ride me?"

Perhaps he did, and what was that about? Pigs did. Sheep did.

"Fergus, I'm an old horse. You needn't be afraid."

The smallness of her body punched him so hard he felt his heart skip.

"I'm an old horse, been riding as far as I can remember."

Sitting up — there was just room enough — she started unbuttoning her coat. She shrugged out of it, and spread it on the bracken. Beneath the coat she wore layers of ragged linen shirts. None of the shirts had buttons, but she had bound them on with soft straw cord wrapped around and around herself, battening the layers of gauzy cloth to her body.

He watched her pick at a knot in the cord. "I'm small but you won't break me. Here, you must help me." She handed him the cord, and he started to unwind it from around her. It took time. She laughed aloud.

Finally she was unwound. She began pulling off her shirts. The top layers still had dye but the underlayers were faded and silvery and came to pieces when he pulled at them.

"It's a kind of hunger, we must feed ourselves," she said, kissing his thumb. He felt her hand rest lightly on his hip. Her shoulders were narrow, her breasts small and sharp. The skin was very soft and pale. Taking his hand she touched his fingertips to her nipples and the softness of each breast.

"There it is, there it is." Her eyes closed.

When she let go of his hand, he pulled it back.

She opened her eyes. "Aren't I pretty enough for you?"

He didn't know how to answer.

"Don't you want to be inside the whirl?"

He said nothing.

"Fergus, there's nothing to be feared. I'm an old horse. I'll show you."

Luke untied the string at her waist. Wriggling her hips, she started pulling down her trousers, and in another moment she was naked. She seized his hand again and brought it along her throat and to her mouth, nipping his fingers and kissing his palm then bringing the hand down the ripple of her ribs. Her belly was flat and hard. He touched the knobs of her hips. He stared at her eyes as his fingers brushed her bush of sexual hair. She flinched and bit her lip then smiled.

"Go on, there's nothing better, Fergus."

She opened her legs a little and he touched the gash, and then with his fingertips wet from inside her he stroked the soft white skin of her thighs. The juicy, meaty smell. He inhaled it from his fingers. She smelled alive. She began pulling at his clothes.

"I'm going to seize you and swallow you alive," she said. "I'm going to give you all your courage."

When he was naked he felt raw, light. Her skin was hot to touch. She took his scarlet penis in her hands and kissed him. When he pushed into her she grunted and wrapped her legs around his hips and licked his neck and said he was a captain. He felt a sense of great distance from everything else but this sharp, hard edge of joy.

Mary Cooley

A FEW MORNINGS LATER he was awakened by the sound of shouting. It was very early. Luke had already left the scalp though he could still feel the impression of her light body curled into his hip.

They were feeding on each other, every night.

How peculiar, the dexterity of passion.

Those things burning inside — he had never contacted such heat before. Vicious, hungry, wild.

He smiled. He felt alive, living in his skin once more.

A girl gave you yourself.

Hearing more shouting outside, he hurriedly pulled on clothes and crawled out of the scalp and started walking along the trench, toward the smudge of the morning fire.

The soldier was on his knees by the fire, blubbing. Luke stood over him, bayonet in her right hand. A kettle of water was seething.

"What is it, Shamie?" Luke cried. "Was it the horrors? Were you dreaming?"

Steel blade in her hand; mess of black hair mobbing her shoulders.

Bog Boys who'd come running at the noise stood coughing and scratching.

"Tell us what it is my love, what has got you so flayed?" Luke grasped the soldier's hair and snapped his head back. "You bleeding bastard Shamie, you devil, what are you afraid of telling? What have you done?"

Suddenly Luke thrust the bayonet in the ground and pushed her way out through the circle of Bog Boys, walking quickly along the trench toward Shamie's scalp. Fergus called her but she ignored him and broke into a run. He started after her.

At the entrance to Shamie's scalp she hesitated, looking back at Fergus. Then, dropping to her hands and knees, she crawled inside. As Fergus came up, all he could see of her were the black soles of her feet.

She was already backing out of the scalp. Extracting herself, she stood up brushing her sleeves.

"What is it then?" he asked.

"Oh my... there is a storm, Fergus." She rubbed the legs of her trousers. Backs of her hands dark from dirt and weather, as if they had been smoked, cured. "Go see."

He didn't want to, but he must. He couldn't shy in front of her.

Getting down on his hands and knees, he began crawling inside. When his head and shoulders were through the opening, he smelled earth and old smoke. He couldn't see at first, it was so dim. He touched skin — a leg. Peering closer, he saw it was Shamie's little maid, Mary Cooley, lying on her stomach on a pad of bracken and leaves, her skirts rucked up.

The dead lie so close to the ground. They seem so heavy.

He smelled the blood. It was smeared on her buttocks, her stalky thighs.

He could hear his breath hissing through the sticks, the wands, the turf that composed the scalp. Yesterday he had watched Mary Cooley fastidiously picking lice from Shamie's clothes, and wondered that anyone thought the soldier worth such trouble.

But she was Shamie's girl.

How old? Nine years? Ten?

He rolled her over. Lips and teeth coated with blood. Eyes open. Blood glued at her chin and throat.

The furry odor of leaf mold was making him sick.

He couldn't feel sorry for her, not really. He didn't feel angry, or anything strong whatsoever, not like before, not like the cabin burning.

He could hear Luke shouting.

He started backing out of the scalp, snagging his trousers on a wand, tearing the cloth.

Veins of light in the sky.

Luke was heading back to the fire, and he started after her.

All his feeling was oriented to her, he realized. Their nights had burned them together. In every situation he would think of her first.

The circle of Bog Boys opened. The soldier was kneeling by the fire and plaintively rubbing his hands and wrists on the ground.

"Shamie, Shamie, what have you done?" Luke cried.

The Bog Boys shifted on their feet, tense as cattle.

Shamie looked up. "I did kiss her, Luke —"

"He has killed Mary Cooley," Luke announced to the Bog Boys. Pulling the bayonet out of the ground, she kicked Shamie, who crumpled up and lay on his side, motionless, looking up at her.

"You fucked her so brutal, you know you did. Tore her up."

"No — for love, Luke. For love. I swear."

"If we have rope we must hang the fellow," Johnny Grace called.

"You used her wicked."

"She wanted me; I was her easy."

"Sentence of death," said Johnny Grace.

"There isn't rope," Luke said, not looking around, but gazing down at Shamie and gulping each breath, her chest rising and falling.

"We can make one!"

Luke placed one foot on Shamie's chest and held the point of the bayonet at his heart.

"Kill me, Luke. I don't care."

"Kill him with the dagger!"

"Only do it quick, and I won't have no flogging." The deserter began unbuttoning his jacket. The boys stood watching, fingers in their mouths.

Fergus sensed the direction they were going now — blood and dying all around, and this was their way. The appetite for violence had been nurtured.

He could not stop feeling the sexual night.

Joy bit your finger like a wasp. You touched her and she was open.

Shamie held open his shirt, exposing his chest. There was a spot of blood on the white skin where the bayonet point had scratched him.

The fire sizzled. Fergus heard a curlew crying in the fog.

"No," said Luke.

She lifted her foot from Shamie's chest.

"Let me then!" Johnny Grace cried.

"No. Shamie's life is spare." She stepped back.

"Get your hands red, Luke!"

She looked around at the Bog Boys. The soldier lay on his back, gasping like a fish.

"I won't have blood on us now. Not when we are about to venture. He is ours and ours now." She looked down at the soldier. "Do you get this, Shamie? You is spare, understand? You had better serve well."

"Kill him, Luke, it's our honor."

Luke shook her head. Jabbing the bayonet in the turf she pushed her way out through the ring of boys and strode to the edge of the camp, where she climbed out of the trench and set off across alone the heather.

Shamie was on his elbows, nostrils flared, breathing in shallow pulses. Seeing Johnny Grace eyeing the bayonet, Fergus stepped forward and pulled it from the ground.

"You snap him, Fergus!" Johnny urged. "Get your hands red. Be our chief."

Looking over their heads, Fergus saw Luke's slight figure roaming the distance.

He slipped the bayonet under his belt. "Get the kettle on. Chop the grub. We'll bury her after."

They were so thin and faint, so malleable, they couldn't resist his orders; Johnny Grace falling in with the rest. Weak as moths, they moved to obey.

HOWLING THE *uilecan*, the funeral cry, the Bog Boys carried Mary Cooley out across the bog plain, then formed a hollow square and watched in silence while Fergus and Johnny Grace dug the grave, using spades left by turf cutters, chopping through bracken, through turf with gauze roots.

"Gently now," Luke said.

Fergus took Mary Cooley's wrists. Luke and Johnny took her ankles. It was still early, but the light had stalled. They swung her out over the hole. Water had seeped in already. The bottom was shining black. They set her down without making a splash.

No one spoke.

He picked up the spade and was about to start filling in, but Luke touched his arm.

"Time for you all to think." She stared into the hole for a few moments, then looked around at the Bog Boys, studying their faces. Luke wore Shamie's soldier jacket, her hands plunged in the pockets. "There is dead and there is life and there is something in between," she said quietly. "I have been living in a strange country and somehow I want to go home again. I suppose us all wants so. Boys, the only way is bravery."

When she paused, he heard wind moving through the bracken. He knew the storm was coming.

"We must take the thing in our hands," she said. "Call it a raid, call it a venture, and make war of it. Make a beautiful battle if they try to stop us."

The cold aroma of fresh turf.

Once, cutting fuel with his cousins and uncles, they had unearthed a strange, white thing. He'd thought it was a fish, but they insisted it was the pure body of a young girl. Later he heard them say she was a queen, with rings on her fingers and a blue stone held tight in her fist. He did not recall seeing any such things himself.

"This girl here," Luke said, "it wasn't Shamie's fucking that killed her. He is a stupid, guff fellow, but I myself have been with fellows worse, much rougher — had them over me, using me; maybe you have too — they were gentlemen, some of them. It hurts, but it don't kill you. No, Mary died because she was too small to live, because she hadn't rations, just like you. And where is the food? Where is it?"

"Where is it, Luke?" asked the Little Priest, one of the smallest Bog Boys.

"The farmer has it. The farmer has hugged all the food of the country. If you are looking for a murderer, why, there he is."

"There he is," Johnny Grace said. "You're right, Luke."

Fergus realized what she was doing. She had put something in the air, a charge, he could taste it. Gunpowder.

But her plans were vapor. She had no plans, only wishes.

She had courage but no patience. Hers wasn't the temper of a hunter.

"So, Mary Cooley," Luke said, "here you are, girl, into the ground."

The Bog Boys were standing almost soldierly, their feyness and weakness disguised behind solemn faces.

"Let your soul keep us. Keep us strong and brave, guide us as we go for war. Make them old farmers answer —"

"Answer in blood," whispered Johnny Grace.

"Answer in blood, for what they've done."

"Answer in blood," the Bog Boys murmured.

"Strength and courage," Luke intoned. "Watch over us. We're your soldiers now."

Luke nodded at Fergus, and he threw the first spadeful of soil down upon the dead girl, trying not to look at her face.

EVERY NIGHT, as the old moon was dying, Luke would wrap herself in the teamster's greatcoat and lie on Mary Cooley's grave until Fergus came out and led her to bed.

They could not get enough of each other in those nights before war.

After their convulsions, he lay warmed by the heat flowing from her body. The little scalpeen was suffused with her sexual smell.

"I am full when you're in me, Fergus," she said one night, idly playing with his hair as he lay across her. "Don't feel the empties. No sadness at all. I wish we might stay connected all the time."

In such interludes, between bouts of craving, he too was content.

"Know why I didn't kill Shamie?" she asked him one night.

He shook his head.

"It isn't that I'm a girl and felt soft. I'd have killed him easier than slaughter a pig. But Shamie is the only one who can load and fire. He tried showing me the musket drill, but I couldn't follow. He gets so red in the face — pinched, yelling — I had to laugh. But Shamie, he can put three or four bangs in the air fast as anything. There. Do you think I'm wrong, Fergus? Think I'm cold? Do you hate me?"

He turned on his side to look at her. It was strange how you connected with a girl, violence mixed with peculiar tenderness. And you thought you were deep inside, but you weren't. No one was. Other people, machines of independent mystery.

"Fergus? What are you thinking, boy?"

"We are all cold inside, aren't we?"

Luke seized his hand and kissed the pad of soft skin under his thumb and rubbed her cheek with it.

"We are an army," she said.

Hunger (II)

"TONIGHT IS BATTLE," Luke told them.

The old moon was finally dead. The loam sky glittered with stars. Clutching sticks sharpened at both ends, the Bog Boys stood about the fire.

"After a battle is always a song — always. Do well, behave strong, and we'll be sung from one end of the country to another. They'll be a song with our names stuck in like nails."

Don't need songs, Fergus thought. *Need quiet. A plan. Directness.*

But they all were ready to follow her, even Shamie. Even himself.

And perhaps that was enough of a plan.

LUKE ARRANGED the smallest and weakest Bog Boys directly behind her, at the front of the column, where they couldn't straggle. Shamie carried the musket, Luke a pitchfork, Johnny Grace an iron spade. The others were armed with sharpened sticks.

Impressed with themselves, awed and solemn, the Bog Boys set out on the night march in better than their usual disarray. Shamie brought up the foot of the column, carrying the musket flat across his shoulder, fist around the muzzle. The Little Priest skipped up and down the column, plucking at their sleeves.

"Will I do something mighty?" the boy asked Fergus, touching his hand.

"I don't know."

They were calm and easy, traveling across the bog plain — soft ground, their ground, but he could feel the tension increasing as the column trailed through the abandoned village at the edge of the bog, past the cabin wrecks and the heaps of rubble marking graves.

A dove fluttered off a broken wall and the whole column froze.

"It's all right, only a bird," Luke reassured. "She's wishing us well. Come along now, men. Easy now."

Moving farther and farther from the safety of the bog, the column trailed across frosted pastures and meadows. He heard boys whimpering and pissing the ground. Like cattle, they were uneasy on the move in strange country.

Luke finally led them out on a hard road with stone walls flanking both sides and a grassy verge bearded with frost.

Shamie hustled from the rear of the column, breathless with protest. "Luke! You promised we shouldn't travel on roads!"

"We can slip the walls easy enough, if we have to. We can get lost if we need, Shamie dear. Don't worry."

"Dragoons patrol the roads!"

"No dragoons tonight," Fergus said, "only a few Frenchmen."

Shamie jabbed the muzzle into Fergus's belly. "You'd like to see me flogged, wouldn't you? I know your kind — you're a Feeny, ain't you? You're a Thin Boy, a rebel bastard —"

"Shamie! Get back in line!" Luke hissed.

Swinging the muzzle, Shamie pointed at Luke's chest. Fergus heard a metallic snap as the hammer cocked.

"What is this, Shamie?" said Luke quietly.

"What I please." The soldier's wrists were shaking.

Luke laid one finger against the barrel. "Will you blow my heart out?"

"No roads!" Shamie cried. "You promised we'd keep off the road!"

"Time of war, you tell me what holds, Shamie — what promises." Luke spoke softly. "Rations or a fight — that's all I promised the Bog Boys. That should be enough."

Shamie held the gun level.

If Luke was shot, Fergus decided, he would seize a boulder from the wall and smash Shamie before he could reload. Break his legs, crack his head. But Luke still would be dead.

"Do it, then," Luke said calmly. "Go, Shamie. Get it done, then. Fire away."

The Bog Boys were watching, twittering anxiously, like sparrows on a branch.

"Are you going to or not?" she said impatiently.

Slowly, Shamie lowered the weapon. "You know I'm one with you, Luke — it's only this fellow. Perhaps he is a spy."

"Get back in line now, Shamie," Luke said. "You must save any stragglers."

"The Bog Boys we are," Shamie groaned. "We don't belong to no road."

"Everyone must keep their place in line of march. I'm counting on you, Shamie." She looked back at the Bog Boys. "No stragglers. No voice men. Quiet and carefully. Forward, boys."

She led them down the road, carrying the pitchfork over her shoulder. The column shook itself and stumbled after her. Shamie stood aside and let them pass, and Fergus wondered if the soldier was going to desert the Bog Boys now, and slip away across the fields. He hoped this would happen, but a few minutes later when he looked back Shamie was there at the foot of the column, impatiently herding the smallest boys.

THEY ENTERED the wood where once he had hunted badger with his dog. At night the wood seemed unfamiliar, but the cold, weird smell of a small brook he remembered. The Bog Boys splashed across, ankle-deep, one after another, the water biting cold, the bottom grainy.

"Take the head now, Fergus," Luke said after they had all crossed the brook. "It's your country, after all."

The Bog Boys were clumsy in the unfamiliar wood, stumbling over roots, slipping on greasy leaves. Finally Fergus had each one grab the shirt of the boy in front. The connection seemed to settle them. Holding on to each other, the column curled through the wood, quiet as smoke.

Looking up through networks of branches, Fergus saw yellow stars. They came out on a lane and he recognized gouges left by cartwheels. They were approaching the farm.

Suddenly he doubted if he could be an outlaw after all, if he had the heart for murderous intent. A familiar whiff of manure and chimney smoke left his throat as dry as bark. He wished he was alone and had never met Luke and could disappear.

They passed an oat field where Carmichael's cattle usually grazed on the winter stubble, but there were no cattle out tonight.

He heard a sound and stopped abruptly. The column jammed up behind him.

Hooves scratching.

Leather noise.

A horse was coming up the road.

He gestured for the Bog Boys to skip over the nearest wall. They tumbled across and squatted in thick, cold grass along the base of the wall, their backs to the stones.

The land before them sloped from the road. Carmichael's orchard of small, tough apple trees.

He listened.

"Only one alone," Luke said.

Shamie was using his teeth to tear open a cartridge.

"No firing!" Luke whispered.

Fergus peered over the wall.

"Who is it?" Luke asked. "Travelers? Churchmen? Can we rob them?"

It was the farmer, Carmichael, sitting heavy as iron aboard his beauty mare.

Shamie banged the butt of his musket on the grass, tamping the charge, then brought it to his shoulder.

"Shamie — no!"

The shot was simple and abrupt, like a piece of wood splitting. Shamie was enveloped in dense white smoke.

The farmer slumped on the mare's neck for a few paces before tumbling off. His foot caught in the stirrup and he was dragged along the road by the frightened mare like a fox dragged by hunters.

"Have we killed them?" Johnny Grace asked eagerly.

Boys were hopping up and down to see over the wall.

"Is it dragoons?"

"Where's the rations?"

"Is it fighting?"

Shamie was tearing open another paper cartridge. Fergus felt sick. Luke touched his arm. "There it is, Fergus, there it is," she said softly.

Shamie grinned, his long face stained with powder. "Took him in the brains. Now we may help ourselves."

Luke stepped up to the soldier and Fergus thought she was going to strike him, but she stroked his arm instead. "You must keep up steady firing, Shamie, when we reach the farm, and hold the others off."

"You can't go now," Fergus insisted. "They'll be waiting, he has sons, they have a bell gun. We'll never get away."

"Come on! All of you!" Luke cried. "Over the wall! Boldly now! Up the road!"

Clutching their double-pointed sticks, yelping, the Bog Boys swarmed over the wall as Fergus watched, stunned. Even Shamie went over eagerly, climbing like a spider, his military equipment creaking. Smaller boys struggled to hoist themselves.

"Come on," Luke said, holding out her hand to Fergus. "Here is war, old man. Be sweet, Fergus. This is our night."

Boys were running up the road and disappearing into the dark, screaming.

His throat was painfully dry, as if a fire inside had scorched everything.

"Live or die, don't matter," she said. "Not really. I'd be better with you, Fergus."

He still did not move. She turned away. He watched her throw her spade over the wall. He imagined her torn to pieces, her blood entering the ground. She went over neatly.

He saw her pick up the spade, start down the road. She did not look back.

The aroma of apples filled his head.

He heard the crack of a shot from Shamie's musket and a deep, answering boom from another gun.

His bones felt heavy. He would only have strength to travel a little way alone. He would be sick. He'd lie down in some ditch.

If you lay down alone, you'd never get up. You needed a reason. She was the reason.

Sharp screams, two gunshots, and an undertone of yelling floated down the road.

He climbed over the wall and started down the road toward the shouts and firing.

THE IRON gate at the entrance was swinging loose, squealing on its hinges. He stood by the pillar. The farmhouse was closed with iron shutters except one upstairs window where a light burned.

He could see Luke, Shamie, and a group of boys sheltering behind the storehouse. Boys were being boosted up and wriggling through a narrow window, dropping inside.

Two more boys were lying in the open between the buildings, and he could tell from their flat, uneasy shapes they were dead.

As he watched, Shamie stepped out briskly from behind the storehouse, took aim at the farmhouse, fired, then stepped back to shelter. Acrid smoke hung in the air.

He heard a horse whinnying. The red mare was pacing restlessly in front of the stable, dragging Carmichael on the stones.

As Fergus dashed for the storehouse, a gun fired from the farmhouse window, and he saw bits of iron shot sparkled on the paving. He made it to safety behind the storehouse wall, crashing into Luke, who threw her arms around him and kissed his mouth. Her lips tasted of salt and he felt her quick wet tongue; felt her bones through the clothes.

"They are killing my boys, the fucking farmers."

He was glad for coming after her, glad for courage, if that was what it was. Glad for being ready to die.

Shamie finished reloading and cautiously peered around the corner. "You take care," Luke said, patting his hip. "Don't let them clip you."

"Takes a farmer a year to reload," the soldier said disdainfully.

Stepping out from the wall, he brought the musket smartly to his shoulder, discharged, then stepped back and immediately began his drill of reloading.

"Beautiful firing, Shamie, beautiful!"

The Little Priest was tugging at Fergus's sleeve. "They're eating butter inside."

"Fergus, if you please, go inside and stop the fellows gorging. Start passing out whatever we can carry way. We must get away before light. Shamie and I will hold the farmers off — never I seen such beautiful firing, Shamie! Fergus, you must get 'em started passing out the rations."

"Farmers have pikes," Shamie said. "Don't you go inside, Luke! Stay with me, as cavalry supports the infantry."

"I will, Shamie, I will, I'll spike them and you can shoot off their heads." She turned to Fergus. "Yellow meal, butter, bacon, ham — whatever you think we can carry off. See if there's any axes, pikes, or blades we can use. Quickly, now. It'll be light soon."

Boosted on the shoulders of two boys, he wriggled through the deep little window and dropped into the storehouse. Sickles and scythes hung on the walls on pegs — the same ones he and his father had used, making Carmichael's crop in the sun.

There were unopened crates of nails and sacks of sand, for mixing cement. A rack of fir planks, sorted by size. Sheet iron, intended for the roof of a new pig-gery, lay against one wall. Carmichael worshipped neatness, never trusting what he could not lay his hands upon. Insisting ground was his, even if others had named it and were buried in it. If Carmichael couldn't see something, it didn't exist, as far as he was concerned.

A trapdoor yawed open to a root cellar, once a place of concealment for saints and martyrs hiding from the bloody invaders. It was lit by a yellow lantern that greased the air with its fumes. Peering through the hole, he could see the Bog Boys feeding like maggots on a bone. He started down the ladder rungs.

The floor was awash with spilled yellow meal, and the Bog Boys were feast-ing. They had hacked open sacks, broken into casks, smashed clay jars. Boys were cramming their mouths with ham and butter and fighting over beakers of honey and jam.

He cut himself a slab of ham, then took an apple and rubbed it in butter and ate it before he started dragging the Bog Boys away from their gorging. He could feel his lips swelling from salt and grease. He knew if the Carmichaels rushed the storehouse, and Shamie and Luke were unable to hold them off, the boys trapped in the cellar would be killed like rats.

"Come along, men, we must get as much as we can." Organizing them into a line, he started them passing rations up the ladder to Johnny Grace, who dropped the goods through the window to Luke and the others waiting outside.

They heard a shot and a piercing scream. The boys on the ladder froze.

"She's killed, I reckon," the Little Priest said. "Luke is killed, Fergus. Are you chief now?"

Shoving boys aside, he scrambled up the ladder. In the tool room Johnny Grace was standing on the bench, peering out the window. Pushing him aside, Fergus squeezed out through the opening, dropping feet first into the yard.

She was squatting against the wall, panting.

"Are you shot, Luke?" She nodded to Shamie, lying on his back a few paces out from the protection of the wall. "The poor one, see how he spills."

They could hear the blood gurgling out of Shamie's chest, spreading wetly on the stones.

Little boys huddled along the wall behind them were munching apples. Luke stepped out before Fergus could stop her, grabbed Shamie's ankles, and started dragging him in. "Fergus, fetch the musket!"

He stepped out, snatched the musket, and jumped back to safety.

Luke was kneeling beside the soldier. "He's dead."

Shamie's jacket was black with blood. Both eyes were staring. Luke began unbuckling the white cross-straps and pulling off the ammunition pouches. "You must reload quick, Fergus, they'll be coming for us now. Powder, ball, wad — you seen him do it." She peered out around the corner. "Hurry!"

Ripping open one of the paper cartridges with his teeth, he spilled powder down the barrel then dropped in a ball.

"Here they come!" Grabbing her pitchfork, Luke stepped out.

He knew she was shot before he heard the report — she was turning to him, mouth open, when the pitchfork fell from her hands, and he saw the wound blooming on her clothes.

The noise of the shot sped past like a bird in the dark.

Johnny Grace leapt down from the window and tried to seize the musket from him. Luke lay on her back on the cobbles, snorting, her lips wet. Shaking off Johnny Grace, Fergus looked up to see Saul Carmichael running across the yard, horse pistol in one hand, ax in the other. Without thinking or aiming, Fergus raised the musket and fired. The ball caught Saul in the chest and knocked him backward, the pistol and ax flying from his hands, screeching on the cobbles.

With Johnny Grace's help, he dragged Luke behind the storehouse. Her clothes were steeped in blood. They sat her up against the wall, her legs splayed. He couldn't look at her anymore. Methodically, he reloaded, stepped out, fired at the farmhouse window, stepped back, and began reloading again. A gun flashed from the upstairs window and the iron shot cracked on the stones. Reloaded, he peered around the corner. He kept watch until he caught a shadow of a movement — they were firing from one of the bedrooms. Stepping out briskly, he aimed and fired, hearing a muffled scream as he stepped back to shelter. He began reloading.

When he stepped out again, a shot sang past his ear, snapping on the wall. He fired again at the upstairs window and stepped back again to reload, then repeated the sequence, exchanging shot after shot with whoever was gunning from the farmhouse.

After each returned shot, when they must be reloading, Johnny Grace raced out to plunder Saul Carmichael's body, taking the pistol first, then Saul's beaver hat, then the ax.

Boys dropped down from the slit window and huddled along the wall, cramming food in their mouths and staring at Luke. Fergus could hear her asking for water.

"We must get away, Fergus, it'll soon be light," Johnny Grace said. "You lead us the way, Fergus."

Fergus ignored him. Stepping out again, he fired at the house. He tried to avoid looking at Luke as he was reloading.

Boys began escaping the farmyard in the intervals between shots. Lugging sacks of food, they cleared the walls or raced through the open gate. Johnny Grace was shot dead while trying to pull Saul Carmichael's boots off his feet.

One by one the Bog Boys fled, until there was no one but Luke and Fergus sheltered behind the storehouse. As dawn leached into the sky he could see the dead scattered across the yard. Luke was making coughing sounds. Ignoring her, he placed shot after shot at the upstairs windows, until he noticed she had fallen over on her side. Propping the musket against the wall, he sat her up. He had a handful of bullets left, and four or five powder cartridges, and he began to reload. After firing and stepping back, he saw she had fallen over again. This time when he tried to sit her up, she was dead. He sat her up anyway. Then he peered around the corner at the farmhouse.

He could see the kitchen door had been left ajar, probably by Saul.

He looked down at Luke. Her black hair had come undone, spilling around her shoulders. "I can't put you in the ground. You'd like me to, but I can't." His fingers were busy reloading. "I'll finish it if I can. You'd like that, wouldn't you?"

Instead of stepping out and firing, this time he held his fire and ran for the house. Crashing into the kitchen, racing for the staircase. Abner Carmichael appeared at the top with a bell gun and Fergus shot him then galloped upstairs. The upper floor was crowded with gray, sour smoke. Stepping over Abner's body, he heard groaning and saw dim light spill through a doorway. Coughing in the dense smoke he reloaded hastily then advanced down the hallway.

Cautiously he peered into the bedroom. His eyes stinging, he could hardly see through the smoke. Phoebe Carmichael lay on a massive four-poster. The smoke poured from a smoldering carpet, set alight by a spilled lamp. He began to stamp on it but it was no good; he couldn't squelch the smoke.

He approached the bed. The pillow and bedclothes were brown with blood. Her eyes were fixed on his. As he came close she made sounds. A piece of her jaw had been shot away. He couldn't understand her mumble; her lips were bubbling blood. There was water in the stand, and he filled a cup and tried pouring some in her mouth, but she seemed unable to swallow. He kept stamping the smoldering carpet. Bits of spent shot gritted underfoot; the room stank of gunpowder and burning wool. He fell into a jag of bitter coughing. When he looked back at the bed Phoebe was unbuttoning the front of her dress.

Fingers dirty with dry blood.

"Fergus?" Somehow she articulated his name.

"Yes, miss?"

"You won't leave me lying in pain, will you?"

He barely heard the awful sounds, but understood what she wanted. She had pulled open her dress, exposing her white breast, and was struggling to raise herself up on her elbows. "Please, Fergus."

Slowly he raised the musket, taking aim at her heart.

"Will you lift me up to the Lord?"

Everything stopped. The world stopped.

He squeezed the trigger. Smoke filled the air and the gun roared and she flopped back on the bed, dead as any of them.

Cattle

Summer! Summer! The milk of the heifers,
and ourselves brought the summer with us.

He lay on his stomach, concealed, watching cattle drovers pushing a herd of bullocks up toward the pass. He didn't recognize their song, but it was low and plaintive, like all the cattle songs he knew.

A fat man followed the drovers on a pony. Dressed like a cattle dealer, in a cloak and boots and straw hat, he was swaying from side to side as if he were asleep in the saddle — and perhaps he was, a broad yellow hat shading his face.

Fergus had left the farm riding Carmichael's red mare, blood on her saddle that he'd tried to wipe clean with handfuls of straw. He could ride her well enough but, afraid people would recognize her, he'd dismounted after a few miles and left her grazing along the road, where someone must claim her and feed her.

He'd found his way up the road into the pass, where he had been hiding for weeks, sleeping in a crevice padded with leaves, surviving on wild herbs, rain-water, and eggs stolen from birds' nests below the cliff. Time had become an astringency of cold nights, various kinds of sunlight, handfuls of gathered food. Three or four times he'd painstakingly loaded, primed, and cocked Shamie's musket. With a peeled stick on the trigger, he held the muzzle to his heart while curlews and magpies cawed from the rocks and gnarled shrubs. Despite the birds' taunting he had been unable bring himself to fire, and would unload slowly and carefully, then repeat the sequence a few hours later.

Ashamed of his weakness, he decided to avoid thinking any more than necessary. Trying not to let words form, but feeling his way through the days by sensation, texture, mood, the play of light on the rocks.

There was a string of fine-weather days, which he spent lying on his back on the rough, warm granite, watching clouds float across the country. When it rained, the pass was cut off from the world. He respected that, the precision of solitude, his body in the clouds.

Solitude and constant wind gradually honed him, or numbed him, until he was no longer bothering to reload.

One day a fine carriage had come through. Hiding the musket in the rocks, he had stepped out into the road, begging, and the lady presented him a loaf of bread, butter in a noggin, a hunk of mutton, and a fat little tract, which he used for a pillow.

Pads of white, pulpy skin developed on his heels. The skin of his face hardened. His lips cracked, healed, cracked again. Fissures had appeared in the balls of his feet, frightening him — red cracks into himself, exposures, openings. The blue workhouse jacket, leached of dye so it was almost silver, hung from his shoulders like a husk. His trousers were greasy rags.

Another afternoon, concealed behind rocks, he observed a company of dragoons working up the pass, walking heavy black horses, in perfect silence — all noise being shoveled off the mountain by the wind. He'd kept out of sight, flattened on granite, sighting the musket from man to man — but he hadn't felt tempted to shoot.

He spent hours each day gathering herbs, chewing them soft. Stolen eggs he broke in his fist, licking up raw egg-meat and splinters of shell. Hour after hour, lying on his back, on warm rock, he watched hawks wreaking havoc on smaller birds.

> The yellow summer and the white daisy,
> And ourselves brought the summer with us.

A strange song to be singing in winter, he thought. Perhaps it was the only cattle song they knew. The bullocks were now almost at the mouth of the pass, where the road narrowed between two boulders. Wary of the squeeze, the animals were hesitating, and the drovers started pitching pebbles, trying to force them ahead.

A mistake. Cattle couldn't be forced. You had to respect their wariness. Driven stiffly, they would always rebel.

Pecked by stones, the lead bullock lurched off the road, kicking his heels. He watched the others start to mill and turn. The dealer awoke and bellowed at his men, who were haplessly cracking their little whips. Two drovers went stumbling down the bracken slope after the strays. Braying and frisking, more animals quit the road and wandered uphill, biting at the rough grass.

Watching the disarray, he decided the drovers didn't know their business. Perhaps they were sheep men.

He'd expected to die on the pass but hadn't been able to kill himself, and had let the dragoons pass through without engaging. Weather had flayed him, but not killed him. Perhaps it wasn't the time to die after all. His feet were hardening again.

It was time to go down into the world.

Shamie's musket lay in a crevice, protected from the weather. He decided to leave it there. It was too dangerous to carry — any cattle dealer in the mountains would be carrying a bell gun or a pistol and would be quick to open fire on an armed stranger.

He stood up. Facing the wind, he started picking his way down the slope, and a flash of Luke lit up his brain. The tune of her little voice. The scent of her cunt, like straw burned from a field.

BULLOCKS WERE an awkward set of creatures, difficult to handle, insolent, infinitely nervous. Six were wandering in the rough above the road as he came at them obliquely and started pushing them together, speaking softly, taking advantage of their instinct to herd.

When he had them in a group, he knew he could turn them without getting too close.

He could feel the dealer watching from under the brim of his straw hat. Slowly, steadily he worked the bullocks back to the road, where most of the herd was grazing on the grassy crown.

Once they were back on the road, he snapped off a hazel wand. Cracking it against his leg and clicking his tongue, he started pushing the herd through the narrows of the crest. The bullocks foraging in the rough slope below the road trotted uphill to rejoin the moving herd, the inexperienced drovers floundering after them.

No one spoke to him, but after a mile or so he was included in their pattern of position and calls. The dealer went back to sleep in his saddle.

THEY CAME out of the mountains into country smelling of grass, damp wind in their faces. The dealer awoke. Kicking his pony's sides, he pushed ahead through the herd and cantered off into the dusk.

It was dark when Fergus next saw the dealer, standing in the road ahead holding a lantern on a stick, turning the herd into a field he must have hired for the night. As soon as the gate was shut, the dealer climbed back aboard his pony and rode off to find his supper, and the drovers started a fire of sticks. Wooden noggins were pulled from a sack. Fergus took one, and a wooden spoon. No one stopped him. He helped himself to their porridge of Indian meal, licked his bowl clean, refilled it, and ate more slowly. He had always disliked the Indian meal, each summer he'd grown sick of the taste long before the new potatoes came in, but now it tasted luxurious — rich, greasy, sweet. He felt it softening his tongue, restocking his brain, language returning.

It was dark when the cattle dealer came back, smelling of whiskey. Throwing his reins at Fergus, he pulled a pistol from his saddle and walked off to inspect the herd while Fergus unsaddled the pony and turned it out to graze. A few minutes later the dealer returned to the fire and glared at Fergus as though seeing him for the first time. "Who are you? What's your business?"

Fergus looked down into the fire. He felt the weight of English words on his tongue but couldn't say them.

"I don't need no scamps. Got a tongue? Are you a rebel?"

He felt strained and anxious but he couldn't spring the language. The dealer was looking at him with hard eyes. "Are you one of the reivers? A cattle thief, are you?"

Fergus shook his head.

"I'm driving for Dublin, for Eden's Quay. I could use another fellow that can trail a herd of wild woollies and no fuss. Pay, five shillings, coin of the realm, once they are safe aboard."

Fergus nodded.

"Give me your hand, so." The dealer spat in his palm and slapped Fergus's hand. "You are a vicious-looking scoundrel, have you been living in a hole? Now you're Billy Butler's man — Butler of Slieve Gullion. What name is yours, *buachaill*?"

"Fergus."

"After we get to town, you Fergus rascal, you'll have brass in your pocket, the wee girls will rip you to shreds." Billy Butler sat down heavily, leaning back against his saddle, his thick legs stretched out toward the fire. He placed the pistol on the ground, filled his pipe, and lit it with a wand from the fire. Puffing away, he looked at Fergus.

"Get a feed?"

"Yes."

"No blanket, though."

Fergus shook his head.

"You can roll up with one of the other fellows. Get out there now, *buachaill*. We all stand night guard. Take a round of the fencing, see my beauties is easy."

BILLY BUTLER slept aboard his pony all day, straw hat and canvas cape protecting him from weather. He kept his pistol dry in a greased welt on the saddle.

They began overtaking crowds of people moving east along the road for Dublin. Men and women, with children on their backs, stepped out of the road as the bullocks were driven through. At every halt the drovers cooked stirabout. Wary of reivers, Billy Butler never slept at night, but sat by the fire smoking his pure tobacco, getting up frequently and strolling among his bullocks, pistol in hand.

Dublin Town

"BY THE LIGHT OF BURNING martyrs, I'll drop any Dublin digger tries to turn my herd."

Butler sat in his saddle. Swigging *poitin* from a clay jar, he coughed, spat, and handed the jar around. The drovers were at the edge of Kildare plain. Instead of grazing the herd one last night, they were going to drive straight through the city, heading for the quays.

When the jar reached Fergus, he took a swallow, stamping his foot when the liquor scorched his throat. The men laughed at him.

"The Dublin girls will eat you fellows alive," Butler told them.

As they ran the bullocks in along the black river, Dublin's sharp forms and hardness impressed him. Granite blocks sheathed the water. The moon slapped light on the city's endlessness of stone.

Just at dawn they began passing the quays, the light like gray wool. Ships lay in packs along the river. The road thickened with traffic of drays and barrows and people carrying children and baggage on their backs. The bullocks kicked their heels and threw their heads back, bellowing from thirst. The river smelled of tar and herring.

They drove the bullocks into a wooden pen on Eden's Quay. Dublin was packed with noise of dray wheels crackling on stone, men shouting, whips cracking. Hundreds of people sat guarding their baggage as the winter sun blared orange in the east. Children slept on mountains of baggage: trunks, cases, sacks, grips, casks, bundles of tools, sets of harness, chairs, lamps, stools.

"Where are they all going?"

"Liverpool and America."

He'd heard of them but had no sense of where these places were — across the water, he supposed. Men went across the water to navvy the canals, or harvest wheat in Scotland, but they always returned, as his father had returned.

Billy Butler handed each drover a little tobacco, then went off looking for a buyer.

Intimidated by the noise, the crowds, and the piercing complex of Dublin smells, the drovers retreated shyly to the cattle pen to stand among the warm animals, puffing their pipes.

Fergus walked out on the quay. The caustic disorder was stimulating, the noise a relief from his thoughts. A steamer lay along the quay breathing from a pair of iron chimneys. The steam smelled of moss.

He peered down the black river, trying to catch a glimpse of the sea.

BILLY BUTLER came back with a buyer and went wading through the herd of bullocks, sorting animals with a stick. Fergus watched the two men bargaining then slapping hands for the sale.

"Yes, yes, he's taken the whole bunch for Liverpool," Butler told them. "Come along now, lads, let us run 'em aboard old *Nimrod*, then I'll treat you to breakfast."

The crowd of emigrants waiting on the quay began to stir when they saw a gangway run out from the steamer. A few passengers tried to force their way aboard but the deckhands beat them back with tarred rope-ends. A group of deckhands poured down the gangway and ran across the quay to the cattle pens, shouting and swinging their rope-ends, clearing a way through the crowd.

Billy Butler shouted at Fergus to run the gate open. They began driving the braying, shitting bullocks across the quay and up the gangway onto the deck, where they trampled neat coils of rope and overwhelmed every inch of deck space.

As soon as the last was run aboard, the gangway was hauled in. People on the quay were waving tickets and begging to be let aboard but the men standing guard along the rail ignored them.

"*Nimrod* has sold five hundred emigrant tickets but she won't have space for fifty." Billy Butler shook his head. "Ah well, they've no business leaving their own country."

A TURF fire glowed in the beer shop. Each drover had a pot of porter in front of him. Billy Butler had gone upstairs with the fat woman owner.

It felt strange to be in a room.

Fergus studied himself in a mirror that was mostly a painting of a ship, with little strips of looking glass up and down the sides. A pauper's black face glared back at him. His cheeks almost to his eyes were covered with greasy, downy hair. Another patch sprouted in the middle of his forehead. Hunger fur.

A woman brought out plates with bread and butter.

"It's a proud thing, English food," said the drover sitting next to him. "They said if I'd come to England, I'd eat bread and butter."

"Isn't England here, you poor lost sheep." The woman laughed.

The drover stared at her. Her size and boldness were impressive. "What is it then?"

"You must cross the water for England, as every Christian knows. Dublin's Ireland!"

Ireland. One winter after his right eye had been sore and red for weeks, his mother had taken him to a holy island for a cure, after first attempting to heal the inflammation with poultices of potato peel and juice. As they were rowed across she had dropped a coin and bits of glass into the water. For a long time he had thought *Ireland* was only the small island in that gray lake. Even now his associations with the word were eye pain, damp, and the smell of lake water infused with rotting wood.

The woman next brought out a kettle of soup. Bits of red floated in the liquid.

"What is it, missus?"

"Fish and treacle."

"The red bits, missus?"

"Pimiento."

He did not know what that was.

"Never seen such a woman," the drover beside him whispered. "She is bigger than a king."

They were slurping soup and chewing wheat bread when Billy Butler came downstairs, accompanied by five girls in shawls. "Here you are, men. Very decent girls, and only a shilling apiece."

One girl immediately sat on Fergus's knee, kissed his forehead, and dipped her fingers in his soup. He could feel her thinness, her bones scraping on his thigh.

"That one'll eat you alive," Butler laughed. "Here it is, sir, your wages."

The dealer laid four coins in Fergus's outstretched palm.

The woman licked soup from her fingers.

"That's but four," Fergus said.

"One for the girl."

"You said five."

"You'll get a bath and a lovely jab if you go upstairs."

"Hear him," the girl said to Fergus, poking a bony finger in his chest.

"A bath and a clean girl." Butler smiled. "All for a shilling."

"No. Five, mister, give me five; you said five."

Butler shrugged and dropped a coin on the table. Fergus seized it. The other girls were helping themselves to food and porter, overwhelming the helpless drovers. The girl sitting on Fergus's knee gave up trying to kiss him and began soaking bread in the soup and cramming it in her mouth. Perhaps she had forgotten how hungry she was until she smelled the food. He'd had enough for now. He slid out from under her and stood up, coins in his fist.

"Interested in a passage?" The fat serving woman pulled a sheaf of tickets from her apron, fanning them out. "Here's a passage to Liverpool on *Ruth*. She's leaving Eden's Quay this morning, she is. Have you across the water tonight. Nowhere in this world so rich as Liverpool. Halfway to America."

Red tickets the color of blood.

"How much?"

"Three shillings for the bright world."

Sometimes your heart cracks and tells you what you have to do.

PART III

City of Stone

LIVERPOOL, DECEMBER 1846–JANUARY 1847

Crossing the Water

Ruth was smaller than *Nimrod*. He stood on the quay with a crowd of passengers clutching tickets, watching anxiously as flocks of sheep were driven aboard the little steamer. The tide had gone out and her deck, already crammed with wailing sheep, lay well below the quay.

"We won't get aboard by waiting. We'll have to leap for it," said the young man next to him. He wore greased boots like a navvy and carried his belongings bundled in a red handkerchief.

"We've paid our tickets," a woman said. "They can't leave us here."

"They can't — but they will."

With the last flock driven aboard, the deckhands left the gangway to passengers, and a mob began crushing to get aboard.

Would he be a different person on the other side, with different things in his head? What would feed him, and who would care?

Ruth's black funnels were smoking merrily. He could see dockers throwing lines off the iron bollards on the quay.

"That's it, she's pushing off," the navvy announced. "Anyone wants to get aboard had better jump for it."

The deckhands were hauling up *Ruth*'s gangway, and passengers caught halfway across were scrambling for their lives back to the quay.

The navvy carefully pitched his stick and his bundle down onto *Ruth*'s deck, then looked around. "No one else for it? Well, good luck, you poor sheep, and happy days in Dublin town."

He cleared the gap with his leap and landed hard on *Ruth*'s deck. Fergus watched him scramble to his feet, retrieve his stick and bundle before the deck-hands could interfere, and mix quickly into the throng of passengers pouring off the gangway.

More lines were cast off — *Ruth* was beginning to glide off the quay. He stared down at the gap of black water widening. Those aboard were jamming the rail and screaming at wives, husbands, and children on the quay, begging them to jump for it.

No one begging you.

The world moved, that was the law. Moved on itself like a wheel.

He jumped for the deck, landing hard. Shaken, he got to his feet, afraid the deckhands would grab him and pitch him overboard. He couldn't see the navvy. The deck was jammed with passengers and howling sheep. No one was bothering about him and he decided he was safe. They were drift out, passengers shouting and waving at relatives left on the quay and the deckhands busy laying out their fastidious coils of dripping rope.

He made his way forward as *Ruth* churned downstream, steam snapping from her funnels and the paddle wheel churning. The noise was deafening. No one looked twice at him. The deck was slippery with sheep manure.

Reaching the bow, he stood on a pile of chain, watching the river open to the sea.

You carry everything inside. You carry it with you.

Ruth flailed through the waves, her bow rising and falling sickeningly. He vomited the last of the fish soup, treacle, and scarlet specks of whatever it was. When the wind grew too cold to stand in the bow, he joined the other deck passengers herding around the funnel for warmth.

"Where's our country now?" an old man kept asking.

They had lost sight of land. The ocean was all around, green and silver, wild as nothing. They huddled around the funnel like cattle in a storm and the crash of the paddle wheel and the screaming wind made his ears roar.

"Plenty warm below!" *Ruth*'s master shouted. "Shilling a head buys an hour down below with the engine! Men, think of your women! Fathers, think of the bairns. Down below it's cozy as a cabin. Sure you won't have your people suffer such inclement, nasty conditions for the sakes of a coin? Do the manly thing, gents. Shilling a head."

Spray lashed over them, soaking them. Tempted, Fergus took out his two remaining shillings. He was staring at them in his hand when the navvy touched his arm.

"Hold on to your money, man; you'll want it on the other side. And it only feels the colder after you come up."

"I'll have you whipped! You close that lid of yours!" the master cried.

"Get away or I'll flip you like an egg."

The master glared and muttered and began herding below those who'd paid the fee.

"Where has our country gone?" the old man asked.

As it grew dark, it grew even colder. "Sure we ought to climb in the pens," the navvy announced. "Nice and warm in with the woollies."

"The master will throw us in the sea," a passenger said.

"He'd like to but he won't."

The others were frightened of the master's wrath; Fergus was the only one to follow the navvy, climbing into one of the sheep pens where they stood among the bulky, butting animals, absorbing their heat.

The navvy unwrapped his bundle and shared his cheese and bread. "Now you know what you are — an Irish animal, only not worth near so much as a decent breeding ram."

The other deck passengers began climbing into the pens as cold overcame their fear, and when the master came on deck and screamed at them they stolidly ignored him, hugging the sheep.

"Spike them Irish blaggers out of there, you fellows!" the master ordered his deckhands. "Get the women, get the brats! Hear what I say, you damned Irish mikes, my boys will crack you very sharp and drop you in the deep if you don't step out of the pens! You shall not roost with my cargo!"

The navvy stood among the bawling animals, gripping his stick. On his face, the thin, light smile of a fellow who knew he could put up a fight.

If the deckhands tried to clear them out, the navvy would violently resist, expect Fergus to fight alongside him, and where would it end? With the two of them being dropped overboard? A long silent plunge through a sleek depth of black water. A swallow of death.

Terror; the world is terror. Terror stinging in your fingertips. Inside your mouth, the back of your throat. Terror like a cloud in your head. The world is just kills.

But the hands ignored the master and refused to come near any of the pens and the master, screaming, "Blaggers! Criminals! Ireland's well rid of you!" gave up and went below, leaving the passengers standing amid the packed pens of butting, shitting animals.

It was barely warm enough among the bumbling sheep. He distrusted their bitter black hooves. The wool on their backs stank like lamp oil. Hungry, thirsty, the animals seemed resentful of the intrusion, blatting out furious cries, kicking and prancing and trying to stab his feet.

He was too uncomfortable to sleep although his head was heavy. His stomach growled and spat as *Ruth*'s bow rose and fell, breaking the waves while her paddle wheel whipped the trailing sea to lather hour after hour, until it seemed unlikely the passage would ever end.

After dark the breeze faded and the rolling waves flattened. The steamer kept whacking ahead, her bow plowing up the sea as if it were a turnip field, and he realized the passage must be ordinary to her, no matter how extraordinary it seemed to him.

After a while he caught a weird aroma that prickled the hairs in his nostrils, so dark it spooked him, like smoke to a horse. Rich, thick, heavy as a club. He hoped he might be dreaming it — but he was surrounded by howling sheep, and certainly awake.

Even amid the rancid wool he could smell it; there was no doubt the scent was real, not a product of dreams. "What is it? What is that smell?" he asked the navvy.

"Land," the navvy replied.

The smell of earth, it was. But so ferocious and fresh, as though he had never smelled ground before.

Floating over the sea, it had smelled like an open grave, weird and distinct.

"The ground of England," said the navvy. He stood up, puffing his pipe, sur-rounded by bleating ewes. "We're coming in, so. Go up forward, *an mhic*, and have a look."

Hoisting himself out of the pen, Fergus ran along the wet planking to the prow, where he stood inhaling the scent of the ground of England as it came writhing across the dark.

Ruth was entering the mouth of a river. Standing on anchor chains in the bow, he watched shore lights closing in. The other passengers were climbing out of the sheep pens and crowding along the rails.

The banks of the river were sheathed with stone. Forests of black masts and spars rose up from the stone basins where ships lay.

When *Ruth*'s engine suddenly cut, the stillness was a shock. Picked up by a steam tug, she was warped through a narrow water gate into a basin packed with three-masters, surrounded by stone quays and stone warehouses. As soon as lines were thrown, passengers began heaving baggage over the rails, leaping ashore and passing down wailing children without waiting for the gangway. Fergus joined the people climbing over the side.

Shepherds in white smocks laughed and jeered at the emigrants staggering on the quay. After the sway of the ship it was difficult readjusting to the firmness, the fixity of ground, English ground.

The English were yelping at them, teasing them that they were drunk. "I'd like a drop of what you're having, Mike! Any Irish whiskey for me?"

Runners shouted the names of lodging houses and prices. He saw runners tearing baggage from people's hands, flipping it into their barrows and racing off, emigrants stumbling after them helplessly.

He caught sight of the navvy leading a group of passengers who had closed ranks to fight off the runners. Forcing his way through a flock of wailing sheep, Fergus ran to catch up.

Night Asylum

NIGHT TRAFFIC BEHIND the quays was harsher and more violent than Dublin. Carts rumbled up and down the road, iron wheels grinding and snapping on the cobblestones. It was snowing lightly. The group was straggling. Some of the *Ruth*s were having trouble keeping up.

"Not far now," the navvy said, looking around. "Keep together. Liverpool's full of thieves."

Fergus stared down the dark streets they passed.

Another city made of stone.

"There she is." Stopping at a corner, the navvy was pointing to a stone building across the road. "Fenwick Street Night Asylum."

A long line of people had coiled around the building.

"Is it the workhouse?" Fergus asked.

"They give out soup, so what do you care?" The navvy laughed. He was already walking away. Fergus longed to go with him but didn't have the strength to keep up, and was afraid the navvy would laugh at him if he tried to. He crossed the road and joined the queue.

They were all emigrants off the steamers. He could tell from the shawls and red cloaks women wore, the shapes of men's broken hats.

A soldier in blue uniform stood at the front door admitting people in groups of four or five. The queue advanced slowly.

He smelled soup each time the door opened. He was trying not to think of Luke, who was crowding his mind: her voice, her pale eyes, her bones.

What you wanted must keep you going.

"No talking inside," the soldier warned, holding open the door. Once inside the queue moved slowly down a brick passage to a table where a clerk sat scratching names in a ledger and handing out tickets for soup and a bed.

The scent of soup was intense; he could see the steam of it shining on the bricks. Hunger wetted his mouth.

Poised with his pen, the clerk did not even look up. "Name? Where from?"

"Ireland."

"Whereabouts?"

He hesitated. "Dublin."

"What ship?"

"*Ruth.*"

Gas lamps hummed with light. He could smell the steam and the food. He had never felt so alone.

THE EMIGRANTS fed at long tables. The great room was quiet except for crying children and the scrape of spoons. He was allowed to take a lump of bread from a basket.

The soup was yellow, with scraps of fish. He crumbled the bread into his bowl, looking about him as he ate. Everyone else was concentrating on their food. Even the small children were eating vigorously.

Finishing his soup, he suddenly felt clipped with weariness, and rested his head in his hands. A cramp shot through his belly. When it subsided, he took a breath, then another cramp shot through.

On the pass he had been ready to die, but not here. He wasn't ready to die in England full of poison.

The cramps struck hard, crippling him as he staggered from the enormous eating room.

In the open courtyard, a dozen men and boys squatted on boards over a pit, relieving themselves. He stepped out of the remains of his trousers and squatted. Stinging liquid gushed out of him until he thought his heart, soul, liver, must have liquefied and been voided. He kept hoping there was nothing left inside, but there was.

My share of blood, he thought, my share of poison. I am dying like all of them.

No. He wasn't. The cramps were already subsiding, and his head was a little clearer. After a few minutes he was able to pull up his trousers, hand over his second ticket to another blue soldier and enter the night asylum where ranks of wooden boxes were organized on the floor with men asleep inside them. He walked up and down and stopped when he finally found an empty box. In orange lamplight he could see others drifting up and down the rows, like men culling through a herd of cattle, or examining old headstones.

He hated to think of strangers looking at him asleep.

Too tired to keep standing, he finally stepped into the box and lay down, staring at the ceiling, trying hard to think of nothing, and after a while he slept.

City of Stone

THE GUN FIRED and the smoke was seeded with bits of iron that stung his face and eyelids. It fired once more, and this time a slug spinning came at him, its tip sharply pointed, like a fish spear.

He sat up, violently awake, heart pounding, heat spreading over his legs. An old man coming up the aisle between the pallets was ringing a hand bell with a kind of joy, and men were swarming like ticks from their sleeping boxes.

"Out and out, you farthings, out and out with you! Come, you poor Michaels, shake the leg!"

Herded outside, they spilled into the wet, shiny road. It was night still. His breath steamed. Women and girls flowed from another door, and the crowd began sorting into families that started off into the complex darkness until there was no one left except a few white-faced women suckling babies on the asylum steps.

A plan was needed. Without the spine of a plan he knew he could not withstand the city, it would dissolve him, and he started to walk, aiming for the river, passing pungent lumps of bodies asleep in doorways.

He would find the steamers disembarking cattle and hire on for a drover. Walk those cattle into the mountains of England. Whistling and calls; driving them easy, as he knew how. He had the voice for cattle. He grasped their moods; he could feel the weather they could feel.

Work the cattle trade, save. Buy greased hobnail boots, a straw hat — and then, perhaps, a pony. Or a good red mare, a real hunter: a bounder with thick cannon bones, long back, and a spring to her. A sleek pistol tucked in the welt of your saddle. Gun down any marauders wishing to ruin you.

The world's a rim, a wheel, enclosing everything. A wheel don't look back at what is crushed.

STREETS AND squares of Liverpool were organized, fantastic monsters. Building after building, corners, edges and strict angles — he could never have imagined anything so sharply arranged. The limited sky smoldered and slowly lit, providing some depth to side streets of houses shouldered together. Traffic began to thicken.

Liverpool men walked briskly, wore boots and canvas aprons. Runners pushed barrows piled with sheepskin, coal, and pig carcasses. Near the river, the smells of brine and tar mixed with the scents of burning coal and horses. Everything moved quickly here — pairs of boys trotted along bearing heavy timbers on their shoulders. Men carrying grapple hooks, swinging buckets of nails.

You could smell the ferocity on the street.

WHAT IS Liverpool? A city? A world?

He stopped underneath a carving of a horse hanging on wires above the door of a beer shop. The smell of smoke and meat leaked out from inside and his mouth was wet with hunger, but he felt uncertain. Coinage was fraught. He wasn't certain he knew the ritual of exchanges.

Wary of Liverpool men, massive and unusual. They might pitch him out. Set him a beating.

However, hard money had some power. He remembered his mother kissing each coin on market day.

Life burns hot, Fergus.

Trying to make up his mind, he hopped restlessly from one foot to another, one coin in each fist. The door opened and pack of thick-shouldered men came out, and he caught a tantalizing whiff of the smoky, meaty atmosphere within.

You could stand outside, bootless and chewing fear like a baby; or take the bold plunge. Offer a coin for a feed and see if they would like it.

The world, latent; a gun loaded with chance and mistakes.

The door swung open once more and two enormous men came out, with an odor of hot blood and juice, almost sickening. Ignoring him, they paused to light their pipes, then walked off on their crisp boot heels.

Honor is held by them in boots.

Seizing the door, he pulled it open and threw himself inside.

THE AIR was gray. Liverpool men sat cutting into fuming hunks of meat. The barman, drawing beer, glared at him.

Fear hummed in his blood but he forced himself to return the man's stare.

Luke, make me hard.

"Away with you Mike! No beggars here!" the barman growled.

Fergus held up one of his coins.

"What's that, Irish brass?"

He flinched but kept holding up the shilling until the barman reached out and grabbed it, flipped it, caught it — and dropped it in the pocket of his apron.

"Sit down, you awful savage."

He found space on a bench and sat, ashamed of his bare feet among Liverpool men so preoccupied with their fabulous, smoky eating they hardly spoke among themselves. Men glanced at him then went back to their rations — no one seemed to care who he was.

His beer had a sweet smell, when the barman put it in front of him, like a flower in the sun. The beefsteak had a round of bone in its eye and a rind of charred fat. Cutting the meat into fragments, lifting each delicious piece on the point of his knife, he chewed slowly.

He worried they were watching him but they weren't.

How to ignore the pressure of the rough world?

By the time he had cleaned his plate, there were only two other customers left in the shop — old brown men lying on benches, hats over their faces, snoring. He chewed the last strand of fat and began to soak bread morsels in juice. The barman behind the bar stood reading a newspaper, eating a dish of cooked eggs.

Closing his eyes, he saw Luke propped against the storehouse wall, blood leaking on the stones.

You carry everything inside. Where? In the head. If you could knock it out, would you? If you could scour the brain, would you? Yes. Of course.

Swallowing the last dregs of the beer, he rose, grabbed the disc of bone, and rushed out into the day's smashing brightness.

THE FIRST cattle dealer to whom he applied glared and said, "No, I don't require no more hands, no."

Other dealers on the quays all shook their heads.

"Don't need you, Mike."

Some of them cracking little whips, impatiently.

"No."

"No!"

"This herd is only going across the river, Mike."

He walked the dockland with senses sharply tuned, like a dog unearthing a badger. Sky over the river, blue as clay. At Clarence Dock a steamer was splashing in, and a runner informed him she was *Merrion* out of Newry — wherever that was. Her deck jammed with red cattle. He watched deckhands throwing lines and sodden passengers heaving baggage ashore then leaping down onto the quay where runners descended on them like a horde of wasps.

He approached dealer after dealer, asking for work. Cattle dealers wore side-whiskers, gaudy pantaloons red-and-white striped, plush waistcoats, and cravats. Their jackets were trimmed with ribbons, and their horse boots shone with grease. They puffed their pipes and looked at him steady.

No.

No.

Not now, Patrick.

Don't need you.

No.

Dockland stretched forever along the Mersey. Beggars called out in Irish, soft voices crushed under iron-rimmed dray wheels. Each dock held a basin crowded with ships, surrounded by quays and warehouses. Looking up, he watched ship riggers at work in forests of masts, spars, and rigging. The riggers looked like black beetles, working so high.

Liverpool was a hard place, a stone place; it could grind you.

Embrace of loneliness shall kill you in the end.

Walking up the wide road behind the dockland, afraid of being so afraid. Trying to keep your terror compact and hidden.

Stab the Drum

AT MIDDAY GUNS CRACKED and bells banged all up and down the river. Hundreds of sailors, dockers, and riggers poured off ships and quays into a warren of alleys behind the dockland, lined with eating houses, roast beef stalls, and beer shops.

He was standing in the Vauxhall road with eyes closed, feeling the stream of hungry men pour past him, feeling invisible, when he sensed the vibration sliding through the streets like a piece of changing weather. He opened his eyes and saw that horses and carts were being pulled to the side to clear the way for men who were marching up the road following a drum.

He stood next to a cart horse with his hand on the animal's warm flank, watching the red-bearded giant who walked at the head of the parade bearing a great drum, followed by rank after rank of men carrying picks and spades sloped at their shoulders.

"Who are they?" he asked the carter.

"Scotch navvies, off the railway works. Mr. Brassey's contract."

"Where do they march?"

"Looking for a randy, I suppose."

"What's that?"

"A fight."

"Fighting who?"

"You Irish fellows, I should think."

The red giant thumped his drum with a pair of tasseled sticks, and the boom of it shook the air; it stirred you, made you feel excited, vulnerable, and weak. The drummer was flanked by six guardsmen carrying pick handles.

It was moving to see them, a proud, disciplined army such as Luke had never dreamed of. Pipers were playing in the ranks, the wild bleats skirling up and down the Vauxhall.

As the drummer and guards passed, a figure broke from the crowd of onlookers opposite Fergus and dashed out into the road.

It was the navvy from *Ruth* lunging at the drum with a knife in his hand, slashing the taut white skin and ripping it open.

Suddenly onlookers — men and women — were taking stones from their pockets, pulling out clubs from underneath their jackets, shawls, and cloaks.

The cart horse whinnied. He stroked the animal's warm neck, wishing it were possible to live inside your head, and not out in the world, so surprising and ruinous.

He had lost sight of the navvy — the guardsmen had surrounded him and were flailing their pick handles. The onlookers surging into the road were attacking the Scotchmen.

People at upper windows along the street were throwing bricks and lumps of coal at the marchers and the stuff was clattering in the road.

Peering through the flurry of the fight, he caught a glimpse of the navvy crawling down the middle of the road, the red drummer walking alongside and beating him with a pick handle, working at him the way a turf cutter with a spade would patiently work a piece of ground, or a carpenter the jamb of a door, or the boards of a coffin.

Starting after them, Fergus nearly stepped on a woman shivering on the pavement, blood pouring from her head. Stooping to pick up a spade, he saw the navvy on his hands and knees, wavering while the drummer nudged with his toe, testing to see if he might topple.

Fergus approached them from behind, gripping the spade in both hands. As the drummer raised the pick handle to deliver a finishing blow, Fergus swung the spade and caught him behind the knees with the edge of the pan. With a scream the red man flopped down onto the paving where he writhed and groaned under the bulk of the torn drum still strapped to his chest.

Fergus helped the navvy to his feet. The stones were greasy with blood.

"Give me that whipper," the navvy insisted, reaching out his hand.

Fergus picked up the wooden handle, and the navvy snatched it from him and began to beat the drummer.

You heard the whip and crackle of each blow, but felt neither pity nor anger, only a kind of slow, dense bewilderment as the navvy flailed away, bright blood splashing his face and clothes.

Suddenly he dropped the pick handle, grabbed Fergus by the arm, and began leading him through the mix of the fighting. No one tried to stop them. The people watching the riot shied from their bloody clothes, and it was easy to cut straight through. Coming out the other side, the way was clear and the navvy let go of his arm and broke into a lopsided run.

Not knowing what else to do, Fergus started after him.

Nothing had its fingers on you, running.

A horse might run until its heart burst.

CUTTING INTO an alley, they ran past old-clothes barrows and food stalls and through a web of stinking passages. The navvy was quick, despite his wounds, and Fergus had to struggle to keep up, tasting on his tongue the metallic tang of scorched breath.

A murky passageway brought them out into a courtyard where a cow was tied and children played in muck near a well. A dog with raised hackles lurched from a doorway and flew at them snapping. They threw themselves onto a wall, scrambled over, and dropped into an adjacent court, where a bonfire crackled between raw, unfinished brick houses and two men were roasting a horse's leg in the flames. They ran down more alleys smelling of tar, filth, and food, and finally out into a hard, wide road lined with iron lampposts, stone buildings, and gleaming sets of white steps.

The navvy's neck and shoulders were waxed with blood, his shirt was black with it, and he was beginning to falter.

Finally he stopped running, bent over, breathing hard, spitting while Liverpool people in magnificent clothes snapped past them, ignoring them.

"If they catch us, man, they'll murder us both," the navvy gasped. "We'll go for Shea's. Shea will fix us up."

He straightened up. Seizing Fergus's hand, he shook it vigorously. "Arthur McBride is my name."

Fergus gave his own.

"Never been across before?" Arthur asked.

"I haven't."

"Raw and green, raw and green — Shea will like you. Come along, then."

"Where are we going?"

"Shea's Dragon, where else?"

Whatever that was.

Linking arms, Fergus and the navvy began walking down the road.

As if they belonged there. As if the city were theirs.

Shea's Dragon

"WHY DID YOU STAB the drum, Arthur?"

"Oh, for the honor. I hate to see those fellows swagger."

He could feel the terror in his body soften as they walked arm in arm. It had been there since the night of the farm.

The rub of their two voices warming him.

"Aren't they navvies? Aren't you?"

"They are Scotch, and don't like seeing Irishmen working on the railway contracts. There was a bad fall yesterday, in a cutting on the London-and-Northwestern construction. A few tons came down and buried six of their fellows. They are claiming it's ignorant Irish getters responsible, saying the contractor must let 'em go, which is all wrong, for we are as skilled as they. There was a randy in a tommy shop night before last, and we heard they attacked one of our camps out by Alybury yesterday, the dogs — burned the shanties and frightened off the women. So we were waiting for them. When I heard the drum, that fucking boomer, why, I reckoned I must go for the thrust, and give our men heart."

It was good to have a connection, a companion, and a voice attaching you to the world.

"Have you done any navvying yourself, Fergus?" Arthur was wiping blood from his neck with a handkerchief.

"I haven't."

"It's why you come across, is it? Looking for work?"

"I don't know. Perhaps."

He had not been looking for anything, except to get away.

"Too late for harvest work. Too soon for plowing. Were you looking to be a factory hand? Plenty of Irishmen in Manchester. Have any people on this side?"

People? Arms and legs, rising in flames.

You don't forget anything. That is not how it works.

The dead cross the water, too. They swim.

"A navvy can tramp from Aberdeen to Land's End, railway camp to camp, and always have a feed and a bed. Do you wish to come along with me? What do you say?"

"All right." Better than being alone.

"Boots you'll need, though."

He looked down at his bare feet.

"Never mind — Shea will fix you up. I was green as you, Fergus, when first I crossed the water."

SHEA'S DRAGON was set in a terrace of tall, narrow brick houses in Bold Street, far from the docks. Navvies puffing short clay pipes basked in sunshine on the marble steps. They all seemed to have cudgels or brass-knobbed sticks near at hand.

Arthur was limping badly. An old man stood up to greet them. "You're the brave, Arthur!"

Above white whiskers, the old man's face was seamed and rough, red as berries.

Arthur smiled. "Iron Mike. Have you heard?"

"One of the girls ran back here quick as the devil. Shea thinks they might come to the Dragon looking for a vengeance."

Iron Mike glanced at Fergus then started untying Arthur's bloody neckerchief. Removing his own, he draped it across Arthur's shoulders.

"There you are, Arthur. Steady now. Are you badly hurt?"

Arthur was swaying. "I am feeling a little peculiar, I think."

"She'll want to see you." The old man nodded at Fergus. "Let's get Arthur inside."

Halfway up the flight of steps, with Fergus and Iron Mike supporting him on either side, Arthur stopped. "Don't know as I shall make it, Iron Mike."

His face looked gray.

"Come, Arthur. Yes you will. Hold on to your friends."

"This fellow Fergus is just over . . . saved my hide. He wishes to go navvying."

"Tunnel work down London way, as I hear. They say Mr. Murdoch has got a nice contract in North Wales, a piece of the Chester-and-Holyhead. Come along, Arthur. One step at a time."

They finally stood before the beautiful door. Iron Mike reached for the knocker and rapped it. "You watch yourself now, Arthur. You're a brassy boy no longer, and must respect the house."

"Are you her crusher now, Iron Mike?" Arthur said lightly.

"Porter, I am. They ain't the need for crushing, the Dragon is not that sort of establishment these days." Iron Mike looked at Arthur for a moment. "Grand to see you all of one piece, Arthur."

"And grand to see you, you old muncher," Arthur called after Iron Mike as he went down the stairs.

"Very nice, Shea is become," Arthur said softly, facing the door. "When first I crossed the water, the Dragon was a set of nasty cribs in Launcelot's Hey behind of a beer shop, the Bucket of Blood. She needed a crusher in those days.

"Oh my dear, Fergus, I am feeling a little weathered —" Arthur was wavering again. Seizing the knocker, Fergus banged on the door. Arthur leaned forward so his forehead was touching the wood. "If I die, the fellows must wrap me in the green flag."

"No good talking that way."

"Isn't it? And why not? What will happen?" Arthur smiled. "Is it the goblins? Will the *sioga* cross to Liverpool and eat me?"

"It's no good." To talk of your own death was to roil a certain magic, disturbing the way of the world. It was dangerous and ought to be avoided.

The door swung open so suddenly that Arthur nearly toppled over, but Fergus caught him by the arm and held him up. A plump, pink, yellow-haired girl stared at them with slightly bulging eyes. She was holding a scrub brush. "Look at you, Arthur."

"You always said I was a pretty fellow, Mary."

"You ain't now. We heard what happened. They might have killed you. Perhaps they did, by your looks. Come in."

They stepped inside and Mary bolted the door behind them. The floor was damp from scrubbing. A baby in a crate waved its fists.

Mary was eyeing Fergus suspiciously. "Who's this creature?"

"A friend, never fear," Arthur told her. "Name of Fergus."

"Never seen such a dirty monster."

"Is the mistress disposed?"

"Still in bed she is."

"Has she heard?"

"I reckon so."

"What did she say?"

"Her? Nothing."

In the front hall, water splashed and gurgled in a white fountain. Did they water their horses here? How did they get horses up the steps?

There were green things growing in brass tubs. Looking up, he saw sky. Daylight was pouring in through glass panels in the roof.

"She wants to see me, I expect," said Arthur.

"Well, you can show me your money first, and I'll go ask her."

"Oh Mary, sure, in my condition —"

"It's her rule and you know it, Arthur. One pound, hard money, or find your way downstairs. Go talk to one of them pot girls, I hear they're cozy."

Sighing, Arthur handed over a gold coin. "Not a hero's welcome," he complained.

"No one in the Dragon never said you was a hero, Arthur McBride."

"Oh Mary, you're killing my heart. Come along." Arthur clutched Fergus's arm. "We'll go to see the Dragon herself."

"You can't bring him, Arthur!"

"Mary —"

"You wait. Let me go and ask. If she's disposed —"

"For the love of God, Mary, I've had the life beat out of me."

The baby wailed. Mary walked over to it and picked it up. "Go on then, Arthur, God love you."

* * *

THEY MOVED down a corridor, Arthur leaning on him. The floor shone, and pictures of women, ships, and horses were hung on pale walls. Stopping in front of a door, the navvy let go of Fergus's arm, pulled himself erect, and knocked softly.

"Who is it?" a woman called.

Arthur opened the door. The room was struck with sunlight, smelling of wool, candle wax, flowers. There was a great carved bed with someone in it sitting up and holding a newspaper spread open.

"Are you glad to see me, Shea?"

Lowering the paper, Shea studied them.

Her dark hair was pulled back, sleek. She was older than the navvy; perhaps twenty-five. She had gray eyes in a face so plain it was handsome.

She reached for a cigar that was smoldering in a glass dish on a little marble-topped table beside the bed. "You look deranged, Arthur," she said.

"I've been over the other side —"

"Hell, Arthur? Have you been in Hell?"

"Close enough to Hell. Skibbereen would drive anyone mad."

"Come closer, let me look at you."

Holding himself stiffly, Arthur advanced across the room. Fergus saw bright, fresh blood sponging through the back of his shirt.

"You're looking older," she said.

"Too old for the Dragon?"

"I knew it was you the moment I heard. Why must you do such things, Arthur? So ill considered, so foolish."

Arthur sat down on the edge of her bed. "You mean, *so bold, and done so handsome.*"

"No — I mean foolish."

"Come, Shea — don't drag me now."

"They'll come for us one day, burn us out — they know we're an Irish house. There's more hate parading in those streets every day. There's going to be the devil to pay for your fun."

"Did it for you, Shea."

"Oh blast you. For me? I don't care a damn for your navvy rags."

The navvy grimaced.

"Are you hurt badly?" she said, suddenly concerned.

"I am feeling . . . a little . . . shady —"

"Oh Arthur, you fool! What have they done to you? Let me see."

Dropping her newspaper on the floor, she threw back her covers and swung long white legs from the bed. The gown she wore was unlike any garment Fergus had ever seen, green and shimmering, with dragons and flames embroidered on the sleeves.

"If I'm alive at all, it's thanks to this Fergus here."

She glanced at him. Not knowing what else to do, he bowed deeply.

"Here, lend a hand," she said. "Take his feet. Lie back now, Arthur, and we'll lift your legs."

They settled the navvy onto her bed, blood streaking the linen. Shea pulled off his boots, dropped them on the floor, and began stripping his clothes. When Arthur tried sitting up, she pressed him back. "No, stay down, you fool."

The navvy lay still, his eyes shut. His body was marked with dark, bloody cuts and swollen bruises beginning to show color.

The room smelled like a flower. The walls were carved and polished and there were chairs everywhere.

"Fergus, in a drawer over there — bandages, cotton stuff, salve."

Hurrying to fetch what she asked, he saw his own reflection in an oval looking glass.

Filthy, unspeakable. A savage.

"Is he dead?" Mary had appeared in the doorway, holding her baby and a steaming kettle.

"He isn't," said Shea, "but one of these days he will be. If he thinks I'll be bansheeing over his grave, he'll be sorry."

Mary poured the water into a china basin, and Shea dipped a towel and began cleaning cuts on Arthur's back. Mary nodded at Fergus. "What about this one?"

Shea glanced at him. "Give him a bath. Oil his hide or he'll dry like an apple. Broth, bread, cabbage, but don't stuff him, Mary. Small beer, if he takes it, and squeeze a lemon in."

Shea gave him a quick smile and a dip of her head. "Welcome, sir, our guest of the house."

Once more, he bowed.

Mary snorted. "Come along, your lordship, and scrub away your sins."

"WHERE ARE we going, miss?" He was following Mary through the house.

"You heard what she said — a bath for you. Arthur always has come with trouble. Now he'll expect us all to die for him, which isn't my idea."

"Only may I have something to eat first?"

"She said you wasn't. Nothing but broth."

"But I could eat anything. I could."

She clucked impatiently, but after they had passed a few closed doors, she suddenly halted. "Wait here. Don't move."

She opened a door and slipped inside. Carrying the baby on her hip, she crossed a room where men in clean clothes were playing cards at half a dozen tables. The men ignored her, and he watched her fill a plate with cold meat, onions, and boiled carrots from a side table crowded with food.

She came out and handed him the plate without a word, and he followed her down the carpeted stairs, eating with his fingers. They passed through a noisy, steamy kitchen where half a dozen women and girls were at work, then down a set of narrow, iron stairs that curled around and around.

The baths were in a clean white cave. A fire glared in a stove. There were three copper kettles big enough to stand in.

"What is this?" he asked, holding up a piece of meat from his plate.

"Leg of chicken."

"Is it good to eat?"

"Too good for you, I suppose."

"A bird is it?"

"It's a chicken."

"I've eaten birds. Used to catch a blackbird."

"Take off your rags." Holding her baby on her hip, she reached to twist open one of the spigots, and water began sprouting from the pipe and roaring into a kettle. He stared. The direct violence of water was impressive. And hot — he could smell the steam.

"Will you get rid of them awful clothes, boy!"

He quickly finished his food and started peeling off the workhouse clothes.

"Speeding with vermin I expect," she grumbled.

Skin of my days, he thought, staring at the clothes on the floor, remembering the snowy streets of Scariff, and Murty Larry.

"I won't touch 'em! Throw 'em on the fire." Mary removed her shawl and swaddled her baby, then hung the bundle nearby on a clothes hook.

He stared at his rags, smoldering and smoking on the coals until suddenly they flared up.

"You're more dirt than anything." Reaching overhead, Mary shut the torrent and the room fell quiet except for noise from the kitchen overhead.

He touched the warm copper sides.

"Climb in. Hurry up, don't be such a pecker."

He peered down through the steam. He was frightened of the heat but did not like her to notice.

"Oh climb in, Fergus, if that's your name. Hot water won't do you any harm. You must sit down in it and soak to get the marl off your skin, you cowboy, that's why you're down here. Never bathed in a copper before, have you?"

Her complacence and disdain were annoying. What did she know, all fat and pink, with her enormous pink baby?

"Go on. Climb in. You're quite safe here."

He swung one leg over, testing the water with his toes. It was stinging hot and he exhaled.

"Go on," she coaxed.

He swung his other leg over and stood in the kettle, the hot water reaching to his knees.

"Now sit down."

"I cannot."

"Slowly, do it slowly."

Gripping the sides he lowered himself inch by inch until he was sitting on the copper bottom.

"How is it?"

She was right — it wasn't so painful, past the first sting. He felt sweat breaking out on his forehead.

"Relax. Do you know what that means? Don't think. Let your head go black inside."

She was scrubbing him with soap and a soft red sponge when the door opened and Shea walked in.

"Terrible shy he is, missus," Mary said. "One of them mountainy savages not accustomed to the bath."

"You can go upstairs, Mary, I'll finish here."

"Is Arthur alive?"

"He took a little brandy. The surgeon says there are no broken bones."

Mary unhooked her baby and left. Shea wore a neat blue dress, button shoes. She rolled up her sleeves, knelt down on the towel Mary had placed on the floor, and began soaping his chest and shoulders. He tried to relax as she lifted his arms. Before Luke he had never let anyone own his body. Shea put down the block of soap and began scrubbing with a thick wet brush.

Luke kissing his nipples.

The taste of smoke on her skin.

Shea took a razor from a shelf and clicked it open. He watched her stroke the steel on a strap then test the hone on her thumb and he thought of Luke sitting on the stones but pushed that picture away before it could grip.

The key of lightness and possibility is control of the brain. Don't let terror in your head. If it starts, evict it.

She began to shave the matted hair that had grown on his face almost to his eyes. The slip of the blade along his skin was a relief. He could not speak. She rubbed more soap in his hair, sluicing it off with handfuls of water, laughing at him when he sputtered. Her hands were strong, but tender.

A horse would not settle under weak hands. A horse knew from the touch who to trust.

"Are you going for America?" she asked.

"Don't know."

"That's where they're all going this year."

"Is it far?"

"It's on the other side."

"But this is the other side."

"This is only England — America's another forty days by sea." She dumped another pan of water over his head. "Where are your people?"

He said nothing.

Placing her hand on top of his head, she pressed down gently, and he let himself slide under. As soon as the water enclosed him, he was thinking of the dead.

There is no guidance. Left alone, you find yourself moving farther and farther away from them.

Stop following me.

Let me go.

I'm sorry.

He came up sputtering. Shea laughed. "Who were you talking to — Neptune?"

"What is that?"

"God of the water, god of the sea."

"I'm talking to what's in my head."

Shea plunged her arms into the kettle, soaped his penis and balls and asshole very quickly, delicately, her touch shocking his skin, his prick tingling, then stiffening.

She stood and left the room and he slid down in the kettle, took a mouthful of water and spat at the soapy taste, worried that he had insulted her, and relieved when she returned, moments later, carrying a blue bottle.

"Stand up."

She opened the spigot and warm water gushed down over him, rinsing off the soap scum. Shutting off the water, she made him step out of the kettle, and rubbed him fiercely with a towel.

His skin was pink, his body whining with heat. She made him sit with the damp towel on his shoulders while she clipped his hair, then wiped his ears and nostrils, using scraps of flannel dabbed in oil.

"You've never had it soft, have you? You're a culchie; I hear Clare in your voice. A rugged little culchie. Are you Fergus really?"

"I'm from Dublin, missus. Come over on *Ruth*. With Arthur."

"It's all right, it doesn't matter where you're from. It's where you're going, that's all that matters. Come now. Lay yourself down. I'm going to oil you, you little beast."

She had draped the bench with plush yellow towels. He lay down, and she wiped steam from his face then picked up the bottle and shook fluid onto her hands.

"There's gentlemen in trade in this city would pay five guineas to have Shea oil them."

First she rubbed his face, stroking the bridge of the nose and under his eyes, making circles on his cheeks, streaks of warmth along his jaw.

"Your hide is parched."

The oil smelled like sun on hay.

"Don't think of nothing," she said softly. "Sleep, little baby." She rubbed the gullies beside the tendons in his throat. As she rubbed his thighs, then belly, his prick climbed up stiffly. She brushed it with her fingers, and he felt reckless and vulnerable all at once and pictured the Bog Boys racing eagerly up the road for the farm.

Bending over, she kissed the tip of his prick then began stroking him.

Everything inside that you long to let go.

"Here it is," she said.

It could have been a dream and it felt very close to drowning.

How a horse feels when it can't stop running.

He recalled the salt taste of Luke's skin.

Joy. Poison.

There was something he yearned to give her as she touched him — he couldn't name it, but the exchange was the whole meaning of what they were doing.

You carry the world, within.

He heard himself yowl like a dog stepped on. The convulsion was rigorous and awkward and there was nothing left after.

All his bones, soft.

She cleaned him, made him roll onto his stomach then began rubbing warm oil in his neck and shoulders, up and down the backs of his legs. She rubbed oil into his heels. "Sleep, man, sleep."

It was impossible to stay alive as she rubbed and crooned. He was drifting in a glinting salmon river. Women were calling from the bank, but he was letting the current carry him down, he was floating, he was gone.

Pearl Boy

HE DREAMED HE WAS ABOARD *Ruth*. The sea handled the ship. Green water spouted up a hatchway from the engine room and the master raced about the deck like a squirrel. Passengers and drovers, cattle and sheep, slid from side to side as the steamer rocked on her beam ends. Large blue fish swam loops around the ship, snapping their lips, ready to make a fabulous meal.

He awoke for a few moments and thought he was drowning, but it was only spit in his throat.

HE WAS ill for days, churning with fever, in an attic room of the Dragon.

Once, very early in the morning, he had another vision of Luke's body.

Small soft breasts. Her patch of sexual hair.

How they used to bang each other alive.

Testing.

The way you let her plunge, and you plunged.

It shook him as hard as anything; it hurt from his toenails to his teeth. Unable to withstand the pressure he screamed, but no one came running. He was too weak.

A scream like a kitten yawning.

Forget. Forget them all. Time goes up not down. Money in your fist, boots on your feet. Get strong and hard.

Then you wouldn't be so vulnerable to the dead.

ARTHUR CAME hobbling up the attic stairs and lay next to him, puffing his pipe and blowing smoke rings at the ceiling.

"Are you going tramping soon, Arthur?"

"Perhaps I am."

"When?"

"Soon as I'm ready. Stay here a little while, I suppose. Put a pound or two by." He drew on his pipe. "Fellow don't like to tramp with no brass in his pocket."

Fergus suddenly felt the blood stinging in his veins. Thin, bitter, pungent; like gun browning. The itchy heat it caused in his muscles was intense, and he started writhing on the bed, flailing, punching Arthur's shoulder, kicking at his legs.

Arthur struggled to hold him down. "There, old Fergus, what's got into you?"

He could hear himself making animal sounds. He felt curiously detached from his body. Unbuckled, floating.

The strange fury passed gradually. He looked up at Arthur, sitting on his chest.

"Are you better now, old fellow?"

He didn't mind so much being under the navvy's weight. He felt safe.

"It's your old fever, I expect. The last of your fever kicking."

"Don't leave me here, Arthur."

"Mike says the Scotchmen are lurking. They've a price on my head."

"Don't you go without me."

"Never fear."

"I saved you — they'd have finished you. Don't go without me."

Arthur sucked his pipe and blew a mouthful of smoke at Fergus. "All right then — I won't."

*   *   *

HE SAT smoking a Kentucky cheroot while a black whore called Betsy cut his hair.

"Side-whiskers is what is wanted for effect," she said. "They're elegant."

The Dragon was scrubbed every morning by an army of barefoot, Irish-speaking maids, supervised by Mary. Fleeing the wet mops and steaming laundry tubs, the whores came trooping up to the attic, carrying their breakfast things: jugs of milk and tea, plates of bread and butter, bacon, a basket of oranges. They came yawning, with scraps of oily paper twisted in their hair, wearing print gowns over petticoats, lisle stockings, and soft sheepskin boots. Aromas of carbolic and beeswax drifted up the stairs after them, mixing with the scent of buttered toast, tea, and fruit.

He was passionate for the oranges; he had never tasted more satisfying food.

"He's too small for side-whiskers," said a tall skinny whore called Jenny, watching Betsy cut his hair.

Barbering was a fad with them. Every morning after breakfast, Fergus and Arthur were washed, clipped, and greased with various pomades. The whores oiled their feet and hands, cut their nails square, dabbed on varnish. They were convinced that skill at barbering would win them husbands, and spent their pocket money on cigars, ribbons, and fat little books with pictures of gentlemen's mustachios, side-whiskers, and waxed beards.

"A proper-run house needs a pearl boy," said Betsy. "I'd make him a velvet coat."

"Would you like to stay with us, Fergus?" Jenny asked.

He nodded.

Betsy smiled and kissed his nose. "A man with nowt to say is a gift of God."

The whores lounged on his bed or pillows on the floor, smoking little clay pipes, drinking tea.

"With side-whiskers, he would look like a cavalryman," Betsy said.

Her dark cheeks were rough in sunlight — *rough as a road*, he thought — but she was beautiful, they all were.

"Shall you stay at the Dragon, Fergus, and be our pearl boy?" Jenny asked.

"Down the railway line I'm going, along with Arthur McBride."

"Down the line, down the line!" Betsy said sharply. "Don't you know there's nothing down there but broken heads and broken backs?"

"Arthur says it's the life."

"You oughtn't listen."

"I never meet a railway navvy with any gentleness," Jenny said. "I suppose whatever they have gets knocked out of them."

"Worse than sailors," Betsy said.

"For all the great wages, the navvies are always poor. Never with a penny left, after a spree. Whoever heard of a rich navvy?"

"This house needs a pearl boy," Betsy said. "Look at you, you'll be a handsome fellow when you fill out. The wags would like him, don't you think, Jenny?"

"Very strong they would. Eat him alive."

"He's too small for the railway. They'd drop him in a hole. Stay with us, Fergus. I'll make you a green coat and waistcoat. There, now you are trim." Betsy stepped back to examine her work. "Very *beau*." She kissed him on the cheek.

He loved his sunny attic room, the smoke from their pipes and cheroots drifting and winding in the light. Were all women as generous? Around them the air was always warm.

He thought of Luke in the scalpeen, breathing the smell of cold ground and dry leaves and her —

Drop the past. Drop it.

You can't eat it can you.

The old world's crushed.

Life burns hot.

ON ST. STEPHEN'S DAY the whores were going out driving in the country in a hired coach, with bottles of champagne, their dinner packed in baskets.

Fergus wished to go along, and the whores begged Shea to let him.

"No. You aren't strong enough yet. Not for English air."

"I feel much better." He *was* better, though he still suffered from screams and sweats at night, often awakening near dawn in a bed sour with piss. Mary left extra sets of linens folded neatly on his chair and he would change the sheets himself, with the Dragon safely asleep, and no other sounds but claws scratching wood as the house cats roamed the hallways, stalking mice. He usually went back to sleep, and always awoke feeling hopeful, daylight streaming in his room.

He was hungry now for the taste of the outside, but Shea shook her head. "Soon. Not yet. Arthur won't be coming out neither — there are men watching the house. I don't want him seen. You can keep him company."

HIS ROOM seemed bleak with all the girls away except Mary. In the middle of the afternoon Arthur came upstairs to smoke a pipe and began pacing restlessly, smoke streaming.

"Iron Mike says they have sluggers from Glasgow who'll murder anyone for half a crown."

"We'll be going on the tramp quite soon, won't we?"

"Why? Don't you like the Dragon?" Stopping at the window, Arthur peered down at the street. "I can't live this way much longer, bundled up like a precious."

He sat down on the bed, puffing his pipe in great fumes. The cuts on his face were healing black and small.

"I like it here. But it isn't the railway line, is it?"

"No, thank God."

"When are we going, Arthur?"

"Navvy work would kill you."

"It wouldn't."

"You don't know what a rough business it is."

"I'm stronger every day."

"They don't care on the contracts. If you break your back or burst your heart, why, there's always another fellow to pick up the shovel."

"I could do it, Arthur."

"I'll tell you the truth, Fergus. You'd be better off staying right here at the Dragon and becoming a pearl boy for the wags."

Fergus stared at him.

"Don't look at me so," Arthur laughed. "It's easy money. Wags like the young Irish navvies, but they're frightened of us too. They'll pay extras like mad — I had a fellow once buy me a suit of clothes. It don't hurt much. You get used to it."

Others were never who you wanted them to be. Never so brave, loyal, intelligent. They hardly looked at you. They couldn't see you clearly; they didn't care to.

"Where do you think I got these boots? Pearl boy's not so bad. Not much chance of getting hurt — not like navvying. You can always do a wag pretty easy. It's good money."

"It's good money down the railway line, you said."

"Pearl boy is better money than railway wage. Come, come, don't get all peevish with me. You don't own boots. Not even a hat. You owe her everything you have. Who's kept you alive, after all? You can give it a try, can't you?"

Fergus stared at the wall, trying to hide his tears.

"What you think I did when first I came over? I was green as you. Pearl boy won't bust you, you aren't made of glass! Look at the girls. If they can, why can't you? It ain't so different as on the contracts, Fergus. A railway contractor hires your skin, same as a wag — only the wag pays better. Come now, we're your friends here, are we not?"

"You said we'd go down the line together, Arthur."

"I said I wouldn't go without you, and I won't. If you don't like the business, Fergus, why you can always give it up. Only give it a try. It wouldn't be fair, after all she's done for you, just to up and quit the Dragon, would it? We are your friends here. I tell you, Fergus, you won't find life so sweet down the line. You won't have the girls grooming you there. Come along, it's only sporting. I'll tell Shea to fix you a nice mild old gent. It's not the end of the world. Some of them only want you ten minutes. Nice quick money. Will you do it so? What do you say? Look at me."

He tried but could not look Arthur in the face; had to look away.

"She can't afford to keep you much longer, without you paying your way. She'd have to turn you out. And where will you be? Without so much as a shirt of your own? Don't be angry."

It wasn't anger, and it cut deeper than disappointment.

"Listen, Fergus, there's many fellows do the same. The Dragon gave me good boots, put the meat on my bones and brass in my pocket. Come, Fergus, say you will try. For the love of your old friends."

He remembered the Night Asylum — the emigrant men roaming the aisles, looking for a box to lay their bones in.

"Say you will try it. That's all she asks. Christ, Fergus, everyone needs a stake. You can't get into England with empty pockets and nothing on your feet. England's a killer — don't you know that yet? Come, man, say you will try the business. For the love of your old friends. Who else is there, after all, that cares for you? Say you will try."

Who are you, alone?

Fergus nodded.

"There it is," Arthur said, taking out a clean handkerchief and gently wiping Fergus's face. "I knew it. I told her you was game."

"Only until I get what I need. Only until I pay her back."

"Yes, yes, then we'll go down the line together."

Standing up and returning to the window, Arthur peered out again.

"Do you see them?" Fergus asked.

"See who?"

"Sluggers. From Glasgow."

"I see no one tonight. Will you come downstairs and drink your tea in the kitchen with Mary and Iron Mike?"

"I'm tired. I'd best stay here."

Looking out the window again, Arthur said, "I tell you, man, sometimes I'm wishing I'd never stabbed their fucking drum. It has brought me more trouble than honor."

"It was bold."

"Bold? Yes. Bold it was. And what else is there, eh?" Arthur said, with some of his old cheerfulness. "I gave them all a glory show, didn't I? Never mind that Shea — she's got me down. She's changed too much. She's too careful now. No one ever made his mark, being careful."

AFTER ARTHUR had gone downstairs, he got out of bed and crossed to the window.

It was getting dark outside, and looked cold as iron. Everything quiet. Winter was set now.

Somewhere through Liverpool's passagework of brick and stone was the estuary smelling of the sea. The great stone docks hectic with steamers. Cattle and emigrants pouring out of Ireland, clawing their way.

Using his fingernail, he peeled curls of frost from the glass and thought of Luke. How softly they lay, their bodies connected.

Scent of peat. Crispness of the old, dry bracken. Deep old scent of her, a fire burned down to black.

Could you ever feel so complete again?

No. It didn't seem possible.

Not here, not in this world of stone.

HE WAS to come down to the piano room, for tea. This was where gentlemen peering through peepholes would make their selections.

Shea sent up his pearl boy clothes. Trousers that strapped taut under the arches of his feet. A nankeen waistcoat and a ruffled shirt.

He sat grimly on the stool as Betsy powdered his face and painted his lips maroon. Hating the look and feel of the thin, glossy slippers Shea insisted that he wear.

"You're frightened ain't you?" Betsy said. "Hold still a moment. I know it. I was younger than you when I started in. Still am frightened. Just a little. Just enough."

He looked at her and couldn't speak. Couldn't open his mouth.

"The business won't kill you, Fergus. You can put some money by. She won't use you badly if you play her fair. If you don't cause trouble. Listen, we must all make our way, mustn't we?"

"I'll go on the tramp. With Arthur."

"Is that so."

Betsy was silent for a while, applying waxy red lacquer from a silver pot, daubing it on his lips. The stuff tasted pitchy, like tree gum.

"I'm out of St. Vincent, Fergus — do you know what it is?"

He shook his head.

"An island off in the Caribee, it is. Come to Liverpool aboard the sugar ship *Angel Clare* with a gentleman, a planter's son, who made promises he didn't keep, and turned me off the moment he smelled England.

"Before Shea found me, I was living along the docks, if you call it living. Ship riggers, sailors, and barrow men was my trade. I worked for pennies, or for a cup of gin. Sometimes they wouldn't pay me even that. Many mornings, I'd go down to Woodside landing stage, stand there for hours as it rose and fell on the tide. Watch the butchers' boys rushing cattle on the barges, and think of throwing myself in the river.

"After she found me, she bathed me herself, fed me, and gave me a clean bed, and I didn't do no business at first, but only helped in the scullery. Then she said I could turn to, if I wanted a little pocket money to spend. Otherwise she might not be able to afford my keep. Said she'd never let any man hurt me, and more or less, it's true. I have been going strong almost six years. I have had the jumps, had raging womb twice, and I shouldn't expect as I ever should have a baby of my own since I'm all peculiar down there now — since that last surgeon, who weren't nothing but a butcher.

"All I'm saying, Fergus, is, the Dragon will keep you alive, and it's not so bad here. Only don't stay too long. Not like me or like Arthur."

"Arthur and I are going on the tramp."

"No. Arthur isn't going navvying anytime soon. He prefers life here at the Dragon. And when he leaves, he doesn't go navvying. Hasn't tramped for years. He crosses back to Ireland, cursing Shea, cursing England, saying he never shall return. But he always does, and never gets past the Dragon.

"Never put your time in another's hands, Fergus, or you'll always be disappointed. When you're ready to leave us, don't wait for Arthur. Here, take this." Betsy took something from a pocket of her gown and held it out — a small, pearl-handled clasp knife, no bigger than his thumb. "Carry this. Go on, it's for you. Don't tell Shea."

Opening the little knife, he tried the bright, brittle blade on his thumbnail.

"If a fellow gets too rough, you prick him where he knows you mean business. Come, slip that beezer in your pocket, and let's go downstairs."

SHEA, ARTHUR, and the girls were in the piano room, drinking tea, eating butter toast and apples, ham sandwiches, kippers, and little yellow cakes the girls called lemon drops.

Arthur winked at him from across the tea table.

Shea was staring at him. "You've too much powder on him, Betsy. He looks half dead."

"I'll take him upstairs and do him over if you like."

"No, no, there ain't time. Try not to look such a sad dog, Fergus!" Shea pinched his cheeks. "It's not a hanging! You're here to make money, the key of happiness, so brighten up!"

The girls were noisy, giddy, dipping toast into teacups, slapping one another's hands as they grabbed for cakes, and he could sense they were all frightened.

THE COAL fire sizzled in the grate. Fragrance of butter, toast, blackberry jam, and tea with sugar clouded the room.

What would the Bog Boys have done for such food, which was beyond their imaginations?

Arthur had been selected almost immediately. Shea touched his shoulder, and he stood up and left the room, smirking.

Luke had been a whore in Limerick to feed herself, to put food in the little boys' gawping mouths.

Shea poured the tea and Mary, in a crisp white cap and apron, handed the cups around. He had grown fond of the whores' drink of tea, its smoky flavor. They never had tasted tea on the mountain. Water or whiskey. Milk he'd tasted from Phoebe's pail, or stolen, squeezed from her father's cows in the field. Men drank porter in the beer shops on market day, after selling the pig.

"Here, Fergus, help yourself, take as much as you want." Mary was passing around delicacies on china plates: cakes, herrings, jam on toast, cold fried oysters with salt. He was surprised that he had an appetite.

The whores were wearing their best gowns fluffed with starched petticoats, their hair dressed in ringlets. They blew on their tea to cool it, poured it into saucers and slurped noisily. They lit straws at the fire, then lit cheroots from the straws. They blew streams of smoke at one another, told one another riddles he didn't understand. They took up their needlework for a few minutes then put it down. They screamed whenever they spilled a drop of tea or dab of jam on their dresses, and didn't seem to be the same girls as they were in his attic room in the mornings, daylight spilling in the windows.

* * *

ARTHUR RETURNED and sat away by himself, a little black cigar clenched between his teeth. Catching Fergus looking at him, he stared back coldly, eyes narrowed against the smoke.

A few minutes later, he was chosen again and left the room once more, following Shea.

Perhaps half of the girls had been led away. Those not chosen gobbled more cakes and drank tea and laughed even louder at silly jokes, though it seemed to him some of them were near tears. He couldn't tell if they were disappointed or relieved.

Shea came in, pouring tea and telling girls to sit up straight. Standing behind Fergus's chair, she placed her hands on his shoulders. "What is it, man? Why so sad? Everyone must have a trade, you know."

Empty chairs and abandoned teacups marked the places of those now upstairs wrestling with the trade.

He suddenly knew how afraid he was. His body stiff in the chair. The faces of girls seemed blurry. He wondered if he was going blind from the poison of fear, which he could feel in his blood. He had never been so afraid.

He thought of his parents lying in the cabin rubble. Married people were to be buried in the same grave or one would come looking for the other. By now the rain would have beaten the wreckage of the cabin down to a slick mound of clay.

Jenny, tall and sallow, hair the color of wheat, sat down at the piano and started playing, the notes flying from the polished instrument so bright and hard he could almost touch them.

Gathering around the piano the girls began singing about Greensleeves.

Without knowing any of the words, he opened his throat to join in. They were all as frightened as he was. Some had been summoned from the room two or three times, inspected, sent back. Gathered around Jenny sitting at the piano, they were singing to defend themselves from how alone they felt, how unprotected, while Shea moved in and out of the room softly, touching girls by the arm, leading them away.

Singing gave them a sense of something surrounding and protecting them, and they sang song after English song until Shea, reaching out, touched Jenny's shoulder lightly.

The whore immediately stopped her playing. Closing the lid, she arose, touched her hair, and followed Shea from the room. No one sat down to take her place. The singing was finished and he followed the girls back to the tea table and helped them light their cigars.

WHEN SHEA shook him awake, he didn't know where he was.

Gazing around the smoky warm room he saw girls yawning, and realized he had fallen asleep with his head on the tea table.

"Come, come." Shea was nudging him impatiently.

Thinking he had been chosen, he immediately felt queer and knew he was going to be sick.

"You may as well go to bed before you put the others to sleep!" Shea said sharply.

He looked up her. "What?"

"You're a dreary feature, not doing any good down here! Go upstairs. You're casting a spell on the others. No one wants a boy so grim and unbecoming! You're very poor investment."

Relieved and ashamed, he headed for the door, anticipating the quiet of the attic and the cool, dry sheets on his bed.

"You'll pick up by and by, Fergus." Betsy was sitting in a chair, doing needlework. "He isn't quite well, not yet," she reminded Shea.

"I want him fresh. Feed him some brandy next time! And not so much powder, Betsy! Lively and fresh — that's what gentlemen want."

Fresh fish.

IN THE middle of the night he woke to noisy shouting from downstairs. Racing down through the house, he found the kitchen crowded with excited girls and half-dressed gentlemen. Arthur had chased a wag out into the alley and was beating him with his fists. Standing barefoot in the cold, Fergus watched Iron Mike and three other men dragging Arthur off the man and carrying the navvy inside, kicking and writhing. They laid him on the kitchen floor, and Iron Mike sat on his chest, the others holding down his arms and legs.

"You're breaking me, Arthur!" Shea was furious. "You're ruining the Dragon and everything I built!

"He bit me!"

"I won't let you ruin my house. I'll let those Scotchmen shoot you like a dog."

"I won't have any maggot bite me!"

Iron Mike and the others strained to hold Arthur down. Shea looked at him with disgust. "Put him below. Throw him in the coal cellar. We'll see if he likes himself alone."

NEAR DAWN, Fergus went down to the coal cellar and tapped on the iron door. At first there was no response, then Arthur's voice said hoarsely, "Who is it? Let me out."

"I haven't got the key. She'll let you out in a couple of hours, I suppose."

"You go tell her let me out now. Tell her I'm sorry, I'll be excellent, and she won't have to worry about her precious old wags. You tell her so, Fergus. Go on. Please, man. You and me, we are the railway birds, ain't we? We shall tramp down the line together, by and by. Only you tell her to let me out."

Fergus went upstairs and knocked on Shea's door.

"Who's there?"

"Me."

"Fergus? What is it?"

"Arthur wishes you to let him out."

"Tell him he can rot."

"He's very sorry for the trouble."

After a few moments the door opened. Shea wore the silk dragon gown over her nightdress and held a candle in a silver dish. "He'll ruin my trade. It's always like this. He thinks being wild is glory — thinks we love him for it. He knows nothing of the world."

"You'll let him out, won't you?"

"He's never brought anything but trouble into this house."

But she already had the key in her hand, and followed him downstairs and into the gloomy cellar, where she unlocked the door.

Arthur had been sitting on a pile of coal. He quickly stood up and stepped out without a word.

"This is the last time, Arthur. Don't do it again, I warn you."

"What am I to do when a fellow insults me?"

"Take it — they're paying good money."

"That rabbit bit me, bit my old cock."

"I don't care if he bit it off."

"Sure you do, sure you do." He smiled at her.

Shea shook her head wearily. "I don't wish to see you. Go upstairs, and make sure you're clean before you touch my linen."

TWO COACHES had been hired to drive the whores into the country for their monthly outing.

"And you shall come with us, Fergus, you want some color in your cheeks," Shea decided. "That'll get the old crooks snapping."

Shea refused Arthur's plea to come along.

"You needn't punish me no more, Shea. I am quiet, so."

And it was true — since his night in the coal cellar, he had been gloomy and silent.

"It won't do to show your face. Iron Mike says they have a price on your skin."

"I'm a veal calf, Shea. I must get out! Only for a spin — I need the air worse than anyone."

"Should have thought of that before you stabbed their drum."

Arthur grew so morose that Shea finally agreed to let him come along on their outing if the girls disguised him as one of themselves. They bought fabric and Arthur stood in the attic room glumly smoking little cigars one after another as they measured, pinned, and cut. By Sunday morning they had him outfitted in petticoats and a gray morning gown, trimmed with green ribbon; with a pelouse, bonnet, and a rabbit-skin muffler. They hadn't found slippers large enough for his feet, but the skirts concealed his boots.

"Oh Arthur, you're a bonny lass," Betsy teased.

"I don't give a damn for it. I'd as soon let them kill me."

"Oh, don't say so. If Shea hears, she won't have you come at all."

Betsy and Jenny shaved and powdered Arthur, painting his lips, gradually transforming him into a sullen, pretty young woman.

Fergus thought of Luke's body, a passion between the two of them, a secret.

Sooner or later everyone disguises themselves and where they have been and what they have done.

STANDING IN the street, Fergus and Iron Mike kept a lookout for the hired coaches.

Most of the loitering, lounging navvies had disappeared from the Dragon's front steps when the cold settled in. Iron Mike said they had gone for the railway contracts in Wales, or London for tunnel work, or had crossed the water home.

"When are you going yourself down the line?" Fergus asked.

"Oh, I'm house porter now, Shea's house cat. My railway days are over. Here we are," Iron Mike said, seeing the carriages turning from Hanover Street. "Fetch the lovelies."

The whores came trooping down the steps in a pack, wearing cloaks and bonnets, keeping Arthur surrounded with their bodies and laughter as they piled into the coaches.

Shea nodded to the coachman and they were off, rolling by street corners where emigrants stood guarding lumps of baggage. The sky above the stone buildings was dark blue. Burnished pavement and scraps of frost shone in hard light.

WRAPPED IN rugs, the whores dozed, lulled by the crackle of wheels and the fresh air. The dense stone city thinned out to muddy building sites and bleak new terraces of brick houses standing isolated in fields. Fergus kept awake, alert and watchful, amazed at Liverpool's power and sprawl, the way it lay upon the land.

Finally they reached open country, driving along a metaled road lined with fat gray trees, sunlight flickering through the canopy of bare branches.

The whores awoke famished. There was a hamper and two bottles of champagne in each carriage. They drank champagne out of the bottle and ate ham sandwiches and cold meat pies as the pair of carriages rolled through a country of clipped meadows and soft hills.

After noon the light thinned, the sky slowly losing its luster, and the air grew sharper. In the yard of an inn, the horses were fed and watered, and the whores brought inside and given warm cider and rum cakes with butter. Piling into the coaches again, they started for home, the horses' hooves snapping briskly on the road.

Late in the afternoon, near dusk, the coachmen made a last halt so the girls could run out in a field and pee, while Shea fed apples to the horses, whispering and stroking their necks. Arthur stood in the middle of the road, clutching a champagne bottle, bonnet thrown back off his shoulders.

Fergus had climbed up in the driver's seat to look at the rim of country, the hills of England, the neatly organized rigging of fields. They were close enough to town so he could sniff coal smoke in the cold, still air. Daylight was murky. The whores were squatting in tufted wet grass, peeing and swigging champagne.

Peering ahead, Fergus saw two figures approaching along the road. Jumping down, he stood alongside Arthur.

Breathing the cold, loamy air of England, tinted with smoke.

"Shea, have a look," Arthur said. "Here are a couple of poor Cathleens."

A pair of girls, both wearing cloaks. One limping slightly.

"Good day to you," Shea called.

One girl stopped and the other bumped into her. Both were barefoot. Their faces looked dull with exhaustion.

Fergus said a greeting in Irish, and they started to cry.

"Ask if they've had the fever," Shea said.

He asked in Irish. Both girls nodded.

"Ask how old they are." Walking up to them, Shea stood looking them over head-to-toe. "Tell them to open their mouths."

The two girls stood dumb as cattle. Straw in their hair.

"Go on!" Shea told Fergus impatiently. "Do as I say."

Their names, they told him, were Brigid and Caitlín. They were thirteen and fifteen, and from a townland he didn't understand the name of but near, they said, Tullamor.

They stood with mouths open like birds while Shea squeezed their cheeks and peered at their teeth and their tongues. The two coachmen and the whores watched in silence as Shea felt beneath the coarse workhouse gowns and squeezed their breasts then lifted up their skirts and studied the triangles of hair, white bellies, and thighs streaked in filth.

The bigger girl was shivering. The horses shook their iron hooves and dropped shit on the road.

"What a pair of haggard little creatures," Arthur said.

Shea stepped back, still studying them. "Cheap meat, but I can feed 'em up, I suppose. Need a bath more than anything. Tell them they shall come along with us, Fergus."

When he didn't respond she glanced at him. "They'll have a warm bed, rations, and pocket money. Shall you leave 'em here, then? They're dead in a week."

In Irish he said to the girls "She will give you a roof. Come with us now."

THE CHAMPAGNE was all finished. Cold and tired, the whores wanted to go home. The outing had lost its glamour.

The pauper girls were seated in Shea's coach, and Betsy was tucking a blanket around them. Girls were still climbing in when Fergus heard a puffing, like the warm breath of an animal.

On the edge of the sky, he saw an explosion of white smoke.

"Train!" Betsy called.

Snorting, hissing, clanking, the train rose from a cutting he hadn't noticed, speeding along the rim of the horizon, like a line drawn under everything he hadn't known before.

The whores stood waving their handkerchiefs and bonnets, pitching champagne bottles, screaming.

"Come lay with me you iron monster!"

"Give me a shilling for my breath!"

"Kiss my squeak hole, you old smoky beast!"

Shea sat with a rug around her shoulders, ignoring the train, and the two paupers huddled together, terrified at the commotion the whores made.

A train was an idea, he saw that right away.

Before he knew what he was doing, he had leapt down and climbed the wall and was racing across the wet meadow grass, whooping.

Passion of motion and distance.

Power of smoke, transformation.

Possibilities. Change.

He reached the line just as the train blew past, hard as Hell and flagrant with speed, light bursting from carriage windows. A gorgeous disturbance, breaking up his sense of the world.

Then she was through, leaving the air buffeted, disturbed by the violence of the passage. He bent to touch the rail, feeling the heat.

The whores were calling, waving their bonnets and handkerchiefs. He stood on the track bed staring after the train as it took a bend, ramming across the open country, like a promise of everything you could leave behind.

HE TOLD Iron Mike he was going on the tramp, looking for railway work, and the porter directed him to an old-clothes stall in the Vauxhall where he swapped his button jacket, nankeen waistcoat, strapped trousers, ruffle shirts, and slippers for greased hobnail boots, woolen stockings, moleskin trousers, two linen shirts — one green, one blue — a tweed coat, a good stiff beaver hat only slightly dented with a hatband to tuck a pipe into, and two red handkerchiefs.

"Take the Woodside ferry across the river," Iron Mike advised. "Catch the line for Chester. Don't buy no ticket, but ride the trucks; you'll see plenty of fellows jumping. From Chester you can follow Mr. Telford's road out along the coast of Wales. You'll soon see railway works, the Chester-and-Holyhead. Contracts are let in ten-mile sections, and they will have navvy camps all the way to Anglesey. Mr. Murdoch has one of the contracts, I hear, and you could do worse. I've worked for him in Scotland and in France and he always paid his men in coin of the realm, no scrip, as some of them will try."

SHEA WAS annoyed when he told her he was going. "My God, Fergus, do you really believe you can help yourself by leaving? My girls live as soft as house cats. I'm offering you the life, and you're going to break yourself on the navvy line?"

He nodded.

"Can you tell me why? Have you been so ill treated?"

He shook his head.

"Was it that no one chose you last week? Listen, boy, we shall dress you up a little nicer next time. You already look so much healthier. You have to remem-

ber there is a lot of Irish boys harking the streets these days and they're terrible
cheap, and many with black fever — Irish boys seem a little out of fashion, at
least among my class of gentlemen. But we'll get you a velvet suit and a softer
name — William, Albert, Edward, something squishy like that. We'll tell 'em
you're Scotch. Don't worry, you'll do fine."

"But I was glad I wasn't chosen."

She shrugged. "You were scared, so. That's natural —"

"I can't do that, Shea, what the wags want. Don't wish to be open that way."

She shook her head slowly. "Boy, they'll get into you one way or another,
don't you know?"

"Still, I'm going to leave."

She crossed the room and he thought she was going to slap him and he pre-
pared to take the blow, thinking he deserved it from her, but instead she placed
cool hands on his cheeks and kissed his forehead.

"They'll crack you like mice," she said.

EARLY IN the morning Mary fed him breakfast in the kitchen of the Dragon.
The whores stood around in nightdresses and flannel wraps, sipping milky tea
and admiring his hard new clothes.

Mary fed him toast, honey, tea, and an orange, and gave him a parcel for the
road, tied up in a handkerchief.

"You'll be sorry," said Arthur. "Only when you get down there, tell them
you're the friend of Arthur McBride, best hammer there ever was on the
Manchester lines."

"I'll tell them so, Arthur."

"And don't think ill of your old house."

"I won't."

"Which took you in when you was a scarecrow, don't forget. And look at you
now."

"I won't forget anything."

"You watch out for them navvy kills, man. You're small enough; they'll put
you on the horses. Watch your legs. The horse tip is the wildest spot on any
contract — they are always murdering boys."

He kissed Arthur, and then went around the kitchen kissing them all, his chest tight with emotion, sorrowful now that he was actually leaving. Never before had he left where anyone had wanted him to stay. Such parting was sweet, in a way.

"You're a miserable, ungrateful cur for leaving, after all we've done for you." Shea kissed him, then held open the door.

Grave, excited, confused, he walked out into the smoke before he could change his mind.

THERE WAS power in going forward, but it was vulnerable, it could be broken. The ferry flapping across the gray Mersey was packed with cattle. He studied the tramps leaning along the rail and smoking their pipes — tough men in greased hobnail boots, carrying their belongings in handkerchief bundles.

After the ferry arrived at Woodside landing stage, he followed the tramps up past the slaughter yards to the railway station, where dozens of men sprawled on the platform, puffing pipes, dozing like bulls in the sun.

After the train slid in, shrieking, he watched well-dressed passengers disembarking and boarding carriages. Gentlemen removed their shiny silk hats, too tall to wear inside. The engine leaked steam and an odor of iron and burned coal. He watched the tramps sauntering down the track, pitching their packs and bundles up into open wagons attached at the rear of the train, and climbing over the sides.

A whistle whooped like a bird, and a boy raced along the platform, slamming carriage doors shut. The train shook itself, and Fergus heard the iron couplings banging, one after another, as it began to move.

You throw yourself on the world like turf on a fire.

Picking up his bundle, he started walking along the platform, conscious of the iron wheels rumbling and creaking, the scent of grease, and death so close. Glancing over his shoulder he could see the string of open wagons approaching, each one packed with men peering out over the wooden sides.

He let the first open wagon go by. Walking faster, he flipped his bundle into the second, and saw one of the men aboard catch it. Grasping the iron ladder, he felt the hard power of the train, and suddenly he was running to keep up. His feet left the ground, and he hauled himself up the first two rungs then froze, disoriented by the complex motion, the ground spinning, the wagon trembling like an animal.

A couple of tramps reached over, grabbed him, and roughly dragged him in over the side. He fell onto the floor but jumped up immediately, and a man gave him his bundle. They stood packed shoulder-to-shoulder. The wagon rocked and shook.

Looking over the sides, he saw houses tumbling by, gardens, piles of bricks, ash heaps. A pen of sheep, a fellow waving a hat, a girl dashing liquid from a window. He gripped the flexing sides and stared at the world rushing past like an animal escaping, as though the train had torn a trap open.

PART IV

Red Molly

NORTH WALES, JANUARY–MARCH 1847

The Cutting

HE TRAMPED THE COAST road for four days, out of Chester, singing to himself, light-headed, face burned by bright wind off the sea. Most of the time he was alone. He avoided Scotchmen and English tramps. He knew the Irish by the bent shapes of their hats, and sometimes joined a pack of men for a few hours, learning what he could from their talk.

Thousands of navvies and horses were constructing the railway along the coast of North Wales. The work had been let out in sections, in dozens of separate contracts. Each river was being spanned with iron bridgework. The country was being smoothed out mile after mile in the railway's quest for perfect grade. Cuttings were slashed straight through the Welsh hills, and tons of excavation dumped, spread, and compacted across every soft place, every dip, every bit of marsh.

"A railway loves the level grade," an old tramp told him one afternoon.

They were smoking their pipes and watching a thousand navvies at work in a cutting, hacking with picks and spades. Fergus had wanted to know why they couldn't lay the railway over the slight rise instead of cutting straight through it.

"On a slope, iron wheels don't have any purchase on iron rails — they spin," the old tramp said. "Which is why we make cuttings and fill embankments — to make good grade. The world ain't level, but the navvies make her so."

In some places, the line was almost finished, and he heard the crack of hammers and watched men driving spikes, fixing the iron rails on timber sleepers.

Driving spikes was work looked down upon by the tramps, who said the track-layer gangs were composed of poor Welsh shepherds paid meager wages, drawn down off their black mountains by the promise of hot food.

Making grade — cutting open the hills, laying a streak of perfect level across the old, soft world — was the work the tramps respected.

"No skill or risk in pounding iron," the old tramp said scornfully. "Nothing glory. There's no battle in it. Making grade is our work — a navvy likes to fight the ground."

He understood this. Making grade was a powerful act.

In Ireland the ground had betrayed them all, poisoned their food.

Grade was theirs, human. Grade was like a thought made hard and real. It might last a thousand years.

Grade showed the navvies as strong as the world.

MOSTLY THE weather was clear and hard, but flurries of snow swept in from the sea, rattling the road, scratching his cheeks.

He encountered packs of navvies on the tramp, moving in both directions along the coast road. Contractors were always trying to lure the tramps into hiring on — they were fed at the contractors' beer shops, and slept on clean straw in their sheds. All along the Chester & Holyhead, contracts were shorthanded. Men quit casually, shifting from one contractor's camp to another, staying clear of the Welsh villages, where they were not welcome.

Offered wages at Aber cutting, he kept walking.

At Conwy, the contractor wanted rivet boys on the bridge that plunged like a sword across the neck of the river. Offered two shillings sixpence daily wages, he was stunned, and tempted, but still did not feel like stopping.

Days tramping the coast were short and cold. The sea on one side, like a green glass eye. It was easy enough living inside your head, absorbing the sky, and thinking only of the weather, the next feed.

Tramping was strange and addictive, a kind of perfection, but there came a time you had to stop, or you would walk right out of yourself. It would be easy.

* * *

"I AM needing tip boys. Ask anyone — I treat my fellows square. Here, man, taste this."

The contractor had been standing in the road, waiting with a cart and a cask of beer, willing to hire any tramps that came along. Drawing a pot of beer, he offered it to Fergus. "Wages paid once a month, regular. Three shillings per day. Coin of the realm."

Sipping the tawny beer, Fergus looked across fields lightly flavored with snow to a cutting where hundreds of men with picks and shovels were gouging a right-of-way.

Looking the other direction, he watched the sea smashing the coast. It seemed yellow, so angry in its foam.

"Samuel Murdoch is my name." The contractor wore a straw hat tied under his chin with a ribbon and an old swallowtail coat, weathered purple. Pantaloons were tucked into the tops of horse boots spattered with mud. He watched Fergus sip the beer. "You're a good Irishman — where are you from?"

The days of the Dragon fell away and he saw his sisters and parents, and the white faces of dead girls — Phoebe and Luke — so strangely composed.

Feeling the contractor staring, Fergus looked up slowly.

Man, I'm from Hell. I am dosed in death.

But you had to shove all that down. Conceal it. It was poison to you, possibly a hanging.

"Limerick," he said.

Murdoch nodded briskly. "I'm Carrickfergus, myself. All my fellows are Irishmen, pure and pure, excepting a few little black Welsh and one or two Cornwall miners that don't cause any trouble. I pay coin of the realm, no scrip, and I treat my fellows fair. Is that good beer?"

"It is."

"You're my man, then."

Fergus hesitated, clinging to the freedom of the road. So far his head had been clear, but if he kept on any longer, alone, bad thoughts would return.

The dead unburied, pecking him.

Four days of solitude was enough.

"All right."

"Good man. Finish that up and go see my timer, he'll set you down in his book."

THE CUTTING was a notch in the hill. Hundreds of navvies were digging it wider and deeper, filling horse carts with the excavation.

The camp sprawled over muddy ground adjacent to the right-of-way. He crossed a field where dozens of spare axles, cartwheels, wooden wagon-tongues, and barrels of grease were arranged in neat rows and stacks. In other fields there were dumps of gravel and yellow sand; stacks of building lumber, and timber sleepers; black mountains of coal. A park of wrecked horse carts neatly arrayed had been picked over for salvage.

Heavy drays were squishing along the road in and out of the camp, loaded with casks and crates, bundles of iron tools, burlap sacks of meal.

Despite the abundance, there was an air of meanness to the sprawl. Horses standing bleakly in an icy field stared at him walking by. Looking up, he could see shanties, tents, and shebangs where the men lived, terraced on the muddy slope just below the cutting.

The heart of the camp was equipment sheds, repair shops, and barns, all built with green lumber. Mud alleys between flimsy buildings were deserted except for drays and teamsters unloading stores. He heard a blacksmith hammering and smelled the sour tang of hot iron. Passing an unpainted wooden church, he saw every window was hollow, framed with shards of broken glass.

Every structure in the camp looked temporary, ready to buckle in a hard wind. The air smelled of iron, wheel grease, and pine lumber. He passed a bootmaker's tent, with a pair of old boots dangling from a pole, and a barber's, with a red-and-white sheet flapping in the wind. He met an old man pushing a barrow of apples and asked for directions to the timer's hut.

It stood at the center of the camp, next to Mr. Murdoch's beer shop, which had plate-glass windows and looked light and fragile, as though it might lift from its footings and sail away. The timer's hut was a squat cabin, roofed with a sheet of iron. A brass bell hung outside. He gave it a pull, and a voice yelled at him to enter.

Inside was warm. The timer sat at a rolltop desk. "Close the door, you devil." He spoke without looking around.

A fire glowing in the nickel stove.

Fergus waited, absorbing the heat of the room.

The timer spun around in his chair. A crab-like youth in a dingy white shirt, wearing steel spectacles. "Hiring on?"

"I am."

The timer reached to a shelf and took down a ledger. Opening it on his desk, he dipped his pen, made an entry, then offered the pen. "Step up and make your mark, you heathen."

While Fergus made his scratch, the timer started drawing a pot of beer from a cask in the corner. The scent filled the warm hut, and Fergus suddenly felt dizzy. Had been right after all to stop? Perhaps his fortune was to keep walking.

Walk until you come to the end of the country.

Walk into the green sea.

There is nothing holding you in the world.

"Look smart!"

Blinking, he looked up. The timer was holding out a pot of beer. "Drink up! Mr. Murdoch's best."

"I can't pay for it. Don't have the money."

"Mr. Murdoch treats them signing on. Drink up." The timer took out a paper ticket from a drawer, marked it, and slid it across. "Your sub ticket — subsistence, worth nine shillings, deducted from wages. Find a shanty taking lodgers, and exchange your sub for a week's board. After one week, you may draw another. Pay is made, last Saturday of the month, at Mr. Murdoch's beer shop in the camp. If you are thirsty, you may always take a drink at Mr. Murdoch's — the barmen will mark it against wages. Stay away from the shops in the village — Welshmen are thieves."

Fergus stared at the slip of paper in his hand, feeling overwhelmed by warmth, beer, and an inchoate sense of everything lost.

The sense of spinning.

Like a dead leaf whirling from a tree.

"Try Muck Muldoon's shanty," the timer suggested. "He ought to have a crib to spare. His wife's the pretty red doxie."

* * *

THE SHANTY camp on the Welsh hillside resembled the *baile* on the mountain, if the mountain were thoroughly peeled and stripped, every stream caked over, every well forgotten, every cabin slathered into the ground.

Muddy paths were lined with shanties that had no proper roofs or walls, only scraps of whatever would stand.

The terrain was barren and brown, stripped of turf, trees, gorse, animals. No potato plots. No patches of well-drained limestone ground. Nothing could be raised in such a slickness of mud.

No mysteries. Everything had been scavenged from somewhere else. The whole hillside could have been the ruins of one enormous, tumbled cabin, a giant hump of greasy clay, marled with stones, scraps of canvas, and bits of lumber. Slowly losing its shape, dissolving under the rain.

Overtaking a woman lugging a sack of coal, he asked her the way to Muldoon's.

Red Molly

A RED-HAIRED YOUNG WOMAN was boiling wash in a kettle in front of Muldoon's shanty. Fergus watched her stirring the clothes. Small nose, small hands, wearing an old blue gown.

"They said you take lodgers," he called.

She looked up. Full lips, freckles. "Got your sub?"

He nodded.

"Let's see."

He walked up and showed his ticket.

"Show us your tongue," she demanded.

He stared at her freckled face.

"Come on, man," she said impatiently. "Open up, or go away."

He stuck out his tongue as rudely as he could.

She glanced at it, then nodded. "Come along, I'll show you what it is."

He followed her inside the shanty, resenting her brusqueness.

"There is three rooms. Muldoon and me has the one. The other is lodgers. This here is the cozy, where we eat."

A table and benches on an earth floor. A battered armchair and a couple of three-legged stools in front of the fire, where an iron kettle was seething on the hob.

The girl rapped her knuckles on the table and pointed to a stain in the wood.

"Can you guess what that is?"

"I can't."

"Blood. That's where they laid out Kelly."

"Who is Kelly?"

"Kelly was killed Christmas week." She touched the stain with her fingertips. "Broke like a bowl of eggs. The fellows brought him in here, laid him on that table. They used to say he was rough, but he wasn't, not really." She rapped her knuckles on the wood. "Come, I'll show you your crib. You get a pot of beer with your supper. If you want more, it's sixpence."

He followed her into a sleeping room where clothes hung from nails on the rafter. The crib she showed him contained a straw pallet and a blanket.

"Was it Kelly's?"

"It was." She was small and quick in her movements, smoothing the blanket. She didn't bother looking at him. He sensed her impatience.

"What happened with Kelly?"

"They say he must have slipped while his nag was pulling, and the truck cut off both his legs. Muck found him on the line. I was getting the dinner, nine bits of mutton on string, boiling away. Except they carried in old Kelly, and laid him out on the table. I've scrubbed but it don't go away. Do you want the lodgings or not?"

"Yes."

"Give it over then." She took his sub. "The fellows will be back soon. Mutton for supper, spoileen. You get porridge with milk in the morning, and your dinner to carry along. I will sell you some tobacco, if you want."

"What is your name?" he asked

"Molly they call me."

"Fergus I am."

"The basin for washing is outside, and the jakes."

She left abruptly, and he sat down on the bed, trying to remember what had brought him out here. Mostly the pure, sick desire to keep moving, which he had felt ever since that morning in the snow.

As he lay back on the bed he could hear the girl, outside, stirring the wash.

He stared up at the shabby sticks that were rafters, and the planks and scraps of canvas forming the roof, and knew it could all come down in a good knocking wind, burying him. He could feel the weight pressing his chest, but he made himself stay flat in the bed, though he wanted get up, run outside.

The only true thing is how alone you are now.

You can't run from it or you'll never stop.

IT WAS dark when he awoke. The fragrant steam of boiling meat made him hungry, and he got up and went out into the cozy, where Molly had lit oil lamps and was kneeling by the fire, stirring the kettle.

She looked up and grinned. Her eyes were green — sea green. Water and light.

"Sit down, man. They'll be in soon enough."

Sitting on one of the three-legged stools, he took out his pipe. Now that it was settled where he would live and eat and work, he should feel relieved, but did not. He felt the gloom closing around him and wished he were on the tramp again.

He searched his pockets for tobacco, then remembered he had nothing left.

"I can sell you backer," she said quickly. "That's what you want, ain't it? Sixpence a good handful. Straight backer, too. No junk in it."

"Don't have the money."

"I might advance you enough for a smoke. Would that suit you?"

"It would."

She disappeared into the other bedroom and came out with the tobacco. "You're hired for a tip boy, I reckon?"

"Yes."

"The work ain't so bad if you don't lose your legs. Most of the fellows spill every penny of wages on drink, and jackets, and Liverpool girls." She gave him enough tobacco to fill his pipe, then filled her own. "He may knock you around at first —"

"Who?"

"— but if you can stand it, why, the wages is good."

"Who will knock me around?"

"Muldoon. Muldoon is ganger for the horse boys."

"Does he knock them around?"

"I suppose he does."

"Does he knock you around?"

"Sometimes he does. Ain't that fine backer?"

"It is."

"If you are still here tomorrow, I shall advance you sixpenny worth." She puffed her pipe. "This is fine smoke, ain't it? Don't buy backer at the tommy. They will skin you, give you three ounces for four, and it's rotten old meal besides. A fellow told me they mixes ground old bones with their backer. My stuff is quite pure. Do you like playing cards?"

He had seen the boothmen and horse dealers at fairs playing brightly colored cards, and gentlemen at Shea's with their cards, cigars, and brandies.

"I never have, myself. It's a con, isn't it?"

"It is, and it isn't. Myself, I deal a pretty straight game. Only for amusement really. And a penny here and there." She grinned. "Won't you like to play sometimes? You can always play on tick. I trust my fellows."

"Perhaps I shall."

Drawing smoke, she held it, then let it sidle between her lips. She was looking at the table, where she had already set out supper plates. "I used to deal the fellows cards on that table — do you know the game Pharaoh?"

"I don't."

"It's common. They deal it at the fairs. Me and my old mother, we've lived on the cards. All over Ireland. Working fairs, you must keep moving. You don't like 'em to know you. Poor old Kelly, he liked a hand or two. I ain't played since they brought him down. I scrubbed the table, but it don't go away. He wasn't rough, Kelly, not really."

He heard noises outside.

"Oh, here we are," she said, "I hear the mighty fellows!"

She jumped to her feet and was lifting mutton from the seething kettle when the door opened and a small, wiry man wearing a leather coat stepped inside. He stopped and stared at Fergus.

"New lodger, Muldoon," Molly said quickly. "Fergus the name. This is Muldoon."

Muldoon glared at him with black eyes. Fergus nodded.

Two others, a thin young man and an old man, came in behind the ganger, bringing a smell of cold soil in with them, faces windburned.

"Sit down, Muldoon, you mollusk."

The girl helped the ganger taking off his coat, and Fergus saw her lift a pistol from a pocket and set it on a shelf. Muldoon sat down in the armchair while she knelt and began untying his boots.

"Get his sub?"

"I did."

"Give it over."

She handed him Fergus's ticket.

"God, you are the fucking queen," said Muldoon, sitting back.

"Oh yes I am. The supper's ready of course."

The two lodgers shook hands shyly, muttering their names. McCarty was a horse boy, tall and thin. The other was an old navvy, Peadar. They set their muddy boots in front of the fire then took their places on the bench while the girl began dishing out the spoileen.

The men ate using knives and fingers, silent, as though the cold wind had bowled all words out of them.

AFTER SUPPER, while the men smoked pipes by the fire, he watched Molly chip mud off their boots, working grease into the leather with her hands.

"You're a horse boy," Muldoon suddenly said, "but McCarty there's a boy horse."

While the ganger smirked at his joke, the tall thin boy — McCarty — looked up from his pipe. "Have you come from the south?"

"Liverpool."

"Any news of London? Are they hiring for the tunnels?"

"Why do you care about London?" said Molly. "Ain't I good to you?"

"Heard they was paying well on the tunnels." McCarty shrugged. "Like to see London town."

They continued puffing their pipes, staring into the fire.

He felt loneliness crushing — the unyielding, metallic otherness of the world.

Unable to withstand the weight any longer, he went outside to stand in the cold darkness, pissing and staring up at the sky of stars. The air buzzed with coal smoke. The sting raked the back of his throat and tears lubricated his eyes and dripped down his cheeks while he shook off his prick.

Self-pity. Wet face. Disgusting.

Should have stayed back there, let them bang you.

The world's an empty barrel, full of black air, scent, and nothing.

You're nothing brave. You're nothing.

Where do you go from here?

No answer in the darkness. He felt nothing near. Even the dead were gone.

He was about to go back inside when he encountered the girl stepping out.

"Ate a good supper, did you?"

"I did."

She studied him. "Look, boy, it's hard when you're fresh, always."

"Oh yes. I know."

She walked off into the dark until he could no longer see her.

"I never did like a new place," she called to him. "New always feels wicked at first."

A moment later he heard the sound of her pee zinging in the mud.

"Are you Muldoon's wife, then?"

"Railway wife — they won't have girls in camp unless you must be fixed to someone. My old ma was transported, for stealing tools. They put us both on a ship for Van Diemen's Land — only at the very last, when the she-lags was all wailing, and the soldiers was knocking them about, I slipped down the cable and got ashore. Derry Quay — that's where Muck Muldoon found me. I am a rough chicken, Fergus. Hungry enough to scrap and fight. A rough chicken will get her share and more. A rough chicken don't mind a little blood." Suddenly reappearing out of the darkness she gave him a push. "Let's go inside, man. Fucking cold it is! You're lucky to be off the road."

MULDOON WAS standing in front of the coals, slowly swinging a gold watch on a chain.

"You must warm a watch before winding," Molly explained. "Show him, Muldoon."

Cracking open the watch case, Muldoon displayed the white face with its black numerals and slender hands.

"It's French," said McCarty. "Muldoon won it at Rouen, when we were digging Mr. Brassey's contract, and he knocked a horse down."

"Tell us the time, Muldoon," Molly said.

Muldoon studied the watch face intently.

"Go on," she coaxed.

"Quarter past the eight o'clock." Muldoon looked around, daring anyone to contradict him.

There was something wild in Muldoon, like an animal, a ferret; handsome in a dark disjointed way, with his chipped skin, wide mouth, and thin lips. Eyes pale and lit.

Snapping the case shut, the ganger began carefully winding the pea-sized golden knob.

"What do you like best, Muldoon — the watch or me?" Molly asked.

Muldoon kept winding.

"Trade me on a pair of good boots," Molly said. Kneeling, she began to smoor the fire.

"Never let you go," said Muldoon.

MULDOON AND the lodgers retired, leaving Fergus and Molly alone. He liked the warmth and stillness with the two of them in it. She was kneeling in front of the coals, greasing boots, while he smoked his pipe. "Here, give me a puff," she said, suddenly reaching out. He passed her the clay pipe and she took a draw, letting the smoke curl out between her lips. "I suppose you had a randy up in Liverpool and spent all your wages?"

He didn't feel like telling her about his crossing from Ireland on the boat of sheep. He nodded.

"Did you spend lot of money?"

"Molly!"

Muldoon's shout came from their bedroom. She concentrated on the boot she was rubbing.

"Come to bed!"

She grimaced. "Yes, yes, only I must get done the boots, mustn't I?" Taking up the next, she started rubbing the warm, pliable leather with a lump of fat.

Fergus could hear the lodgers snoring.

"Come to bed."

Looked around, Fergus saw Muldoon in the curtained doorway of the bed-room, wearing a yellowed undershirt that hung almost to his knees.

She kept on rubbing grease. "I must finish your blessed boots, mustn't I, Muck? And set out the breakfast iron. You go down, Muck, I'll be in by and by."

Muldoon stood glowering, small and wiry, bowlegged. "What are you look-ing at?" he said to Fergus.

Fergus shrugged and gazed at the fire. A few moments later he heard Muldoon retreat back to his bedroom. She finished the boot she was rubbing and picked up another. "Old Muck's a little sore. Pay was made last week and he went off on a randy. They found him in a hedge. He'd spent every farthing, or the Welsh cats robbed him. Sold his hat, for drink. Sold his best waistcoat." Her hands, shiny with grease, were flying over the leather. "He'll fight, and slag, and pour beer down his gully — die in a hole one day, Muck will."

Finishing the boot, she set it alongside the others at the grate where the warmth would keep the leather open and the grease would soak in.

"I don't like night anymore," she said firmly.

She began banking the coals with a poker. "Old Kelly, I can't hardly recall his face. See him dead on that table better than alive, and we knew each other pretty well, Kelly and me. He always said he was going for Indiana. Do you know where it is?"

He shook his head.

"It's America."

"I used to think Liverpool was America."

"Indiana is in America, somewhere near enough Quebec. Last year it was three pounds passage for Quebec. New York fare is twice that or more, on the Black Balls. Kelly's brother had a stone house, and a great many sheep, accord-ing to letters. I never seen the letters. It could have all been a story. Kelly was always going on about how he was to buy a farm and grow Indian corn, raise pigs, and keep bees as well. However. He's dead."

"Molly! Come to bed!"

She arose quickly and moved into the shadows. Fergus heard the curtain rus-tle as she disappeared.

* * *

HE LAY awake in his crib unable to push the girl — her quality of tension, anger, suspense — out of his head.

Old Peadar's snoring rattled the dark.

Thinking of her in bed with Muldoon was troubling.

He tried not to see Luke moving along the edge of his thinking.

It took a long time to sleep.

The Tip

"GET UP, YOU BEARS, get up."

He had been involved in a dream but all he could remember was wind blowing through a sea of grass, and horses, seen from miles away, moving across open country.

Molly stood in the doorway holding a candle. McCarty and the old navvy were groaning and hacking.

Molly left with her candle and the room went black.

Might be anywhere. Might be dead.

LATER, BY the fire, while the men ate porridge, he watched her slicing bread and cold mutton, wrapping the food in their clean handkerchiefs.

He consumed his breakfast, trying to let go of everything he remembered. Porridge with milk was luxury. His boots, cleaned and greased, were placed along with the others in front of the fire. That was good enough.

The boots felt supple and warm when he pulled them on. Molly stood by the door with their dinners.

You were safer without some girl leading you into the wild.

Putting the pistol in his pocket, Muldoon accepted his bundle. Placing a finger under Molly's chin, he tilted her face and kissed her on the mouth.

"Go on, leave." She was impatiently pushing Muldoon away. The ganger grabbed a fistful of thick hair and gave it a tug.

"Like kissing a fish!"

"Let go of me, Muck! Don't be a beast."

"You want some better manners I think," Muldoon said, grinning at the other men.

"Oh go away, Muck."

Fergus could see her cheeks flaming with what — anger?

Humiliation.

The worst is to have someone own you. His father had once owned him, but as soon as he was old enough to resist, he did. Carmichael, it turned out, had owned them all. The farmer would have preferred they were cattle, not souls. He would have fed his cattle.

Muldoon gave Molly's braid another sharp tug then walked out the door. "We'll see you tonight, though," he called back at the girl.

As the lodgers followed Muldoon outside, she handed them each their dinners.

"Spare the horses," she told Fergus, handing him his bundle. He nodded. He wanted to say something consoling, but before he could produce the words she was shutting the door.

The gray morning, raddled with coal smoke. Weak sun licking the rim of the world. Men were silently streaming down the hillside, heading for the works, every man carrying his dinner tied up in a handkerchief.

MCCARTY TOOK him through the camp and out to the pasture to collect a horse.

"You want to catch the strongest nag you can, though none are any good."

Forty or fifty animals stood in the barren, muddy field, ice on their backs, looking bewildered.

"Don't let Muldoon catch you standing about. You must always be pulling. Twenty tips a day. Fast is how they like it."

"Poor horses."

"They're poor, yes — they're cheap old nags. They don't last long neither. A railway contract is founded on the murder of horses. Come now, let's choose our pullers — catch the best as you can, and lead him into the stable for oats, then I'll show you how to hitch him to a string of trucks. You watch me, Fergus, you'll see how it's done."

They joined a line of tip boys slowly advancing across the field. There was a fluff of snow on the crisp mud. The horses stumbled before them, wary of capture, then crowded nervously along the fence as the boys closed in, calling softly in Irish, holding out handfuls of hay, rubbing it between their palms to release its scent.

Fixing on a gaunt black horse, less famished looking than the others, Fergus began slowly working the animal into a corner of the field.

"There you are, good man. I ain't seen a one like you. No I haven't."

It doesn't matter what you say; they must hear softness and flexibility in your voice. Also power of will, firmness. To capture a horse, you feel what he is feeling, anticipate his thoughts. Distance must be respected, negotiated. A horse doesn't hate a voice that is steady. Shrieks and yells frighten them.

"That's all right. You're a rugged old fellow. I shall treat you well."

The horse snorted and flared, then abruptly relinquished, extending his neck to bite at the poor, silvery hay. The brief show of spirit seemed to have exhausted him. He was docile as Fergus knotted his fingers into the mane and led him into a big, noisy, gloomy barn where the farrier had a red fire pumping in a small hearth and was banging ferociously on horseshoes. Dozens of horses stood at a tin trough noisily munching oats while the tip boys buckled on leather harness collars and pried stones out of their horses' feet, using sharpened sticks. Muldoon prowled impatiently.

The horses all looked thin, wretched. Coats were dull. Manes were wild, feet shaggy, backs glazed with ice.

Using his fingers, Fergus curried and scraped the ice off the horse's back and flanks. McCarty showed him where the harness sets were kept, hanging on iron spikes driven into barn beams, then helped him fit the harness collar over the horse's neck and showed him how to arrange the buckles, straps, and cinches.

The horses shivered as they munched, their hides steaming.

"That fellow of yours is new," McCarty said, eyeing the horse. "Ain't seen him before. The gypsies drive old cart horses out from Chester, and Mr. Murdoch buys twenty, thirty at a go."

"His feet are good. He's strong enough."

"He won't last."

"Come on, come on! It isn't a tea party!" Muldoon yelled.

"I'm showing the new man the ropes, Muck," McCarty protested.

"Get those nags cracking."

MCCARTY SHOWED him how to hitch to a string of empty trucks. The trucks ran on iron wheels along flimsy, temporary rails that had been laid along the half-finished railway grade.

"Drag your trucks up just below where navvies are excavating. They like to undercut to make an overhang. You pull your trucks underneath, then they can chop at the overhang until it breaks off and slumps and fills your trucks in one go — that's called *knocking the legs out*. That way they fill trucks fast, without having to shovel any.

"Soon as your trucks are filled, you pull them down the line to the tip. Don't spare the horse; don't even try. Everything fast, remember. Tons of ground we shift — tons! My God, Fergus, when I think of the ground in Ireland, how we sucked and paid rent, all for a little plot of limestone soil, to raise a few spuds. It makes you wonder. I've tipped more ground than there ever was in bloody Ireland, I'll wager."

THE NAVVIES worked fast, men driven to atone for something. If a slump broke off and filled a truck successfully they cheered, having saved themselves the labor of shoveling. But slumps often came down bigger than expected — he saw boulders bouncing like apples down the slopes of the cut, while navvies and tips ran for their lives, shouting and laughing.

There was always a moment of silence and limpid, perfect calm after each big slump. It was shattered by the screaming of horses, just as the cloud of dust started to rise, billowing up the slope. Horses were always caught in the slumps. Hitched to the trucks, they couldn't get out of the way fast enough.

Before the dust settled, the navvies had scrambled back to their stations, and the rattle of picks and shovels started up again.

The horses kept screaming until Muck Muldoon came around to execute them with a single ball in the ear.

THE TIP was at the head of grade, a half mile up the line from the cutting. To make a tip the horse had to be hitched offside like a tow horse on a canal path, then run briskly until the front wheels hit the balks at the ends of the rails with enough momentum to tip the load.

Next in line, Fergus watched McCarty start his horse then run alongside, whipping at its flanks.

Just when it seemed the horse was going to run straight off the tip into midair, McCarty jerked a cord, pulling a pin that disconnected the horse and the truck. The horse turned away just before the wheels slammed the balks, and the load tipped violently, spewing down the embankment.

Fergus's horse was wheezing, neck down, already exhausted from the heavy haul along the grade. Muldoon was watching them, hand on his hip, hat pulled low over his eyes.

Some men are like tools, or weapons. Minds stiff as leather.

Suffering attracts them.

Clutching the cord, Fergus cracked his horse with the halter, and the animal threw itself against the harness. The truck wheels groaned and creaked and started rolling.

He ran alongside, whipping with the halter strap. He could see the flimsy iron rails flexing under the truck wheels.

The tip was approaching too fast. He gave the cord a sharp tug but nothing happened. He jerked again, but the hitch pin was stuck. Then he stumbled, and as he fell the cord and halter were jerked from his hands. Sprawled on the gravel, he looked up in time to see the horse plunge over the tip then the truck smash the timber balks and plunge over after it.

Anger you taste, on your belly in railway gravel. Purely hating everything. Their bloody throats. You'd have murdered them all over again.

Poor Phoebe in her bed, whispering mercy.

The insides of your skull, so rotten and unkempt . . . death stored everywhere.

The cord had cut a stinging streak across his palm. He stood up slowly. A dozen horses and trucks were backed up along the grade. Tip boys waiting. sucking stubby clay pipes.

Picking up his hat, dusting it off, he walked to the edge of the tip and peered over.

Halfway down the embankment, his truck was upended, the wheels creaking as they spun. The black horse, half buried in the spill, was scratching weakly with his forelegs, trying to stand.

"I lose horses every day. I don't give a fuck for horses."

He turned and saw it was Muldoon.

"Go fetch another nag. Speed I want. Twenty tips a day."

Muldoon stepped off the edge and started slipping and sliding down the steep face of the embankment.

Two tip boys with sledges were already spiking in fresh balks. The hammers made a sharp, clinking noise.

Dust had settled on the black horse, giving him the patina of something curious and permanent.

Reaching the wreckage, Muldoon took out his pistol and began loading.

Wild and alone is the way to live.

Cold and wind to burn the thoughts off you.

The black horse was pawing weakly. No sound worked its way up the slope. The ganger extended his pistol arm. There was a flash, a puff of white smoke, then the report of the shot, faint and insignificant.

Fergus turned away and started walking back along the grade, feeling weaker than ever. He caught up to McCarty who was walking alongside his horse, pulling a string of empty trucks.

"Don't matter you lost a nag," McCarty told him. "Mr. Murdoch don't care. Horses are cheap. Some they only want to die. You can't blame them."

The image of the girl, Red Molly, slipped into his head.

Red hair, small hands, white neck.

In your hunger, a girl draws you like a fire does. You feel her heat. Feel her light licking your face.

*   *   *

HE WATCHED a blue gelding moving restlessly up and down the fence line, tossing his ugly head. The horse was deeply galled, but there was good action there. A bit of spring left in his haunches. The galling meant a cart horse, but he could have been a saddle horse in his younger days, even a hunter — he was tall and thick enough.

He showed more spirit than any of the other ghosts, flaring and whinnying, then trotting away when Fergus tried to approach.

"Ain't going to harm you." He followed the horse patiently, giving him room, holding out a fistful of hay.

Perhaps it was true, that any horse chosen for the tip was doomed. But at least the animals that were worked were fed a little oats, while the rest were left to starve in the barren pasture.

"Why have I come here?" he said to the horse.

No longer sure why. Only knowing you couldn't go backward.

"I'm after wages. Want them gold clinkers, man — sovereigns. But I shall care for you regular, I promise. I'll try to be favorable."

The horse, gradually cornered, finally extended his neck, pulling his lips back and reaching for the hay Fergus held out. Knotting his fingers into the mane, Fergus started leading him to the stable. The galls stank of rotting fish.

The horse suddenly bit him on the arm.

"Ow!"

The horse ignored him, ambling peacefully now. The pain was shrill. Rubbing his arm, Fergus caught up and took another handful of the mane, wary this time.

"Don't waste that gumption on me. Save it for yourself."

He watered the horse, fed him a pan of oats, then got ointment from the farrier and rubbed it in the galls. As Fergus scraped mud from the thick legs, the horse suddenly lashed out with a kick that would have broken bone had it connected.

He couldn't help admiring the animal's spirit.

Anger gave you strength.

Disquiet kept you going.

*   *   *

RUNNING HIS first tip, the horse broke into a gallop. When Fergus jerked the cord the pin flew, the horse leapt clear, and the load spewed down the embankment in a tumult of dust.

The blue horse was a puller.

That first day on the works, Fergus saw horses break their legs and burst their lungs. When they collapsed, they were dragged off the line, stripped of harness, and left in ditches along the grade. He never saw one get back up on its feet, and Muldoon came by eventually and shot them all.

Names

AT THE END OF THE DAY, the timer's bell rang. The tips unhitched their horses and walked them back along the grade to the stable, where they were unharnessed and fed a ration of oats. Fergus got the pot of ointment again and rubbed it into the stinking galls before turning the horse back out into the field. He walked through the camp with McCarty — navvies were streaming off the works. McCarty pointed out the broken windows of the unpainted church.

"A Welsh preacher tried to convert us, only we smashed him up. In Ireland people must give up their religion to get a taste of soup, but we don't stand no soupers here."

They saw Muldoon and the old navvy, Peadar, heading inside the beer shop.

"You can get a beefsteak, if you want, for half a crown," McCarty said. "They take it from your wages. Do you want to stop?"

"No."

"Myself neither. I'm saving money to buy a good farm."

Fires were burning, and the smoke hung low. Looking up, he could see the shanties clustered on the brown hillside above the camp.

"Did the Moll try to sell you tobacco?" McCarty asked.

"Yes."

"Beware. She marks it high. And don't play her at cards. The worst of it is, she don't even keep the money she steals; Muck gets it out of her. The feed is good enough, though. At Muldoon's we don't do so badly, considering. I'm saving pretty well. Not like some. That is an ugly fellow you have."

"Strong, though. He pulls."

"For a while. None of them lasts."

He wished he'd been able to give the horse better rations. The farrier was stingy with oats, and the hay they fed was cheap old silvery stuff.

An elderly Welshman was hawking penny newspapers from a stack on a pony cart, and Fergus was impressed to see McCarty dig into his pocket and buy one.

"I take a paper sometimes, it's improving," the horse boy said proudly. "You find out you're in the world. It's not all mud and slaughter. Do you have the letters, yourself?"

"Not really."

They started up the steep, muddy path to the shanties. Cold had stiffened the mud, and he thought of the horses standing all night in the bald, barren field.

"I'm going to pick up a nice farm," McCarty was saying. "There's leases going for nothing in my country, in Fermoy. I'll have sheep and a proper house, not a cabin —"

"The hay is bad hay."

McCarty glanced at him. "What's that you say?"

"It's all silver — there's nothing to hay like that. May as well feed them straw."

"He's only a tip horse after all, Fergus. He won't last long."

MOLLY WAS kneeling at the fire, stirring the kettle, when they came in.

"Muldoon's in the beer shop, I suppose?"

"*Certainement,*" McCarty replied. "That is Frenchy for, yes, Muldoon is in the beer."

Removing their boots, they stood in front of the fire warming themselves.

"Will you read me some news, McCarty?" she said.

"Perhaps I will afterward — if the feed is good enough."

"It's too good for you."

Fergus could smell the mutton seething but there would be no supper until Muldoon came home. McCarty sat down in Muldoon's armchair. Lighting his pipe he began describing Fergus's blue horse to Molly. "A buster, he is. Vicious. A beautiful killer —"

Fergus interrupted. "Not beautiful."

There was something particular about the horse but it wasn't beauty.

"God, he has a yellow eye, though. He is the devil of them all."

"Why choose him if he's a killer?" Molly asked.

"He's strong, I suppose."

"Do you know horses, then?"

"A little."

"Muck says they are all broke-down."

"Mostly they are. There's a few good ones, I suppose."

"I hate to see 'em. Makes me angry."

"Why?"

"They're all going to die. They know it, too."

To extend the mind that way, feel pain outside yourself, is troubling. Thrilling.

It's like a dare. It opens you.

Rolling up his sleeve, he displayed the half-moon bruise the horse's teeth had left on his arm. "My fellow has a spirit, at least."

"So, if they're wicked, that's a great thing, is it?"

"Well, it hurts. But at least you know you're alive."

"When Muck's wicked, I ought to be grateful, I suppose?" Molly turned away and went into her sleeping room.

Fergus looked across at McCarty, who shrugged and puffed smoke. Fergus wondered if he had offended her — but she returned, carrying an envelope that she dropped in his lap.

"What is it?"

"What do you think it is? Your tobacco."

"Thank you, miss."

"It's not a present! You'll owe me on the Pay, understand?"

"That ain't tobacco," McCarty said, "it's pig manure dried with bits of straw. She's a pure vessel of greed."

"Never mind him. My smoke's a mile finer than what you'd get in the village or from Murdoch's tommy shop."

"How's that? You buy from the Welsh, Moll, you know you do, and they sell you shit and shavings, since it's only for wild navvies."

"Well," she said carelessly, "you may buy your fill anywhere you choose, boy."

"The Welsh take cash money only," McCarty told Fergus. "There's no cash in camp between Pays, so if a fellow wants something there's only Mr. Murdoch's tommy shop, or greedy wenches like this one."

"I ain't selling tommy rot," Molly sniffed. "I sell good gear."

"Ah Molly, such a softhearted little piece. And how much straw did you cut in?"

"I feed you better than your mothers did! If you don't like it here, then go away!"

"But will you and Muldoon give me back my sub?"

"Oh you dog! You've no right to snap at me, McCarty!" Molly said, then burst into tears.

"Don't mind," Fergus tried reassuring her. "I like your tobacco."

"I do my best . . . I prefer a little straw in a mix . . . I smoke it myself," she said between sobs. "I do . . . for flavor . . . it's genteel."

"Oh come, come, sit down, have a puff with us, don't be such a baby." McCarty tried to grab Molly's wrist, but she jerked it away.

"I cherish you, Moll," McCarty said. "Come sit between your friends and have a puff."

"You're not my friend, you always been against me! I don't know what a friend is!"

"Have a puff with us, Moll. No hard lines." McCarty grabbed her wrist and pulled her onto his knee, where she sat, sniffling. The horse boy brought out a handkerchief and Molly, seizing it, blew her nose violently.

"Don't buy tobacco from the Welsh," she told Fergus. "And don't buy at the tommy shop. Mr. Murdoch makes more profit selling tommy rot than building the line."

Snatching McCarty's pipe from his mouth, she took a puff, letting smoke stream out between her small, even teeth. "You're vicious," she said to McCarty.

"Ah, Moll, I'll make a song of you one day."

She laughed. "Don't sing it near Muldoon — he'll cut your string."

"If I'd had you in Ireland, Molly, I'd never have gone walking."

"Oh, go fetch your old paper and give us a read."

She stood up, and McCarty rose obediently and went to fetch his newspaper from the table.

"So proud of his letters! If you can read, McCarty, why do you want to go back to Ireland?"

"What shall I read first?"

"Read us a good hanging." The girl sat down on the bench.

McCarty examined the paper.

"Once I went to Nottingham for a hanging," she said.

"I have seen in Cork the men hanged," said McCarty. "And two navvies, when we were building the line to Aberdeen. Killed a policeman with a spade."

"Muck says a hanging is a lesson as good as you'd get in church. Only there was such a crowd we couldn't see much, and a snapper lifted Muck's best handkerchief."

"No hangings that I can find today," said McCarty. "Very sorry. Would you like to hear about the Mexican Question?"

"Read us the shipping."

"What will you pay? A kiss?"

"Oh just go ahead and read it! You needn't look so puffed! Anyone in America can read, even the babies."

"Do you want to hear 'em or not?"

She stood up, crossed the floor, and bent to kiss McCarty on his cheek. "There. Now read 'em, if you please."

He tried to grab her wrist but she returned to the bench, sitting down beside Fergus, and leaned forward to listen.

McCarty rustled the pages. "You're wanting America, I suppose? It's always America. How about New Zealand for a change? Or India? Always plenty of shipping for India."

"No, America."

McCarty sighed and examined the page, then slowly began to read.

" 'Brig *Laconia*, one hundred eighty tons, sailing March tenth thereabouts for Philadelphia. Captain Shelby, master. Neat and dry. Passengers apply to W. Tapscott and Co., Liverpool.' Like the sound of her, Moll?"

"That's not all. Read the others."

"'For New York, *Fox*, two hundred fifty tons, Black Star Line, Captain Coxom, master. To sail March twentieth. All foodstuffs provided —'"

"Weevils and cat's meat," said Molly. "But go on."

"'For Quebec, brig *Na . . . Na* —'"

"*Naparima*," Molly said impatiently. "I knew a fellow went out on her last year."

"*Naparima*, yes. 'One hundred seventy tons, sailing April seventh, Captain Shields. For Philadelphia, *Malabar*, two hundred fifty tons, sailing April seventh, Captain York. For New York, *Centurion*, *Fidelia*, and *Carolina*, sailing April first . . .'"

As McCarty droned down the shipping list, Fergus watched Molly lean forward, chin in her hand, listening.

The curious names of the ships had incantatory power. Nothing he could touch, but something he could feel. They had radiance.

"'Ships of the largest class,'" McCarty read, "'commanded by men of experience who will take every precaution to promote the health of the passengers. *Miramishee*, one hundred eighty tons, for Quebec, April fifteenth . . .'"

Molly's mouth was open slightly, and Fergus understood she was dreaming of her passage to America. She was no older than him, was in no better position — worse, perhaps — but she was living on the taste of a dream.

What you lost weakened you, could kill you. What you wanted kept you going. What you wanted gave you strength.

Muck Muldoon

THE CUTTING GOUGED DEEPER and wider every day as the slopes were peeled back, tons of excavation filling the trucks. When it rained the mud was soft, and when it froze the mud was stiff. Horses struggled and floundered trying to pull trucks along the temporary grade. The sleepers had been poorly ballasted; sometimes a truck derailed and tipped over on its side, dragging the horse over with it.

Plodding up and down the line between the parallel rails, horses cut their legs on the wooden sleepers. If the nicks weren't cleaned and salved, the horses went lame and Muck Muldoon shot them along the right-of-way or they died in the bald field overnight. Every morning when Fergus went out with a handful of hay to collect the blue, there were nags lying dead in the field.

"WHY NOT get out your pack and deal the Fergus a hand or two?" McCarty said to Molly one evening while they waited for Muck to come home. "She can teach you the ways of the world," he told Fergus.

"What's the use?" she said. "Muck takes it all. You know how it is."

"It's your winnings, so. I don't know why you stand it."

"He's not so bad."

"You let him rule you too much." McCarty puffed his pipe contentedly.

"Oh, and you stand up to him? Very brave I seen you, McCarty. Very bold."

McCarty shrugged and waved smoke away.

"Never, McCarty. Not once." She went back to chopping turnips and leeks.

Fergus smoked his pipe, staring into the slow fire. Muldoon was an oppressive presence in the shanty, even when he wasn't there. Molly seemed always to be listening for his footsteps, always waiting for him. No supper could be put out until the ganger was in his chair, eyeing every plate, making sure that no one had a bigger portion than his. They each had to sit in the same place at the table every night — it was another of Muck's rules.

Men like to rule — girls, and others. Rule animals; rule the ground.

He remembered Carmichael distributing the plots each year. Telling them where they could dig their beds and plant the sets.

Muck ruled her. Also ruled him, and McCarty. It was no good pretending he didn't rule them all.

In order to live, you had to submit to rule. It was what you did in exchange for wages. What a horse did for food.

You could try telling yourself you weren't in submission; navvies liked to pretend so. Men had their pride. Tramping had seemed like freedom, but that was an illusion. What was a tramp except a road slavey, always hungry, looking for a place to fit himself in? Six days a week when the timer's bell sounded three hundred or so ex-tramps picked up picks and shovels, which they were not permitted to put down again until the noon bell rang — when they were allowed twenty minutes to eat their dinner. Then they worked until another bell rang at the end of the day.

The Bog Boys had thought they weren't in submission. At least Luke had imagined so. Misappreciation killed her.

Molly, interrupting his thoughts, handed him a package wrapped in newspaper. "Here."

"What is it?"

"Turnip tops."

He immediately thought of that gray, cold day with Luke, scouting, when they had gleaned a turnip field.

Turnips, hunger food on the mountain, only eaten in bad times.

"Do you want 'em or don't you?"

He looked at her blankly.

"For your blue horse." Impatiently. "Still kicking, ain't he?"

"He is."

"Muck don't care for the nags so don't tell him."

I'm only a horse myself. So are you.

"And here he comes," McCarty warned them.

The door flew open and Muldoon entered, followed by old Peadar, both of them smelling of beer.

"What are you doing with these fellows — having a game?"

"No, nothing, Muck — only waiting for you. Sit down, I'll take off your boots."

"What supper have you got me?"

"Mutton it is."

"Mutton, mutton . . . I'm tired of your old mutton. Why don't you feed us beefsteak like Englishmen?"

"Well, mutton's what there is."

"English eat beefsteaks. This is England here, let us feed like English. Give it to us red. Sick to death of your old mutton."

"It isn't England anyhow. Wales it is."

"Damn you for saucing me!"

"I'm not, Muck. Sit down, let me take off your boots."

Muldoon's hungry, rampant look made them all uneasy. Molly started pushing the ganger into his chair. Suddenly he threw his arms around her in a bear hug, lifting her feet off the dirt floor.

"Set me down, Muck, you idjit."

Instead he began swirling her around the dim, crowded little room. "You ain't Kelly's — you belong to Muck."

"Oh, go on, Muck! I can't breathe. Let me down! The fellows want to eat. Come, let me go . . . I've made you a good supper."

"You're my sleeper, ain't you? *Druid mna*, little witch."

"Let me down, you lugger."

Then Muck stumbled and released her. The girl nearly escaped, but he seized her wrist. "Give us a kiss, angel."

"No, let me go." She was turning away when Muck cracked her.

Suddenly the room smelled very bad — not different than before, only stronger: the stench of half-burned trash, men's dirty clothes, and sweat.

Her lip was cut, there was blood in her mouth and on her chin, and Muldoon was pushing her roughly across the room.

"Muck, don't — there's the supper, I cooked you good supper. Meat on the hob —"

He gave her a shove through the curtain of their bedroom then went in after her, disappearing.

Fergus looked at McCarty, who shrugged.

How unfinished and shapeless you feel. How lewd.

They could hear Muldoon cracking her, again and again.

"I'll show you down, you little witch."

The iron bedsprings bucked and creaked. Muldoon owned the only set of bedsprings in camp — he'd boasted of them. Molly was proud of them as well.

Fergus caught McCarty's eye again, and the horse boy slowly shook his head.

He could hear the thrusts clearly.

She didn't make a sound.

Kneeling by the hob, Peadar, the old lodger, sighed and picked up a spoon to give the boiling mutton a stir. "Come, this looks quite ready. We had better eat." He began dishing out the mutton onto their plates.

McCarty sat down.

"He'll kill her," Fergus said.

"She's a rugged little thing, tough as a pony. Come, take your feed. It ain't your affair, Fergus."

He sat down reluctantly. Staring at the mutton on his plate, smelling the steam, and disgusted by his own appetite.

The question is, who rules, and why. These arrangements can change. You don't need to accept. You can struggle. You may bust out of one set of rules into another.

He made up his mind he wouldn't eat. While he was staring at his food, smelling it, hunger licking his mouth — the ugly sounds from the bedroom stopped.

"There it is," McCarty said, relieved. "All blown over now."

"I would nail that fellow's tongue to a tree," Fergus said.

McCarty looked up. "Don't you give him no spark. She's the one will pay for it."

He was still staring hungrily at his untouched food when Muldoon sauntered out, buckling his belt. Spitting into the coals the ganger helped himself from the kettle of boiled meat. "Ain't this fine spoileen?"

Old Peadar nodded. "It is, it is."

You butcher a pig by slitting its throat. At first, hung by its heels, blood dripping, a pig retains its shape. White strings of muscle and the force of whatever it was that binds flesh to bones. As you butcher, the shape dissolves, until there is nothing left except a pigskin attached to a heel caught in a loop of rope, a soak of black blood on the ground, a pair of eyes.

He heard her come through the curtain and cross the room. While she was helping herself from the kettle he saw her gown was torn. Sitting down, she started to eat. She had cleaned the blood off her chin.

No one had noticed his foolishness, his pathetic gesture of solidarity. He hesitated, then began to cut up his food.

"I said you'd be eating meat every day in England," Muldoon told her.

"You did," she agreed.

THE BLUE horse filled out. New drafts of animals came in, but never any with the bones as good as his. The galls were slowly healing. Feeding on oats twice a day, his coat had taken on a shine. Fergus soaked the cuts on his legs with brine, applied salve, then wrapped them in clean rags overnight. He persuaded the farrier to replace two missing shoes. They were tipping sixteen, eighteen, twenty trucks a day. The blue was a puller, strongest on the contract, but the other tip boys, fearing his evil temper, left him to Fergus.

The better he fed and cared for the blue, the meaner the horse became. Going out in the field in the mornings with a handful of hay, Fergus could sense the animal's distrust as it backed away from him, snorting and pawing, slashing his tail. Captured then led inside, fed and watered, he tried to bite at every opportunity. Each time they ran a tip, he could feel the horse's anger uncoiling. Sometimes he thought the blue was going to dash off the embankment and carry him along but at the last moment the horse always let himself be pulled away.

Ashes

ONE SATURDAY NIGHT in Mr. Murdoch's camp, Muck Muldoon was battling a tramp called Greaves for a prize of one sovereign, put up by the contractor.

All the tip boys wanted Muldoon to defeat the navvy.

"Muck is our boy," McCarty said. "Greaves, who's heard of Greaves? A tramp, a shifter."

Three hundred navvies formed a hollow square in the muddy street outside the contractor's beer shop. There were no ropes; four tip boys with torches stood marking the corners of the ring.

In his corner Muck studied his gold watch, then slipped it into his coat pocket and took off his coat, waistcoat, and shirt, handing the clothes to Molly. In the opposite corner Greaves had already stripped off his shirt and was slapping himself briskly against the cold.

At the sound of the timer's bell, the two boxers approached the center of the ring warily, Greaves massive and yellow, Muldoon wiry and dark, lean and agile as any horse boy.

They touched knuckles, stepping back as if they'd been stung. Muldoon began dancing around the ring, darting in to throw little hectoring jabs at the navvy's face, like a bird stabbing nectar from a flower. Greaves seemed bewildered, shaking his head, spitting blood from a split lip. He began working Muldoon steadily into a corner, ignoring the jabs, pressing ahead stolidly. Once he had Muldoon trapped, Greaves stood and fought like a mountain. Muck kept jabbing but his quick, light punches didn't seem to have any impact on Greaves, who was working the ganger's head and ears with high, hard blows that must have hurt his own hands.

But Muck stayed on his feet, and Greaves was visibly tiring, slowing. When the tramp dropped his hands for a second, Muldoon quickly placed a jab below each eye. Greaves threw up his hands to cover his face and Muck hooked him once on the belt then took the opportunity to escape the corner.

The crowd was breathing steam that floated and spun in the gaslight. He could see Molly yelling for Muldoon.

If men hit so hard for so long what is left? What is inside? Where is your spirit? Where is your voice?

Greaves suddenly caught the ganger with a blow that knocked Muck on his rump, but he sprang up while the crowd was still roaring. Both men had foam dripping from their lips. The tramp had open cuts on both cheeks; the skin below his eyes was puffy. Muldoon was unmarked except for a trickle of blood from his right ear.

Suddenly he stopped prancing. Taking position at the center of the ring, he beckoned Greaves, taunting the tramp to stand and fight, toe-to-toe, man-to-man. This was what the navvies wanted to see and they began howling at Greaves to meet the challenge.

Greaves approached warily.

Once they were toe-to-toe, both men began driving their punches. They fought like two engines — slamming, stamping; not really human.

The sight of two men using themselves brutally, blood and spit flying from their mouths, was wildly stimulating to the crowd, cawing like crows.

The nearness of death provokes. The smell of blood. Violence drives you from yourself.

Suddenly Muldoon fell to his knees. Greaves stopped punching and stepped back, nearly tripping over his feet. Blood streamed from a cut on Muldoon's scalp, drenching his eyes, blinding him. On his knees Muck was still swinging wildly, punching at air while Greaves paced back and forth and the crowd roared. Molly stepped into the ring and came up behind Muck with a towel.

It seemed the fight was over. Greaves had retreated to his corner, where his friends were rubbing his shoulders while he gulped from a jug of beer.

Fergus watched Molly clean blood from Muldoon's eyes while Greaves stood with arms raised, acknowledging cheers.

Men were turning away, going inside the beer shop, when the crowd gave a roar — Muldoon was on his feet again, roaming the ring, feinting punches and barking at Greaves, who stood with hands on hips, chest rising and falling.

Something terrible in the scene, desperate, and something you understood.

We are all trying to break out of something.

Shrugging, Greaves threw away his towel and started into the ring after Muck. The ganger wouldn't let himself be cornered. Weaving and ducking, he dodged each cumbersome punch, skipping around the ring with the tramp rumbling after him like a loaded truck.

Then Muldoon made a stand at the center of the ring once more, and beckoned Greaves.

The tramp closed in and uncoiled a punch, but Muldoon dodged it. As Greaves stumbled, thrown off by his own momentum, Fergus saw Muldoon fling a cloud of dust or ashes into the tramp's face.

Roaring in pain, Greaves raised both hands to his eyes and Muldoon landed two jabs at his kidneys, then two more under his eyes when the tramp dropped his hands. Then Muck got behind him, leapt onto his back, and began punching his ear and clawing at his face while the tramp staggered around the ring trying to throw him off.

Fergus saw Molly jumping up and down in the corner, screaming for Muck. Didn't she think the violence applied to her?

He's a killer, don't you see? He could kill you. Easy he could.

When Greaves stopped, Muldoon knelt on top of him, hammering his back, neck, and hip until the bell rang and men surged forward and dragged the ganger off.

They washed Muck down with a bucket of beer sluiced over his head. Fergus watched him accept his prize from Mr. Murdoch, who clapped him on the shoulder and said he was the roaring boy, the lion of the line, and a credit to the Milesians.

They were throwing water over the prostrate tramp, Greaves.

Men like a rampage.

FERGUS AND MCCARTY walked up the path with Molly. She was carrying a bucket of beer, and Muldoon stumbled after them, muttering and clutching the sovereign in his fist.

"What was it you passed him?" Fergus asked.

"Whatever are you talking about, boy?" She grinned at McCarty.

"When you were in the ring. What he threw."

"All's fair," said McCarty. He exchanged a glance with Molly, both smirking.

"In France the Scotch navvies would carry iron spikes into the ring," McCarty said. "What's a little sanding? Old Muck won clean enough, for a railway bout."

THEY CARRIED the laundry kettle inside, and Muck stepped in. She began washing the blood off him while he stood docile.

"What's wrong with Muck?"

"Punchy. That fellow put some hurt on him." After washing him down she rubbed him dry and settled him on a stool in front of the fire. Using Muck's steel razor, she carefully shaved a patch on his scalp and began cleaning and dressing the gash.

"Ashes," she said suddenly.

"What?"

"Ashes I give him. To taste on his tongue. When he's lagging. The bitter sparks him up — there you are, hold still, Muck. You're a broken egg."

"To toss in Greaves' eyes, you mean."

"What do you suppose a bout is, after all, Fergus? Do you think it's country feast, a dance to the moon?"

"A fight's to win." McCarty spoke without looking up from the newspaper he had spread open on the table.

"That's right," she agreed.

"Perhaps you want ashes then. For you don't seem ever to win," Fergus said.

Molly ignored him, carefully winding a cotton bandage around and around Muck's head.

McCarty looked up then went back to his paper.

A girl was a mystery. You wanted to protect her, also destroy her a little. You wanted her to ruin you in exactly the same way.

Tired Horses

THE WELSH SABBATH WAS ENFORCED by magistrates and no work could be performed along the line. Even the beer shop was shut. The navvies and the tips spent the day sleeping, or drinking at blind pigs — shanties where the women sold beer. Others went roaming the country looking for fresh eggs. A few men with guns went out poaching.

It was his second or third Sunday in the camp. Molly gave them black sweet tea at breakfast, and in the middle of the morning Fergus and McCarty were still at the table, eating wheat bread and honey. Molly was piling up clothes for a wash. Muck and Peadar had dragged the bench outside where they sat in the watery sunshine smoking their pipes and drinking beer.

"Who feeds the horses on Sunday?" Fergus asked, thinking of the blue standing out in the barren field.

"Feed the nags? No one, I suppose. Sunday's the day of rest."

"I'm going down, then."

"They aren't your creatures," Molly said. "You're not responsible."

"Feed bins are locked," McCarty reminded him. "They're always afraid of gypsies stealing. Muck keeps the key."

"I'll get it from Muck, then."

"He won't give it to you."

"Can you get it?" Fergus asked Molly.

She shook her head. "He keeps keys on his belt — he'd murder me."

"Then I'll drive them out along the road. It's free grass along the ditches. I'll give them a graze. Will you come with me?" he asked McCarty.

"I'm going to sleep all day and mend my clothes. I seen enough of nags."

"Let it be, Fergus," Molly said.

"I can't let it be."

THE CAMP felt desolate on a Sunday morning. It seemed abandoned, and the stillness made him think of Cappaghabaun. Were Carmichael's cattle surviving the winter up there without hay for their browse, with no one driving them from pasture to pasture?

Browsing cabin wreckage. Rotten potatoes were cattle feed, perhaps.

What wild things had seeded over his plot?

When ground lay open, you never knew what would take.

He passed a few lumps of men lying where they'd collapsed the night before, on the spree. Asleep not dead, but they may as well have been.

It doesn't take very long for a body to start looking as though it belongs to the ground.

You will stay on your feet. Keep moving. Those are the rules.

THE HORSES in the field looked dazed. He tried the feed bins but they were bolted and locked. Searching the racks of harness, he found one soft rope halter. There was some loose hay, and he grabbed a handful and went out to capture the blue.

The horse was hungry and came to him easy. Slipping the halter on, Fergus led him out through the gate. "I'm going on your back. You won't like it but that's how it'll be." Climbing the fence, he threw his leg over before the animal had a chance to shy. He gripped with his knees and kept the halter loose while the horse angrily tossed his head.

"There it is . . . easy now. Not so bad, is it?" Kicking heels lightly, he started the blue walking down the road, and looked back at the gate he'd left open. Horses hated being driven; why wouldn't they? But they would follow one another, follow their curiosity and instinct for companionship.

He smiled as he watched the tip horses ambling through the gate.

* * *

HALF A MILE along there was a stream flowing under the road in an iron cul-
vert. The water on either side tasted fresh, and there was good thick grass along
the ditches.

He stretched out on the blue's back while the horses cropped peacefully. It
was like being back on the booley — feeling the sun on his face and watching
the sky, spinning himself into childish, self-conscious trances. That was before
he'd understood the world existed, firm and real, careless of him or anyone.

It was as if he'd spent all that time on the booleys asleep.

Tramps stopped to drink at the stream and light their pipes and ask the news
of Mr. Murdoch's contract.

"Are they hiring on the cutting?"

"How many killed so far?"

"Any fever in the shanties?"

He felt the slow, sweet calmness of the world that afternoon. Tramps lay
down in the grass, content in the sunshine, puffing their pipes, and it didn't
seem the same world where girls died choking on their own blood.

Watching over grazing horses allowed a feeling of peace.

All you are is hunger.

SNOW LIFTED from the flanks of the Welsh mountains. Some days the wind
came off the sea tasting soft and wet, and he could smell grass growing.

The next Sunday, he met Mr. Murdoch coming along the road, riding a pony
too small for him.

Pulling up, the contractor eyed the horses grazing. "Well, man, are those my
nags?"

"They are, yes."

"Ah. I thought as much. What are you doing, so?"

"There's no browse left in their field. It's all cropped down. You couldn't keep
a rabbit there."

"And do you expect to be paid wages for grazing these poor old bucks?"

"I don't."

"That's wise. Because Sunday's Sunday, you see. The law says I can't pay a fellow Sunday wages, even if I would. Kindness must be its own reward. But here, have a cigar." Reaching out, Mr. Murdoch handed him a cigar. "That's a decent-looking animal you're sitting on. Good bones. Is he one of mine?"

Fergus nodded, sudddenly afraid that the contractor was going to claim the horse for himself.

The blue raised his head and shook his neck.

"He looks well set up." Mr. Murdoch eyed the horse critically. "Might have hunted him — in his better days."

"He'll run twenty tips a day. Got his own mind. Wicked biter."

"Is he? Well, it's always sad to see a gentleman come down in the world."

Mr. Murdoch rode off. Relieved, Fergus reached down to stroke the blue's neck, and the horse twisted around and tried to bite him.

Perhaps meanness was the reason he'd come down from saddle horse to cart horse to tip horse on the railway — or perhaps his misfortune had made him mean. The world didn't require a reason for things to fall apart. He knew that, and the horse knew it too.

Her Sorrow

IN THE MIDDLE OF THE NIGHT he was awakened by one sharp cry. He kept very still, heart knocking in his chest. Wind squealed along the walls of the shanty. It was a hard, cold night. He tried convincing himself it was only wind that he'd heard.

He'd been beaten, often. The open palm, the fist, the stick. Speechless violence, what men seemed to admire most of all. The humiliation almost unbearable, far worse than the pain.

Her next scream flickered so fast, like a startled bird, he almost believed he hadn't heard a thing.

The musty smell of night with fear flowering in it, which is the smell of being alone.

With nothing around you but cold, you perceive the world coldly, realizing anything else is a lie you've told yourself.

When she cried out again, it wasn't loud. A small shout, quick. A fox caught in a leg trap.

He got out of the crib, dressed quickly, and crept out into the cozy, causing a dispersal of startled mice.

A few coals were glowing in the grate. Dishes sat in moonlight.

He could hear the iron bed creaking.

Crossing the room, he lifted Muldoon's pistol from the shelf. Powder and bullets were in a leather bag. Conscientiously, he loaded.

You smell a girl coming at you, like apple blossom on the wind. Excitement and demands, transformation, danger. A girl awoke you and suddenly you were walking in the startling forest of your dreams.

He crossed the room and stopped in front of the curtain.

He could hear nothing from inside, no voices, only the ticking of the ganger's watch.

The wind had died. After a while he could hear Muck's deep, steady breathing.

Only make a sound. Cry out. I shall walk straight in and shoot the fellow.

Muldoon began snoring.

Fergus stood just outside the curtain, shivering, his resolve slowly leaking away. Finally he unloaded the pistol, replaced it on the shelf, and returned to his crib where he fell asleep and dreamed of Luke fleeing across the bog, her boys chasing her. She was covered in scratches and they had been licking her blood.

The Cliff

IT WAS THE LAST SUNDAY before the Pay and he was grazing the tip horses along the road when he saw her walking out from camp. He'd never seen her away from the shanty before. Muck did not like her to venture.

McCarty said the road was death for girls, with all the famished tramps and gypsies.

She was a solitary figure, wearing an old bonnet and carrying a basket. As she came closer he saw she was barefoot.

"Where are you off to?"

"Gather seabirds' eggs."

He was astride the horse, and she passed by without saying anything more.

He continued to watch her. She had a way of walking, resolute. She owned herself.

He saw her leave the road and start across the grid of small, enclosed fields. She was heading for the clifftops above the sea. Kicking his heels, he started the horse ambling along the road. Dismounting at the gate she'd passed through, he started after her across the fields.

The grass was thick. Sheep bawled at him. Climbing the last stile, he lost sight of her. Fearing she had fallen over the cliff, he was hurrying to the edge when she reappeared, crawling out under from a clump of gorse.

"Muck says we'll sell eggs for a penny each. I see them but I can't reach them."

She didn't seem surprised that he had followed her. She stood up, brushing off her gown, and walked to the edge of the cliff. "There's Ireland out there, man." She pointed. "If you was a seabird, you might fly the way."

He couldn't see anything, just sea. The sky fast with clouds.

"No use going back," he said.

"No. No use."

Standing beside her, he could feel some tension in her. She was near the edge, her toes out over the grassy tufts at the very lip of the cliff. Waves smashing white on the rocks far below.

"I'm thinking I'm going to jump, Fergus," she said suddenly. "Give these old goners a splash. I'm ready as Hell."

He took hold of her hand.

"No. Let me go."

There a white patch of sail, far off, quite small on the silver plate of sea.

"Look, Molly, a ship."

Stepping back from the edge, she sat down in the grass.

He sat beside her. Wetting his handkerchief, he wiped her forehead, temples, cheeks. At first she balked, then shut her eyes.

"If you want to get away," he said, "I'll take you to America."

She said nothing for a while, and he kept dabbing her face.

"You haven't the money," she finally said. "No more than three pounds coming to you, I suppose. A fare's three pounds each, even to Quebec. And you must have supplies for a passage. Warm clothes. Extra rations — you can't make it on what they feed."

"We'll go down the line, another contract. London tunnels. Soon we'd have enough."

Her eyes were unreadable. "He'd find me on the line."

"He wouldn't."

"You don't know Muldoon. You're no good next to a fellow like that. You're only a boy."

"I'd take care of you, Molly."

"Muck's not so bad — he brought me out of Ireland. I was living like a finch when he found me."

"He beats you."

"I can stand it."

"He rules you, though."

She looked out to sea. Seabirds circled below the cliffs, wailing.

None of it thought out. No plan in your head. No words before you said them.

"You want to get away of him. Don't be afraid. Come with me."

" 'Don't be afraid'?" She laughed, mocking him, but he saw how terrified she was, and he felt strong. Muldoon was nothing, Muldoon was bad sky; he would walk right through Muldoon.

She suddenly stood up, brushing grass and twigs from her gown and picking up the basket, which contained two paltry pale green eggs. She stepped to the edge again. He could hear birds crying and sea breaking on the rocks far below.

"If you are going to jump, Molly, then jump with me, to America."

She looked over her shoulder. He felt exhilarated and strange, as though he were living outside himself. "Will you come?"

The huge, empty pan of sea. The motion of things.

"He mustn't find out. You mustn't say a word to anyone. Not to McCarty or anyone else. Keep away from me — don't be whispering at me, never! Keep apart, or Muck will know. The Pay is when. Night of the Pay — we'll get away then, Muck will be on a spree. How much will you have on Pay Night?"

"As you say; three pounds nearly."

"It's not enough."

"It will get us to London."

"Muck will be drinking and roaring on the Pay. Can your horse carry us both? To Chester?"

"Yes."

"Go to the stable after you collect your pay. Wait for me there, get your horse ready. I'll get clear of Muck somehow; once he's on the spree you could shoot him, and he wouldn't know it. We'll go for Chester and catch the Southern Express. Only don't say nothing. And don't come at me, no whispers, no sweet talk; don't look all moony. If Muck is giving me trouble, knocking me about, you stay out of it. I can take it. If he finds out, he'd kill us both."

He felt like a ship, powerful, restless, moving. Standing up, he placed his hands on her shoulders. She stood still, her gaze fixed at a point on his chin.

When he bent to kiss her she accepted it, but her lips were dry and closed.

"Moll —"

She clapped a hand over his mouth, kissing his chin, then cheeks, his ear — then his mouth. Their teeth clashed. The juice in her mouth tasted sweet. She began unbuttoning his trousers. She pushed him down on the cold grass, lay down beside him and, siezing his wrists, pulled him on top of her, licking and biting his hands, thrusting his fingers into her mouth and sucking them, then dragging one hand up under her skirts and rubbing his fingers between her legs. Grasping his cock she directed him. When he was plunged in her she began bucking her hips.

Joy overwhelms the capacity to make sense of it.

For a few seconds as the juice was leaping out of him he believed he was seeing the shape of life clearly, but when the climax passed and he collapsed on her his brain went cloudy and the vision did not sustain.

She lay still for a few moments, then began wriggling out from under. She stood up, shaking down her dress. "Don't come after me now."

Before he could say anything she was gone. He sat up and watched her striding over the meadow, climbing the stiles.

Turning, he looked out to sea. Pale sun glinted on the waves. The sail had disappeared.

Could you see America, when the air was clear?

No. Too far.

The hard-looking, empty sea made him feel empty and alone.

It lay out there, the mystery.

Of course you couldn't see.

HE FOUND a piece of Molly's clothing draped on a stool by the fire, drying. A little undershirt. Flimsy white Manchester cotton.

She was outside, bucketing through more wash.

Afraid to be seen with him. Afraid Muck would somehow sniff out their plan.

He took the soft little thing, lay down in his crib, and covered his face with it, the dampness and the softness.

A girl turned you inside out.

The Pay

WEATHER CAME IN SLEET the night before the Pay. Snow covered the grade and greased the rails in the morning so that the first trucks ran almost in silence. The sky began to break at dinnertime and was dark blue by afternoon. The navvies cheered when they saw the wagon with an iron strongbox aboard pulling up at the timer's shed, a policeman in a leather cape sitting alongside the teamster. The timer emerged to escort them to the beer shop where the Pay would be made.

After feeding their horses and turning them out, Fergus and McCarty walked back through the camp, passing the beer shop, which was closed, with curtains drawn over the windows.

It was very quiet in the camp. The navvies had came down off the cutting at the sound of the bell and headed straight up the hill to the shanties to get themselves ready.

"What will you do with your pay?" McCarty asked.

He was tempted to share the secret, but resisted. "Don't know."

"I'd like to get a girl," said McCarty wistfully.

A secret makes you strong.

PAY NIGHT supper was cheese, bread, and onions, eaten quickly. Then the wash tub was dragged in front of the fire and filled. Muldoon bathed first, dropping his old clothes on the floor and stepping gingerly into the tub. After he finished it was old Peadar's turn, then McCarty's. After bathing, each man stood naked in front of the fire rubbing himself with the clean rags Molly had set out, then went into the sleeping room to dress in clean clothes.

Fergus was last. She was greasing boots as he undressed. She'd paid no attention to any of the men bathing except Muldoon, who had her scrub his back. Fergus was about to step into the gray, soapy water when he looked up and saw her across the room staring at him.

Naked, holding her gaze, he felt charged and reckless.

During the weeks on the line his body had been transforming, hardening. He felt fresh with power as he held her stare.

She was such a small person, small bones, hands, feet.

His prick was arousing, thickening in its pad of curious hair. Her eyes on him, wary.

Suddenly he felt capable of killing Muldoon. Knife or stick or fist or gun.

Finishing him, pitching his body out the door.

"You want hot water," she said. Wrapping a handkerchief around her palm she lifted the kettle from the store and began pouring the steaming water into the tub.

"Get in," she said. "You certainly need it."

THE MEN sat in front of the fire in clean clothes, smoking their pipes, waiting for the timer's bell, and he tried not to look at her.

When the bell sounded, the old navvy clapped his hands. "That is the sound of joy, men! I wish you all the joy of your pay." The old navvy and Muldoon arose and shook hands. For a few moments, they were all shaking hands with one another.

She kept back, watching them.

The ganger lit a torch from the coals, and they all pulled on coats and boots and followed him outside.

Men were streaming down the hill, groups from each shanty silently joining in the flow. The only noise was the squish of boots in the mud and the bleats of a few whistles. All were dressed in finery, hats brushed, boots freshly greased. Men wore yellow leather gloves.

He felt a little stunned by the nearness of money; perhaps they all were.

The beer shop glowed from inside. They joined the queue wrapped around the building. The curtains had been flung open. Pressing his forehead to the glass, Fergus saw the timer making the Pay at the table covered by a red blanket, the policeman standing behind him, holding a pot of beer in his fist. After taking their pay, men were crowding at the bar, drinking beer and calling for beefsteaks.

"I'm feeling strong tonight," Muldoon called out to Greaves as the tramp walked by, his face still lumpy and purple. Ignoring Muck, he joined the queue.

"No takers," Muck said, sounding disappointed.

"Someone will turn up," said Molly.

On his way inside, the contractor stopped and spoke to Muldoon. "You are looking dapper, Muck."

"Boisterous I am, mister."

"We'll get a challenge then. Who do you like?"

"Ach, there isn't a man in camp now."

"Perhaps they've a fighter on the Conwy job."

Muldoon was springing on the balls of his feet, snapping punches at the air. "Only tonight I feel itchy, my lord!"

"Who's game?" the contractor called out to the men in line. "Who'll get up on his hind legs with Muck Muldoon? Two pounds for the last man standing."

No one stepped forward as Muck hummed and danced, feinting punches.

"I'd take you on myself if I was any younger, just to see you box," the contractor said thoughtfully, putting his hands in his pockets and going inside.

SOON THEY were inside. The atmosphere was rich and warm with tobacco smoke, burned fat, the stench of beer. He watched her step up to the table with Muldoon, who received his pay and exchanged the lodgers' sub tickets, sweeping the stacks of coins into his pocket then heading for the bar.

Molly stood by the pay table to collect tobacco money from her lodgers as they took their wages.

When it was his turn to step up to the pay table, he couldn't stop smiling.

She ignored him.

"Name?" the timer barked.

Surprised the man didn't remember, he gave his name. The timer studied the ledger and made a scratch. "Three-and-six on twenty days, less three subs, nine shillings each, with no other debts outstanding, equals two pounds five shillings." The little man piled the coins into neat stacks and slid them across the table. "Pay is made. Next!"

"Three shillings tobacco money." Molly was holding out her hand. "Pay up, man, before you drink it all away."

You are the brilliant, he thought, watching her pick the coins from his palm.

She was good at disguise, at concealment. They would be strong together. She wasn't so bold as him, but more deft.

You are the light.

She took her money and moved away. As she was leaving the beer shop, he saw her standing next to Muck in a crowd of shouting, drinking gangers and wives. One of the other women was giving her a light for her pipe. Muck was starting his spree; soon he'd be insensible.

No one will ever hurt you worse than I will.

Goodbye you devil.

The Bout

EVER SINCE THE SCATTERING, he had often wondered if he was still alive, or if the days and nights so strange and wild were actually the world of the dead.

He'd felt dead in the workhouse and in the Night Asylum. On the bog, his scalpeen, when he slept alone, had smelled very close to the grave. He could have been dead wandering the weird stone streets of Liverpool.

With a girl you knew you weren't.

He caught the blue and led him inside, rubbed the frost off his back and slipped on a bridle. There was no saddle.

The feed bins were open, and he gave the horse a pan of oats.

Sitting on the anvil, smoking his pipe, he watched the animal noisily feeding. He could hear the other horses outside, clacking in the mud.

He loved the blue, despite the horse's unrelenting meanness, his wicked sense of himself, his determination to bite the hand that fed him. He loved it that the blue owned himself.

Feeling unusually content, he smoked through three pipefuls. It was as though he had never really wanted to get away with her after all, but would be content to wait in the stable forever with the horse who, finishing his oats, stood whisking his tail impatiently.

As though the dream of leaving — leaving with her — were enough.

What was the world, except scent, feel, light? Was there something touchable in sorrow, loneliness? He could almost feel the past in his hands — warm, weighty, like a spade of earth from a good, loamy field.

Hearing footsteps approaching, crackling through the icy mud outside, he stood up.

That moment when you join your life, you're thrilled. Your head spins. You feel a little sick.

The stable door opened with a groan.

"Molly?"

"Jesus!"

It was McCarty, peering into the dark.

"Who is it? Who's there?"

"It's me — Fergus."

McCarty snorted. "Idiot! You give me a spook —"

"Where's Molly?"

"Fuck, you give me a scare. I've shat meself . . . oh mercy. Mr. Murdoch is looking for you, man. You would have half a crown, but they have given it to me instead. Jesus I'm jingling tonight I swear." McCarty took a coin from his waistcoat pocket, flipped it, and caught it with a slap.

"Where is Molly?"

"Scare the gas out of me, you did." McCarty kissed his coin then peered at Fergus. "Muck's going to fight your horse. It is all arranged."

"What?"

"No one will stand up with Muck, and we need a blaster. Fellows are wagering like mad. Mr. Murdoch sent me to fetch him. Everyone likes a good fight, so."

"Where's Molly?"

"Having a time with the Moll, are you?" McCarty shook his head. "Beware, Fergus. Remember old Kelly."

"We're going away."

McCarry shook his head slowly. "Kelly was taking her away — for America. Only Muck found out. Next time we saw Kelly, he was dead, and Muck had her washing him down." McCarty unwrapped the halter from the post. "No, give it up, Fergus, Muck will never let her go; he will snap you. Listen — you can hear the fellows yelling from here. Nothing like a Pay for stirring up. And Muck

knocked down that horse in France, he did." McCarty started leading the blue
from the barn. "One good crack. That's all it took — here, you devil, none of that!"

The horse, writhing, had tried to bite his arm and he gave the strap a vigorous jerk, then held it out to Fergus. "Here, you lead the fucker."

He took the strap, feeling disarrayed, disarmed by confusion, and for the first
time, vulnerable. Had Muck somehow learned of their plan?

He could hear the noise down in camp, men roaring. He could ride away,
but he knew he couldn't leave her, so he started after McCarty along the
muddy path.

Sometimes you walk in the dark aware of everything you have lost, and you
feel lost, but you just keep going, because you haven't the strength to stop or
turn back or run away.

THE NAVVIES had formed a ring to watch a pair of wrestlers grappling, but
when the crowd saw Fergus leading the blue horse they began shouting and
whistling. Drenched with mud, the wrestlers gave up their match and stood
back as he led the fuming horse into the ring. The night air was greasy with
smoke from torches, and the blue bleated and tossed his head nervously,
spooked at the flickering lights.

Something made you do this: hunger, desire, a sense you had to gamble
everything to win.

Molly was beside Muldoon, who began taking off his coat. Fergus kept looking at her until she met his eye and gave a little shrug.

He struggled to hold the horse steady while Muck began prancing in his corner, cutting the air with punches.

Mr. Murdoch in muddy horse boots stepped into the ring, holding up his
hand while the men cheered and whistled. The contractor let the noise continue
for a few moments, then raised his hand again. The crowd fell silent.

"Rules of engagement! A win is by knockdown! Nothing else will serve!" The
contractor looked at Muck, then Fergus. "Ready, men?"

Muck nodded. he was flushed with beer and exercise.

Molly was looking at Fergus, but he couldn't tell what she was thinking or
feeling.

Kelly. Of course she'd wanted Kelly to help her get away. You couldn't blame her for that.

It cracked you to realize you weren't the only.

The timer's bell sounded and Muck came out quickly, dancing.

Feeling strange, as if he were moving in a dead world, Fergus let go of the halter. The blue started trotting around the ring, looking for a way out. Snorting with fear. The heavy mud was sucking at the horse's feet. He kept trying to break out of the ring but the navvies kept him in, screaming at him, waving their hats, slapping at his flanks.

Suddenly the frightened horse dashed straight for Muldoon and reared up, clawing the air with his forelegs. His right foot snagged Muck's shoulder and knocked the ganger down. In a flurry of stomps and kicks, the blue horse trampled Muck in the mud then resumed his frantic dashing around the ring, wild-eyed and fluting steam, the mud sucking at his hooves.

The blue had already forgotten Muck, on his back, chest crushed, spouting red blood.

The dead lie so soft. Souls yielding they hug the ground. What is it that's taken out of them?

The men would need to kill the horse, he knew, in vengeance for their champion.

Sometimes the future flies straight at you. Your brain reaches out and takes what it wants.

The blue was dashing from one end to the other when Fergus ran out into the ring, seized the halter, and threw himself up on the horse's back. He could feel the blue's exhaustion as he steered him across the ring. Looking down at Muldoon's corpse, he saw the railway spike still clenched in Muck's left hand.

When he leaned down for her, she hesitated only a second before grasping his arm and pulling herself up behind. Kicking and wriggling, then getting a leg over.

With her arms around him he kicked hard and rode straight at the men at the far end of the ring. The faces fell back, yelling and cursing, and then they were through. Trotting past the bootmaker's tent, the ruined church. He caught a whiff of iron, tangy and rough, as they crossed over the grade, the horse moving between his knees, Molly's arms around his chest, her breathing hot on his neck.

You felt so strong. Felt so pure.

You carry yourself inside, don't you? Dry, like a handful of seeds.

You thought you'd been redeemed.

THEY HAD the road to themselves. Through the dark villages, dogs yelped in surprise, and Molly held on with both arms across his chest as though she trusted him completely and believed he would never do her harm.

They barely spoke. She seemed internal, untouchable, made of thoughts. The night was bitter, ice lacquering the fields, but the thrill of leaving burned like a good fire and he was never cold.

Who wants anything but to travel at night with a girl? Night of the Opening Road. You don't care if you are awake or sleeping, alive or dead — you just keep going.

You tell yourself you want to protect her, but of course it is more complicated than that.

The Road

DAWN WAS BLURRED, smelling of old blankets and snow, when they rode across the bridge at Conwy. While he watered the horse at an iron trough she spread Muldoon's coat on the ground and sat examining an object in her hand.

"Look here." She held up Muldoon's gold watch, dangling on its chain. "It was in Muck's pocket, of course. And here, his pay." She showed him the handful of coins. "There's enough for a passage. Needn't go south, so. Straight to Liverpool and buy a passage."

He should feel glad but did not. The watch tied her to Muldoon.

Molly held the instrument to her ear. "Still alive. His time she is beating. Listen."

She pressed it to his ear, and he heard the small, dry noise.

"We shall let her run down, and that marks the finish of Muldoon. When she has good and stopped, I'll wind her up again." She fixed the watch chain around her neck. "Poor old Muck. He was good for something at last."

Dawn was filling in. He could see a rocky headland and the plate of sea. On the other side of the road, beyond the fields, heavy mountains caught the light.

"In America there is woods so thick, Fergus, they call it the Nightland."

"Why?"

"So heavy you can't see light. But it's good browse for cattle."

"They have their cabins there?"

"No cabins, they all own farms." Molly lit her pipe. "We'll go straight for Liverpool, flog the watch. Must be careful whom we deal with, or they'll nab us for reward. Say I stole the thing."

"You didn't. You're Muck's wife —"

"Railway wife don't signify. No, have to be careful or we'll end up on the iron gang. Convicted and sentenced for transportation. Van Dieman's Land!"

"I've friends in Liverpool."

"Can they help flog the watch and find a ship?"

"Shea can. She knows sailors, I am sure."

"A sailor is only a navvy on the sea."

He used to think the navvies were powerful, but the railway was powerful, not the men.

Could he find his way back to the Dragon? They were the only ones who could look at him now and not see a stranger.

The city's streets, courts, and alleys were scattered in his mind like bits of iron shot.

Explosive Liverpool.

"Here." Passing him the pipe, Molly lay on her side wrapped in her cloak, facing away.

"I'll own cattle," she said.

He touched her hair. If she felt his touch, she didn't respond. He could hear the watch beating — regular verse of the hard new world. He wanted to put their new relationship into words but didn't know the words. Taking off his coat he lay beside her, pulling the coat over them both. Molly muttered and wriggled closer for warmth, kerning her hips into his.

God, he was so near.

He lay absorbing her heat, watchful and hungry, listening to her breathe.

WHEN HE awoke, he knew right away she was gone. He stood up quickly. Frost shone on the ground. The horse gone as well. The pockets of his coat were empty; she'd taken all his pay.

Scrambling up to stand on a flinty wall, he gazed down the road.

It was empty. Mountains and empty sea. Hard wind, the light shifting nervously.

He felt stunned. He didn't want to think. Jumping down off the wall, he started along the road.

Anger and grief live in the throat. They're always there, always ready.

Walk, keep walking. Crack of hobnails on stone.

An animal is all you are. And the world's just ground and light.

Keep moving. Open your mouth wide, the wind screams right in.

THE SUN warmed the road and he stopped to drink at a stream.

He wondered if she'd watered the horse. Probably not. She'd be pushing too hard, going fast, breaking him down.

He smelled brine. The wind was whipping the sea, flecked with whitecaps. The cold water he had drunk burned into his chest, and he felt it like a cut in his belly. He started coughing, couldn't stop. He bent over longing to spit his life on the road while the coughs racked him. But then it passed, and he wiped his eyes and kept walking. An hour later he came to a long, sheltered stretch where the road turned away from the sea and cut through a soft green valley with meadow on each side, dotted with sheep. He saw the blue up ahead, eating grass under a hedge.

The horse was lame, hobbling.

No sign of her.

The horse wanted to shy away, but he managed to catch hold of the bridle. Raising the blue's right leg he saw that the lameness was only a shoe knocked loose by the hard surface of the road. All the nails but one were still in place. Using a stone for a hammer, he drove them in tight. It wasn't perfect but would hold a few more miles. He threw himself aboard and started down the road. The horse was tired, needing rest, water, and feed.

After a couple of miles he caught sight of her up ahead, a lone figure walking the road. He kicked his heels until the blue horse broke into a tired canter.

She heard them coming and turned around, shielding her eyes from the sun.

He halted when there was still a distance between them.

"You're angry, I suppose," she said.

"Why'd you do it, Molly?"

"Thought he was gone lame."

"Why'd you run away?"

"I don't know." She was still shielding her eyes. "Your horse woke me. Stood over me, he did, but quiet and easy. Before I knew it I was up on his back. Then I was looking at you, thinking sure you'd open your eyes — only you didn't."

"You stole my pay."

"It all just happened, Fergus, I swear. It never was a plan." She held out the coins, wrapped in a handkerchief. "Here's our stake. Nothing I've spent. Only a shilling for some eggs. And tea. And jam."

"Give me my money." That she could have left so easily, so lightly, shocked him.

Approaching the horse, she held up the bundle of coins.

"Mine — I want only what's mine," he said coldly. "You may keep Muck's — you go hang with Muck's. Give me what's mine. Count it out and give it over."

"Man —"

"I don't wish to hear your rattle."

"It was only to be alone awhile —"

"Count me what's mine!" Even in the seethe of anger he understood why she had fled. It stung him but why wouldn't she? She'd been banged about by hard men, and hard she was.

Molly stroked the horse's neck. "I had my thoughts to order — you know how it is. But I was thinking on you while I were walking, Fergus — thinking on you quite sore."

"Count me out mine, and clear away."

"Don't get all harsh, man. You'd only hurt yourself as well as me." She touched his leg with her knuckle

"Get out of the road!" He began to cry.

"You're such a boy now," she said softly.

"Clear away!"

"We're strong together, man, you know we are. And I was going to stop and wait for you. I would have, sure." She tugged his trouser leg. "Come, Fergus, give me a lift. We're stone partners. You know it."

A flock of guillemots were circling and howling over the shore.

He did know it. They were stone partners. Each had tasted the world and tried to spit out the taste and couldn't.

"I was going to sit down and wait for you, man, soon as it got a little warmer. I knew you'd be along." She touched his leg again. "Come, Fergus, give me a lift. We need each other."

Leaning over, he held out his arm. She seized it to drag herself aboard, kicking and struggling to get a leg over.

She was dark as him, she was rough, they knew the same hard things.

Astride, laughing, she wrapped her arms around his waist. "Oh, man, I like it up here!"

Gently he kicked, and the weary horse resumed walking.

AT ABERGELY they paid a couple of shillings for beer, cheese, wheat rolls, and feed for the horse. They sat with tramps on benches outside the beer shop, eating and drinking in the sunshine. The men peppered them with questions, wanting news of the line. Was there fever in the camps farther west? Would the work at Mr. Murdoch's last until summer?

"Where is Muck Muldoon?" a tramp asked Molly.

Fergus flinched at the name.

"Dead," she answered.

The tramp wore a smashed lady's bonnet and had his bundle tied on a stick. "How did it happen?"

"Oh, he tried to clip a horse, but the horse clipped him."

"Poor old Muck. He was a terrier."

"Poor old Muck," she agreed.

They boarded the horse and rode on. After they had gone a mile or so, Fergus looked around at her. "Did you care for Muldoon?"

"What do you think? What a *gommoch* you are."

They encountered sheep, being driven west to sell in the railway camps, flowing nervously around the horse, pushed by fierce-looking Welsh drovers and heeled by fanatic dogs.

"Muldoon I met on Derry quay when I was lurking there after my ma was transported. I was feeding off the Quakers' soup — poor scran it was. Didn't know how I'd keep alive.

"Me and her, we used to run palsy games at the fairs, with our bones, our shells, our playing cards. You should see me cut sixpence off a farmer when I have got him feeling bold — how stupid men get at a fair. We hardly stole nothing that summer, only a bit of what come our way. Then she took some tools from a fellow making wagon wheels in Enniskillen, thinking we could sell them, and that was on account of a debt of honor, for the fellow had been promising we could live in his house, only he had a wife, which he didn't tell us.

"So she was hooked by the law, and the magistrate sentenced her for being an evil, idle wretch, which she wasn't. Twelve years transportation. I sometimes wonder where she is, lost at sea, or playing the game in Van Dieman's Land? But it don't matter. Them transported, you never see again. They are good as dead.

"Anyway, I was hungry. Muldoon asked, would I like a bite to eat. He was kind for a while. 'Machree,' he would say, 'you were lost but I have found you.' He had cold mutton in his pail, bread, and a little butter. A little *poitín* jar. Gave me his hard cloak to wear, paid my fare across to England, and said I'd be his *cailín dhas*."

His sweet girl, his pretty.

"Do you suppose they have buried him by now?"

"They plant fellows quick before the farmers try to stop them. In some field if the digging's soft, or under the grade. Poor old Muldoon."

"You say so but you were frightened of him."

"Ach, he wasn't so bad, I've seen worse."

The horse was jogging along, iron shoes scraping the road, when Molly tugged sharply at Fergus's sleeve. "Stop!"

He pulled the reins and stopped the horse. She had Muldoon's watch out, holding it to her ear. Then she pressed it on Fergus's ear. "Hear anything?"

Listening strenuously, he could hear nothing but wind through gorse, and the horse's breathing. "No."

"That's Muck's time has run out. Dead he is. Quite dead." She began twisting the knob between her thumb and forefinger. "Here, you give it a lick. Don't work it too tight. Just go easy, easy, and fill her in slow."

He wound the knob, feeling resistance increase with every turn.

"That's good enough."

Holding it to her ear, Molly smiled with satisfaction. "Now it's our time."

THEY STOPPED at a contractor camp and bought hay from the farrier. Molly asked the time and set the watch. While the blue horse was feeding, Fergus watched a team of horses pulling a giant wooden roller up and down the grade, compacting.

"When you die on the passage they feed you to the fish. It's better to be buried under the line." Molly was standing beside him. The farrier had offered her warm water to wash in. The sun was warm, and she had taken off her cloak. Her feet were bare, her breasts pressing the thin cotton gown. Dry, pink lips.

He felt clumsy and vulnerable, standing so close. A swell of tenderness he did not know what to do with.

Shea would want her, he realized.

The Dragon was softer than anything Molly knew. Safer than rocking for Muldoon; more real than America. He ought to keep clear of the Dragon and its temptations, but he knew he had to see his friends, and see himself in their eyes. They were the only ones who knew him now. They were his people and he could not relinquish them.

OUTSIDE CHESTER, with the light fading, Molly spat into her palm, slapped hands, and sold the blue horse to a Welsh farmer for six shillings. Fergus stood watching as the animal was tied behind the farmer's cart and led away.

No use trying hold on to any part of the world. Let it go, forget it, or be demented from sorrow.

THEY HURRIED to the station. A Southern Express stood huffing like an important dream while passengers slipped into the carriages and navvies swarmed the trucks. The Northern Express had already gone through, an agent informed them. The next wasn't due until morning, eight o'clock.

"We'll doss in a churchyard," Molly decided. "No use wasting money."

They bought bread, cheese, and herrings at a victualer's shop and ate as they walked. At the churchyard, tramps scattered among the graves were already asleep, rolled up in their blankets. Spreading out Muldoon's coat on the grass behind a tombstone, they lay down, spooning for warmth. She held his hand close to her mouth and he felt her breath, warm and damp, on his thumb. He could feel his prick getting hard.

After a while she rolled onto her back and looked at him. "I know what you want."

Seizing his hand she drew it under her skirt.

Curious, tentative, he touched her.

"Cold!"

She seemed unable to relax her body. After a few moments, confused by her stiffness, unwilling to be rough, he withdrew his hand.

"Do as you please!" she said. "Go on! It don't matter! Go ahead."

"It's no good unless you want to."

"That's all talk." She jabbed him with her elbow. "Do as you please — I don't care."

He fumbled with buttons on the front of the gown and got a few undone. Underneath, she wore a gray woolen vest. He slid one hand under the layer of greasy, strong-smelling wool. The skin of her breasts felt warm and soft. He started kissing her again. She did not open her mouth. After a few kisses, she sat up, pushed him back, and started unbuttoning his trousers.

Taking his cock in her fist, she began rubbing it briskly. As the shaft became slippery with fluid, his hips began to buck, and he felt very close to death or some new understanding. How angry and strange everything was, how unsettled the world.

She took it between her lips, and an instant later he was jarring inside her mouth.

After the last convulsion, he lay exhausted.

She spat out the junk.

"That was deadly good, wasn't it?" she said.

"It was." But something was missing. He felt estranged, hopeless, falling through the world.

"Is it what you wanted, so?"

"I want you."

"Well, I'm here, ain't I?" She wriggled close, dragging her cloak over them. "Go to sleep, strange fellow."

IN THE morning he was awakened by the noise of her being sick on the grass.

He got up and rubbed her back until the convulsions had stopped. "Oh man, there's black in that." She was peering at the mess. "I'm sick, I'm sick. Oh man, I can't follow this life no more."

He knew the first sign of black fever, typhus fever, was usually headache, thoughts tangling and blazing. Then violent sickness. Skin flushing dark, so the victim was black in the face. Chills. Overnight, fever sores blistering. Every joint swollen and tender. Terrible sleeps, like sleeping in fire.

She was weeping. Wetting his handkerchief on the dew, he began cleaning her mouth.

"I want to be warm, Fergus. Everything's wrong. I'm never warm. There's more to life than this."

"Have you never had the fever?"

"Don't talk to me of fever." She made herself stand up straight, and shook out her skirt. "I'm all right. I'm better now — I'll be all right. We'll have our ship by tonight, won't we?"

"I don't know. Perhaps."

"I tell you, man I won't never more sleep on the ground."

"What time?"

She cracked open the watch. "It's time. Let's go, let's catch our flier."

IN THE mist, well-dressed railway passengers stood clutching their parcels and waiting for the Northern Express. At the far end of the platform, a group of navvies sat on their packs.

No train in sight.

"We've rations left from last night, don't we? I'm famished, man. Give us a fill, I need something." She was peering down the line, impatient.

Her face showed good color, nothing feverish.

He gave her bread and cheese, which she ate greedily, watching the line. "Here she comes, man."

He could see the engine, furling white smoke. "Look at that beauty!" Molly cried, hopping like a bird. People began collecting packages as the train clanked into the station, smothering the platform in steam, cinders, and the stink of hot grease and iron. Navvies were getting to their feet.

"Come on, Fergus, let's find a place, she won't stop long." Without waiting for him Molly started down the platform, heading for the open trucks at the end of the train.

If he stayed there, standing on the platform, she'd still board the train. He'd not see her again. He'd be alone. Safer. Watchful. Using solitude like a drink.

Another tramp in a world of tramps.

Alone, you lose your sense of yourself. Your thoughts slur. Eventually you'd vanish, like those ejected; like them dropped into the sea.

"Fergus! She's starting to pull!" She was beside one of the open trucks. "I can feel it! Come give me a leg-up, man!"

Rejecting solitude, you follow what is warm.

He hurried down the platform. When he reached the truck, he bent and cupped his hands. Laughing, she stepped up neatly and scrambled over the side. He climbed over after her. The tramps were packed shoulder-to-shoulder but Molly brusquely elbowed for space. "Make room, make room, gents — we all shall fit nice as fleas." The whistle screamed and couplings slammed down the length of the train, and the truck gave a jolt and started rolling. It left the station quickly, clattering over switches. Smoke and red cinders fluttered over their heads. Past stables, wagon yards, and the backs of houses, they broke out into the open country.

Molly was crouched out of the wind, lighting her pipe. He stood holding on to the truck's swaying sides watching the fields of England flipping past.

Great speed makes you feel powerful, as though you possess what you see, but the feeling is a delusion.

City of Stone

DISEMBARKING AT BIRKENHEAD, they followed a crowd of navvies past slaughter yards reeking of smoke, blood, and shit, down to the landing stage, where they paid a penny each and boarded the ferry.

The Mersey teemed like every thought in his head spilling out. Dozens of steamers and ships trafficked up and down the river or lay waiting to enter the stone fortress docks on the Liverpool side.

At midstream he caught the sharp aroma of the sea just as a three-master crossed their bow, her yellow sails flapping. She was headed out under tow from a steam tug; her deck was full of passengers capering and cheering and waving their hats.

"Look at them going for America," Molly said enviously.

The sound of cheering was cut and garbled by the wind.

As the ship crossed their bow he stared up at passengers lining the rails and felt the mystery of life on them, radiant.

You don't know where it is, the other side, you can't imagine.

"I WILL get clean," Fergus announced.

"Let's find your friends first."

"No." They were watching people with damp hair and shining faces coming out of the public baths on Georges Dock, a few steps up from the landing stage. "We'll bathe first, and new clothes. Look out —"

A runner was coming through, pushing a barrow piled with baggage. Yelling traffic out of his way, trailed by a pack of emigrants who looked stunned by what was happening to them.

Liverpool no longer stunned him, but it was a hard place and used people hard, if they were unprotected. Ruined them.

"Come on, Moll."

He led her to an old-clothes cart, one of a dozen on the quay. He longed to change his skin, to clean up, to impress Shea. They began sorting through hats, boots, and clothes piled on tables and pegged out on lines, flapping on the breeze. The better dressed, the stronger he would feel. Shea must see him as the hard fellow he had become. If she tried to take Molly, he would fight.

"Do you like this, Moll?" He held up a shirt, Manchester cloth, red-and-white checked, with small, hard, white buttons, but she was absorbed trying on boots. He found a pair of duck trousers, sky blue in color, stiff from washing, with two rows of black buttons down the front. Linen and cotton underclothes. Woolen stockings that smelled of lamp oil. Studying a table of hats, he saw a beaver sleeker and even taller than his own, but his own was still good enough, still stiff enough and more or less straight, without the crazy dents and angles of Irish hats. He picked out another cotton shirt, checked black-and-white, missing a collar button.

"I feel like a duck," Molly said staring down at the boots on her feet.

"Boots make you strong in the world, Moll. Nothing like it."

She held up a pink gown with blue ribbon at the neck and a split seam. "I ought to burn my old thing; I smell of turnips." She turned to the old-clothes man. "Tell me what it is for this gear."

"A pound the lot."

"That's no good."

"It's fine gear."

"Spun of gold, I suppose?" she sneered. "Come along, man, I'm not off the boat. Six shillings I'll pay."

You're too small for a whore, he thought, watching her bargain with the dealer. *Too bony. You don't want strangers inside, they will tear you open, will bust your thoughts.*

They settled for a price of nine shillings, with a canvas grip included, and raced for the baths. Tickets were a penny each, paid at the wicket. She paid for them both — she had their money, rolled up in Muck's handkerchief. As he watched her heading into the women's baths, another fear nipped him. Would she be waiting when he came out? He was about to call after her and ask for the money, for his share at least, but stopped himself.

He didn't know what she would do, but he wished to know.

In the men's dressing room white bodies of men and children appeared and disappeared through a gauze of steam. He stuffed his old clothes in the grip, which he left with an old attendant, receiving in exchange a brass disc on a cord that hung around his neck.

Walking the tunnel to the baths, the noise of water splashing reminded him of that first night at the Dragon, how clean that bath had scraped him; and of Shea, oiling him, then coaxing him.

He had been ill for weeks, and they had taken good care of him. Never before had he received such bounty and affection.

The tiled bathroom was crowded with steam and men's bodies. Hot water slashed from nozzles in the ceiling. Stepping under a torrent he felt a shock of heat, and stood for a couple of minutes hanging his head, like a bull dozing, absorbing the drench, before he began scrubbing.

If she went off with the money she would swim like a fish in the streets of Liverpool and he would never find her.

After rinsing off the soap, he stayed under the torrent while a stream of bathers flowed in and out of the room.

Betrayal was what it was — the timing didn't matter. He was in no hurry to find out.

Most bathers seemed to fear the ferocity of the pounding, drenching deluge. They ducked under for only a few seconds, gasping and howling, slapping their chests and thighs, then rushing away.

He could go for the Dragon, even without money, and Shea and Arthur and Mary and Betsy would welcome him; would take him in if he had money or not.

Perhaps there was a room somewhere within the Dragon — somewhere in the warren of passageways, staircases, kitchens, card rooms, and bedrooms — where he could hide, and no one could ever find him. An unvisited room, dusty and forgotten. A space concealed by the living house, surrounded, and perfectly safe.

Of course such a room couldn't be.

That was your grave you were thinking of.

"WHAT A Liverpool jockey you are," she said, teasing.

She had been waiting for him outside the baths, wearing her new gown, combing out her damp hair with her fingers.

Looking down, he noticed with satisfaction how neatly his new trousers broke over his boots.

"You're the navigator, lead away," she said, taking his arm. "All I know of Liverpool is shit and death. Find us some friends."

Threads attaching you to another person, to a woman, are biting and intense. You try to gather them in your hand and they are almost invisible but how they sting and cut.

THE ALLEYS up from the dockland were lined with victualers' shops and crowded with sailors, ship riggers, and the smoke of roasting meat. Every wall was plastered with bills and pictures of sailing ships.

"If I had my letters like old McCarty, I could read them bills for what they say and find us on a ship tonight. If we stay long in Liverpool, Fergus, we're bleeding money — I can't wear these boots any longer, man, they are biting my feet." Taking them off, she tied the laces and strung the boots over her shoulder. "Don't know how you stand it."

Following spaciousness of light they came out of the alleys and into Custom House Square, where streams of traffic slashed past, drivers cracking whips, everything excited. Crossing the square, swept along in a sea of umbrellas and silk hats, they started up Hanover Street where girls and old men hawked pilchards, roast apples, and grilled nuts from carts and barrows.

"We have the coin, we can get a bite to eat, man. Who knows how far it is."

"Waste of money. They will feed us at the Dragon."

"Are they clever? Can they help us bark the watch?"

"I suppose they can. There are gents with money at the Dragon. Merchants and all."

"Sounds like a big, fat fuck house." She sounded amused. "Were you a fuck boy, Fergus?"

He shook his head and walked faster.

"Why'd they keep you then?"

He ignored the question.

"Oh, don't look so queer! Come along, tell me, what did they want you for, if it weren't the old fizz? Did you stoke fires? Clean boots? I reckon they wanted something."

"They were my friends."

"Oh ho, they were going to put you to work, a fresh boy like you! Of course they were. You can't blame them." Molly tightened her grip on his arm as a glossy tide of people carried them along. "Hang on to me, man, or I'll drown in this road."

Tousled and hungry, a sparrow she seemed, furious for something. He said nothing of his fears. They were carried along, buoyed on the crowd. If he told her he was afraid of losing her, it might come true.

"WHAT IS it, Fergus?"

They were standing in Bold Street, staring at the gap in the terrace where he was sure the Dragon had once existed. Now there was nothing between two adjacent houses but a flight of white marble steps leading nowhere, and heaps of bricks and charred beams, and a gap of sky.

"Perhaps you have it wrong. These streets look all the same."

Molly looked over her shoulder and called out to the butcher's boy walking down the other side of the street. "Boy, do you know the Dragon?"

"What happened to them inside?" Fergus called. The boy wore a white apron and carried a paper package stained with blood.

"Burned out, they was."

"Come, man, let's get away," Molly said, tugging Fergus's arm.

"Burned out and sent to Hell, every single one. Hey you, Mike, are you one of them?"

"Come on, Fergus, it's no use, let's get out of here."

Drawing a steel knife from his belt, the butcher's boy stepped out into the road.

"Where are they?" Fergus asked.

"Nest of murderers and traitors it was — they got what they deserve."

"Are they dead? Shea? Mary? The baby? All of them?"

The boy shrugged. "Big pawky funeral they give 'em, very grand."

"Come on, come on." Molly began pulling Fergus away. He looked back and saw the boy capering in the road, slashing the air. "I'll fix your Irish bollocks!" He was still shouting as they turned the corner into Hanover Street where the rush of traffic, hundreds of carriages, thousands of people, drowned everything.

Letting go his hand, Molly plunged ahead, slipping and dodging so neatly through the stream of well-dressed people coming at them that he almost lost sight of her.

Stunned by the murders of his friends, he had no sense where they ought to head now.

Neither did she, but she wasn't looking back. Moving so lithe through the heavy crowd. It was taking all of his attention to keep up, not to lose sight.

Letting go of everything else, he gave himself up to the pure motion, pure forward, two of them struggling like salmon against the stream of Liverpool.

Tim the Jew

ON THE QUAY AT CLARENCE DOCK they stood watching a steamer slip into the dock basin. "These are only the monsters back and forth for Ireland and I would rather drown than go back there," she said.

A wall behind them was plastered yellow with shipping bills. She looked at the runners leaning on upturned barrows smoking penny pipes and waiting to dive upon the emigrants. "Foxes they are. Muck said they run baggage wherever it suits them. Whatever lodging house or ticket broker pays their tip."

Even before the steamer had tied up, the people were pitching their trunks and baggage over and leaping onto the quay, and the runners came alive, moving in. Fergus watched a boy wrestle a grip out of a woman's hand and fling it in his barrow. "They're thieves!"

"They're quick boys, and we ought to engage one to find us a clever fellow. Someone who'd take the watch off us without getting all fussy."

Arthur would have known the business; Shea would have helped. He watched the runner dashing away with the grip in his barrow, the poor woman howling after him.

Without friends you are vulnerable. Anyone can take a jab at you.

"Can't we sell it to a navvy, or a sailor?"

"Show gold to sailors? We'd be robbed, murdered, and thrown in the river. Anyway, no sailor nor navvy's likely to have the price, is he?"

"I don't know. What is the price?"

"Yes, well, I do — trust me."

"Why did they have to kill them, Moll — it was only Arthur they wanted."

"I don't know, Fergus. No use asking why things happen. They do, that's all. Only you must think what is going to happen next. Now, we might try selling the watch to a sea captain or a gent, but it's risky, he might turn us in. No, we really want a clever fellow, and must hire a runner to find him. Come on, man, let's cruise."

Leaving the quay, they started up one of the alleys. "It's a fierce old town. The stomach of the world," Molly said. "Don't think about them, man. Leave them behind."

PASSING A victualer's shop in the alley called Launcelot's Hey, she studied a group of runners outside, leaning on their upturned barrows, laughing and smoking.

"Too risky, a pack of them. Turn on you like dogs these fellows."

It had started raining. A pungent whiff of noise, liquor, and beef smoke leaked out from the beer shops and spirit vaults in the alley. The whole world was guzzling.

"We need one fellow, alone, who we can handle, if he tries to sharp us. Wish we had a knife or a blagger. Then we could handle anyone."

A runner came rushing through the alley, bawling the way clear, trailed by a pack of emigrants trotting like cattle.

Fergus thought of Arthur, gently shepherding the *Ruth*s from the savage dockland to the night asylum.

Molly clutched his arm. "Here's our fellow" — indicating a solitary runner standing in the doorway of a spirit vault, keeping out of the rain. He was munching a sausage roll. His barrow parked on its nose.

As they passed by Fergus studied him quickly, trying to calculate whether he could beat him in a fight.

He felt physical power flush through his muscles like a pure dose of rage.

"He's alone all right," said Molly, looking back over her shoulder. "He's a meager-looking fellow — I wonder if he knows his way about."

They walked on a little farther, stopping where the alley ended at a busy street. A dray rumbled past, headed for the docks, freight strapped down under canvas. The teamster held the reins between his knees and was eating his dinner from a pail while rain streamed off his hat.

"Ever wish you was goods, Fergus?"

Molly's bonnet was soaked, and the skirt of her gown was black from the rain. Smoldering, pelting, pavement Liverpool. Through a lit shop window, he could see a man slitting a wheel of gold cheese. Everyone else in the city seemed to be eating.

"Used to wish I were a horse."

"Horses are treated worse. I've wanted to be a wheel," she said. "I've wished I were a crop of wheat standing in a field." She gripped his arm. "Come on. Let's see what this fellow knows."

The runner had noticed them, and as they came back along the alley he was watching them. Close up, he looked even slighter. Narrow skull, thin blond hair, eyes darkly rimmed.

"What are you looking at?" Some illness or delicacy lurked behind the sharky Liverpool face. "Get away, you awful micks. Clear off."

"We've some business."

The boy wiped his lips with the back of his hand. "What business?"

Molly held out Muck's watch and the runner glanced at it. Taking a splinter from his pocket, he began picking his teeth with elaborate indifference. "That's a common, cheap old guzzard, Mary. I don't want the thing."

Fergus saw Molly hesitate. They glanced at each other, and she slipped the watch back into her pocket.

"We ain't barking with you. Bring us to a clever fellow."

"What price? If I might ask."

"Fair price."

"Come along, Mary, what price?"

"Bring us to a clever fellow. You'll get a chop."

"Say your price. Perhaps I'd buy her myself."

Molly said nothing. The runner looked at Fergus, who shrugged.

"Let me see her again." The runner sighed.

This time he picked up the watch, and Fergus tensed, afraid he might try running off with it.

He held it to his ear, then handed it back. "Well, I might give you five shillings for the thing."

"It is French," Fergus said. "It is a watch. You wind it. It never shall stop."

"Is that so? And can you tell us the hour, Michael?" the runner, smirking.

"I cannot," he admitted.

"How do you know she works?"

"Listen to the tick! Sure she works!"

"Seven minutes after five o'clock," said Molly. "Shut up, man. Let me handle this."

The runner laughed. "Six shillings, then."

"No. I ain't selling to you. Take us to a clever fellow —"

"Seven I shall give you," the runner said. "You won't do better. You'd better be careful, barking stolen goods in Liverpool, there's fellows would turn you in for the pleasure —"

Fergus stepped between the boy and Molly. "Don't threaten."

The boy stepped back. "What's in it for me?"

"Five shillings," said Molly. "If we get our price."

Fergus stared at her, shocked. Nearly two days' pay on the tip.

"What price?"

"You'll know when we get it."

"Tim the Jew," said the runner. "He's the fellow you want."

"Lead away," she said, "lead away."

A MILE from the docks, the runner turned into one of the raw, new streets off the Vauxhall road. Isolated terraces stood in fields of mud; Fergus could smell the clay of new brick. Turning his barrow on its nose, the runner peered through the window of a corner shop. The interior was gloomy, but they could see a man, woman, and child eating by candles at a table in the rear.

The little runner knocked on the glass and the man, without looking up, waved them away.

"Tim's eating his dinner — he's very nice about his food, Tim is. We'll go for a guzzle and come back later. I knows the beer shop that'll do you fair."

Molly rapped impatiently. The man ignored her.

"Damn your eyes. You greedy fellow! Come and do business." She kept rapping, and the man suddenly arose and came across the floor. They heard the door unlocking. It cracked open a few inches.

"What is it?" Tim was a young blond man with a neat beard.

"You remember me, Tim — it's Walter. We done business together? Silver spoons."

"Come back tomorrow."

"No, listen, Tim, I have brought people with business —"

"They're strangers. I don't do business with strangers. Go away."

"No, Tim, I think you'll want to," the runner said hastily, turning to Molly. "Show him."

Molly held up the watch.

The man glanced at it. "Come back in the morning."

"Tim, Tim! I only brought them as I knew you liked the good stuff —"

"No, let him eat his supper," Molly said. "We'll do our business someplace else."

"We'll have to go down the street and give Terry's a snap at it, Tim, or one of them little disaster shops in the Goree. These people are going for America, they're in a rush."

Molly turned to Fergus. "Let's go."

Tim stared at them through the crack. "How did you come upon it?"

"My man's."

"Where is he?"

"Dead on the line."

"How?"

"Killed by a horse."

"Which line?"

"Chester-and-Holyhead."

"Which contract?"

"Mr. Murdoch's."

"Where did he acquire the watch?"

"France."

"Where in France?"

"Rouen when they was building the line."

Tim glanced at Fergus. "Who's he?"

"Off the line. Wages in his pocket. We ain't knockers, we're going for America."

Opening the door, Tim stepped aside for them to enter.

The little shop was crowded with clocks, barrels of swords, and the coarse smell of polish. A chorus of mechanical chirping sounded like a summer's night in a field. There were clocks on tables, clocks standing in shiny wooden boxes the size of upright coffins, and solemn white clock faces clicking on every wall.

Swords in scabbards hung on the wall. Dozens more were crowded into wooden barrels.

Taking the watch, Tim lit a lamp and sat down at a crowded workbench, Molly standing at his shoulder.

Fergus extracted one sword from a barrel. A slightly curved, slender thing, short blade — a rapier, gleaming in its nickel sheath. He started drawing it and the blade came out smoothly, with a pleasing rasping sound. Blued steel, a little greasy. He touched the edge; it seemed quite keen. Testing the hone, he scratched his thumbnail, peeling off a filament of tissue.

Purely sharp it was.

He made some brisk cuts and flourishes and the blade sang sharply, slashing the air.

Tim's wife and child were eating supper. Beef, bread, hot onions, and the sweet aroma of beer. The child stared at him glumly.

Walter the runner stood picking at calluses on his hands.

It was powerful to hold a rapier. You immediately began to consider the meaning of death.

He made another slash.

"Gallant," Walter smirked.

The blade cutting the air made a sound like bedsheets tearing.

Molly glanced over her shoulder. "Stop goosing."

"Not French," the clever fellow said. "Swiss — L. F. Audemars. A robin escapement, see?"

Clutching the rapier, Fergus approached the bench.

"A two-arm compensation balance, that's very nice." The clever fellow held the exposed machinery in his palm where it trembled like the warm insides of a small animal or bird freshly killed. "Spiral steel balance-spring and regulator, very nice."

"I told 'em you was the mince, Tim," Walter said with satisfaction.

"A pleasant piece of equipment."

"Nobody knows the tickers like Tim," the runner said.

Opening the lid with his thumbnail, the clever fellow studied the face. "Enamel dial, very nice. Very Swiss. And the hands, blued steel —"

"It's made of gold, ain't it?" Molly said sharply.

"Yes." Tim smiled, hefting the watch in his hand. "Engine-turned gold case." Snapping it shut abruptly, he held it out to Molly.

"Don't you want it then?"

"That all depends. What price?"

"Ten pounds."

Fergus saw the clever fellow glance across the room at his wife, then back at Molly, then at the watch in his hand.

"Fair enough. Done." He unlocked a drawer, and Molly looked dismayed — she'd asked too little. Tim took out a purse. "Hold out your hands."

Instead, Molly pulled off her bonnet and held it out. Tim began counting coins and dropping them into the bonnet, one by one.

A rapier in your hand gave a feeling of power. The weight was pleasant, organized, nicely balanced.

He watched the clever man dropping coins one by one. Clink, clink, clink.

Killing is an action, only an action. Less effort than whipping a horse. Less than fucking.

Rush the steel right through his heart.

The smell of food was rich, cloudy. Fergus glanced at the woman, cutting meat into little pieces, feeding herself and the child. The child stared back.

It wasn't pity. You knew your brain would be ruined by another murder, you'd become inaccessible to yourself: sectors of your thought stripped, ruined, untouchable. That was what stopped you. That was all.

Germans

OUTSIDE THE SHOP MOLLY COUNTED five shillings into the runner's hand. Nearly two days' pay on the line. "Now bring us to a lodging house, Walter, and I mean a fair place. None of your vermin shrouds. Someplace clean, civil, and not too steep, and we shall pay you a good strong tip."

"Maguire's," said the little runner. "Maguire keeps Germans; they've all got money. It's clean there."

"Is it far?"

"Not so very. Just up from Princes. Come along."

They had to run to keep up with Walter, who seemed incapable of any other pace. Gasping, out of breath in an alley not far from the quays, Fergus and Molly stared up at the countless windows of Maguire's lodging house. River mist and the scent of ship tar hung in the air.

"I don't often bring trade here," Walter said. "Maguire don't pay commish."

"Looks fair," said Molly.

"Fair? Fair it is, I'd say. Best emigrant keep in Liverpool, I'd say."

Molly flipped him a coin, and he shook hands with both of them, then seized the handles of his barrow and trotted away, quickly vanishing into the gloom.

They looked at each other, then back at the building.

"Great block of a monster she is," Molly said.

"Will they have us?"

"Oh Jesus, yes. We have only to knock the bloody door. Go on."

The building's size and hardness were intimidating. He hesitated.

"It's only money. Go on. They all wants our money, Fergus."

Sucking in his breath, he stepped to the door and hammered with his fist until he heard it unlock. It swung open. An elderly porter scowled.

"We're after lodgings —"

"We can pay," Molly added.

They were grudgingly admitted. "Stand here." The porter tugged on a bell pull then glared at them. The house smelled of tea and washing. A door opened at the end of the hall and another old man approached, cowhide slippers slurring on the floor.

"Yes? What do you want?"

"This is a lodging house, ain't it?" said Molly.

"William Maguire, at your service."

"Lodging we want."

He studied them. "We're a little dear, I'm afraid."

Molly shook the bonnet bunched in her hands and they all heard money jingle.

"Shilling a night," said the man. "Porridge for breakfast."

"Can you do us any kind of supper?"

He shook his head. "My kitchen help is dossed down. We get an early start here, feeding Germans."

"Really, mister, we have come a long way."

"Where from?"

"We're off the Chester-and-Holyhead."

"Where in Ireland?"

"All abouts. Derry."

"I am Fermanagh myself. Well, miss, perhaps we might do you something cold. Follow me, but quiet."

They followed him through the house, past people sleeping on upholstered benches in the hallway and wrapped in blankets on the floor.

"This lot just came in from Hull, and Bremen before that. There is always a few won't sleep in a crib because of a few bugs. Do you know what a German is?"

"I don't," Fergus admitted.

Some of the people had tied themselves to their baggage with rope.

"These are all for New York on *Humphrey*. They ship from Hamburg or Bremen to Hull, then by train to Liverpool. I have pushed through thousands of Germans for New York and St. Louis. They use their own German brokers and stay clear of the thieves on the Goree. They use the Black Ball packets."

Maguire led them into a large, chill kitchen. When he turned up a lamp, they saw plates and noggins stacked in enamel cupboards and steel knives arranged on a rack by a cutting table. A bag of onions dangled from a beam. The kitchen had the smell of a clean stone. Maguire opened a locker and brought out a dish of cooked onions and a shoulder of mutton covered with sacking.

"How much these days for a passage on *Humphrey*?" Molly said, casually.

"Seven or eight pounds. New York packets are expensive this year," Maguire reached down two plates from the shelf and brought out a dish of butter and loaf of bread.

"What about Quebecs?"

Choosing a knife, Maguire stropped it briskly on a steel. "The ships in the timber trade are starting to cross, hoping the ice will be out when they get there. They like to fill with emigrants. But Quebec and St. John can be a brutal crossing, as I hear."

Whisking off two slices of mutton, he laid one upon each plate and added a spoonful of cooked onions.

"There it is. Go on, eat."

The meat was tough to chew but tasted fresh and delicious. Fergus shoveled the salty, slippery curls of onion onto buttered bread while the landlord stood with his arms crossed, watching them. "Do you want a mug of beer? It's fresh."

They both nodded.

Having money changes everything.

Money, the hard power of the world.

THEY LEFT their grip in a boxroom crowded with German leather baggage, crates, sacks, and bundles of tools.

"Germans are good farmers and prosperous men. I have emigrants through here — Germans — with machines for making glass lenses; with violins and brass horns and every kind of musical box; with crate after crate of books; and one fellow had a machine for pulling teeth from horses. They're not like the Irish, all sputter and luck, most of it bad."

Maguire gave them two clean blankets. Molly was leaning heavily on Fergus's arm as they followed the landlord upstairs. "I'm beat, man, my soul is dead."

"We'll find you a bed," the landlord assured her. "Only a wee bit farther, miss."

"My bones are even sore. I can't walk much longer."

They following him along a corridor, where more Germans roped to their baggage were sleeping on the floor. A woman nursing a child watched them balefully. Maguire began opening one door after another, shining his lamp briefly into each sleeping room before going on to the next. The people asleep in the corridor wore beautiful cloaks, leather jackets, embroidered aprons and nightcaps, woolen stockings, woolen mittens. Good boots were scattered everywhere. "This lot are going for Illinois, they've already purchased their farms." Maguire opened another door. "Here we are — top shelf, over there," he whispered, holding up the lamp. "Go on, climb aboard."

Men were snoring. Bodies were stretched out on two of the three sleeping shelves racked on each wall. The uppermost shelf, on the far wall, was unoccupied. Maguire shone the lamp to give some light as they crossed the floor, jumbled with baggage and boots. Molly tripped and nearly fell but Fergus grabbed her arm and steadied her.

"I'm so tired, man, past the end of the world."

He helped her step up onto a German trunk from which she could climb into the sleeping shelf. He climbed up after her.

"Safe ashore? Good night."

Maguire shut the door softly, and the room went black. Struggling out of their coats, they knocked their heads on the ceiling and bumped against each other while struggling to spread a blanket over the straw pallet. She bundled Muldoon's coat to use for a pillow while Fergus untied his boots and strangers asleep sighed and moaned in the dense, sweet darkness. He finally got the boots off. Dropping them on the floor, he stretched out on the straw pallet, spooning alongside her.

"Molly?"

"Sleep, man, sleep." Her voice was thick. She was already half asleep.

He felt alert and excited, smelling her skin, feeling her heat.

Longing burns down fear, consumes hesitation, ignores danger. You wish to lie open as a field.

But people can't be truthful, not all at once.

THE HALL where they were fed breakfast was noisy with Germans speaking their storm of a tongue. Girls brought kettles of porridge from the kitchen and German graybeards at the head of each table served it out while Maguire and his porter went around the hall pouring tea. Fergus felt his body relaxing in the German noise. He felt safe in the hubbub. He liked the salt smell of their leather clothes.

When breakfast was over a tobacco pouch went around the table and all the German men helped themselves, stuffing the carved ivory bowls of their pipes. He was offered the pouch and filled his clay pipe, then passed the tobacco along to Molly. A candle came around for a light.

The German smoke was mild and sweet. "Better gear than what you used to sell, Moll."

"That old railway shag was nasty goods. How it crackled though. You could smoke my stuff under water — stop scowling at me, you old hare!" She stuck her tongue out at a German woman staring at her across the table.

None of the German women were smoking.

Eyes half shut, Molly leaned forward, elbows resting on the table, puffing contentedly. "You know what I am wishing, Fergus?"

"No."

"Wishing I had my pack of cards. German farmers, man . . . Pharaoh could make some money here."

"Have some tea, miss." Maguire was standing behind them, holding a big tin jug.

"Tea, tea!" Molly cried. "Oh mister, you are a very gift. Tell me, where do we go to buy our Quebecs?"

He filled their noggins with tea. "Go down the Goree piazza, where they used to buy and sell the blacks. All the brokers selling Quebecs hang loaves of bread outside, meaning the vessels they sell follow British navigation laws, which isn't much — a pound of food per day per passenger, ship's biscuit or Indian meal with bugs. The fast packets and the Yankees, of course, feed much better. Try Crawford's on the Goree. They will not cheat you any worse than the others."

The Goree

PASSAGE BROKER SHOPS FLANKED the Goree, with their loaves of bread dangling from poles. Long queues of emigrants extended from each shop and snaked around the piazza. They asked for Crawford's, and joined a queue of ragged, wet emigrants who looked straight off the docks and the Irish steamers.

The boy standing directly in front of them said he was going for Cattarackwee, in Upper Canada, where his brother owned a farm.

"Has he any cattle?" Molly asked.

"Cattle I cannot say, but he owns one hundred sixty acres, some in wheat, some barley, some in timber. He is feeding pigs and selling off his timber and a kind of honey they draw from trees."

"How will you reach there?"

"Steamer, three or four days up the river from Quebec."

"Three or four days!"

The boy nodded. "They've so much land in America they don't know what to do with it, they give it away. It's not like Ireland at all."

"I want a piece!" Molly gave an excited little skip.

"Ah yes, well," the boy said somberly. "Myself as well. Hungry for land. What I wouldn't do. My brother will be surprised to see me, I'll tell you."

"I have heard they die of the snow at Quebec," said an old brown-faced woman.

"Don't tell me so, mother." Molly laughed. "I've heard enough bitter news. Don't wish me no more cold!"

"Wish it or not, what's coming will come."

It was midday before they got inside Crawford's shop. The walls were slathered with shipping bills. Three clerks at wickets were selling passages.

After waiting in line another quarter of an hour they finally stood before one of the clerks.

"We want a passage for Quebec or St. John." Molly held the money, rolled up and knotted in a handkerchief.

"I've got *Laramie* sailing for Quebec tomorrow."

"How much?"

"Steerage?"

"What is that?"

"You aren't requiring cabin passage, I suppose?" the clerk sneered.

Neither of them could grasp what he meant. "Listen, man," Molly said nervously, "we want tickets for Quebec —"

"Steerage fare, three pounds a head."

"How many days across?"

"Long as it takes. Come along, Mary, let's see your money now."

Molly untied the handkerchief and spilled out the coins. The clerk counted them briskly then swept them into a drawer and pushed two slips of blue paper across, their tickets. "See the surgeon outside, have them stamped. Next!"

Going back out, they joined another queue, standing behind the old woman. It was cold and windy on the open square.

The surgeon was a plump young man wearing horse boots with mahogany leather tops, lolling in an armchair dragged out from one of the broker shops. Stepping forward one by one, emigrants showed him their tickets and opened their mouths. The surgeon glanced at each one, asked a question or two, and nodded to pass them.

His clerk, sitting at a portable table, stamped their tickets.

"Thinks he won't let fever aboard," the old woman grumbled. "Only he's not looking very hard is he?"

"What if he won't stamp me, Fergus?" Molly looked worried.

"You're not ill. Don't worry. He's turning no one away."

"He trusts himself to see the humors, but he can't," the old woman said. "Fine fellows like him never can."

"What if he won't?"

"But there's nothing wrong with you."

"You'd leave me here, you'd go without me."

"I would not." He was shocked.

"I'll die in bloody Liverpool."

"No, Molly, you'll pass fine. Everyone is."

The surgeon had one leg hooked over the arm of his chair. He kept wetting a handkerchief from a flask and dabbing at his upper lip.

"How delicate he is! Frightened of smells!" the old woman said. "How can he know fever or sickness without catching the scent?"

"I reckon he only gets paid for them he passes — do you think that's so, Fergus?"

"Yes." He had never seen her so jittery.

"In Derry if they thought you had fever, they would leave you under the hedge."

They were nearing the head of the line, and people in front of them were removing cloaks and jackets. When her turn came the old woman stepped forward, smiling and nodding at the surgeon.

"Are you feeling quite well, mother?"

"Blessed I am, going for America."

"Hold out your tongue. Passed. Next. Come along, miss."

Molly hesitated and Fergus gave her a little push. The surgeon glanced at her. "Are you feeling quite well? Show your tongue."

She seemed unable to respond.

"Come, come," the surgeon said impatiently. "Show your tongue or I can't pass you!"

She didn't step forward and didn't open her mouth. The surgeon snorted and got to his feet. The old woman, having her ticket stamped by the clerk, glanced back at Molly. "Come across, come across," she called out, "don't fear the country of the waves! The day has its feet that will see you on the other side."

Frowning, Molly stepped forward. "Now hold out your tongue!" the surgeon said. She stood stoically while he peered into her mouth, then unbuttoned the top of her gown and roughly pushed up her sleeves, searching for fever rash.

You look at a girl and it's like seeing a road. *My life*, you think, *here is my life* — curling away into distance, far beyond what you can see.

"Passed." The surgeon sat down with a grunt. "Next! Come along, man. Are you feeling quite well?"

Fergus stepped forward. "I am."

"Hold out your tongue."

"Passed. Next!"

FOR TEN shillings they bought a battered sea chest at a chandler's shop on the Goree, along with three pounds of tobacco and some gray felt stuffing for extra warmth. Molly bargained for knives and spoons at a tinker's cart in the Vauxhall, along with a pair of tin dishes, two noggins, and a mended kettle.

Packing everything into the chest, they lugged it to Maguire's, fighting off runners trying to seize it for a fare. Halfway there it started to rain, cold rain sliding down their necks. When they finally reached the lodging house it was noisy with a new set of German emigrants in from Hull. "One hundred twenty," Maguire said proudly, "all going for New Orleans and Missouri."

They were surrounded by Germans with mountains of baggage, the women with their squirming, red-faced babies. Shivering in her wet cloak, Molly looked white and exhausted.

"The supper is almost ready. Take off that cloak, miss, come get a piece of the fire." Maguire took them each by the arm, leading them into the parlor. "I'm burning coal, it's like burning money." There were Germans on every chair and bench, and some sitting on trunks, smoking their enormous white pipes. Children were playing on the floor. Mothers nursing infants. A coal fire buzzed at each end of the long room.

"Let the fire warm your bones." Maguire helped Molly out of her cloak, settled her on the bench closest to the fire, then took the cloak to the kitchen to dry.

"Are you feeling all right, Moll?"

Rubbing her hands and knees, she was gazing at the coals. "Cold," she whispered. "Cold."

Maguire returned with a mug of lemon tea for Molly and a blanket he wrapped around her shoulders. "There, better, is it not?"

"Yes. Better."

"Don't let anyone push you away from the fire. Soak up the warm." He beckoned to Fergus. "You — come with me."

Out in the kitchen, the landlord indicated a pile of supplies on the table. "These provisions I have set aside. You'll find you can't live on ship rations."

"How much does it cost?"

"Turnips, carrots. Here are onions, a few apples, leeks. A jar of whiskey. A cheese — cut off what rots, and eat the rest. Some hard bread. Plum preserve in this jar. Honey. Salt and sugar in those sacks. Juice of lime."

"How much, mister?"

"All this you can have. My gift. I won't charge you nothing. No I won't, God help me. I'm rich enough to spare."

"Thank you, mister."

"Only see to that girl of yours. Do you remember *mi an ocrais*, the hungry month?"

Fergus nodded.

"The old spuds is always finished weeks before you lift the new. Well, your crossing may have its hungry month, so save what you can. If they feed you the yellow meal for rations, make sure it is cooked soft or it'll kill you with the gripes. Keep the berth fresh as you can. Bathe whenever possible. Change the straw. And pack everything with felt, and don't let her freeze to death. What ship?"

Fergus showed the landlord their tickets. "Do you know *Laramie*?"

"No. Ships in the timber trade are old scows, they're not famous. Sailing when?"

"Tomorrow from Princes Dock."

"You be on the quay at daybreak, boy. There's early tide tomorrow."

"The clerk says she won't sail before midday."

"He don't know and don't care — a clerk will say anything to get you along. Any master collecting his crew in Liverpool will try to slip out on the first tide, before they all change their minds and run away. No, you be on the quay, bright and early. Watch that girl of yours! She's fragile!" Maguire gave him a push. "Go in and sit with her — I pays for fire, it's a crime not to use it. See she gets plenty to eat."

AS HE came out of the kitchen, Fergus saw Molly heading for the stairs. "Don't you want any supper?" he called.

"No."

Bewildered, he followed her upstairs and along the chilly corridor. She went into their room.

It was much colder in the upper reaches than down in the parlor, by Maguire's opulent fire. The sleeping shelves were empty — everyone was downstairs.

Unbuttoning her gown in the dim light, she stepped out of it, letting it fall on the floor.

"What's wrong, Molly? Do you have a chill?"

"No." Wearing her linen shift, she climbed up into the crib.

Worried, he picked up her damp gown from the floor. She had wrapped herself up in a blanket. She didn't look flushed or feverish. She wasn't shivering anymore.

The supper bell began clanging downstairs.

"Come downstairs, Molly, get a bite of food. It's warmer down there. We'll feed you up."

"No."

"I'll bring you something, then."

"I don't want it. Just go away."

"Well, I'll put your gown by the fire —"

"Go away."

"Molly —"

"Go away! I need my thoughts."

EATING BLOODY beef with the German farmers, he decided that she was afraid of the sea. Of course she was. That was her trouble. It was only natural. She feared the crossing.

Nothing human in the sea.

The fear was in him too, but he had managed it by not thinking of it directly, not handling it in his mind. He looked around at the farmers and wives and children eating. Cheerful they seemed, blithe, despite the awful journey before them all.

He remembered the old man on *Ruth* sobbing after they had lost sight of land. And that crossing had been one day at sea, not forty.

WHEN HE brought her supper on a tray she was asleep, or pretending to sleep, facing the wall. Leaving the tray, he went back downstairs and spent an hour in front of the fire, mixing ashes with kitchen fat, rubbing the paste into their boots. Working coat after coat of grease into the pliant leather with his hands.

He wished he might rub her with a healing wax, something to protect her, to keep her warm and safe.

When he came back upstairs she hadn't touched the tray. Germans were preparing for bed, rustling their heavy clothes, women undressing underneath cloaks, boots dropping on the floor. People sighing in the dark as they settled in bed.

She didn't move when he climbed in beside her but lay facing the wall, with her back to him, her little shoulders, frail white neck.

The last candle was blown out. Soon he could hear the long, rolling breaths of the people asleep.

Longing burns down fear, consumes hesitation, ignores danger. You would die for a passion, easy — for a scented, gluey cunt — but you want something more from a girl, and can't name what it is.

HE AWOKE in the middle of the night. She was asleep but her body was burning, her shift soaked with sweat.

The air in the crowded room was moist with the breath of people unconscious.

He thought of the ship waiting. How dark was the ocean, forty days out?

It sounded brave, saying you would go for America.

He didn't feel so brave.

After a while he climbed down carefully from the crib, making as little noise as possible, and picked a path through the clothes and luggage on the floor, taking care not to awaken the sleeping farmers and their families.

THERE WERE no Germans in the corridors. In darkness he felt his way carefully, and came down the stairs. The only light in the house came from an oil lamp glowing in the little vestibule where Maguire's night porter was snoring on his bench.

Fergus went quietly to the boxroom and tried the door. It was locked. Going back to the vestibule, he lifted the key from its hook without disturbing the porter's snores, then returned to the storeroom and unlocked the door. After lubricating the iron hinges with spit, he eased the door ajar.

The storeroom racks were crowded with canvas sacks, bundles of tools, sea chests, casks, wooden crates the size of coffins. The crates were nailed shut and the chests fastened with locks and iron straps or bound with knotted rope. Canvas sacks, lumpy and heavy with the goods inside, were sewn shut.

He found their sea chest, opened it, and took out the steel knife. Groping at the canvas sacks, he tried guessing what might be inside. Slitting one open, he began pulling out woolen shirts and woolen stockings. The soft German clothing smelled clean. Some of it was wrapped around books. Laying the books aside, he began stuffing the woolens into their sea chest.

Slitting open another sack, he found a set of embroidered blankets wrapped around jars of pickled onions. He packed the blankets and the onions into their chest, then slit open another sack and found a great yellow wheel of cheese wrapped in yards of fine cloth. He added the cheese to their chest and began rearranging the sacks so the room would appear undisturbed. Locking the door, he replaced the key without awakening the porter and went upstairs quietly.

Climbing in beside her, he felt new and strange. He put his arm around her, his hand on her little round belly, pushing his leg between her warm thighs.

PART V

A Ship I Am

A Ship I Am

IT WAS STILL DARK when Maguire summoned them. Pulling on their boots and coats, they went downstairs quietly in the dark. The Germans were asleep.

In the kitchen the landlord gave them slices of bread smeared with butter and honey. The night porter was still asleep when Maguire took the key from its hook and unlocked the box room. Fergus slung the canvas grip over his shoulder, and he and Molly each took one handle of the chest.

Maguire held open the front door, saying "God be with you," then shutting it firmly the moment they were outside.

It was cold. They struggled along the glistening street, lugging the chest between them.

"It seems so very heavy. We ought to hire a runner, Fergus."

"Waste of money. We can do it ourselves."

"No, it's too heavy, I'm going to bust my arm."

As soon as she saw a runner lurking in a doorway she hired him to bring their baggage to Princes Dock. Hurling the chest and the grip into his barrow, the fellow set off at top speed and they hurried after, afraid to lose sight of him. The white mist was crammed in the alleys, and Fergus tasted the salt of the sea.

WAITING IN the pack of emigrants on the quay at Princes Dock, he told himself that no matter what hand reached out for the rest of them, he and Molly would survive. Their boots were greased, their clothes stuffed with felt, extra woolens in the sea chest, excellent stores; he and Molly would preserve themselves. They could live in the coldest thoughts, in the dark bottom of themselves. Whatever was necessary. Stone partners they were, tough and hard. They would survive.

THEY STOOD all morning on the quay, guarding their baggage and watching dockers humping sacks and barrels aboard *Laramie*. The dock basin was surrounded by warehouses, "built of iron, with no lumber in their works, not a twig, so they never will burn down," the Cattarackwee boy informed them. "Full of treasure. Packed."

"What sort of treasure?" Molly wanted to know.

"Everything. Cotton, sugar, black men, gold — but here we are, here's the push!" The boy eagerly picked up his satchel. An officer was paying off dockers who were quitting the ship. As the last man came off, the crowd surged for the gangway and a fight broke out. The crowd kept pressing from behind. They were getting squeezed, and Fergus could hear small children caught in the crush moaning like cattle.

A few people began heaving their baggage over the ship's rail and clambering aboard. An officer in a black suit and an old man observed from the afterdeck without trying to stop them.

"Come on, no use waiting like sheep," Molly said.

Dozens of passengers were now scrambling over the sides, passing baggage and hoisting children across.

Dragging their chest to the edge of the quay, they hoisted it onto the ship's rail, then scrambled over themselves and lifted it down. They were aboard.

The deck was a tangle of ropes, hatches, spars, and boats. Passengers anxious to get below were shoving and fighting at the head of a hatchway while sailors perched in the rigging laughed at them.

"Come on, Fergus, we must claim a berth, and we'll only get what we fight for."

They joined the crowd at the hatchway fighting to get onto the steep ladder that led to the 'tween deck hold. A chest had been dropped and was smashed open at the foot of the ladder where the owners were frantically trying to salvage their goods, which were being trampled and crushed by the passengers pouring down. Molly raced forward to claim a berth while he dragged their chest over the wooden floor. The 'tween deck stank of mildew, and iron rust, and was fitted with berths, three tiers on each side. It was dark except for the daylight that fell down the hatch.

He found her lying in a slatted berth, hands clasped under her head, pipe jabbed in her mouth. When she saw him, she drummed her heels violently on the slats, taking the unlit pipe from her lips. "America!" she whispered.

He smiled and sat down, then stretched himself out beside her. Strange to think they were afloat. The ship felt amazingly solid, without any sway or roll.

"Does it suit you, Moll?"

Their hips were touching.

"Man, this is it," she said warmly. "Waited for this all my fucking days."

"Is he a ribbonman, Father?"

Fergus looked out at a little girl who had stopped at the berth and was staring at them.

"Why don't you ask him?" Her father was dragging a sea chest across the deck.

"Are you a ribbonman?"

Fergus shook his head. There was a boy, the same size as the girl, and their mother. "Deirdre, be still," the woman said.

"They are very curious on ribbonmen," the man said. "Every unhappiness in our part of the world is laid to ribbonmen, never the landlord —"

"Stop it, Martin," the woman said sharply. She wore the red cloak of a country woman.

The man wore town clothes — a hairy brown suit, more or less clean. "Coole is my name, Martin Coole. We'll take the lease above, if you haven't any objection."

"We haven't."

Tall and stooped, he reminded Fergus of a riverine bird, an egret or heron. His wife was already lifting blankets from her chest. The man gave Fergus his hand, then Molly. "There's something I'm wondering. Perhaps you know the answer. How is it that Irish beasts are shipped for England, while Irish people starve?"

"Martin, don't!" the woman said. She was spreading blankets on the two upper berths.

"It's a crime somewhere." The deck was too low for him; Coole had to slouch awkwardly, neck bent. "These are close arrangements, very close indeed. How do they propose to feed two hundred souls? Yellow meal has to be cooked soft. Kill you otherwise with bloody flux. Where are the stoves for two hundred people? What about water? I counted but sixty-one casks taken aboard and I'm sure —"

"Martin, don't start. Calm yourself."

"Have *you* seen any arrangements in the way of cooking?" Coole turned to Fergus. "Stoves, grates? Seen any kettles big enough for two hundred?"

"I have not."

"I really can't think —"

"Get ahold of yourself, Martin! Think of your children."

"Yes, yes, yes. The children." Extending both arms, Coole flapped them in a strange, nervous gesture, again resembling a stalky, riverine bird.

"Think of Carlo and Deirdre. Get ahold of yourself for their sakes, and don't go to pieces now."

Coole twitched his arms, shook out his wrists and big hands, raised each foot and shook out each leg — then shook his entire body, from his neck to heels, with extraordinary vigor, like a wet dog.

Suddenly there was shouting from the main deck, and feet rushing overhead.

"Sinking!" Coole gasped.

"No, mister," Molly said. "I reckon they are throwing off. Leaving, it is. Come on, man!" She elbowed Fergus. "Let's go up and see."

THE BREEZE tasted sharp after the rottenness below. Girls with trays slung around their necks strolled about the deck selling oranges, nuts, and pocket mirrors.

Fergus watched as the gangway was hauled aboard. Sailors dragged in the dripping lines unleashed from bollards on the quay, coiling with frantic neatness and singing weirdly as they worked.

He studied the men up on the afterdeck. A man in a cowhide jacket — the river pilot, he overheard a passenger say — was giving orders to a sailor manning the wheel. A man in a black coat clutched a brass tube in his hand. Next to him an old man wearing a shaggy fur coat stood with his hands clasped behind his back.

A dozen sailors were singing as they worked a machine, winding a thick, wet cable that was warping *Laramie* off the quay. The taut cable drew her sluggishly across the basin toward the water gate, where a footbridge had been raised so she could slip out into the river.

Passengers arriving too late for boarding had raced for the water gate, hoping to leap aboard as she slid through, but it was a terrifying jump. As the ship passed through the gate, he saw the old woman from the Goree in the cluster of anxious faces. A few men and boys made the leap, caught the rail, and were dragged aboard, but others were hesitating, too apprehensive to try.

"Come across, mother!" Molly screamed to the old woman. "Country of the waves! Come across!"

Without hesitating further, the old woman pitched her bundle then leapt across. They caught her by the arms, dragging her in over the rail as *Laramie* nosed into the river and began swinging about when the current caught her bow.

Wheezing and coughing, the old woman pounded her chest and spat voraciously.

"You're all right are you?" Molly asked. "That was a fair jump."

"I'm old but I'm fleet." The old woman pulled out a clay pipe she carried in her hair. "Spare me a pinch of backer, daughter? Never dreamed I could fly."

A STEAM tug was towing *Laramie* out through the busy traffic of steamers, ships, and barges.

Sailors armed with pikes went below, hunting stowaways, while the emigrants were herded up a pair of ladders and squeezed into ship's narrow foredeck. Sailors stood guard at the ladders and a clerk from Crawford's shop began calling out names, checking them off against a passenger list.

They were packed so tightly on the peak that people were lifting children up onto the rails.

"Oh man, this is awful business, I don't like this at all," Molly gasped.

Never would he have pressed cattle so close. To distract himself from the grasping panic he could feel rising in his throat he stared up through masts, spars, and rigging to the white sky.

Can you control the song of fear in your head? It never really goes away. You're wound with it, like a French ticker.

After hearing their names and displaying their tickets, they were allowed to climb back down to the main deck, where they stood along the crowded rail. Tugs were buzzing up and down the river. Paddle wheels flashing, iron muzzles smoking. Laramie's bow sliced across the Mersey ferry's wake, a track of yellow fizz. The ferry was packed with red cattle and tramps, some heading for the railway works, probably; some for Murdoch's cutting.

The sailors who'd gone below hunting stowaways returned empty-handed. The river was opening, wide and green, marled with whitecaps. Their bow began to rise and fall, and some people were seasick on the deck or over the side. Looking up, he saw sailors walking out the yards, high above the deck, bare feet on footropes. The sails were still bundled in long white canvas rolls. Seabirds floated over the ship, crying bitterly.

The breeze smelled of salt and kelp.

The ship ahead of *Laramie* dropped her towline and filled her sails, clouds of pale canvas blooming as she started to roll.

Im long mé méasaim, he thought. A ship I am.

A little boat was maneuvering alongside. One of the boatmen tossed a line that was caught by a sailor and the orange-seller girls began going over the side on a rope ladder, dropping neatly into the boat. He watched Crawford's clerk swinging down to take his place. The little boat fell off, raising a red triangle of sail and making for the Birkenhead shore.

"Good-bye, old England, you fucker," Molly said. "Good-bye, iron men, hard roads, bad sleeps, sickness."

He looked at her profile, small nose, strong chin. She was gall, she was bold. Her warm skin he loved, her scent, her clear, tough directness of thought. She was passion for staying alive.

"Good-bye, old Kelly," he heard her say. "Good-bye, you heartless fucking Muldoon."

Laramie's yards were braced, the sails filled with a cracking sound, and the ship began to surge. The towline was cast away and passengers began cheering wildly as the tug fell off. *Laramie* began to roll and the cheering turned to terrified screaming as the world dipped. He heard Molly whoop for joy.

Cutting loose the old, the everything. The country of the waves now, green and wild.

The Poison Cook

THE WIND WAS COLD. Molly soon went below but he remained on deck, fascinated by flocks of ships coming in under sail, eagerly crowding for the mouth of the Mersey.

When he finally went below he found her sitting on their berth while the old woman placed drops of tincture on her tongue, using a straw. Mrs. Coole, hands on hips, stood watching. The contents of the old woman's bundle — bunches of dried herbs, little jars and bottles — were spread out on the berth.

"What is it? What are you feeding her?"

"A healing potion. Medicine for women."

Molly's face puckered from the taste. The old woman touched her forehead. "Now let the dose find her way in."

Molly opened her eyes. "Tastes rough, mother."

"It stings. Yes it does."

"Here." Molly handed her a pinch of tobacco for payment, then lay back, and the old woman began gathering up her goods.

"In my own country of Faha, I am well known," she boasted. "I am Brighid of Faha, you ask them in my country. *Cailleach feasa* they say."

Wise woman. He sat down on the berth. "Are you ill?" he asked Molly.

"I am," she whispered. "I have the grumps. But improving."

"It's the ship rocking, perhaps. You'll get used to it."

"Perhaps — oh mother!" Molly suddenly groaned, clutching her belly.

"Let the potion do its work," Brighid of Faha said, taking her hand. "We must dose you every few hours. If you wish to help her, man," she told Fergus, "rub her feet and ankles. Keep her warm down there; heat brings down the blood."

The ship was tossing and swaying and he could hear passengers being violently sick, the stench starting to bite the air.

Untying her boots, he began to chafe her ankles and feet. Molly's eyes were shut; her face glistened.

"In my country of Faha they come to see me," the old woman was saying. "I have a blue bottle and can see ahead what hasn't happened if you pay me a shilling, or two pounds good butter. And I have the healing stones to cure the pig —"

"Ignorant old witch! An old poison cook is what you are!" Mrs. Coole snapped.

"Oh don't say so, missus! Don't speak so harsh — you don't know me."

THEY STOOD in a queue while Mr. Blow, the master, distributed rations: half a pound of yellow meal, half a pound of ship's biscuit, and a piece of salt beef, with two quarts of fresh water pumped into their pails or kettles. Children received half rations.

The old woman stood behind them. "You must soak the awful beef in fresh water or the salt will burn your mouth," she warned. "Blisters the insides, and you'll shit yellow sprue."

Coole was ahead of them in the queue. "What arrangements for cooking?" Fergus heard him ask the master.

"We ain't a packet. See for yourselves. You'll have to rough it."

"Yes," Coole persisted, "but where are the stoves?"

"Two cabooses to be set on deck. You'll have one hour at morning and another at evening to cook your mush, weather permitting. If I see any fuss about the fires, I'll have them doused."

"Two hundred souls aboard, and only two stoves?"

"You watch your tone with me, you damned Irish rebel, or you shan't have no fire at all. Step away now. Next!"

* * *

AS SOON as they smelled smoke, passengers seized their pans and kettles and raced up the ladder to the main deck where the two cabooses were smoking. Wooden boxes, the size and shape of coffins, lined with bricks and set with iron grills, they had been stuffed with coal and lit by a sailor carrying a pan of red embers from the galley.

Passengers mobbed the stoves, fighting for space to cook their food. He was ready to join the fight but Molly touched his arm.

"No use, man, you'd only get spilled."

Sailors were laughing at them. Kettles were knocked over, yellow meal and water sloshing on the deck.

"I could sort out this riot in ten seconds if they'd let me." Molly sounded frustrated.

"They'd never let a woman," Mrs. Coole said.

"Get back from the stoves!" The master appeared at the afterdeck rail with a speaking trumpet. "Step away!"

Sailors were lowering buckets over the side and hauling them up full of seawater. As they dashed the coals, yellow steam blanketed the deck and the riot broke up, people coughing and wiping their eyes and searching for their children.

"Get below! I'll keep you below like a cargo of niggers if you won't behave!"

Sailors swinging tarry rope-ends were starting to drive people below when Molly called up to the master on the afterdeck. "Let me organize the rations mister! I can tell you how it's done."

The master was young, with raw pink skin and yellow hair. He glared at her. "Don't screech at me, you harridan; I know how to handle an Irish mob. They'll serve up very meek when they're hungry enough."

"All they want is fairness." Her voice was just firm enough to carry. "Divide us into shanties — call six berths a shanty. Cook-of-the-day to collect all rations and do the stirabout for the others. That way you've ten cooks instead of fifty at the stoves, and you won't worry about them knocking into one another and fire being spilled."

"They can live on biscuit and see if they like it!"

"We only want things fair, the rations cooked soft enough. You'd kill us off with raw yellow."

"Go below, miss," the young master said wearily. "I've had enough Irish."

"WE'RE CROSSING, ain't we?" she whispered. "Tell me it's so, man."

"It is. We are."

The old woman had dosed her, and she'd wept for a while, but now seemed hazy, near sleep. He had curtained off their berth with a German blanket. For his supper he'd gnawed weird, thick biscuit and some cheese and onion, but she'd had no stomach for food.

"No sea monsters, man," she whispered. "No storms nor glooms nor ship fever shall stop us."

"No they won't, not now."

"My God," she whispered, "we are rocking for America, Fergus, and nothing in our way."

Nothing, only the sea.

She fell asleep after a while but he couldn't. More than half of those lying in the hold were ill, and the air of sickness was pungent and nasty. He lay looking up at green lumber framing their berth. Berths had been fitted crudely into the real build of the vessel, her solid timbers. Passengers did not belong aboard this ship; they were an afterthought, an encumbrance. The master was disgusted by them. Sailors pushed them about like cattle.

Cattle would have been easier to handle, and might sell at a profit, too.

The slats above his head creaked, and he heard Mrs. Coole being sick in a pail. "Oh give me some water, Martin," she groaned.

"Here, my sweet," Coole whispered. "Let me rub your lips a little."

The air was clogged with stink.

Fergus pushed back the blanket and swung his legs out of the berth. Molly muttered and rolled over and he tucked the blanket carefully around her. The only light came from an oil lamp swinging on a beam as he groped toward the ladder. The floor was slippery, but the motion of the ship thrilled him, its energy and sway; he climbed up through the hatchway and out into a cold, smashing breeze.

The Constant Sky

THE MAIN DECK WAS DESERTED. On the afterdeck, he saw two sailors manning the wheel, and the yellow-haired master prowling back and forth.

Forward, he saw light in the galley, where the crew's rations were cooked. Hoping for a light for his pipe, he started that way.

Inside the little galley shed he found a black man and a little one-eared sailor sitting by a stove, puffing their pipes.

"May I take a light?"

The black man studied him then nodded. Using tongs, Fergus lifted a coal and lit his pipe.

"Did you ship plenty of tobacco, Mike?" the one-eared sailor asked him.

"A little."

"Any liquor, any of that wild Irish fume?"

Fergus shrugged.

"I'll try your backer, so." The sailor held out his pipe. "Come, come, give us a fill."

He gave them each a pinch of tobacco.

Braising in the fiery heat of the stove, they smoked in silence, the noise of the ship filling in for talk. Hemp squeaking. Canvas snug with wind. The splash of the sea, racing along her side.

The men had nothing to say to him and after a while he went out to stand by the bulwark, smoking, looking at the sea.

The world is strangers.

"Can you spare a light?" a voice called.

Looking up, Fergus saw the old man who had earlier been watching the passengers swarm aboard. He was standing at the head of the afterdeck ladder, an old silver man in a fur coat; he looked like an enormous badger.

Fergus drew on his pipe to make it crackle, and the old man swung himself down the ladder, quick and lithe for an old fellow, and came forward to light his cigar. "Thank you."

"Are you the captain?"

The old man shook his head. "Cabin passenger. Out of Ireland, like the rest of you. The master, young Mr. Blow, he's your captain."

The earthy aroma of the cigar recalled the Dragon and faces of girls probably dead.

"They're quite ill down below, I suppose?" the old man asked.

"Yes, some of them."

"Get worse before they get better."

Spray broke over the bow, crackling on the fo'c'sle and deckhouse.

"There will soon be no one left in Ireland, only the crows," the old man said. "All I mind about leaving is having to sell off my horses. Sold off three good animals, to squireens who won't use them well."

They smoked in silence for a while. The sea unsurprised, careless of their existence. A ship was small out here, and Liverpool unreal in memory, as if his experiences there had all been a dream.

"They run wonderful strong ponies, up the country where I'm headed," the old man said suddenly.

"What country is that?"

"The *pays d'en haut*. Athabaska. A rich man, a hunting chief, will have a hundred buffalo runners. Not so grand as the Irish hunter, but wiry and rugged. Plenty of heart."

"I had to sell a horse myself."

"Yes, well. The world is cruel to horses." The man drew on his cigar.

"Good long bones he had," Fergus said, thinking of the blue. "I wish he don't end up back on the railway contracts. I'd rather have shot him than think he was back there."

"When I was at Fort Edmonton, war parties used to come up the river, to barter with us. The Blackfoot steal the best horses from a thousand miles around. Called us *old women*, for I wouldn't send apprentices out to trade with them, but made the hunting chiefs step into the palisade, one at a time, leaving their guns and knives outside."

Stories always started this way, suddenly, and set within a strange world. Patience is required, to let the stories unroll.

This is how people explain their lives.

"Ponies, pemmican, and slaves was what they had for trade. The Blackfoot aren't trappers. They make no fur, theirs is not a beaver country. And their young men — the brave dogs — despise to hunt anything but buffalo. A Blackfoot brave dog won't kill if he can't kill from horseback."

None of it was clear — black dogs, on horseback? — but he kept his ears open, listening.

"The slaves were captures — Cree, Crow, Kiowa. Sometime I'd buy 'em on the Company account, just to spare their lives. Buy 'em cheap — a few grains of powder. Bought my son for some powder and ten pounds of lead."

"You bought your son?"

The old man nodded. "A brave dog has no use for prisoners. No use for most trade goods. Oh, their women like a kettle. English woolen blankets they demand as presents. But all a brave dog cares for is a good gun, and only the best English makes will do. No trade muskets for them. A good gun, powder, lead for bullets, a little brandy. You'll never see better horsemen than the grass nations. Ride rings around the dragoons. My boy running buffalo at the full gallop would spit the bullets into his gun."

He struggled to get a purchase on the old man's story. "Blackfoot . . . ribbon-men, are they?"

The old man grunted. "An Irishman might call them so."

"Is it the landlords they are after?"

"No, they own their country themselves, or think they do." The old man puffed quietly for a few moments. "Where is it you're heading for?"

"America."

"Anyplace in particular? Any people?"

"No."

"William Ormsby is my name. My son was Daniel. Such as we called him anyway. His name in Blackfoot was Many Gray Horses. His Crow name was the Constant Sky. Well, good night, good luck." Swinging up the ladder with some agility, he disappeared on the afterdeck.

Fergus remained at the rail, watching the sea slashing along the hull.

America you thought of in strident ignorance as a summer country, booley pasture in the mountains.

You saw yourself working the stream, spear in hand.

Striking the great fish as it rose for the light.

Cailleach Feasa

IN THE MORNING, with the first sliver of light falling in the hold, the little one-eared sailor came halfway down the ladder and informed them they were to divide themselves into messes. "Orders of Mr. Blow. Six berths to a mess, one cook-of-the-day from each mess to collect the rations." Hanging on to the ladder, the sailor peered around the dim hold, where most of the passengers lay helpless in their berths, too sick to think of food. "Poor old mikes — but you shall feel better when we're out of this rocking sea and into the western ocean. Anyone wishing to do a little trading, of tobacco say, or spirits of any sort — see me in the fo'c'sle. Nimrod Blampin is my name."

Molly's upper lip was raw and flaky, and there were dark clouds, almost bruises, around each eye. She was too weak to climb out of the berth.

"Wish to die, man," she whispered.

"No you won't, sweetheart."

The blanket he'd rigged for a curtain was suddenly pulled aside, and the old woman peered in on them. "Get away, man! Let me see her."

Mrs. Coole, arms crossed, stood with Fergus as they watched the old woman run her hands over Molly, feeling her throat, breasts, belly, under her arms. Molly writhed and groaned.

"Drink this now, lovely." Removing the stopper from a little bottle, Brighid tapped amber liquid into a spoon.

"Fergus?"

"Here I am."

"I'm not well, man, not well, I've got the grumps."

"You'll feel better soon, though."

"An old woman of my country would put poison in a well, then you must pay her to cure your cattle," Mrs. Coole said loudly. "When the farmers found out, they wanted to hang her."

Ignoring them, the old woman raised Molly's head.

"This old ship is rocking me to death, it is!" Molly whispered.

"Take this now." Brighid held the spoonful to her lips.

"I want to walk on the ground —"

"There, there," the old woman crooned, "just a drop more."

"I want to walk on the ground!"

COOLE'S SON slipped off the ladder and fell down into the hold, giving a scream that broke off abruptly when he landed. Passengers gathered around the little boy, lying on the 'tween deck, perfectly still.

"Is he dead?"

"Does he breathe?"

When Fergus knelt and touched him the boy's chest moved, a kind of sigh.

Onlookers parted, letting through Mrs. Coole. Stunned, she knelt by her son.

"Better move him to a berth," one of the onlookers said. "If it was my boy, missus, I'd wrap him warm and keep him still."

Martin Coole stood by, gulping and wringing his long, thin hands.

Forcing her way through the crowd, Brighid knelt and began running her fingertips over the lifeless boy. "A cold, wet sheet is what you want," a woman passenger advised. "Wrap him up tight and if he still won't come around you'd better bleed him."

Paying no attention, Brighid continued her examination while Mrs. Coole hovered anxiously. When Brighid finished she stood up with a grunt and pushed her way out through the ring of onlookers.

"Look at his color," the woman passenger was saying. "Wrap him in cold wet cloth, missus, and carry him up and give him a dose of the cold air."

Mrs. Coole kept stroking her son's arms, and a moment later Brighid returned, shaking a brown bottle. Pulling out the stopper, she began waving the bottle under the boy's nose. Fergus could see her lips moving in incantation.

Poetry, he thought. A spell.

"You won't revive him with whispers! His blood wants stirring! You ought to bleed him."

The boy's eyelids suddenly fluttered. The crowd murmured.

The boy stirred. His eyes flapped open and he looked around wildly. Taking his hand, Brighid kissed it.

"A sore head, and a bruise — he'll have the flowers of June on his hip for a while, but nothing broken." She nodded at Mrs. Coole, who gathered up the frightened child and hugged him tight, her shoulders shaking with ugly sobs.

"GOOD FOR her, the damned old juice," Molly said. She was twisting and grimacing while Fergus rubbed her belly and legs to ease her cramps. "She'll sell her gunk for a good price now."

ALL DAY *Laramie* had been caught in a pack of ships moving restlessly up and down a mountainous coast, stalled by rough seas and light winds. He stood on the main deck looking at the snowy peaks. The old man, Ormsby, was on the afterdeck, peering through a brass tube.

"What country is it?" Fergus called.

"North Wales."

The railway country.

"The last of Britain we'll set eyes on," Ormsby said, "and good riddance."

Good-bye to you, poor horses.

If they dropped her into the waves, what would become of her?

She'd have been better off staying in the camp.

She'd have been better off with Muldoon, safer.

Hearing children's voices up in the bow, chanting the ABCs, he headed forward, feeling the wet smack of wind on his face. The voices came from the windlass housing, a small shelter on the foredeck, exposed on the lee side.

Underneath, protected from rain and wind, Coole was sitting with long legs crossed and a red book in his hands. His two children were perched on coils of rope. Coole was giving them a lesson.

Fergus recognized the red book, the *Dublin Universal Speller*. The old Waterloo hero, his occasional schoolmaster on the mountain, had owned a copy.

His rare days as a scholar he had loved — walking across the mountain, carrying a penny for the lesson and a lump of turf for the schoolroom fire. The Waterloo hero had told them stories of battles and smoke, Frenchmen, cavalry on enormous horses, cannon shining gold in the sun.

Coole's boy and girl finished chanting through their letters, then Coole passed the book to the girl. She started reading aloud in a piping voice that didn't carry well across the deck. Coole beckoned to Fergus, but he shook his head and took a step back.

He watched the little girl finish the passage then pass the book to her brother, who began reading aloud.

He kept watching them until he heard the bos'n's whistle, the signal that daily rations were being distributed. Then he turned away, heading for the hatchway to collect their water cans and kettle. He yearned to read; it was another hunger.

What you wanted would keep you going.

"THAT BEEF will be fresh enough now," Brighid said. "Go ahead, cut it up."

The salt beef had been soaking in a pail of fresh water. Pouring off the water, he started cutting up the meat and adding it to the stirabout cooking in a kettle on the grate.

Looking up, he watched a gang of sailors run straight up the ratlines.

Laramie had finally caught the wind. The companion ships had fallen off, and they had the green sea to themselves.

Did the sailors hear commands the bos'n and the master were shouting, or did they work through a coordinated feeling of their own, a sense of wind and terror?

Brighid tossed another handful of herbs into a simmering can. She wasn't cook-of-the-day, but no one had tried keeping her from the cabooses. They respected, even feared, her powers.

"What are you cooking there, mother?"

"Syrup."

"What's it for?"

"To calm the passions of the womb."

Like many old women, she spoke obliquely and seemed to cultivate an air of mystery. She'd sold the Cooles a salve for their boy's bruises, made with crushed herbs and mutton fat she had from the galley cook.

He gave the kettle another stir.

Sailors called the yellow mush *slop-and-grindings* and said the passengers' salt beef was *monkey's paws*, not fit for Christians to eat. But the crew's beef came from the same casks and their stirabout — called *burgoo* — was also made with yellow meal, the only difference being it had molasses in it, and was cooked for them by the black man.

Floors were *decks*. Walls were *bulkheads*. Ropes were *sheets*, *halyards*, or *lines*, depending on function.

The *booby hatch* led down to the passenger hold, which the crew called the *'tween deck*. Passengers' cribs were *berths*. The crew slept in *hammocks* strung from beams in the *fo'c'sle*, a dank hole at the front of the ship — *before the mast* — that was entered by a *scuttle*.

Other words and phrases were still mysterious, but he had resolved to learn their meanings by listening and watching, not by asking.

Men dislike being questioned. They sense you're trying to rob them of something.

Looking up, he watched sailors walking out along the yards, treading on footropes they called *horses*.

So high the men looked like squirrels. Above them the slender stick of the royal mast at the very peak of the ship, rocking back and forth, scratching the sky.

Every sailor belonged to *port watch* or *starboard watch*, depending on which side of the ship his hammock was slung. While one watch was on deck, the other slept in their hammocks, though both watches were ordered aloft when sails were being set — *bending sail* — or if the yards needed *trimming* and *bracing*.

Laramie was speeding now, wind singing off her sails. While she had been beating up and down the Welsh coast, he'd overheard passengers complain of her sluggishness, wishing aloud they'd spent the extra money for a Black Ball packet and a racy, easy crossing to New York.

He'd heard people calling their ship *an old Canada cow*.

A *wreckage*.

A *coffin ship*.

He started a lump of biscuit roasting on the grate, and when the bugs came crawling out, he scraped them off into the coals.

Brighid tasted the stirabout. He had watched her collecting pennies and tobacco from passengers in exchange for her potions. The sailors paid with oily little herrings called *old soldiers*.

"It's done, man," she said.

"Wish we had the potatoes."

"You will not see those sweethearts again."

Fianna

WITH THE FOUL ATMOSPHERE in the hold, all the passengers who were strong enough to climb the ladder had come out on deck to eat their supper. Crouching under the bulwarks, trying to stay out of the cutting wind, they spooned stirabout into their mouths.

He went below with a bowl for Molly but when he tried feeding her, she turned to face the wall. "I won't have that awful goo."

"Come, Moll, only try a little."

"No. Go away."

She was weeping again.

Brighid, pushing open the curtain, peered in. "Give her only what she'll take. Don't force her."

"What's wrong with her?"

"It's only the sea — she'll come back to you. Here, let me try."

Molly accepted a few spoonfuls from the old woman then shut her mouth. A few moments later she was violently sick. While the old woman was cleaning her, he went up on deck to scrub out the kettles, pans, and dishes. Sniffing resiny smoke, he looked up and saw Ormsby on the afterdeck, puffing a cigar.

Going below again, he found Molly lying with a blackthorn stick by her side.

"What is this?"

"What?"

"This stick in our bed."

"She says to sleep with it between us."

"Why?" He looked around for the old woman.

"The *fianna* used to sleep with their swords, man. Sleep with their swords between them — they'd keep pure that way."

Fianna were the soldiers in the old stories, giant-killers.

"We're not *fianna*. I don't want that pure. I want you."

"Only until I am better. I'll have you then, man. I promise I will."

Many Gray Horses

BY THE FOURTH DAY a few more passengers had found their sea legs, and news flew around the ship that if the winds continued favorable they would be seeing the cliffs of Newfoundland the following morning, and Quebec itself a day or two later.

Fergus recalled Maguire saying it was forty days across, but when he came below all the passengers well enough to get out of their berths were packing trunks and crates and tying up their baggage with ropes. The Cooles had dragged out their sea chest and were busily packing it. Molly sat on the edge of the berth, holding the blackthorn stick. Brighid was dosing her with a spoonful of black syrup.

"Feeling better?" he asked.

"Ugh! Wretched!" She made a sour face. "Tastes like bad milk!"

The old woman looked at her balefully. "Pennyroyal and horehound, nip and marigolds — poison for a cure."

"Cure of what?" he asked.

"Juice to draw down the blood," Brighid said.

Molly gasped and coughed. "Well, that is strong gear, ain't it? I want to be strong for America."

"What you need is smoke. A dove's stomach, or an ass's dung, smoking on red coals —"

"Yes, well, no dove's stomachs available." Molly placed a pinch of tobacco in the old woman's hand. "I hope there is something to this gunk, you old poison cook, not just cat piss and pressed dandelions, like the nasties they sell at fairs. I hope you ain't going to murder me."

"Don't you say it." Brighid was offended. "You'll see, you'll see."

"What does it look like upstairs?" Molly asked him. "Can you smell ground? If we see Newfoundland we'll see Quebec, won't we."

"Don't know."

"It's the favorable winds as we've had." Martin Coole looked up from the chest he was lashing with rope. "A lumber boat like this travels fast with only a lightish cargo of people in her hold."

Fergus shrugged. He really did not know. Some families had already planted themselves at the foot of the ladder, where they were sitting on their baggage. Everyone wanted to be first ashore in America.

"Man, tell me I'll see it, though," Molly whispered.

The potion the old woman had dosed her with seemed to be making her ill again. She lay back, clutching the stick with both hands. When he touched her brow, she felt cold.

"Tell me I shall, Fergus."

"You'll see the other side."

"DO YOU suppose we'll see Newfoundland tomorrow?" Fergus asked the old man, Ormsby.

"Where did you hear that?"

Unable to sleep, feeling the stick between them every time he moved, he had come on deck to find the old man leaning at the rail. It was a soft night with thick, damp air. He heard canvas flapping as *Laramie* wallowed in a rolling sea.

"Down below it's what they say."

"You don't believe it?"

"I don't know —"

"Well, don't. We've hardly started. We've been knocking back and forth looking for our wind. It's often so. We're nowhere."

They smoked in silence for a while.

"Tell me of the horse thieves. Tell me how you bought your son."

Ormsby looked sideways at him. "Can't you sleep? Is it so bad below?"

"Pretty bad."

Ormsby drew on his cigar, slowly exhaled the smoke. "The horse thieves were Bloods. One of the Blackfoot-speaking tribes.

"He — my son — was Crow. The Bloods captured him on a horse-stealing raid down on the Missouri. He was eleven or twelve years old.

"He was night herd, looking after two or three hundred ponies, buffalo runners belonging to a hunting chief. One night those Bloods came down whooping and firing, killing the other boys, and stealing the herd right out from under him.

"He was too ashamed to face his own people so he set out after the Bloods. He trailed them to Fort Benton, where he saw his first steamboat. That was summer of the year 'thirty-seven. There were five thousand dead of smallpox at Fort Benton that summer — smallpox came up the Missouri on the steamers, and killed off the grass nations, so that the Americans could start trapping for themselves in the Rocky Mountains.

"Once he was exposed to the smallpox — he had heard stories, so knew what it was — he realized he could not return to his people without carrying them the plague, so he decided to attack the Bloods, who were still driving north, and steal his ponies back, or die trying.

"He'd picked up a trade musket at Fort Benton, and a little ammunition. He chose to attack while they were watering at the Milk River. He killed one brave dog and was charging the others, only they shot the horse from under him. He begged them to kill him, but they laughed and said he was too small for a bullet. He would not give them his Crow name, of course, so they called him Many Gray Horses. You'll find men in that country have many names. The Bloods brought him up to Fort Edmonton and sold him to me for three pounds of lead."

"Where's your country?"

"Rosses Point, Sligo, but spent my life in the fur trade, in the Athabaska country. Have you heard of it?"

"I haven't."

"The greatest fur country in the world. I joined the XY Company at fourteen, the Northwest Company at sixteen. Made partner at nineteen. Fought and lost a war against the Baymen, made and lost a number of fortunes, and retired from service of the Hudson's Bay Company at sixty and went home to Sligo. Here, let me see your hat."

Fergus handed it over.

"Beaver fur felt — that's what a good hat is made from. Good beaver felt is hard, doesn't drink up water, and you can always brush it clean. Nothing like it." Ormsby gave the hat a vigorous brushing with his hand then handed it back. "When I came home I bought a couple of hunters at the sales in Derry and Kildare and set myself up for a gentleman on a place inherited from my father. In my absence it had been badly managed, the agent robbed me blind, and I found the whole operation sinking under debt and bad drains.

"During all the years upcountry, I'd thought of Sligo as my home — but I found a melancholy life there. I told myself it was the rain. But they say that worn-out Indian traders are the most useless, helpless class of men. When I wasn't buying girls in Sligo town, I was worrying that one of my tenants was going to shoot me from behind a hedge. The best thing about Irish rain is they cannot in the cabins keep their powder dry.

"Poor drains and grand horses took most of the capital I had. And I missed the country. I missed the snow. Missed my friends and my women. So last month I went across to London and begged Sir George Simpson himself — the Little Emperor, the governor of the Hudson's Bay Company — for a position, any position, in the trade. I told him I'd build boats at York Factory, go out as an apprentice clerk — anything. He offered the factorship at Fort Chipewyan.

"I was to sail straight for the Bay in June, on the annual Company ship. Then the Company changed its mind, and now my orders are to take charge of the spring brigade of canoes from Lachine, nine miles above Montreal. The northern brigades want a fresh supply of boatmen, and I'm to lead the Lachiners up the country.

"Canoes have set out from Lachine for two hundred years; a child could follow the route. It is clear and plain as any road in Ireland. The camps and portages have been in use for centuries. Every rapids is named for drowned men.

"I don't say the trade is what it was when I was a youngster. Even the fur ain't what it was. The men are different too. And when I think of gentlemen wearing silk hats in Dublin and London town! Silk! I suppose steamers and iron rails will one day reach even Rupert's Land. Before that the Yankees will have grabbed it, as they grabbed the Oregon country, which belonged to the Company. Meanwhile I am to bring my Lachiners as far as the Stone Fort on the Red, sixteen hundred miles or so from Montreal — does this make any sense at all to you, or are you nodding because you're a sleek, duplicitous ribbonman?"

"I'm listening, ain't I? I suppose it makes sense, eventually."

"There's a lot that don't, never. Life comes running at you, trailing gaudy streamers, and you can't make them out until it's too close — are those ribbons, or is that blood? Very little makes *sense* to me, but I know I like to sit in a canoe, I always have."

The High

AT DAWN FERGUS CLIMBED on deck with Coole, who was very eager to see land. The fires had been lit in the cabooses, and there was no land in sight, just the plate of pewter sea.

Coole called up to Mr. Blow on the afterdeck, asking when they should see the rock of Newfoundland.

"Newfoundland? We aren't even in the western ocean, you fool."

HE BROUGHT her food, but she turned away and would not speak.

"Where is your tongue, Molly?"

He straddled her on the berth, searching her eyes, the heels of his hands pressing down on her shoulders. Her face, small and white, defiant in its stillness. He had never looked at anyone so closely before.

"What is wrong with you? Tell me how you're feeling. What is wrong inside?"

He couldn't penetrate. He knew by her eyes that she could hear him, and her willful silence frightened him. Silence made her untouchable.

"It's fear of the sea has taken her tongue," the old woman said, looking in. "See if she'll take a little taste of food."

He sat on the edge of the berth, holding spoon and bowl, while she stared at him. He tried to talk to her, as if nothing had changed. "Good scran today,

Moll. I have put an apple in yours. Cut it up in pieces. It's very good, gives it a taste."

She wouldn't open her mouth.

"A spell of the sea." Brighid shrugged. "She'll come back to you." She patted Molly's hand. "You take your time, lovely, and come out when you're good and ready."

"Why can't she say what it is?"

"But she can't speak." She looked at Fergus. "You know nothing much about women, do you?"

"I know her."

"Well, she has gone away a little while. If you are patient and kind, she'll come back."

HE WATCHED sailors at work high in the rigging. Wishing he could get up there somehow, ride so high. Watching them, he couldn't help thinking of her. In her sickness she was like a bird he couldn't reach.

It looked very wild, up so high, but you'd be able to see like a hawk. He'd overheard sailors saying there was ice on the rigging, but from the deck he couldn't see any. He'd rather be living up there, in the high, than down below in the hold. All his life he had lived in holes of one sort or another: cabins made of stones and turf; scalpeens made of sticks, shanties, steerage holds. Burrows smelling of earth and bodies.

He'd rather live where it smelled of the sky.

Nimrod Blampin was sitting on an overturned bucket, working with a spiky tool, deftly kneading together three strands of line into one.

"What's it like up high?" Fergus asked.

Nimrod glanced at the men aloft. "That ain't *high*," he said scornfully. "They is only bending topgallants. *High* is the very last wriggle, the tip of the skinny — capping the royal mast."

"What's it like?"

"Fine if you don't fall. Curious." The sailor grinned. "There was once a young gentleman — very rich — wished to climb the peak of his father's ship, an Indiaman, never having been. Said he would cap the mast, and made a wager with another passenger, for fifty pounds. Up he goes, climbing like a spider, until he must work up around the mainsail tops — see? — hanging on by the futtock shrouds."

Nimrod pointed up to a circular wooden platform halfway up the mast, supported by iron struts — the futtock shrouds — fixed to the mast.

"It is a devilish place and yet only halfway to the peak, or less. To get out around the platform you must climb straight out, while hanging upside down, which is a funny feeling, the first time.

"Well, the young gentleman, he goes the dead cat there, hanging on upside down at the futtocks. Sixty feet above deck. Won't be coaxed to move another inch. Deadest cat I ever saw."

"What happened?"

"He hung there all night. The watch brought him up a dish of lobscouse and fed him with a spoon, but he couldn't be persuaded to let go the shrouds. Then a wicked storm came on and he froze solid as iron, then died. And they could not work him off even then, and left him until he was leather. Hands going aloft, they would kiss him on the lips for luck. Two years later, when that Indiaman come into Clarence Dock, he was still seized to the shrouds. The ship riggers finally worked him off by use of tar oil, which softened him nicely."

Patches of fog were swirling over the deck. Fergus peered aloft. "Do you suppose I could cap the peak?"

"No!"

"I think I might."

"You're a very lubberly fellow." Nimrod sounded annoyed. "You may start for a lark, but a passenger's lark won't carry you far. You would do a dead cat or fall into the sea. Takes a seaman to cap the mast."

Fog had swallowed the ship while they were talking, and when he looked up again he could see nothing of the rigging or the men. They had been cut off completely by the white pillow of mist. He could hear them shouting to one another, and the sails flapping. *Laramie* was beginning to wallow on her beam ends as her canvas softened and the hull gradually lost way.

He went forward to the bow. Standing on a pile of anchor chain, he peered through the white fog, trying to catch a scent of America, the heavy aroma of ground, animals, people. But all he could smell was the chilly blankness of the ocean.

AS SOON as his eyes adjusted to the dimness of the hold, he saw the curtain had been drawn shut on their berth.

Brighid was shaking a potion bottle. "Come here, man, you must help me dose her."

She pushed the curtain aside. Molly writhing on the pallet, her linen shift rucked at her hips.

"Sit her up so I can dose her."

He could smell the sweat glistening on her white legs and patch of sexual fur.

"I'm going down, man!" she gasped as he put his arm around her.

"I will bring you through, dear," the old woman crooned. "Oh, you are lucky to have me. Only I wish I had a drop of lamb's blood and the black cohosh. Here, angel" — holding out a spoonful of syrup — "you must take another dose."

"I know, I know — only I can't."

"Darling, it will give you some heat."

"I don't want any more . . . Can't . . . no more. Please!" She was weeping.

"Is it black fever?" he asked Brighid.

"Hold her, man, she must take the potion, though it tastes bitter — it does, I know it does, sweet angel." Slipping the spoon between Molly's teeth, she pinched her lips together until she had swallowed. "Now let her down."

Fergus let her down gently until her head was on the pillow, one of the German blankets he'd rifled from Maguire's storeroom.

"Now this, baby." The old woman shook drops from a little bottle onto Molly's tongue.

After a few moments she stopped thrashing and lay still. Her eyes were glassy. Drawing a blanket up to her chin, the old woman began stroking her cheek with the back of her hand.

"I have all the juice — I always have," she boasted. "I am famous in my country. 'Go see Brighid of Faha,' they say. 'She will cure the cattle. Bring her wheat bread. She likes a cup of honey. The whiskey in the cool blue jar.'"

"Is it black fever?" Mrs. Coole asked, when she came below and saw Molly. "Oh my poor children."

The old woman told Fergus he should sleep on deck; she herself would stay the night with Molly. "She'll rest better if you're not here. Go up on top, sleep clean under the stars, and wish for her."

She was trying to spare him, he knew. He had no wish to be spared, but suddenly felt too exhausted to resist. Struggling to empty his mind, to feel as little as possible, he took a German blanket from the sea chest and climbed up on deck.

A Seat in a Canoe

HE MADE A BED IN THE WINDLASS housing on the foredeck, but couldn't sleep. The pressure of loneliness screeched and howled through the cracks and kept him awake.

He tried to recall the tip horses, grazing softly along the Sunday roads. He'd been alone then and content. But he could not find sleep, and finally crawled out of the windlass housing and went aft to the galley. It was the hour when watches overlapped. The wind was blowing steady and the enormous sky was sprinkled with stars.

The galley was packed with sailors drinking mugs of tea with rum. Handed a steaming mug by the black cook, gripping its warmth in his hands, he got a light for his pipe then went to stand at the rail, watching the black sea splashing white along the hull.

Why should being alone be so hard to bear?

"I've been playing cards with our captain."

Looking up at the voice, Fergus saw the old man leaning with his elbows on the afterdeck rail.

"Won two pounds off the gentleman." Ormsby swallowed the last drop of liquid in a tumbler, dropped the glass into a pocket. "Care for a cigar?"

"No."

"I'll trouble you for a light."

Ormsby swung down the ladder deftly, the unlit cigar clamped between his teeth. Fergus gave him a light and the old man puffed and blew until the tip was glowing red. "How are you tonight, Fergus?"

"Well."

"And down below? How are they keeping?"

"There's some of them sick."

"Seasick or fever?"

"Can't say."

"So early on a passage, fever wouldn't be a good sign."

They smoked in silence. He could see the red tip of Ormsby's cigar glowing, hear the sputter, smell the smoke.

Ormsby knew nothing of Molly, probably had never seen her.

"What prospects, Fergus?"

"What do you mean?"

"Do you have people? Friends in America? Do you have a trade?"

"My people were murdered by the landlord. Carmichael his name."

Ormsby was looking at him, expressionless, his face a mask.

Saying the word *murder* felt like setting up a kind of gravestone, hard and permanent, marking the truth of what had happened to them. It felt intensely satisfying to say it.

Ormsby was still looking at him. A landlord himself.

Finally Fergus broke the silence. "Cattle I know. Horses a little. Navvying. I drove the tips. I'd like to get some ground."

"Navvying's no trade! Do you have any capital whatsoever? Any savings? Every Irish emigrant thinks he'll have a farm in America, but farming takes capital."

He was hardly listening. He couldn't really think of America. His head was full of her.

"You'll need to find a place. America is not for the poor. You could starve to death at Quebec or Boston and no one would know your name. It's no different than anywhere else. In Canada they hire Irishmen for cutting timber, but winter is the season for work in the woods. In spring, the camps are all shutting down. Cotton mills down the Boston states pay a dollar a day for hands so I'm told. From Quebec you might walk to Lowell or Manchester in nine days."

He remembered them leaving the camp together aboard the blue horse. The memory caught in his throat and made him cough.

"Are you all right?"

"I am."

Ormsby tapped his cigar, and a trail of embers streamed off into the dark. "There may be a place with the spring brigade."

"A place?"

"A seat in a canoe. I can promise nothing more. Seven weeks' hard travel from Montreal to Rupert's Land."

"A canoe, what is it — a *púcán*?"

"More or less. Our freight canoes are birch bark on red cedar, seamed with pitch. If you make the trip with me, and present yourself to Company council — with a character from me — they'd offer you an apprenticeship."

"Why mister? You don't know me."

"We travel hard, I warn you. A young Irishman with no capital but brains and nerve can make himself a place. Get rich in the trade."

"What do you want, mister?"

"What do you mean?"

"What do you want of me?"

The tip of the old man's cigar glowed red as he drew on it, then breathed out a cloud of fragrant smoke. "Do you play cards?"

Fergus shook his head.

"You'll have to learn. I like to play a hand, traveling up the country, it passes the time.

"The spring brigade — think it over, Fergus. Perhaps it's your fortune I'm offering you. Perhaps it's death in the woods. Who can say? I'm going to bed. Good night."

HE RETURNED to the windlass housing and tried to sleep but the wind creaking through kept him awake. At first light, sniffing smoke from lit cabooses, he crawled out feeling stiff and groggy.

Morning light the color of iron. Clouds bloomed low, and the ocean was greasy with calm.

Was it death he felt in his bones, or just a wretched night? He felt sore all over.

On the afterdeck, Mr. Blow was bellowing orders and sailors of both watches were scrambling in the rigging. There wasn't much wind — he could hear the sails billowing and cracking. When the wind was soft, they made a great deal of pointless noise. When they hardened there was a vibrant, strumming sound, the sound of speed.

He watched the sailors climbing the ratlines hand-over-hand. Men aloft were walking out the yards on footropes — *horses* — slung beneath. From out on the tips of the yards, there would be a clean fall to the sea.

Only a few passengers were on deck, cooks-of-the-day starting the breakfast, or people using the heads in the bow. Though the air down below was awful most people disliked coming up on deck because the endless sea terrified them.

When you were ashore the sea seemed to have a relationship to the land. Aboard ship, you knew the sea was nothing but itself.

Ormsby appeared at his usual spot at the afterdeck rail. "Weather coming in," he called down. "I hope you have found your sea legs. She'll be rocking in a while. We'll get some speed coming out the other end, perhaps. Anything to get us out these murks. Two weeks and we ain't seen Cape Clear. Never had such a pallid ride."

This morning he wore a Scotch bonnet and velvet jacket. Without the bulk of his fur coat the old man looked small and wiry, a rugged little peck of a fellow sipping coffee from a noggin, the pungent, gorgeous scent steaming. He had a shock of white hair and pale blue eyes. His face was pink and freshly shaven.

"You cook yourself a good ration this morning. Don't suppose you'll be allowed fire while the storm lasts. And our captain will nail down the hatches if there is any weather, so the people will have to ride it out in the hold. You tell them there's no need to be frightened, though. The ship is sound. She'll withstand. I suppose there's few of them below have ever ridden out a storm at sea. The Irish have always kept their backs to the sea."

The sea looked placid enough, though darker than usual.

He could see the sailors up high taking in sails, gathering and bunching canvas and bundling it in long fat rolls, which they were lashing to the yards with dozens of small ties.

"Have you given any thought to what I said?"

There was a smile on Ormsby's lips, but his eyes were appraising.

"Will you take a seat in a canoe, and see what the country brings you?"

"I can't go with you, mister, I am traveling with a girl."

Ormsby was silent for a moment. "Are you now?"

"Yes."

"I've not seen her."

"She's keeping down below. She's been ill."

Ormsby nodded and took a sip of coffee, looking out at the sea. "I'll wish you luck then. I hope you both land on your feet."

Sensing the old man's disappointment, Fergus was afraid he had wounded — even insulted — him by refusing. Pride hones disappointment into insult, and Ormsby was proud. Such a caustic old man would know how to cut.

Ormsby hadn't said so, but Fergus assumed that the son with the changeable names — Many Gray Horses, Daniel, the Constant Sky — was dead. If Ormsby was after a replacement for his son, he'd never find it.

The living won't stand in for the dead. The thought of it fills them with revulsion.

Bonaparte's Retreat

THE OLD WOMAN and Mrs. Coole were rubbing Molly's ankles and soaking her feet in warm brine. Her stupor reminded him of small animals he'd found alive in his traps — not yet dead, but ready to die; numb with the foretaste.

"She's in a violent purge," Brighid told him. "All her sense is occupied."

When Molly began to writhe and moan, Fergus helped the two women hold her still, and Brighid placed two drops of tincture under her tongue.

When he leaned over to kiss her lips, he could taste the acrid decoction. Her eyes were open, but she wasn't seeing him.

The ill are consumed by their illness, it swallows them.

THE CATTARACKWEE boy, his face spangled with the red nick of fleabites, stood on the foredeck, fiddle tucked on his chin, playing a familiar tune, "The Bonaparte's Retreat." Passengers were dancing on the deck, determined to burn off the murk and gloom infesting the ship. They danced to warn off the sailors and impress the master with their noise and their power, and Fergus had joined in, trying to defeat the dread he could feel growing inside, slowly paralyzing him.

Like all the dancers, he had taken off his boots. As he jigged and twirled on the slippery boards, he could sense *Laramie* changing course. All day she had been sloughing in a fat sea. Now the wind was picking up and the sky had darkened. Looking aloft, he saw the sails had tightened and filled. He heard the strumming noise of speed.

The fiddle tune kept spinning faster, as though the fiddler was trying to dance them straight into the eye of whatever was coming.

When Molly's cry came, he heard it through the deck boards. It nipped at his bare feet and sent him crashing into a pair of dancers who ignored him and kept on dancing. Pushing his way out of the crowd, he grabbed his boots and raced for the hatchway. No one else seemed to have heard her.

SHOVING OPEN the curtain, he looked down at Molly lying on bloody straw with a mound of bloody rags crammed between her legs. Brighid and Mrs. Coole were sitting on the berth, Mrs. Coole wiping Molly's legs with a wet rag while the old woman chafed her ankles. They looked up at him.

"Go away, man!" Brighid whispered. "Go away! You don't belong here!"

"Is it the fever? Is she dying?"

"Go away! Come back when we've cleaned her up for you. You must go away!" The old woman gave him a push.

"What are you doing with her?"

"Cleaning her, can't you see. She'll be better if you go. It isn't for a man. Go!"

"Poison!" Mrs. Coole hissed.

"Don't say so," said the old woman.

"Look at the mess coming out of her! Poison!"

"Go away," the old woman retreated. She sighed, as if she knew he wouldn't obey, and resumed rubbing Molly's feet and ankles.

"What do you mean, poison?"

"This one has poisoned her," said Mrs. Coole.

"Ach." Brighid's face twisted in contempt.

"She is, she is — an old poison cook, I told you so."

"Poison cook? Who brought your little boy back? You knew how far he was gone, didn't you? And I called him back —"

"What's wrong? Why is she bleeding so — tell me."

"Go away, man. Go away, you don't belong here, you'll spoil her." She glared at Mrs. Coole. "What are you saying, you bossy crag — you've a face like a hawk, missus. Cruel you are, vicious."

"I'm telling him the truth," said Mrs. Coole.

"The truth? The truth is your boy's alive, ain't he, thanks to me."

Both women were silent.

"What is it?" he asked. "Will you tell me, please?"

The women looked at each other.

"Go on, tell him, you." Brighid sighed. "You've ruined him now. Only tell him the truth."

Mrs. Coole looked at him. "She was carrying a child, she was, your child."

"What?"

"She couldn't keep it," Brighid said, wearily. "She wasn't ready. Thought it would kill her. What are you doing here, man? Go away."

"This one has been dosing her with syrup of pennyroyal."

"Pennyroyal? What is it?"

"Poison, man."

"To draw down her blood," Brighid said.

"Draw down this man's baby, you mean."

"No baby it was — she hadn't quickened. Only a few days gone. There, there, daughter," Brighid crooned at Molly. "Nothing to fear. Old me is here."

"Don't say you didn't know what you were doing," Mrs. Coole said.

"It isn't my baby — it's Muck's."

They both looked at him.

"Muck Muldoon, the ganger. He was her man. Before me. It must be his she couldn't carry. She didn't say so on account of being afraid that I would cut her loose. Which I would not, Molly," he whispered, picking up Molly's limp hand. Hot tears filling his eyes, spilling down his cheeks. "I swear it."

Both women were watching him.

Brighid shrugged then turned back to Molly, placing a hand on her brow. "Sometimes it comes down very easy but I warned her, I said it might be rough —"

"You wicked, lurid creature, and to think you were doing your black art in the same berth with my babies —"

"Don't speak ill of me, missus. Black art indeed! You know nothing." Brighid looked up at Fergus. "Forget what you've seen, man. Your girl will get better now. The poison is come out. I told you — she'll come back to you. She'll give you another, by and by."

Reaching up, she drew the curtain and shut him out. He could hear the women murmuring but didn't want to listen to any more. He ran to the ladder and quickly climbed up on deck.

POOR OLD Muck, you're twice dead now.

The sea had broken open, and the wind was aggressive. Waves were cracking over the bow, water sweeping the foredeck.

The passengers were still dancing. The old man, Ormsby, had joined in and was cutting capers, hands on his hips, head thrown back, yipping like a rooster. A dance so crowing and sexual that even the young men and buxom girls were shying away, giving old Ormsby plenty of room — their quick, light stepping so demure next to his jagged leaps and spins.

"Passengers below!" the master shouted through his trumpet. The weather was beating hard at the ship but the Cattarackwee boy kept fiddling and the passengers kept dancing, glad to disobey Mr. Blow.

Two sailors ran up to the foredeck and attempted to seize the Cattarackwee boy. Dodging them, he ran around the deckhouse still with the fiddle on his neck, scraping out music, until the black cook stepping from the galley headed him with an iron pan. The boy crumpled on deck, and a sailor seized the fiddle and swung it against the foremast, smashing the instrument into splinters then dropping the wreckage over the side.

A wave broke over the side, bursting seawater at their feet. Panicking passengers began pushing for the hatchway, trying to get below.

The carpenter appeared with a hammer and bucket of nails, and Fergus saw the hatch was to be nailed shut. He stepped back but the bos'n caught sight of him. "Below with the rest, Mike."

He seized of a shroud and refused to let go. They began beating him with rope-ends but he kept his grip on the shroud until a blow caught him just behind his ear. Stunned, he let go the shroud and felt the sailors dragging him across the deck. They threw him down the hatch and he heard the oil lamp swaying and squeaking as he fell, then nothing.

Letters

CABIN PEOPLE WERE AFRAID of the dark. They lit bonfires to welcome a fresh moon, and hated venturing out alone on a black night. If a man must go out, he carried a torch. If he didn't have a torch, he lit his pipe and kept it burning. Any fire was some protection.

He came to, staring at the flame of a candle. Molly held the candle, and Brighid was pressing a cold, wet cloth to his forehead. Confused, he tried to think his way back into himself, but it was difficult.

The flame entranced him. Insubstantial it seemed. Flickering. So near to going out.

WITHOUT ANY light, time slurred, days lost distinction. Even when he was fully conscious, he couldn't guess how long they had been trapped in the hold. The air was rank. He heard rats scrabbling in the ballast, but nothing from above, except the wind. He wondered if the crew had abandoned ship.

The 'tween deck leaked and dripped. He felt the weight of the sea punching *Laramie*, the ship staggering from blow to blow.

When a tier of berths collapsed, the framework cracking and splintering, spilling people out of their cribs, he thought she was finally breaking up — but no; she held.

There was nothing to do but lie in the darkness and wait for what was going to happen.

"MRS. COOLE said at Quebec there is nuns, Fergus."

They lay in their berth, the blackthorn stick between them.

Even in the fear and darkness, he could tell she was recovering her strength. Her breath, so close, smelled deep and sweet.

"Nuns?"

"Black gowns, ever seen them?"

"No."

"They take girls in, feed them, teach them."

"Teach them what?"

"Letters. I don't know. What there is."

"A workhouse is it?"

"Oh I don't know."

"Open up! We need air! We need water!" Martin Coole had climbed up the hatchway ladder and was pounding the hatch cover with his fist, but no one responded. They had pooled supplies with the Cooles and the old woman; the stores Maguire had warned him to save for *mi an ocrais*. Most of the German cheese was rotten but he cut out an edible portion. The apples were soft but sweet. The Cooles had crackers, figs, rotten oranges, two quarts of lime juice. Brighid had oily little herrings bartered from the crew.

Molly ate a little, lay poised and still, breathing softly.

Aren't you hungry for me? he wanted to ask her. *Don't you feel strong when I'm beside you?*

THEY WERE sleeping when the hatch opened and a shaft of white light bounced down into the hold. Molly poked him with her elbow. "Wake up, man, smell the air. Let's go up, before they close us up again."

He swung his legs from the berth and stood up, feeling strange and dizzy. Dozens of white faces peered down from the tiers. Most passengers were too stunned or weak to move.

"Give me your hand, man, pull me up."

He helped her up out of the berth. She stood wavering, clutching his arm. He thought she was going to faint.

"I'm walking to the sun. Come on." Heading for the ladder, she seized hold and started climbing into the white air, so bright it stung their eyes.

Laramie was making way, her sails packed with wind, her bow biting the waves. There were tags of mist lingering on the sea but the sky above was blue and the sun was an engine warming their faces.

More passengers began crowding up through the hatchway and spilling onto the deck, blinking in the light and moving stiffly after their long confinement, flapping their arms like pigeons, skipping and laughing, begging lights from the sailors to start their pipes.

When Fergus held out his palm above the hatchway, he felt the pressure of foul air rising from the hold.

"Sweep up the old straw and throw it overboard!" Mr. Blow called. "New fresh bedding you shall have. I'll serve out no rations until your quarters are clean and pure."

The passengers set to work scouring the hold, raking filthy straw from the berths and piling it into canvas slings that were hauled up through the hatchway and dumped overboard. Soon there were tawny islands of straw and refuse bobbing behind them on the bright blue sea. The mania for cleaning had seized the entire ship — even the sailors were scouring out the fo'c'sle, bringing their hammocks on deck to air, scrubbing their clothes and pinning them to dry on the ratlines and in the rigging.

In the hold an old man had been found dead in one of the uppermost berths. The widow could not be coaxed down.

The couple's two grown sons seemed stunned. When the old man was finally lifted down and laid on the floor, Fergus noticed how small and yellow were his hands and feet.

"Bring him on deck directly, Mr. Blow says," Nimrod Blampin instructed. "No bansheeing."

Washtubs had been set out on deck and filled with seawater. The sky was cluttered now with clouds but the air tasted soft and rain, if it came, would be easy. Passengers were scrubbing their clothes and their blankets. The collapsed

berths were being repaired by the ship's carpenter, while passengers scrubbed the
'tween deck with brushes and buckets of seawater, then sprinkled clean sand
and vigorously swept it up.

When all the trash had been raked out and the boards were glistening wet
from scrubbing, one of the cabooses was lowered into the hold on ropes and lit
so the thick, tart smoke might purify the air.

The corpse lay on a board on the foredeck, wrapped in sailcloth; their first
death at sea. He watched the sailmaker place two ballast stones inside the
shroud then sew it up with his awl while the dead man's sons stood by, puffing
their pipes.

Warm silver rain began to fall. Passengers began stripping off their filthy
clothes. He watched Molly pull her gown over her head and stand in her shift
with arms extended and face tilted to the rain, her hair black with it, her nipples prickling under the wet linen.

Mr. Blow climbed onto the foredeck with a book tucked inside his jacket,
protecting it from the rain. "I shall perform the service now."

"*You* mean to say the prayers, master?" The dead man's sons were staring at
Mr. Blow.

"Of course."

"But we can't have *you* say the prayers."

"What do you mean? I am master of the ship. I have the proper authority."

"It wouldn't be right."

"Are you being impudent?" Mr. Blow was getting angry.

Martin Coole had joined the little group standing by the shrouded corpse.
"Only a priest for burying, Mr. Blow. That is their custom."

"There isn't any priest, you fool! I'll read the service as written, right here in
this book!"

"Without a priest, it is improper," one son muttered in Irish.

"What does he say?" the master said, furious. "I won't stand that goblin talk."
Coole translated.

"You tell me, they mean to bury their own father," said Mr. Blow, "without
a word of Christian prayer?"

Mr. Coole translated this into Irish. The brothers looked at each other, then
nodded.

Mr. Blow slapped his book shut and stalked off.

The sons' wives began keening dutifully. From the foredeck ladder Mr. Blow shouted, "Put him over! Put him over right now!"

The sailors lifted the board to the rail and tilted it slowly. The corpse began to slide, and then it tumbled. It hardly made a splash, spinning for a few moments, then disappearing.

"*Land ho!*" — the shout came from Nimrod Blampin in the tops.

In a moment the passengers were all crowding along the rail, elbowing and shoving. Molly was next to him, her face glowing. She grabbed his hand, gave it a squeeze. Mist parted for a moment, revealing a white line of surf and a rocky shore.

The passengers began cheering.

Coole grabbed Fergus's hand and shook it vigorously. People were shouting with joy, and men were throwing hats in the air.

America looked green. He could see lines of fences and white specks of cabins. The land divided into fields. So there were farms already.

Had you expected empty land, free for the taking?

"That ain't America, you ninnies!"

Looking up, he saw Nimrod Blampin twelve feet above the deck, hanging from a ratline.

"That's only Ireland! Old Cape Clear!"

The celebration died immediately. The people accepted the news without question, as if disappointment was their real faith, all they really believed in. Turning away from the sight of land, men picked up their hats and joined the crowd pressing for the hatchway, retreating below.

"Newfoundland it is, surely," Martin Coole kept insisting, but people pushed past him, ignoring him. Mrs. Coole and her children joined the others going below.

Soon Fergus, Molly, and Coole were the only passengers left on deck, staring at Ireland.

"Don't look so cut up, Fergus," she said. "It's worth a laugh, I suppose."

"Perhaps it is, but I can't."

"You with your Newfoundland talk!" She laughed at Coole. "You don't know so much, mister, do you?"

"I'm not familiar with the sea, miss, and don't pretend to be."

"You do, though — that's the point."

Coole shook his head sadly. He went into the bow and stood peering ahead, as though he still expected to catch sight of America.

Molly slipped her arm through Fergus's.

Her body so near giving him a kick.

That warmth of her.

"Let it go, man. Forget it. What's coming is still coming."

"Why didn't you tell me that you carried a child?"

Staring back at Ireland, she didn't reply.

"It was his, wasn't it, Molly?" He hated the sound of his voice.

"It's nothing now." She sounded tired.

"It was Muck's, though, wasn't it?" He was afraid she'd see his eyes and think he was crying; think he was soft, which he never would be. He rubbed his eyes with his sleeve.

"If it was mine you'd have kept it."

"If I told you I'd got rid of Muck's baby, as I got rid of Muck's watch, you'd understand? You'd be strong for me, then? You'd say it was still on between us?"

"I would."

Her face was tight. "Do you want the truth, man? I'll give it to you whether you want it or not. Could have been his. Could have been yours. That time on the cliff. Could have been. May have been. Wouldn't make no difference."

"Mine?"

"I won't carry a child. Not now. I don't trust the world."

"You're the witch. Not her. You're the witch."

"Did you want a lie? Is that what you wanted? You asked. I don't mind a lie, Fergus, I would have lied easy —"

"Get away from me, witch."

She left him then and he watched her crossing the deck.

His hand had curled into a fist and was beating on the rail as he watched her going down the ladder step by step. She was still weak, unsteady.

Nimrod Blampin came up and stood next to him along the rail. "Look see — the damned old place is well behind us now. And there she goes." The Irish coast was falling away fast, disappearing into mist. "We're for the western ocean now. What are you doing, Michael? Knocking down the ship?"

Fergus opened his fist. The edge of his hand was raw and tender where he had been beating it on the wood, and he uncurled the fingers slowly.

Anger, what is it? It's nothing pure. It's yourself you despise.

Chance

IT WAS A STRANGE, fast life: day after day of singing wind and empty sea, with America somewhere off the stem.

Had there been a berth unoccupied he might have taken his share of the blankets and claimed it. It wasn't anger he felt, but awkwardness. He felt awkward near her body.

If it was anger, he would refuse to make use of it. If it was anger, he would carry it around like a dull little knife.

The tiers were packed; there were no empty berths. So he remained with her, sharing their blankets, lying with the blackthorn stick between them. While her body was recovering strength, at night she was often burning with heat.

They were quiet with each other. Perhaps she, like him, felt too sore to talk.

The miles chopping past; the seas changing green to blue to green again.

MARTIN COOLE said, "I must charge a fee for lessons."

"How much?" Molly asked.

They were on deck, scrubbing their clothes and blankets in buckets of seawater.

"Knowledge, it cost me a lot to get, such as I have," Coole said. "And like anything else, I must make it pay. I have my children to think of. Do you have schoolbooks?"

She shook her head.

"No matter," said Coole. "I have the primers — the *Dublin Universal*, and the *Goff's* for doing sums."

"If you give me a book, man," Molly said fervently, "I would eat every word."

"Were you ever a scholar?"

"I can do sums — had fellows at the fairs teach me. What's your fee for learning us our letters?"

"You can't say I'm not qualified. I had charge of the famous school established by Sir William Hamilton to educate the sons of his tenants. Have you heard of Sir William?"

She shook her head. "I have not."

"A great man in north Tipperary. Paid me a handsome salary, and gave us a cottage to live in."

"Why have you come away?" Fergus asked.

Coole grimaced. "At the start of the winter, two landlords in the district were shot down in cold blood. The miserable, shucking little priest went running to Sir William declaring I was responsible for the outrage."

A shagairt a rúin, his mother used to call out, when she saw the young priest, on his rare visits to the mountain. O dearest priest!

"Did you? shoot them?"

Coole looked at Fergus with horror. "No, no, what makes you even ask such a thing?"

"I don't know."

"I never knew the gentlemen, except by reputation! I never touched a hair of their heads. That priesteen was always jealous of me; he had a school of his own. He told Sir William that I was educating a nest of ribbonmen."

"Were you?"

Drying his hands on his trouser legs, Coole pulled a thick little book from his pocket. "I was for Repeal, and have shaken the hand of the Liberator himself, Daniel O'Connell. Lately I am — was — am a Young Ireland man. I have the national feeling. That priesteen had Sir William's ear, and Sir William closed the school. We lost our dear cottage. My wife had a beautiful garden she was very sorry to leave. The spuds were blighted, but we had turnips, strawberries, peas. When our benefactor threw us out, we had nowhere to go, and were put out directly on the roads. It was very hard on Mrs. Coole, to see her children suddenly as little paupers — wild little paupers. We followed the road to Cork, begging for food to put in the children's mouths."

"What will you do in America, will you have a school?"

"Mrs. Coole says my opinions have put us on the famine road. A man with mouths to feed cannot afford opinions, she says. I have sacrificed her babies for what? For nothing. The patriot game. The national feeling." He slapped the thick little book upon his knee. "This was given me at a soup kitchen in Cork. It is a Bible. Do you know it?"

They shook their heads.

"Did you ever think that the species of time that is commonly called *the old days* were, in fact, the new days? These here we're living are the old days. Today is certainly the oldest day the world has seen. Tomorrow will be even older. At this instant, are we not living the farthest removed any human has ever been from the act of Creation?"

"It'll be different in America, you think?" Molly asked.

"It will, and it won't." The schoolmaster smiled. "I'm sorry but that's the best answer I can think of, and I may be wrong. I usually am. Did you ever feed at a soup kitchen?"

"In Liverpool — at the Fenwick," Fergus told him.

"Did you get a wide-awake with your supper?"

"Don't know what that is."

"Was there a gentleman shouting, 'Do you want to go to Hell tonight?'"

"No."

"The soup kitchen that took us in was right there on the Parade in Cork, a very decent house it was, with a chapel attached. Lodging, very clean and warm. Food for the children, milk and honey. The preacher was a North of Ireland man, a very fierce fellow. He preached twice a day, extravagantly vehement. He could describe the last feeble, fainting moments of human life and the process of decay up to the last loathsome stage of decomposition. He was rather good at making you see Hell.

"After we were there a week, he offered us passage to America and a piece of land in Indiana where I might have a school. Only we must renounce the pope and the saints to be baptized again. And the children were little papist sinners and must be baptized too. He said he wasn't in the business of sending papists to the New World." Coole slapped the Bible softly on his knee. "I did as he asked. I sold my children's souls for passage to America."

The sun was bright on deck, the light splashing off the sails. Coole went silent, brooding. Molly looked at Fergus. They had two pounds and twelve shillings, wrapped in a handkerchief at the bottom of the sea chest.

"What fee will you charge for lessons?" she asked Coole again.

Coole looked up. "Sixpence a lesson."

"That's steep."

"Sixpence for the two of you."

"Can you really teach me to read?" Molly asked.

"I can teach. Can you learn, is the question."

"LETTERS GIVES you the handle, man," Molly said. "Excepting old McCarty, I never met one fellow on the line who could read."

They were lying on their berth, the blackthorn stick between them. She was shuffling a pack of playing cards she had borrowed from the black cook in exchange for a few thumbs of tobacco. They were dogged, dirty old cards, smudged and soft, but the faces were colorful.

"Speaking of which, did I ever tell you, Fergus, when first I seen a train?"

He watched her split the deck and shuffle again, the cards flying from hand to hand, realizing how deft she was.

"It was when I was tramping out of Bristol with Muldoon. We'd just come across. Muck knew how to live by stealing food. Apples, honey — I knew how to steal milk from cattle, but he taught me to steal the milk from sheep. We were scrounging wheat when the train appeared. Have you ever done so? I mean gathering from a standing crop, not gleaning."

He shook his head.

"It's risky. Any farmer would shoot you dead for stealing a crop standing in the field. Any magistrate would transport you. We didn't care. We were hungry. We were threshing heads of wheat with our fingers, rubbing out the corns, making a paste.

"Muldoon saw steam on the sky. I heard her coming, then saw the engine, hauling four green wagons, pretty as paint.

"I watched her slope down into a cutting — only I didn't know what a cutting was then. She just ran down into the ground until all I could see was her funnel, then not even that — only the smoke, floating over the field. It give me such a feeling.

"*Why, everything moves!* I thought. *Everyone flees! Not just you. It's no one that is fixed.*"

He remembered the glee, the sense of lightness and release he had experienced, seeing his first train storming over the country. But that was before he'd met her.

"You said we were stone partners, Molly."

She briskly cut the deck and shuffled. "Never played cards?" The pack clicked and riffled as she flipped it from hand to hand.

"No."

"Man, they must have been simple in your part of the world. Didn't you go to fairs?"

"To sell the pig. Never had money to spare, never tried the booths. There was a tinker fellow I saw once at the fair at Gort, walking barefoot on red coals. Very bold he was."

"Pharaoh shall pay for lessons. My old ma and me kept alive on cards and fairs, dealing Pharaoh for the cabin johns. I can make the cards pay — you'll see.

"I remember one day at the fair in Louth, a horse dealer from Belfast wished to have me. My old ma said he couldn't. We had already won all his money, and she always said she'd get a bonny prize for me. But that afternoon she had a bad run and lost all our stake, and the Belfast fellow dug up one gold sovereign from somewhere, which was as much money as we'd ever seen, and she let him take me behind the tents. My first jump it was. My first man. Awful old beseecher he was. Miles worse than Muldoon."

Suddenly she spilled the pack of cards, over her legs and stomach, over the berth.

"Are you my man, Fergus?"

"I don't know if I am."

"Say you are. Just say it."

"I'm your man."

She began gathering the spilled cards. "My thoughts? I have such wicked old thoughts, Fergus, if I told them, you'd want to ditch me."

He wanted to reach out for her but the black stick was still between them and he'd promised himself he would not remove it, she would have to get it out of the way.

She finished gathering her cards and resumed her shuffling and the stick stayed exactly where it was.

THE SCHOLARS met in the lee of the foredeck, warm in the bright sun. Coole's children, Carlo and Deirdre, were bent over their slates, scribbling with stubs of chalk.

The schoolmaster held out a box of carved wooden letters to Molly. "Now take one, any one. Help yourself."

She selected a figure Fergus recognized as the letter *A*.

"Now yourself." Coole offered Fergus the box. Feeling ignorant and clumsy, he chose a *D* from the jumble.

"What is it?" Coole asked him.

"*D!*" the little boy, Carlo, shouted before Fergus could answer. The boy had hardly glanced up from his slate.

"*D* for . . . ?"

"*D* for dead," said the little girl, sounding bored.

"Well, yes," said Coole. "Spell it out, Deirdre."

"D-E-A-D, dead."

"And, miss, what letter is that you're holding?" Coole asked Molly.

She smiled, shaking her head. "Why don't you tell me?"

"*A* it is," Deirdre called.

"*A* for agony," said her brother.

"Come, Carlo, if you say it, you must spell it out," said Coole. "Step up here and choose the letters."

The boy stood up and began picking letters from the box. "A-G-O-N-N-Y."

"I think not. Deirdre?"

She stood up. Inspecting the jumble of letters in her brother's hand, she picked out one and threw it back in the box.

"A-G-O-N-Y," she spelled.

"Excellent. Now," Coole told Molly, "you may choose another letter."

Molly picked one out.

Carlo glanced at it. "*P* for . . . " He faltered.

"Come along," his father coaxed, "we've plenty of superior words that like a *P*. Try it now — any word that starts with a puh! Puh! Puh!" He made the pushing sound with his lips. "Come on, you misers."

"*P* for potato," Fergus said.

"Excellent! Spell it out."

He shook his head. "I cannot."

"Deirdre?"

The little girl quickly chose the letters from the box. "P-O-T-A-T-O."

"Excellent. Now you, sir." Coole nodded at Fergus. "Choose another letter. Let's see if you can pick the ones to compose your name."

THE FIRST game of Pharaoh was played in the galley. A hogshead with a blanket smoothed on top served for a table. Passengers and sailors crowded into the little shed, watching Molly shuffle then cut the pack. Fergus stood behind her.

"Are you going to give us a fair shake, miss?" the bos'n asked.

"A little pleasure, sir, that's all."

"I warn you it had better be. We don't like sharpers in the middle of the ocean."

Molly smiled demurely. She raised her voice a little, speaking to the crowd. "If I can have your attention, please, gentlemen?"

She waited until they were quiet.

"I'll tell you how I play this game, which is low stakes and four players at a go, so everyone has their chance." She was speaking so softly they had to strain to listen. "Tobacco is good for stakes, one thumb valued a ha'penny. I shall be banker, and turn up cards one by one. Do you get it? A punter can set any number of stakes — agreeable to the limit, which is sixpence shall we say — upon one or more cards, from ace to king. Stakes are set either previous to dealing, or after any number of coups are made."

She took a deep breath and smiled.

"Or you may mask bets, or change cards when ever you choose, or decline punting — except a deal is unsettled when not above eight cards are dealt. Bank wins when a card equal in points to the stakes card turns up in my right hand — bank loses when it turns up in my left. Punter loses half the stake if his card comes up twice in the same coup. Last card neither wins nor loses. Who shall be first?"

Four men sat down. She played the cards out quietly. He couldn't grasp enough of the game to follow the action, but some of the punters beat her on the coups and some of them lost. After four deals the punters had to give up their stools to the next in line.

During the next hour's play Molly lost almost two pounds, most of their stake. He felt the loss, the shock of it, down to his toes, in his throat and in his belly. She was small, she was light, she did not know these sailor men. They weren't her dumb cow-boys, leering and losing at the penny fair. They were traveling men accustomed to sharps, ruses, and near dealing, and they were happy to beat her at her game.

After the last coup turned up against her, and the bos'n swept up his winnings, she sighed, "That's enough for me. No more deal. I'm over."

"No, miss," Nimrod begged. "Play us some more. I ain't had a turn yet."

"I'm nearly bust. Can't get my magic in this sea air."

"Here is the captain. Make way for the captain."

The sailors and emigrants were standing back to let Mr. Blow through. He stopped in front of the table.

"A ship ain't a gaming house, miss."

Mr. Blow was even younger than he seemed on deck. An overgrown boy, ugly, gawky, and rawboned. A thatch of yellow hair sprouted under a shiny beaver hat so big it seemed about to swallow his head.

"A little amusement," Molly said softly.

"Yes, very amusing. And you're helping yourself to these poor men, I'm sure."

"Come along, Mr. Blow," said the bos'n. "There's no harm. We ain't a Sunday ship after all."

"If you let an Irish jade like this cheat you, you'll be sorry."

"But she's played square."

"I'm only after a little sport," Nimrod whined, "only want a bite. It's nothing wrong."

"Let the girl be," called one of the sailors.

"Let her play!"

"Nothing's wrong," Nimrod told the master.

"The girl has lost most of her stake, Mr. Blow," the bos'n explained. "Hardly what you would call a jade."

"Expensive fun. You'll be sorry."

"She's none of your noisy, belligerent wenches that I know very well. No one's being clipped, sir," the bos'n insisted. "We're having a bit of fun."

Molly cut the deck and looked up at Mr. Blow. "Would you care to try a hand, mister?"

"You're a sharp little bird, miss."

"Sure you don't mean *sharp*, mister," she replied evenly.

"Go on, sir, take a hand," the bos'n urged. "No one's been clipped. She's only a poor emigrant lass. No harm."

"Go on, sir, take a hand!" Nimrod cried.

"You're not frightened of me, are you, Mr. Blow?" Molly smiled.

"Try a hand yourself, Mr. Blow," said the bos'n. "There's nothing wrong with her cards."

The sailors began to cheer and whistle as Mr. Blow dug into the pocket of his black coat and came out with a few coppers. He placed the coins on the blanket, pulled out the stool, and sat down. Molly smiled and cut the cards again, shuffled through them, and began the deal.

She won the first deal, lost the second to Mr. Blow, won the third hand, and lost the fourth. They ended dead even.

"That's enough for me," said Mr. Blow after the last coup played in his favor. "Very steady, very cool, miss." He stood up, taking up his money from the table. "You are a snap. I feel lucky to get away so cheap."

"You see, sir?" cried the bos'n. "It's a fair game, ain't it?"

"You had better play fair. If I hear of you sharping on my ship, I'll drop you on the loneliest rock of Newfoundland, miss, and you can cheat the bears." Mr. Blow turned and left the cabin.

Another punter had already sat down, but Molly shook her head and began sweeping up the cards.

"Come along, miss," said the bos'n. "Don't fold now."

"There's money in the house wants to play," Nimrod said. "Play it out, miss."

"No, I've had enough. You fellows have ruined me nearly."

"Come along, miss," said the bos'n. "Say there'll be a few hands tomorrow."

"Here." She offered him the deck of cards.

"Don't dip your colors, miss. You'll win tomorrow."

"You may have the use of 'em — they won't work for me."

"No, it's not the same — we like a girl to deal. If you are hard up, we will play very light, a penny or two. Come miss, say you will deal us another day."

She hesitated, then shrugged. "Oh, very well."

"Tomorrow?"

"If you like."

"I *let* them win a little extra today," she told him.

They were lying in their berth with the curtain drawn and the stick between them. "Did you expect me to clean them up in a day? A ship is not a fair, Fergus. I can't clip them and disappear, can I? These sailor men would cut my throat, yours too, if they thought we were sharping them. No, no — when you start a house game, you feed the fish some line at first. Work 'em slow! It's good business! Don't worry, man, I'll tighten up."

"You're cheating —"

She put her hand over his mouth. "I ain't! Don't even say it. The deck's not marked; there's no cod, nothing up my sleeve. I'm just letting the cards work for us, Fergus. I'm house — and the cards is always in favor of house, if you play long enough. That's the sweet thing about Pharaoh: If you're house you don't have to clip 'em, and there's no way to lose. We'll do well by Pharaoh, don't worry."

And she was right.

Over the following days the game became a fad on the ship, with sailors from both watches and most of the male passengers who had a few pennies to spare crowding into the galley each evening to play. After a second day of losses, Molly began winning, slowly, and never by a large margin. Some days she fell behind, but most days she came out ahead.

He seemed to have left the weight of fear behind, along with so many vicious dreams, killing dreams. He slept clear of terrors, clear of the fights, and when he came on deck in the mornings the emptiness and radiant light of the western ocean struck him as a surprise and a joy.

Winnings were adding to their stake, which she counted every night, wrapping the coins in a handkerchief, tucking them into the sea chest. By the time they encountered the first ice castles, the stake had grown to nearly eight pounds, and Pharaoh was popular still.

A Vision

"Mouse," she said, looking across at Fergus. They were sitting in the lee of the deckhouse and she was reading from a list of words in Coole's *Dublin Universal Speller*. Every morning they took a lesson with Coole, and in the afternoons, basking in sunshine, they practiced. The schoolmaster gave them use of the speller in exchange for a thumb of tobacco.

Fergus began scratching at his slate with a stub of a chalk, making one letter, erasing with his sleeve, making another, pausing to consider, moving ahead with yet another. At last he held up the slate, frustrated that it had taken so long. "M-O-U-S-E, it is — ain't it?"

"Ach, yes. Brilliant."

Fergus rubbed out the word. "Next, Moll. Fire away." Looking up, he saw she had shut her eyes and turned her face to the light. She seemed to need the coaxing of the sun to feel well again.

"Sun's as good as butter," she said sleepily.

"Come, Moll. Throw me another word, if you please."

She sighed and opened her eyes. Glancing down at the speller she read the next word.

"Flour. The eating kind, not the blooming."

He began scratching. Spelling was easy enough. He had memorized the alphabet in the first few days and was beginning to grasp the composition of words, which were nothing but little hulks of letters, growling and shifting together. Sentences were another matter. Reading a sentence was the very hard ground.

Molly had picked up reading especially fast. Scanning a sentence and reading aloud, she would plunge ahead boldly, not afraid to guess at words she didn't recognize, laughing at her mistakes.

Words that gave up their meanings easily standing alone could conceal themselves very deftly in the blur of a phrase. He had trouble when he couldn't fix every single word perfectly — he didn't like to guess.

Coole's little children could rattle through paragraphs in the *Universal* without pause. Molly was catching up to them — he was the only one who had to grapple.

His chalk broke as he was finishing F-L-O-U-R. Suddenly sick of the business, he threw the bits over the side. "I don't care for spelling if I can't read! Something's bust in my head."

"There is nothing so. You're just rough, that's all. You are spelling along quite nicely."

"I feel poorly with it, feel small. I shall give it up."

Molly had closed her eyes, leaning back against the deckhouse with the red book open on her knees, her face tilted to the sun. "No, you'll pick it up, it's dogged as does it, Fergus. Work them slow, man, they'll come out. Your head ain't bust."

She wore the blue gown bought in Liverpool, dye so leached now it was almost silver. Her feet were bare — she disliked to wear her boots aboard ship. She said she preferred the feel of *Laramie*'s boards under her bare feet, and boots were better saved for walking on the American ground.

Every night they lay in their berth with Brighid's blackthorn stick between them. The stick he hated like bad music, like a killing, like the thought of Muck, and the Belfast man, and Kelly whoever Kelly had been. All those men hammering on her, wrecking her, making her tough but strange.

He wondered how long the *fianna* had been required to sleep with their swords.

Looking up, he watched Nimrod Blampin approaching, holding something in his hand, looking for a swap.

"Three old soldiers for a smoke?" Unwrapping three oily herrings from his handkerchief, Nimrod held them out for inspection.

With the shortage of cash and, lately, tobacco, the little herrings the sailors received as rations had become a currency on *Laramie*.

Molly took out a bundle from her pocket, unwrapped it, and offered Nimrod half a thumb of tobacco.

"The weather is sweet, ain't it, miss? You are lucky to have such a run." Stuffing the tobacco in his pipe, the sailor went off to the galley in search of a light, and Molly handed one of the little fish to Fergus, wrapping the others in a handkerchief.

"Aren't you hungry yourself?" he asked.

"Not so very."

She sat back, closing her eyes.

"My head's not in order. I wish I could get the letters faster," he complained.

"You're saying you are stupid, but I don't believe it."

He heard the bos'n's pipe twittering. The wind had shifted. Looking up, he watched sailors running up the ratlines. Looking at the men so high, he thought of the weird, silver days high on the Pass, hiding from dragoons. The air had a clean taste up there, when he'd lived so bare and rigorous; so narrow in his thoughts. Sucking herbs in his mouth, until they were soft enough to chew. Not letting his mind hold anything.

The sailors up highest, near the peak of the main, were bending royals, the smallest, uppermost sails.

"A deck looks very small from so high."

Fergus saw it was Ormsby who had spoken, the old man standing by the rail in his velvet coat and rawhide slippers, carrying a cane with a silver knob.

"The sea seems enormous," he continued, "and the ship seems like nothing at all."

"Have you been up yourself?" Fergus asked.

"When I was young."

"Perhaps I shall."

"No!" Molly said. "You'll break your head."

He looked her.

"I see it clear. I can! You'd fall and break your head and where should I be then?"

"I won't fall —"

"Don't you even say it. You'd leave me alone, wouldn't you? For the sake of nothing, for a stupid boy's game?"

He felt embarrassed in front of Ormsby by her passionate intensity. "Molly —"

"Promise you won't try it. Promise me, man."

"Molly . . ."

"It's no good, you should never have said it, you should never have thought it nor looked at it — now you must promise. Swear it."

"It really isn't so treacherous —" Ormsby began.

She cut him off. "Swear it, Fergus, you must." Reaching out, she grabbed his hand.

"All right, all right," he said peevishly. "Though I tell you I could have —"

"It spooks me, man, it does. I wish you'd never said nothing of it, that old stick, or looked up it, now we're so close. Now we're nearly to the other side, and I won't have you fall. I won't."

"All right, all right."

She kissed his hand.

"Will you introduce me to your friend?" said Ormsby.

Fergus introduced him and the old man made a bow to Molly, tipping his hat. "You run a very neat game, so I hear, miss."

"Neat enough. Neat and clean." She sounded irritated.

"Perhaps we might have a flutter sometime. Thirty One, *trente-et-un*, do you play?"

"You're a gentleman, mister. You're high stakes. I'm not that sort of a game."

"We might play a few hands very lightly. Just to pass the time."

She shrugged. "If you like."

"Excellent."

The beaky old man seemed to have nothing else to say, but he lingered by the rail.

"Are you an American?" Molly asked.

"I'm not a Yankee, miss, but I've spent most of my life on the other side."

"Tell us what it is like, then."

"What do you wish to know?"

"Can we get a farm?"

"That depends. Land can be cheap enough, rough land especially. It's clearing it and farming it that requires capital."

"Clearing?" Fergus said. "You mean drive the tenants off?"

"No, no — clear the timber."

"And the tenants? Are there tenants?"

"The tenants, if you call them so, are Indians of one kind or another."

"And they must be cleared? Is that what it takes to get a farm?"

"Farmers will clear Indians, yes, or sickness does the work. Cheap land is night-land, the backwoods of Illinois, or the Huron Tract. Pulling stumps and getting in a crop to feed animals over the winter, even if it's just Indian corn. You can acquire one hundred sixty acres cheap enough but you'll find it's rough work to farm."

"I don't want ground that's been cleared!"

"See how you feel when you have the cash."

Was it true? It would be terribly easy to make any piece of ground seem your own, by working it. It always had. As much your own as your hand or fist or head.

"How much capital do you reckon it takes to go farming?" Molly asked.

"Three or four hundred pounds. To start in a small way. My advice to you, miss, is try the cotton mills. Lowell, Saco, Woonsocket, and Fall River — the mills seem to have an endless appetite for hands."

"I could have stayed at Derry to be a hand! I wasn't born for mills, mister, I'd lose my mind."

"Well, when we get to Quebec, you'll see ladies on the quays, looking for girls —"

"Looking for slaveys?" she said bitterly.

"Yes — a lady's maid or some such."

"And how much wages do they get?"

"Oh, a dollar a week, perhaps. A couple of *louis*. Three or four shillings. German servants always preferred to Irish."

"I'm not nice enough for a slavey! I want the sweet wide-open, mister! I want land!"

"Then don't get snagged in the large towns. Start west, and keep going. If you're far enough ahead of the crowd you've done well. Go too far, of course, you stand to lose your hair."

"Lose my hair?"

"The savages on the western plains count coup by lifting a scalp. That lovely shade of yours would be valued considerable, so take care you keep it." Ormsby turned to leave, then stopped. "Shall we play a hand or two, miss, tomorrow afternoon? Cards on deck, right here in the lee, if the weather stays fine? I'd invite you both into the aftercabin, but Mr. Blow would make himself disagreeable."

"Here is good," she told him curtly.

Ormsby nodded, tipped his hat, and resumed his strut around the ship.

"He's a funny little bird," said Molly. "Lose my hair, indeed! Never I shall. Sell it, more likely — I wonder what they'd pay."

"He says he will follow a river like a wide road to the west, and if I go with him, I'd find a place in the trade, he says, the fur trade."

She studied him. "And what did you say?"

"That I couldn't accept."

"Why not?"

"On account of you. Because of you and me, Moll."

She was stuffing the bowl of her clay pipe. Not looking at him, tamping the tobacco with her thumb. Perhaps she thought him a fool for turning down Ormsby's offer.

Looking at her profile, her brown cheeks, small nose, small mouth — the strong jaw and mess of dark reddish hair streaked and filigreed by the ocean sun — he wondered what she'd have done if Ormsby had offered *her* a clear chance, an opportunity. Would she have left him — easily, lightly — as she had along that road in Wales?

Sheltered between the bulwark and the deckhouse, the wind cut very little. The planks were warm in the light, and a pungent, sweet scent of tar hung over the deck.

"Tell me, man," Molly said suddenly, her voice small with intensity. "Tell me what it is, tell me what will happen, tell me something, because it's getting fucking near, and I'm scared, I can't stand those navvy camps again."

"I am thinking we'll buy horses, Moll."

He had not framed a plan in words. Desperation, the pressure of her anxiety, had sprung the notion out of him. Almost instantly he could see it whole.

"Horses?"

"I trust my horse eye, Molly. I'd choose old stringers I could turn into something. Pick them carefully, looking for the bones, and get them cheap. Feed them up to sell at a profit. I reckon we could do worse than trading in horses."

"There it is, there it is," she murmured, "a fellow with a plan."

Taking up his hand, she brought it to her lips and kissed it.

He still had the herring in his other hand and ate the little fish in two bites, licking salt and oil from his fingers.

"We might move along, so." He felt the pressure of her hand squeezing his. "Build up a string. Might have a cart. Find the fairs. You could whirl them with a pack of cards. What do you think, Moll? Trading horses, and a pack of cards."

"It's good," she said firmly, keeping hold of his hand. "Might build up a stake that way."

Keep moving, he thought.

Horses and a girl.

ROLLED UP in her cloak, she lay with her back to him, asleep in the berth, while the ship creaked and sighed.

With the stake from Pharaoh, they could begin a string by picking up two or three cheap, sound animals, selected carefully, and a cart. He would graze them along the roads until they were worth more than he'd paid. All the while moving west. Selling animals to farmers. Buying more. Feeding them up and selling to carters, to liverymen.

Plow horses, cart horses, dray horses. Carriage steppers, saddle mounts.

Hunters.

Big roan hunters if he could get his hands on any.

Martin Coole was snoring in the berth above.

Lumps of sea ice bumped and scraped against the hull, very near their heads — perhaps a warning not to think so far ahead so glibly. You never knew what was coming.

But he couldn't sleep. His mind piling up riches, adding and accumulating.

With profits of trading, he'd keep adding to his string, until he was driving a herd of one or two hundred animals, like the hunting chiefs.

He could hear old Brighid snoring in her uppermost berth above the Cooles. Somewhere in the hold an infant was stirring. Not full-throated crying, not yet anyway. Only a little scratch of noise.

If life is so valuable, why is it invisible, practically weightless, like a cup of air?

He touched the blackthorn stick with his fingers. The wood felt cool and smooth.

Cold sank down the hatchway and was sidling through the hold, through the thick atmosphere of people sleeping. Their breath made white plaque along beams.

People coughing.

Horses, land. You want everything opening.

Her.

You want everything.

The Labrador Current

THE AIR HAD TURNED COLD, and the sea ran dark, nearly black. With the Cooles they were standing at the rail, peering over the side, looking for fish, when Fergus heard cries and, looking up, saw seabirds circling above the peak.

Martin Coole insisted that the cold, the birds, and the black water were all indications *Laramie* had struck the Labrador Current. "We shall be passing the rock of Newfoundland any day now. A few days more and we'll see Quebec." Coole put his arm around his wife, hugging her. "You'll see — we'll establish our school in Indiana — we'll bring the learning to their red minds."

"I'll not see my own mother again, that's all I know. I want my garden — and your children want shoes more than red men need books! We're thrown upon the world, thanks to you, like a pack of cabin johns — I hate America!"

"You're weary of the passage, dear." Coole tried to embrace her but she wriggled free, grabbed her children by their hands, and fled for the hatchway.

The schoolmaster watched his family disappear below. "She'll have a sweeter garden in America, sweeter by far, than ever she had in north Tipperary."

"How do you know, mister?" Molly asked.

"I have faith."

"Perhaps she won't have nothing so again. Perhaps she's right and there's nothing there, not even a pair of shoes."

"I don't believe that and you don't either, miss, or you'd not be aboard."

She was silent for a moment, considering. "I believe nothing's for sure and nothing comes as you think you want it."

Coole shook his head and turned to the rail, resting his elbows and gazing out to sea.

They had lost the blue of the western ocean. The sky was low, streaked with gray and yellow light. Fergus met Ormsby stalking the deck, wrapped in his fur coat.

"Nasty waters here, ice as big as houses," the old man said. "*Desdemona* out of Dublin was smashed by an ice castle in the Lab Current. Went down so quick, there was only six or seven of them and a monkey that survived."

THE FIRST ice castles appeared on the following day, butts of white ice as big as the ship, cruising gently in the black, calm water. *Laramie* had lost the hard wind, the strong way, of the western ocean. With a wintry thinness in the air, sails were loose, the yards creaking and squealing as they swung aimlessly, banging in stays. The sun was weaker than mid-ocean, and there was plenty of bitter fog. The rigging was sheathed in white ice, and the sailors smeared their hands with sticky tar before going aloft, and wrapped rags around their feet.

The cold, thin air seemed to exhaust *Laramie*. She was sluggish.

He couldn't smell America, all he could smell was ice on the wind, but Nimrod said the country lay close enough now. "If the old barky don't run into an ice castle and break up and drown us, you shall see the corner of Newfoundland any day, if it ain't for this wretched fog. If we don't get caught in pack ice in the gulf, but find the leads and the open water, we'll slip the mouth of the St. Lawrence soon enough. Then it is only a matter of beating the current and the tides on the pull up to Quebec."

It began to snow. By the time the cabooses were lit for supper, heavy wet snow dazzled the ship, thickening on every sheet and shroud, piling up on deck, drifting into knee-deep piles against the bulkheads.

Sailors kept lookout during the night. Fergus stood with Nimrod Blampin in the foredeck, peering through the thickly falling snow, trying to spot ice castles looming. The sea was flat and the ship was moving very gently on cold, weak air, almost adrift. Ranged along both sides, the lookouts smoked their pipes and sipped hot coffee. "By the time we see anything, it's too late to change course," Nimrod told him. "We're hardly making way enough to steer."

But *Laramie* crept through the night safely and the next morning a wind came up to blow the snow off the ship, shake the ice from the rigging, and rustle the sky clear.

Crossing the Mountains

THE OLD MAN GAVE Molly a buffalo robe to wrap herself in, and they played cards sitting on deck, in the lee, in bright, cold sunshine. She dealt Pharaoh, but the old man soon tired of that game and taught her to play *trente-et-un* for penny stakes. The play was even, the coins going back and forth.

Ormsby paid the black cook to bring them hot tea from the galley, and plates of toasted biscuits, slathered with Irish butter and honey from Ormsby's own supplies.

Fergus sat on another buffalo robe, working at the letters, using the *Dublin Universal*, frequently breaking off to watch the sailors aloft, fascinated by the shifting pattern of canvas being set and taken in; the speed and daring of men so high.

Ormsby was taciturn, drinking tea, smoking cigars, and dourly flipping cards. But he paid attention to the weather, looking up every time there was a change in the wind's force or direction. Fergus realized Ormsby was feeling the ship, anxious for her — as he was himself. He loved to feel they were grabbing every scrap of wind.

The buffalo robes were only a small part of Ormsby's baggage. "I have all my silver and china down below, ready in canoe packs. Forty-two panes of glass sunk in molasses barrels — I'll own the first glass windows in the Athabaska country. I only hope I reach Montreal in time to catch the brigade."

"Are your friends in America?" Molly asked.

"My friends are dead, miss."

After he had played out his hand and lost, the old man sat back puffing his cigar while Molly shuffled the deck.

It was warm enough in the sun. The buffalo robes smelled of old dust. Every now and then a shear of ice broke off the rigging and shattered on the deck.

"You don't have any people?" Molly asked the old man.

"None left."

Looking aloft, Fergus watched the seabirds circling. For the past few days they had been spattering the decks with white globs of dung.

"Shall I tell you how I met my wife?" Ormsby asked.

"If you like." Molly was dealing the fresh hand.

"I was leading a brigade from the bay across the Rocky Mountains. Bringing twenty packs of otter skins to the Russians in California. In those days, the Russians allowed the Company certain rights on their territory, and we paid in otters.

"It was October, late in the season for crossing the mountains. At Jasper House we fitted out a string of packhorses and started climbing for Howse Pass. However, the winter came in. The horses were no use in snow, and we were too far to turn back. We had to turn the horses loose and drag everything on sleds. At the top of the pass, the air was gray with snow. It was driving so hard, you could barely open your eyes.

"You don't often meet Indians in the mountains, but we came across a party of Peigans. Some on foot, others leading their ponies. How they got them up there, I do not know. They were not people we traded with. None of the grass nations are much for trade. The furs are of little value, and the people are brave, daring, and restless, never to be insulted with impunity.

"At first, I supposed it was a war party — until I saw they had women with them.

"They had been trading for tobacco with the Flathead Indians, on the western side of the mountains.

"We all took shelter there in a little notch, and brewed up tea. Not that it was a good place to stop, but some Indians, especially the grass nations, will prick easily if you don't do the right thing.

"She was wearing her winter robe when first I saw her. She was small, she was fine, and right there I appealed to her father, old Yellowtail, a famous horse thief. 'Why, I will have your daughter for my wife,' I said. 'I'll pay you an excellent gun, a barrel of powder, three pounds English money, a case of tea, treat her well, and honor to your family.' We smoked a good pipe on it, and she was mine."

"What happened then?"

"What happened? My life happened. Everything up until then, I can hardly remember. Everything after I cannot forget. I took her with me over the pass, made it to the boat encampment, and traveled down the Columbia without losing a man. We wintered in the Oregon country that year I remember. In the spring a Company ship arrived at Fort Vancouver, and I was ordered to sail for the Sandwich Islands — the Company wished to open a post. She came with me. She delivered our child on the island of Maui, but it did not survive. Three more babies, all sickly . . . none of them lasted. We were at Maui two years; then back to Oregon; over the mountains again in fall; into the Athabaska country. I became factor at Fort Edmonton. Daniel we bought from the brave dogs — Many Gray Horses, the Bloods called him, and his Crow name was the Constant Sky, though one must not speak it, now he is dead, and generally I don't — he became our son, our love, our child. Six winters past, he was killed on the buffalo hunt. On the Pembina Plains — the party was attacked by Sioux. Then my woman had a cancer in her heart, and after she was dead, that was when I went home. Home to Ireland." Ormsby scowled.

"We have had different kinds of life," Molly said. "I like yours better."

Ormsby rubbed his face briskly with both hands then looked at her. "You ain't had yours yet, miss. It is still coming at you."

Tenderness and Violence

A DRUNKEN PASSENGER was beating his daughter. No one interfered — they lay in their berths, listening to her bleating.

Outside Muldoon's door with a loaded pistol it wasn't fear that had stopped him from interfering, though fear was part of it — everyone in the shanty had been afraid of Muldoon. What had held him back was a sense that interfering between a man and a girl was trespassing. Though when it came to horses he'd have interfered, gone at a fellow with anything — fists, a knife, a gun.

He was unused to reflecting on his own inconsistencies but there suddenly seemed something so shameful in this one — so cold, weak, and unprocessed — that he sat up, bumping his head on the underside of the Cooles' berth.

"What are you doing, man?" Molly whispered.

Without answering, he pushed the curtain aside and swung his legs out, finding the deck with his feet. In the pitch of light from the one oil lamp hanging on a beam he saw the man circling the girl, who cowered with her legs drawn up and head tucked between her knees while he lashed her with a belt.

"Here, take this." Molly held out the blackthorn and he took it and started toward them, both hands gripping the shaft. Every curtain in the tiers was drawn shut but he knew the people must be awake. The stick had flex and felt light in his hands. With a blade fixed to its tip it would have made a passable pike.

Wiping his mouth with his sleeve, the man paid no heed as Fergus began prodding him with the stick, trying to drive him away from the girl. His eyes were embedded in yellow fat and his clothes stank of *poitin* and sweat. Suddenly he dropped the belt and grabbed the end of Fergus's stick, holding on to it with fists tight as gnarls, like deformations on the wood. Fergus tried to twist it from him then shoved it straight at him and speared him in the belly. He released his grip, and Fergus began striking him with flurried blows, beating the backs of his legs as he flung himself up the ladder and disappeared on deck.

The girl's mother and sisters crept out and half carried the whimpering creature back to their berth.

Are you a part of the world, like a bird, an apple tree, a fish, or the sea itself? Or are you here to judge it, everything in it, yourself included?

He had snapped the blackthorn stick with the last flurry of blows. He picked up both pieces and returned to the berth. Molly was sitting up, clutching the German blanket around her shoulders.

"There it is, your keep-away magic, I've bust it now."

He dropped the broken pieces on the bed, then climbed in.

Reaching across him, she drew the curtain shut, and he felt her breast touch his arm.

"He'll come after you, you know. You'll have to look out now." She stretched out on her side, pulling the blanket over herself, facing away.

He could feel the sick, wild heart bumping in his chest, an engine of grief. Why had she offered him the blackthorn, why had she placed it in his hands if she didn't wish him to break down what was separating them?

PASSION. HE awoke in the dark with her fumbling at the buttons on his shirt. She began pulling her gown over her head, then her shift, and he sensed the heat of her skin. Then she was naked. He touched her slowly, soft breasts and rough nipples. Her kisses were delicate, then hungry. Her teeth were wet and cool. She undressed him roughly, hauling his shirt over his head, tearing buttons from his trousers, dragging the trousers off his legs, grasping his prick with her fist, kissing the anguished tip of it. When he was inside her, she was whispering, touching his back with light, fluttering fingers. Pressing teeth on his ear, biting gently, and moving her hips with his.

Is this what it feels like, holding life in your hands?

As near as you'll get.

Practically everything.

Kissing the Peak

HE AWOKE AT THE SOUND of the ship's bell, lay listening to the sailors' feet scraping on the deck overhead as watches changed. Weak daylight and a tang of smoke filtered down through the open hatch. Molly was asleep, her body pressed close. Her delightful warmth and scent carried a charge. He felt a responsibility but it was unclear. Something he owed, but what and to whom? Without awakening her, he pulled on his clothes, swung himself out of the berth, and climbed up through the hatch.

Laramie was slack in a chill calm, making very little way. The man he had chased from the 'tween deck was sprawled by a bulkhead. Someone had thrown a blanket over him. Perhaps he'd come seeking vengeance. Or perhaps when sober he was soft and mild, like so many drinking men on the mountain.

Ormsby, swaddled in his fur coat and peering through a spyglass, was the only other passenger on deck.

Gripping a shroud, pissing over the side, Fergus stared at the slurry of ice and water rubbing along the hull.

Don't send me down to the fish.

Nimrod Blampin poured a shovelful of smoking coals into a caboose. "Look at him," the sailor said, nodding at the man under the blanket. "He's got the sweats, the florids — face all black — been barking all night. That's Irish fever, Michael. You better hope we raise Quebec before it spreads. I seen *Wandering*

Jew run aground at Mobile Bay with all aboard dead — passengers, master, and crew." Nimrod called to Ormsby, "What do you see there mister? Is it Cape Race?"

"Cape Race is out there." Ormsby lowered the glass.

"Can you see it?"

"No, but you might from up high."

"America, is it?" Fergus asked.

"Nearly enough — Newfoundland," Ormsby replied. "Captain Blow ought to send up a lookout. If I was ten years younger —"

"I'll go." Fergus spoke quickly, eager for the first sight of America.

"A lubber like you?" Nimrod said. "You'd fall and break your head."

"Wants a light foot up there. You won't need boots." Ormsby was already shucking off his rawhide slippers. "Here, you can wear these."

The wind was coming up, pressing like a weight at his ear as he knelt to untie his boots, a little stunned by how readily his offer had been accepted.

Your life doesn't weigh so very much, not for others.

"Your girl won't like it when you're smashed like a bowl of eggs." Nimrod sounded peevish. "You're a lubber, you've no business up there. You'll be feed for the birds. Takes a hand to go aloft."

The promise Molly had extracted.

Her lack of trust.

There was a piece of anger, he knew exactly where it was, like a splinter of glass.

"You'd better rub your hands with pitch. And take care where you step your feet," Ormsby said. "Don't trust the rungs; they look rotted through, half of them. Keep your grip on the shrouds, not the rungs."

Fergus slipped his feet into Ormsby's thin rawhide slippers. Fear was twisting in his stomach but it was too late now, he couldn't shame himself in front of Ormsby.

"Give me your hat, it'll only get in your way up there."

He handed it over — would he ever wear it again?

"You can't stop once you get started," Ormsby was saying. "Rub some tar. Avoid looking down."

Nimrod kicked the tar bucket. Fergus dipped his hands.

"Go now, go quickly," Ormsby said. "See what you can but don't stay too long or you'll freeze too numb to climb. Up and down while the sea is calm."

Light-headed and queasy, he crossed the slippery deck. The first ratline was seized to shrouds running from the starboard bulkhead to the main mast, just below a circular wooden platform the crew called the *top* though it was only the head of the mainmast, halfway to the peak of the ship.

Hoisting himself up onto the bulwark, he grabbed the shrouds and swung out. His body hung out over the water for a moment, then his feet found the rungs and he started climbing quickly, hand over hand.

The mainmast top was a wooden platform, size of a carriage wheel, braced to the mast by iron struts — the futtock shrouds. He could feel tension of wind singing off the mainsail. Reaching the underside of the top, he stopped, too disoriented to make the next move. Getting around the top meant letting go of the ratline and grasping another, seized to the futtocks, then crawling out, upside down, his back to the deck forty feet below.

His fingers were clenching onto the shrouds with a will of their own, and he stared at them and cursed them. Finally he was able to uncurl them and for a sickening instant held nothing, then grabbed the ratline seized to the futtocks. He started crawling out, hanging upside down. Reaching the rim of the top, hooking his right foot around a strut, he seized the topsail shrouds and dragged his body over the wooden rim, wriggled himself aboard the mainmast top.

The ship was rocking stem-to-stern, trying to throw him off. Hugging the mast, he forced himself to stand on the top. He looked down and saw Molly down on deck, in her blue cloak, standing next to Ormsby, the old man pointing up.

Above, the topmast was doubled to the main for six feet or so, hooped with iron, then the main ended and the topmast arose until it was doubled to the slender topgallant mast, which was doubled to the royal mast, which looked no thicker than a stick.

He could feel the mast trembling with energy humming off the sail. The golden wood was greasy from the buckets of tallow the sailors slushed on it continuously so yardarms could always be smoothly raised or lowered in their collars.

"Up . . . up . . ." Nimrod's shouts came at him all disjointed, like the wails of seabirds.

The next climb was thirty feet of narrowing and nearly vertical ratline seized to the topmast shrouds. Many rungs were broken and one snapped underfoot, but he clung to the shrouds and kept climbing.

He reached the topsail yard and stepped on it gingerly. The honey-colored wood was glazed with ice. The sail was bent to an iron rail along the top of the yard.

Ice sheathed the upper shrouds, but when he beat them with his fist the ice crumbled in his face. His face felt thickened and stiff from cold. The wind droned as it was forced off the sails.

He scrambled up the next twenty feet on a ratline seized to the topgallant shrouds. The rungs were hardly wide enough for his foot. From the yard he swung onto another ratline and kept climbing. Now there was just a toe-width to the rungs. He looked down at the deck, one hundred feet below, trying to catch a glimpse of her but could not.

He sat out on the royal yard clinging to the ludicrously slender royal mast, which rose another eight feet as narrow as the whip of a young tree and was topped with a round hardwood knob — the peak of the ship. To kiss the peak he would have to stand on the frail royal yard and shinny up the last couple of feet.

Is courage just the awareness that gestures, journeys, lives have intrinsic shape, and must, one way or another, be completed? That there is a path to be followed, literally to the death? Awareness is harsh but better than being unaware, never sensing a path. Better than a life of stunts, false starts, dead ends. Better than the irredeemable ugliness of the halfhearted. Better than feeling there is no shape to anything — there is. The world knows itself.

He stood up slowly, balancing on the narrow yardarm, clinging to the frail mast. He began shinnying up, the wind whipping his hair. He kissed the cap, then clung to the mast as *Laramie* heeled to port. Letting go he'd plummet straight into the sea. Through low-slung clouds, he caught a glimpse of rocky headland. An image of his father's face — cheekbones, lips, blue eyes — came before him, and he began shouting "Land ho! Land ho!" into the hustle of the wind.

The Coffin Ship

AIRS IN THE ST. LAWRENCE GULF were cold and thin as *Laramie* worked her way cautiously, keeping south of a mottled plain of pack ice.

Each night in their berth Molly came up out of herself as if she had never before tasted joy. He found he could stir her up easily. She didn't seem to care what anyone overheard.

They lunged at each other and he felt the ship moving underneath.

Passion was charged and disorienting, like banging on the door of the world.

FOUR DAYS past Cape Race, *Laramie* dropped anchor in a cove on the south shore of Anticosti Island. Three sailors and the bos'n rowed ashore to fill water casks while passengers along the rail peered at slabs of ice lying on the beach like wrecked ships. A sour aroma of fir reached out across the cove.

"Where are the people, man? What's become of the people?" Molly demanded.

There were no openings in the curtain of evergreen forest, no smoke or animals. Mrs. Coole wept at the bleakness of it.

The water casks were slung aboard and the passengers jostled to fill their pots and kettles. The water's stinging coldness made him think of Luke.

Astringent water squishing out of the turf as they walked.

Filling his mouth again, he felt the cold water tear at his gums. He splashed his face then reached out, dribbling water on Molly's head.

"What's that?" she cried.

Passion drives you forward. The future is available and you order yourself to relinquish the dead.

NEXT DAY the gloomy gulf clouds lifted, and cooks stirring porridge at the cabooses glimpsed the snowy mountains of Notre Dame on the Gaspé coast. The schoolmaster insisted they would be raising Quebec itself in a matter of hours. Passengers spent the day packing then sat up all night guarding their baggage, but the next morning there was nothing to see except the endless forest along the north shore.

He kept going to the rail. Where were the emigrants who had sailed this way before them?

It was as if the country had consumed them, but he didn't feel discouraged by the emptiness. There was something in it that he trusted. The pleasing glitter of the daylight.

Of course, light didn't matter, it was only light. It was the absence of darkness; but you couldn't eat it.

Whales rose hissing in the river. Thousands of black-and-white ducks beat across the flat bays, their wet wings making a whirring, groaning noise.

Sips of cold water bit the tongue.

Finally they saw one cabin in a clearing, with a red cow and calf grazing around stumps and smoke curling from a heap of burned timber. A sort of *púcán* boat was drawn up on the beach where a man and a boy were repairing a fishing weir staked out into the river.

"Is it Indiana?" Fergus asked Ormsby.

"We're coming into old Canada now."

But the clearing slipped behind quickly, and there were no further marks of settlement along the shore.

In the lee of the deckhouse Molly, gorgeous and burnished, was basking in humid sunshine. He sat down beside her.

"We can handle half a dozen horses, easy, on a string. One for you to ride, one for me, and four to trade. We'll tie flowers around their necks, water them at the river, and graze them along the road."

"No roads I see," she murmured.

This was true, but passion makes you hopeful and tough.

"A horse wants open country and dry feet. I'll make a world of this, Molly."

THEIR STAKE was kept at the bottom of their sea chest, rolled up in hand-kerchiefs. When she went to count it that evening, it was gone.

"Sure, it's there," he insisted.

"No, it isn't I tell you, it isn't!"

"You might have missed it."

"I wouldn't — I've missed nothing — it's gone."

They turned out the chest and pawed through the contents: their steel knife, Molly's boots, two last sprouting onions, blankets and woolen clothes he'd stolen from Maguire's Germans. They couldn't find the money.

Standing on the edge of their berth, Molly pushed open the old woman's curtain. "Where is our money?"

"God help you. Are you asking for a look in my blue bottle or are you calling me a thief?"

"You old poison cook, I know you took it. Tell me where it is."

"You are a bad girl. You haven't a heart for them that has helped you."

Molly began poking and prodding the old woman's straw pallet. Brighid climbed down with an air of injured dignity, drew on her shawl and headed for the ladder, leaving Molly furiously shaking potion bottles, searching for coins sunk in the fluid.

Finding none, she confronted the Cooles. "You wanted money for your school."

The schoolmaster began turning out his pockets.

"Stop it, Martin," his wife said. "You humiliate yourself."

"I'll humiliate him if he has my money —"

"You watch your gash with me, miss! *Sraoilleog!* Hussy! Clipping the cash off poor men! He hasn't taken your swag and if you say it again I'll smack you down, what you deserve!"

"Well someone's got it!"

"They don't," said Fergus wearily, "they are our shipmates."

"Well who then?" White faces were peering down from the tiers. "Who has our money? Do you? Do you? You wretches, which of you has stolen our money? God help me if I find you, I'll whip you blue —"

"Quench it, Molly, it's no use."

She flung herself into their berth and lay in stormy silence, wrapped in her cloak, until Mrs. Coole went up on deck to cook the stirabout. Then Molly crawled out and began digging through the Cooles' trunk while the schoolmaster lay in his berth not lifting a finger to stop her. Finding nothing in the trunk, she began to poke and feel the straw pallet where he lay.

"Stop it, Molly." Fergus began pulling her away. She struggled, then broke free and ran up the ladder.

After helping Coole repack the trunk, Fergus climbed on deck. There was little wind. The sails were flapping and banging. Smoke from the cabooses hung over the deck. Mrs. Coole glared at him.

Seeing Molly up in the bow, he went forward. She was alone, smoking her pipe. He stood next to her, resting his elbows on the rail, watching *Laramie's* prow split the black river, curling back a froth of white.

"I'm sorry for your horses, Fergus."

How different was the river from the sea. Sweeter. He could feel the country drawing in, the scent of trees and ground.

"There will still be horses."

"Hold on to me, man."

Her body light and warm, like a candle.

THE MAN he had chased up the ladder died with his face dark and swollen. *Fiabhras dub*, black fever. The sailors called it *ship fever*.

It was snowing so thickly they couldn't see either shore. Two of the man's daughters shivered as the sailmaker sewed up the corpse in a piece of canvas, along with a chunk of iron. Mr. Blow didn't try to read any prayers. The hands set the bundle on a plank, carried it to the rail, and quickly tipped it into the river.

"Call it what you will, it's typhus," Fergus overheard Ormsby telling Mr. Blow. "Scour the ship, scour what can be scoured and throw away everything else, then lower a caboose to smoke the hold and hope to God we raise Quebec before it spreads."

For the first time since Cape Clear, they were ordered to collect the filthy straw from the hold and pitch it overboard along with blankets, old clothes, rags, and garbage. There was no fresh straw; they would have to sleep on the boards. Sailors were made to throw away their hammocks. The passengers scrubbed the ship from stem to stern using hot water, straw brooms, and clean yellow sand from the ballast.

He was helping dump straw and trash into the river when he saw a bungled hammock passed up through the fo'c'sle scuttle. The sailors placed the bundle on deck, the sailmaker folded it open, and with wet snow driving in their faces they all stared down at Nimrod Blampin's naked corpse, his chest and arms covered with maroon blotches. "He went quite hard, poor fellow. Very warm, terrible headache, sweats, then blisters."

Nimrod's hammock was sewn up with a lump of iron ballast inside and Mr. Blow was summoned. The sailors removed their tarpaulin caps and stood in silence while the master read English prayers then slapped his prayer book shut with a last, distracted "Amen" and hurried back to the afterdeck. "There it is, Nimrod dear," cried the sailmaker as the hands raised the plank and tipped it. The bundle stuck for a moment then slid off abruptly, knifing into the current and sinking quickly so that when Fergus looked back he saw nothing in their wake but the tawny flotsam of straw and garbage.

"IF IT's spread to the crew, we'll be next," Mrs. Coole said. "See what your politics and your false religion have done? My poor children!"

"A good douse will preserve them." Coole clapped his hands. "Come, Carlo! Come, Deirdre!"

The Coole children peeked out from the uppermost berth where they had taken refuge with Brighid. A few passengers were still scrubbing, but most were occupied packing and repacking their trunks and sea chests.

"Clean they must be. Come with me, children!"

"No, the water's too cold, Martin."

Ignoring his wife, Coole lifted down Carlo and Deirdre. He began leading them to the ladder, but Mrs. Coole grabbed Deirdre's hand.

"You cannot wash off what you have done to us, Martin!"

"Clean they must be," the schoolmaster said doggedly. "It's filth that kills."

They tugged the little girl back and forth, both children howling, until Mrs. Coole let go suddenly and the schoolmaster began herding them up the ladder.

"Stop him! Whatever I say only makes him worse!" Mrs. Coole begged Fergus. "Don't let my babies come to harm!"

Reluctantly, he climbed onto the deck where Coole was looking agitated and disheveled, his jacket, wild hair, and beard flapping in the wind. "Don't you say, Fergus," the schoolmaster shouted, "there is nothing healthier than a freshwater bath?" Carlo and Deirdre were crying as they undressed, and Fergus wondered if the schoolmaster intended to pitch his children overboard. Then he saw that Coole had dropped a bucket over the side and was hauling it up.

"Too cold for bathing, mister."

"Never! Hurry! Hurry now!" Coole shouted at the children. "Peel off your clothes! Pluck off your hideous things! Time to get clean!"

"Why not Mama?" the little girl whined. "Why isn't she come with us?"

"She will, she will!"

"Come on, mister," Fergus cajoled. "You ought not to soak them — it's too cold."

"Too cold for pure water? It's not cold that kills, it's filth and the poison air, the miasma down below."

Setting one full bucket at his feet, Coole quickly lowered another. He turned to the afterdeck where the figure of Mr. Blow could be seen, standing near the ship's wheel.

"I have seen Hell, and Hell is a ship! Hell, sir, is your ship! Can you hear me, sir?" the schoolmaster roared. "That makes you the devil, don't it? The Satan of the pits! I curse thee, Satan! From a thousand tombs I curse thee!"

The wind was blowing strong off the beam. It was doubtful the master could hear.

"Cold is clean. Come, come, Carlo! Who shall be first? It must be you."

The little boy stood with arms by his sides, fists clenched, and eyes squeezed shut as his father drenched him. Picking up the next bucket, Coole approached the little girl, who was naked and shivering. He dashed the bucket over her and the child began to dance and howl, slapping herself.

"There it is, my turn now!" Coole cried, throwing off his coat. He tore his shirt over his head and was kicking off his boots when his wife appeared at the hatch.

"Martin!"

Both children ran to her, howling.

"Douse me, for the love of God!" Coole cried to Fergus. "Douse me!"

Flinging away his trousers and his drawers, the schoolmaster stood naked. "For the love of God, will you give me a drench! Satan, I renounce thee!"

The bos'n and a party of sailors were approaching — the bos'n holding a cargo net. "I renounce thee, Satan!" Coole screamed. "Get behind me, imps of Hell!" Fergus picked up a bucket and pitched it and the schoolmaster whooped when the water struck him, then, slipping on wet planks fell onto his hands and knees. "Again!" he screamed. "Douse me again! Douse me!"

The bos'n flung the net, and the sailors quickly seized him up like a lobster and started carrying him below. Fergus followed, sickened by the schoolmaster's howls as the men crammed him into a sail locker, ruin burst open for strangers to see, humiliation exposed to the world.

The Wager

OVERNIGHT THEY HAD SLIPPED into settled country. The Canada sun shone with strange ferocity as *Laramie* beat her way upriver.

Soaked with spray, he stood out on the slick, wet bowsprit, clutching a buzzing stay and watching farmers with ox teams working fields running back from the river in black and yellow stripes.

The St. Lawrence River threw herself at them in brilliant splashes. The moan of wind on canvas.

Passengers stood packed along the starboard rail, holding up babies, laughing in the light, pointing out farmhouses with chimneys leaking smoke, wooden barns, stone churches.

The new country dousing them awake.

He saw children tending cattle, driving flocks of sheep. At a wooden jetty two men stacked cordwood into a scow.

"Here it is, man, here it is!" Molly stood in the prow, small and soaked, her hair black from spray, the wet gown clinging to her body.

The passion in her voice was the bead of life. She was scanning the country like a hungry owl, absorbing it.

Men and women need each other, don't they.

* * *

FORTY-ONE days after clearing Clarence Dock, *Laramie* dropped anchor below the quarantine station at Grosse Île, an island in the St. Lawrence twenty miles downstream of Quebec. They had two fever cases aboard: the girl Fergus had tried to protect, and her sister.

The line of ships at anchor stretched two miles in the river. A few had been inspected and flew the green flag of quarantine, but most were awaiting medical men to come out and remove their fever cases to the island so that their days in quarantine could begin.

Ormsby was pacing the deck impatiently. They had been at anchor twenty-four hours, with no sign of inspectors. "Dammit, we'll be floating here all summer! I must reach Montreal before the canoes leave!"

There were swans in the river. Even the quarantine island looked green and pleasant from the ship. The fever lazarettos — long white sheds — were isolated at the eastern tip, and the rest of the island was covered in broad-leaved trees that were coming out soft and green in the heat.

In the middle of the second afternoon at anchor he watched a noisy little steamer beating away from a jetty at the western end of the island, carrying emigrants who had passed through quarantine upriver for Quebec and Montreal.

Three more emigrant ships hove into sight and dropped anchor that afternoon. The powerful heat of Canada enclosed *Laramie*, pungent with the stink of liquefying tar. A scum of trash and straw floated on the river — masters hoping to impress the medical authorities were cleansing their emigrant holds.

Skiffs and flatboats worked between the ships at anchor selling provisions and water. Leaned over the rail, Fergus listened to Ormsby haggling in the Canadian tongue with a boatman who wore a red stocking cap. The old man handed down coins bundled in a handkerchief, and the boatman passed up a cheese, a loaf of fresh bread, and a pot of honey.

At twilight the cabooses were fired. They sat on coils of warm rope and ate stirabout. Martin Coole had kept to his berth since his release, not saying a word, eating only what his children spooned him, taking water only if their hands held the cup. "Is there a potion you can dose him?" Mrs. Coole had asked the old woman. "Something to deliver him back — he's no man at all now."

"Get him on the ground. If he can walk on ground he'll be cured, if you can keep him alive so far. I want nothing but ground myself."

They anxiously waited for the inspectors. Since Cape Race everyone had been alert for the coughs, blushes, and headaches that might signal fever. No one wished to be taken off the ship, though the island looked pretty enough, birches growing down to the shore, bright and fresh, without the darkness of Anticosti.

At dusk the sun was red and fat. When it grew dark, Fergus heard *uilecan* laments, funeral cries, drifting across the water from the other ships. It seemed there was fever on the anchorage.

THEY LAY spooned on the bare boards of their berth. Molly slept after a while, but the stillness kept him awake, listening to the anchor chain gnash at the hawsers.

Finally he swung out of the berth and climbed out onto the main deck, where the air was a little livelier.

The sound floated across the water, so low and soft he thought it was an owl. Somewhere on the anchorage a woman was keening.

The sound cut off abruptly, as though someone had shushed her. A moment later he heard a splash. He couldn't see anything but knew it must be a body going into the river from one of the ships near them, getting rid of their dead before the inspectors came out from the island.

He spent the rest of the night moving around the main deck and foredeck, sleeping in snatches on various coils of rope. When dawn showed, he headed for the galley, intending to trade tobacco for a mug of coffee.

"*Laramie! Salût, Laramie!*"

He looked over the side. The boatman who'd bartered with Ormsby stood in his scow, which bumped lightly against the ship. Seeing Fergus, the boatman threw a line, which Fergus caught and made fast as he had seen the sailors do.

"*Prenez garde, Michaud.*" Ormsby had appeared on the afterdeck, wearing rawhide slippers. "Keep everything quiet, I warn you."

The bosn'n appeared with three sailors, who began quietly passing Ormsby's trunks, casks, and wooden crates down into the scow.

"I'm glad to see you — I have something for you. Come with me." Taking Fergus by the arm, Ormsby led him to the other side of the ship. There were swans clucking in the river. Ormsby took out a purse and snapped it open. "Hold out your hands."

"What for?"

"Just do as I say."

Ormsby turned out the purse, and the coins tumbled into Fergus's hands, clicking and heavy.

"What is it?"

"Eight pounds. It's yours, I believe."

"Mine? You stole our stake? You?"

"I won it. Fairly, mind you."

"You won it?"

"Ask your girl." Ormsby clicked the purse shut. "That morning you went up, she asked if I thought you'd make it down alive. I said you weren't the first passenger to climb a peak — I'd done it myself, half a dozen times. *Then*, she said, *we must make a wager on it, for I believe he'll fall and break his head.*

"*What makes you think that?* I asked. *A feeling*, she said.

"*You'd bet against your own man's life?* I asked.

"*I'd better get something out of it*, she replied.

"I thought this very cold.

"*Eight pounds even money*, she said.

"*Done*, I said. That evening she had the money wrapped in handkerchiefs." Ormsby hesitated. "It is strange winnings, I feel. It's your blood money. Better you should keep it."

Suddenly turning away, Ormsby crossed to the other side of the ship, where they were still lowering his baggage into the scow. "Easy there, men," he called softly. "There's beauty glass sunk in them tubs."

Betrayal tastes cold on the tongue, but you don't feel it so much, right at first; you're trying to pull yourself inside.

IN THE dimness of the 'tween deck, a few mothers were nursing their children, but most people still lay in the berths, with their curtains drawn open in the breathless heat.

Coole lay on his side. Mrs Coole was asleep. The old woman was snoring like a frog in the uppermost, with Carlo and Deirdre snuggled beside her.

Molly was wrapped in her cloak, her mouth slightly open. She looked peaceful. She looked happy.

As he began laying out coins on the berth, she stirred, sighed. He added coins softly. A carpet of metal. A shield. He knew he was letting go of something but didn't know what it was. The lightness was making him dizzy.

You betray only yourself, you turn away from yourself.

He wanted to touch her neck, spine, hip, buttocks. Reach between her legs and open her up.

Her eyes opened suddenly. She gazed at him.

He turned and headed to the ladder.

What does it matter, the souls of others? Inside your head you're alone. Nothing's real but your own brain talk.

He heard the coins jingling as she sat up. "Fergus!" He grabbed the rungs and ran up the ladder. The last load of Ormsby's goods was being passed over the side as he came out on deck.

"I'd like to go with you."

Ormsby looked at him keenly for a moment, then nodded. "Your baggage — fetch it quickly."

"There's nothing. Let's go."

A minute later he was sitting in the scow with the river breeze on his shoulders. He glimpsed her at the rail wearing her cloak and heard her calling his name, but he looked away. He didn't wish to feel anything; he was tired of feeling. He wondered if there were salmon in the river and how to catch them.

PART VI

The Law of Dreams

CANADA, MAY 1847

Grosse Île

THE CANADIAN BOATMAN was shouting in his peculiar tongue as their little vessel bobbed and smacked against the current.

"Michaud says *les Irlandais* are dying like shad flies, this year." Ormsby was studying the quarantine island through his looking glass. Fergus saw long, low whitewashed sheds in a clearing, iron roofs glinting in the sun.

"Lazarettos. Fever sheds." The old man lowered his glass. "Don't feel feverish, do you? Got the shakes? Moldy tongue?"

"I don't."

"The flush? Any bones aching?"

"No there isn't."

"Good. Michaud is taking us direct to the point on the island where the Montreal steamer puts in. Quarantine never was intended for gentlemen."

MICHAUD PUT them ashore at a little cove. There was a wooden jetty, and dozens of emigrants scrubbing their clothes in the shallows.

"Michaud says these have all passed their quarantine. *William Molson*'s due in an hour. We'll see Montreal tomorrow."

The boatman quickly unloaded Ormsby's boxes and trunks.

"Sure you don't want to come with us, Michaud?" the old man teased as he paid the Canadian. "We'll find you a pretty Blackfoot wife up the country."

Michaud shook his head and bit the coins before wrapping them in his hand-kerchief. Fergus helped push the boat off the beach. The line of ships riding at anchor stretched as far as he could see. He couldn't tell which was *Laramie;* they were all three-masters and looked alike from this distance, and he wasn't accustomed to seeing her from without.

"My legs want a stretch," said the old man. "If we walk up around the point, we might see the Montreal boat coming in."

Another town hard as Liverpool would smash you.

Didn't have the wire for it, did you.

HE KEPT stumbling and tripping, his legs not adjusted to the buck of solid ground. The old man walked serenely. It was raining. Ormsby seemed younger, more limber, now, in his own country.

To get around the tip of the island they cut in through a thicket of fir, red willow, and birch not yet in leaf, the old man slashing at branches with his stick. There were fiddleheads waiting for the sun to open and lumps of grainy blue snow in the deepest shade.

They finally came out to a little headland with a view upriver. He could no longer see the ships downstream. Ormsby hoisted himself onto a boulder and began striking a steel to relight his cigar.

The green St. Lawrence seemed electric and forceful, flaunting a sense of hazard.

All she is, is a parcel of information traveling inside your brain.

You could always find another girl couldn't you? Buy yourself another girl.

Pulling off his boots, rolling up his trousers, he waded out a few feet. The water was terribly cold.

What happens to the dead dropped into this river?

What he'd enjoyed was her smell. The sweet smell of her neck, nose, and lips. Also, her toughness; and her wicked determination to stay alive, which had been so powerful, and capable, he had believed, of carrying both of them through.

The bottom was pebbled and sandy. He made himself stand quite still while the water was numbing his feet and shins.

What you must do: Struggle. Watch. Proceed.

When he looked straight down, the water was a dozen shades of green.

He kept still, waiting for a fish.

After a minute or so, he saw one swimming. Almost near enough to scoop with his hands if only he were quick enough.

A fish knew what it wanted. A moving case of hunger.

Wading ashore, he began searching for a stick that was supple enough and sufficiently long for a lister.

"May I have use of your knife?" he called to Ormsby, perched on the boulder, puffing his cigar.

The old man dug into his pocket and tossed him down a clasp knife, and he began peeling the stick to the bright green underneath, then the heartwood. In a couple of minutes he had whittled one end to a sharp point.

You do not want feelings, but emptiness inside. Resilience, poise. No attachment.

Gripping the springy lister, he waded out until the water reached halfway up his thighs. He waited, letting the cold bite.

A kill is patience.

He saw a flash, and then the salmon rose almost to the surface, writhing through the water with a couple of elegant twitches.

A fish was always hunting.

He could feel Ormsby observing from his perch.

That old man knew enough to be silent.

Come, sweetheart. I will treat you nice.

Was Molly sleeping? Dreaming? Was he part of the dream?

Ought not think of her. Ought to turn her off.

Get another. Sure.

Feelings weigh nothing. Sorrow is a vapor.

A girl gets inside, though, just as a thief does.

Men get hard, don't they? They coarsen.

He raised the lister and was about to thrust when the silence was broken with the shriek of a whistle. Glancing up, he saw the Montreal steamer, perhaps a quarter mile off, water cascading off her paddle wheel.

Even as he plunged the spear he knew he'd missed his chance. The fish touched him, writhing between his legs and swiftly out of reach.

Upriver

FROM MONTREAL IT WAS SEVEN weeks' journey on to Rupert's Land. "Make the trip with us and you shall have your apprenticeship," Ormsby promised. "Apprenticeship leading to clerkship. Clerkship to factorship. You'd count for something then. Men get rich in the trade, see if you don't."

The old man had paid for a cabin with two neat berths. It was two days to Montreal by steamer, with stops at Quebec and Three Rivers. Emigrants slept on deck, and the only other cabin passengers were two pink-cheeked English officers traveling to join their regiment at Montreal, and willing to play cards all night with Ormsby in the captain's saloon while Fergus lay in his uppermost berth, unable to sleep, aware of the seethe of *William Molson*'s boilers, the machinery of iron arms and gears turning her paddle wheel, stroking them upriver.

What would you feel in the heart of a fire? The roar of the blaze hammering your ears, smoke packing your throat, flames dabbling at your skin. What would you feel as everything was collapsing? Whom would you see in those flames?

A THUNDERSTORM shook the sky after midnight. He heard rain beating down and knew it must be soaking them out on deck under their little shebangs of blankets and baggage. The old man's berth was empty; he was still at cards, with the pair of shiny soldiers.

Men get rich in the trade.

He wouldn't mind being rich. Being noisy in a carriage. Feet in glossy boots.

Shea's gentlemen, in beautiful clothes, selecting girls.

Shea's kindness to him. The memory of which would die with him. The world buries everything.

He did not wish to review the dead; it was painful sorting, no use.

He was for entering a trade.

Luck had kept you alive so far, and was holding.

A girl climbs inside your skin, though. It can be difficult to breathe.

Never very good at holding on, was she? Not constant. Didn't have that in her.

ORMSBY RETURNED at dawn, red with victory. Sitting on the edge of his berth and counting his winnings, he was full of plans.

"We'll find you a wife up the country. Fort Edmonton, the Christmas dances, Blackfoot girls on the hop — how they dance to a fiddle — you'll not see a foot touch the ground. Passion is necessary, man! Nothing like warm feelings!"

Lying in his upper berth, none of the talk could touch him, it was insubstantial, it had no grip or feel. It was just noise. What was real was the pressure singing in the steam boilers and the crazy throbbing of the wheel.

His engine of days was bust, somehow. The world no longer convincing.

AT THE breakfast table the captain said eighteen fever cases had developed overnight among the deck passengers. Even the two English officers sipping coffee looked seedy and disarrayed, coats unbuttoned and hair unbrushed, whispering *if you please* and *thank you* to the little steward filling their cups.

"I'll tell you what's wrong with *them*," Ormsby said as he walked the cabin deck after breakfast, clutching Fergus's arm like an old, powerful bird, a hawk with talons. "I beat 'em! Beat 'em all night and something ferocious. Losing a hundred at cards will give any young fellow a poor color, especially on his way to joining a regiment the dear old pater can't afford in the first place."

From the rail they looked down at the fever cases lying out on the main deck, wrapped in their blankets in the bright, hot Canada sun.

"God have mercy," Ormsby shivered. "All my life, Fergus, I have watched people die, of broken necks, plague, fever, cold. Never understood what to make of it, or if there's anything there. Only that it's a ruthless sort of a business, and the secrets are all buried."

THEIR FIRST death was off the town of Three Rivers. The victim had no friends aboard, his wife and children having died on the Atlantic crossing. From the cabin deck Fergus watched the bos'n sewing the dead man into a piece of oilskin with chunks of iron for ballast, then the deckhands picking up the shrouded corpse on a board, lifting it to the rail, and letting it fall into the river.

Three more of the fever cases died that afternoon between Three Rivers and the St. Mary's current. He heard the captain tell the hands to put them over quickly, but this time their relatives refused to let crewmen near the bodies, insisting the dead be left in peace until they could be carried ashore at Montreal and buried in the ground like Christians.

Water's always moving, you can't lie there. There's no ending, down there. Perhaps for fish.

A body wants the ground.

Montreal

FROM THE CABIN DECK, he watched a collection of iron roofs and steeples panning white in the evening sun, and the hump of a mountain rising behind the gray stone buildings of Montreal town.

The captain had told Ormsby steamers were not permitted to land emigrants at the city quays; instead they would be put ashore at Windmill Point, where fever sheds had been erected. "Montreal certainly don't want the Irish," Ormsby remarked.

The current at Windmill Point was awkward and *William Molson*, coming in with steam up and paddle wheel flashing, banged into the quay with such force that passengers were knocked off their feet. The deckhands were already throwing lines ashore, making fast, and before the gangway was run out he could see people pitching their baggage onto the quay, and lodging-house runners seizing it up and throwing it into their carts.

Everyone screaming.

Fear, haste, thievery.

They had arrived.

THE OLD man paid the deckhands to carry his boxes and trunks onto the quay, then hired a horse cart and told the driver to deliver his baggage to

Donegani's Hotel on Notre Dame Street. *William Molson*'s fever cases were being carried off to lazarettos, long wooden sheds exactly like those on the quarantine island. The English officers had hired a carriage and were offering a lift to town. "No, we'll walk, gentlemen, thank you kindly," he told them. "I want to find my land legs."

The fever sheds were newly built and stood in a midden of mud and sawdust. In a sheep meadow out beyond, long fresh ridges of brown soil had been planted with whitewashed crosses, and gravediggers at work in a trench were so deep that only their hats showed, and the bites of soil flinging off their spades.

A blinkered horse stood placidly harnessed to a cart with six yellow coffins stacked aboard.

"They have come a long way to die," Ormsby remarked.

You imagine her heat inside one of them boxes, nailed shut.

IN THE open fields that lay between Windmill Point and the town, emigrants were sheltering in hundreds of shebangs made from scraps of lumber, tin, and sailcloth. Traffic of drays and carts, wagons, and barrows began thickening as they came into Montreal. At every street corner were emigrants perched on piles of baggage, men sucking their pipes, women nursing red babies. All wore the same bewildered expression.

"I always expected to die in a river," Ormsby's voice sounded small, or perhaps it was just the noise all around, teamsters cracking whips, wagons groaning. Fergus looked at him. Something had lit inside the old man, a yellow energy burning. He gripped Fergus's arm. "The North River, the French, Rainy River," he gasped, "the Winnipeg, the Churchill, the North Saskatchewan. Columbia herself. We used to take any kind of chance, run any kind of a chute, to save ourselves a carry."

"You'd be clean in a river," Fergus said.

"Yes. You'd be clean."

Fergus looked at him closely. His face had flushed pink. "Are you not well?"

"A little bit of a heat." Ormsby began to laugh, the laugh became a sputter, then Fergus had to support him while coughing racked his body.

"I'll tell you what it is," the old man sputtered. "My knees . . . ache. Something dreadful. They do."

That was fever.

Of course it was.

"How far is it to go? Shall I hire a cart?"

"No, no. I must walk it . . . walk it out. Dreadful cramps, that's all. 'Tis all those weeks aboard . . . not natural. Come along, Fergus, come along, I ain't stopping here."

Wind fluttered the scent of hay through the muddy street. Horses and muck. Stone buildings with iron shutters. Flies humming.

The old man had halted again, this time on a little iron bridge humped over a canal; the canal lined with factories, their chimneys smoking. In the factory yards he could see organized stacks of yellow lumber and ash heaps big as houses. Dozens of workmen swarming over a steamboat that was being constructed.

"Busy is money," Ormsby wheezed. "This is all upriver trade." Taking a handkerchief from his pocket, he mopped his brow. "Sometimes the world resembles an animal, Fergus. A bull. A lost sheep. A gray wolf. I've seen the world at Red River looking like a fox in autumn."

Fever talking.

He watched a timber raft, sculling along the canal.

Thinking of Molly's smell, touch, noise.

He remembered lying on his back in bracken on top of the world, hearing cattle, knowing every sound. Shadows of clouds speeding across the mountain.

But the past is nothing.

The world cuts you open. You don't close.

"Plenty of Irishmen working in the timber." Ormsby's voice had a low, strained urgency. "The Canadians fight 'em . . . the work's in winter . . . flooding out of the backwoods now. Drink up their pay . . . we'll have a few of 'em for the brigade."

Talking for the courage. Talking to hear himself alive.

"Here, you'll need something in hand." Taking out his purse, Ormsby withdrew a gold sovereign and held it out.

"What do you want out of me, mister?"

"You'll need money for the town. Tomorrow we'll get you a decent suit of clothes."

"What do you care what happens to me?"

"You must learn to accept a gift. There is fortune as well as misfortune, you know."

Fergus took the coin. "I'm a loose rock, mister. I'm a ribbonman for all you know —"

"You put me in mind of my boy, Daniel. Many Gray Horses, in the Blackfoot language. The Constant Sky of the Crow. Not in looks. In spirit, perhaps."

"— I might get a gun and shoot you in your bed."

"You might. That's a British sovereign, mind," the old man whispered, "worth six Yankee dollars at least. Put it away — don't flash your money — don't let the quackers cheat you. If they offer French *louis* take fifteen at least. As for Spanish dollars, I wouldn't touch 'em."

Peering down through iron grillwork, Fergus watched the raft sweeping underneath the bridge. "I like money."

"It's very useful," Ormsby agreed. "Here give me your arm again, Fergus, I'm not the fellow I was."

They kept walking. The old man was stringy, rocky, tough. The fever hadn't smothered him yet.

A red-haired girl passed, carrying a duck in a basket. He heard Molly's voice

I've wanted to be a wheel

and then her whole shape — sleeping, disordered, sexual — was plangent in his mind.

Late-afternoon sun skipped off the river. Iron roofs stuttering light. In Notre Dame Street a small barefoot girl in a shawl and muddy skirts grabbed at his sleeve. "Come along, *a ghrá*, have a suck, only a shilling," but he put her off and kept walking, the old man saying nothing but leaning heavy on his arm. He saw a horse dealer leading a string of black ponies and a pair of pretty girls swinging sacks of turnips off the back of a cart. Smoke of coffee leaking from somewhere.

The world is hard and real, the world is not private.

DONEGANI'S HOTEL
Wines Baths and Carriages
to
Pleasure Travelers
&
Men of Business

"No good comes of no good, Mr. Ormsby," said Donegani the innkeeper, a thick man in a black jacket, wearing cowhide slippers. His small black eyes studied Fergus. "I don't like the look of this fellow, Mr. Ormsby, to tell you the truth. Town is thick with Irish come up the river. Pack of wolves. It's not the trade I'm used to in my house."

A weak fire of logs sizzled in the grate — Donegani had been working his accounts when they arrived, and a ledger was spread open on the high desk, with a sheaf of bills alongside, a pot of ink, and a steel pen.

Ink's aroma recalling the shack where he'd scratched his mark, before walking up the hill to Muldoon's.

Seeing her outside the shanty boiling wash.

"I told you, man, if you would listen: we are shipmates, traveling together from Liverpool." Ormsby signed the register with a flourish. "He goes out a clerk with our spring brigade. Are you saying a young gentleman in the service of the Hudson's Bay Company ain't custom for your hotel?"

Ormsby was holding himself together but Fergus could see the flush on his cheeks.

You could fight fever for a while but it couldn't be renounced.

"With the Company, you say?" The innkeeper smiled. "Well that's another matter, of course."

Perhaps they didn't see the fever on Ormsby because he was a gentleman.

"Put him in one of those small rooms at the front," Ormsby ordered. "Fix him a bath. Give him a fire if he wants one. Myself as well. And he'll dine with me." Taking a sovereign from his purse, he flipped into the air. The innkeeper snatched it like a frog grabbing a bug.

A man has to lie down and die somewhere, doesn't he.

* * *

A BRASS bed, made up with linen sheets and clean blankets. The servant girl, after opening the window and thumping the pillows on the bed, asking if he wished the stove to be lit.

A shock to find yourself alive in a new country.

Standing at the window, listening to birds clicking on the iron roof, he could see a narrow piece of the river.

"Mister! Will you have a fire, or won't you?"

"No, it's warm enough."

"We had snow on the ground last week. Have you only just come over?"

"I have."

"From where?"

"Liverpool."

"But where in Ireland?"

"Dublin."

"Aughnish, in Fánaid, that was our country. Do you know it?"

"No."

"I come out four years ago with my father and brothers. Taken up farms on the front, they have."

"Is it good land?"

"Good for bears. Did you have a rough cross? They say it's always rough, so early in the season."

"I don't know, I suppose it was."

"Fever aboard?"

"There was, yes."

"They dropped them into the water?"

"Yes."

"Who's the old fellow?"

"I met him on the ship."

"He's money, he is. Are you going for the states?"

"For the fur trade. For Rupert's Land."

"What is it? Do they pay wages?"

"I reckon so. If your people have a farm, why aren't you with them?"

"What business is that of yours?"

"None I suppose."

"I could tell you a dozen different stories," she said, beating the pillows with her fist, "and most of them would be true. I'll tell you this. My father, the old pincer, wasn't the man to leave alone what he could easily take. What he figured was his own. Do you get me?"

"He was jumping you."

"I was nine years old when we come out of Fánaid. Our mother died on the crossing. That was leaving me with three caustic brothers and Father, who is just a big jug-eared dish of a man. They've been hacking, chopping, and sawing for seven years up there on the last range, in the township of Rixborough, country of Megantic. You'd barely call it a farm."

"What would you call it then?"

"Sheer Hell is what I'd say. I quit last spring, soon as the roads were fit to travel, and I won't be going back. I'm for the Boston states. Here, look."

Taking a piece of paper from a pocket of her apron, she unfolded it carefully before handing it to him.

OPERATIVES WANTED

Young persons of Respectable Character

seeking Employment at GOOD WAGES

enquire at the York Manufacturing Co.,

at Factory Island, BIDDEFORD, MAINE, U.S.A.

GIRLS & MEN needed

GOOD WAGES

He read slowly, parsing each word until he had the sense of it, then he handed it back and watched her fold it and tuck it away in her apron like something precious.

"They say you can walk there from here. They say you might meet a bear along the road. Are you sure you don't want your fire lit?"

"No."

As soon as she left, he fell back on the soft, clean bed and lay with hands clasped under his head, staring at the high ceiling, which like everything else in that room was painted white.

How do men speak of women who have betrayed them? Whom they have put aside or left behind? He tried to imagine that language.

That little piece. Dodged her.

She weren't respectful.

Oh I dropped that cunt.

Only a railway wife, man, they count for very little.

The windows facing the river hung on the wall like silver blocks of light.

Pulling off his boots, he dropped them on the floor. He had never lived much in rooms. Up the mountain, a cabin had no *rooms*, nothing private. Nothing solitary, except what was in your head.

His attic room at the Dragon, Bold Street; he'd felt safe there. For a while. Women fussing, and the scents of butter toast, oranges, and honey. Black Betsy, carefully varnishing his nails.

I come across on the sugar ship Angel Clare.

Burnish fading slowly from the windows.

Life honed to the very edge. Sharpened on the whetstone. Chopping through the days. Working time like it was a sweep of hay.

Feeling restless, he arose and went back to stand at the window, peering out at the narrow slice of river. He remembered seeing Farmer Carmichael shoot a bird from the sky, a merganser. Wing shattered, flapping on the surface of a little lake, waves of madness rippling across the calm.

I have eaten too much the world. I am not hungry no more.

HE KNOCKED on the door of the old man's room. When there was no answer, he went inside to find Ormsby lying helpless across the great black bed where he had collapsed without removing his coat or his beaver hat, which had rolled onto the floor.

You could smell fever in the room.

The baggage was in the box room downstairs except a single trunk carried upstairs and left at the foot of the bed, unopened.

"Fergus? Is it you, Fergus?" The old man stirred, licking his lips.

"It is."

The eyelids fluttered. Any light was most painful, to a fever.

"What will you do with yourself?" His voice was papery and thin.

"What do you mean?"

"I mean you're walking like a ghost, *an mhic*."

An mhic, my man, my fellow, my son.

The old man licked his lips again. "You've had the fever yourself?"

"I have."

"Black fever?"

"Still here, aren't I? You'll come through."

"You were young."

There was a jug of water and a cup on the washstand by the window. He filled the cup, carried it to the bed. Sitting on the bed, he raised the old man's head a little. "Here, take a swallow."

Most of it spilling down his chin.

"Old," the old man whispered, "too old, can't go the fight." He gripped Fergus's wrist with surprising strength. "Don't let 'em know downstairs! They'll put me out. Don't want to lie in the sheds."

"All right."

When he pulled off the old man's boots he grumbled and moaned, the delirium of fever starting to bite. Unbuttoning the coat, Fergus found the purse, and his cigar case, and two leather envelopes heavy with money. He unrolled one on the dressing table and studied the rows of glinting gold coins arrayed inside.

He closed it up again. Stripping off Ormsby's, he began sponging him with a damp towel. His skin fluttering with heat. Mumbling nonsense, weakly thrashing.

Quite thin he was.

He dried Ormsby off and was trying to get him in between the clean, rough sheets when he heard a knock on the door and a girl's voice "Shall you be wanting tea, sir?"

He crossed the room to open the door a crack. A servant girl, a different one, stood with a tray.

"Will your master take something for his tea?"

"No, he don't want nothing. He is quite tired from the journey."

"Does he want me turning down the bedclothes and making things nice?"

"No, I'll see to it, he's a tired old fellow. He'd likely sleep through until morning if we let him be."

"I won't be disturbing him. Will you take something yourself?"

"I won't." He closed the door and went back to the bed, looking down at the old man.

Lighting one of Ormsby's cigars from the lamp, he pulled up a chair next to the bed, and sat down to wait.

Everything ends in smoke.

Men are born to get lost, it seems.

"An mhic."

He had been dreaming, and awakened with a start, thinking it was his father, Mícheál, calling him, starting off for the north with a crew of cousins, the barn builders, the wall menders, and summoning Fergus to join him.

"Daniel."

It was the old man gasping his son's name. The noise as small as the last drop of water falling from a cup, in America, in the middle of night. It was quite dark in the room, and he could smell the fur trader's fever breath and the sweet, salty scent of his hair pomade.

"Daniel . . ."

Fergus leaned over the bed. The odor dense and wicked.

"Is it really you, Dan?"

"It is. It's me."

HE SAT up the rest of the night, watching over Ormsby, cooling his brow with wetted cloths. Giving him water when he would take a little.

Opening the trunk at the foot of the bed, he looked to see if there was more money, but there wasn't. Sorting through clothes and linen, blankets and clocks and table silver, he tried on what might be of use, studying reflection in the window glass.

Outlaw. Bog Boy.

One of the houghers, come to open a vein.

Where do they come from, thoughts?

Like wrens, out of the sky.

They arrive.

Noisy, hungry, perfectly themselves.

What about Luke? You don't think of that now.

THE OLD man lasted through the night but his face was quite dark, his tongue thick and stiff. He hadn't much strength, really. There wasn't a lot of flesh on him.

"Hey mister," Fergus said quietly. "I'm going to take your money."

Ormsby was twisting and grunting on the bed and didn't hear, of course.

He stopped breathing as soon as first light showed in the window.

"Give me your hand, so." Fergus picked the dead man's hand up from the sheet, held it. Surprised how heavy it was, how warm. That wouldn't last.

What do you remember now? he thought, looking at the old man. *Everything?*

EARLY MORNING in busy, noisy, narrow streets crowded with horses hauling loads of silver hay, last year's cut, to the hay market.

He wore a clean linen shirt, a fine suit of clothes that fit him pretty well, and his own beaver hat, well brushed. Ormsby's boots sounded crisply on pavement.

He carried a hundred gold sovereigns and another suit of clothes wrapped in the blanket roll slung from his shoulder. In his coat pocket, the purse with more sovereigns, and shillings, pennies, Yankee dollars, and French *louis*.

The weight of solid money kept you in the world; Molly had known this.

Farther along Notre Dame Street, past merchants' coffeehouses, a morning girl stepped out of the blue shadows of an alley. "Come along, sojer, try a bit for a shilling?"

Small white face, tartness of voice. Her feet bare on the cobblestones. "Come, follow me, *ma chroi*."

Perhaps you had to bang life just to know you were among the living.

You needed to work yourself back inside.

He let her take him by the hand and lead him into the alley between a livery stable and a church.

"Now let's see your ready."

He started to unbutton his trousers, but his fingers couldn't locate the unfamiliar buttons.

"Not your jerry!" the girl said. "Your money, sojer! Show your money first."

He fished a shilling out of Ormsby's purse.

"There it is. That's nice. Now give it over."

He handed her the coin.

"You're just over, ain't you, sojer? Where from?"

"Mountain of Cappaghabaun, near of Scariff."

She quickly unbuttoned his trousers, fishing out his prick with her fingers. "There you are, sojer."

Crouching she took him in her mouth. His prick responded, stiffening.

As she worked him, a set of bells began ringing *Angelus* from the church. He heard the shuffling of feet in stalls and smelled the horses in the livery stable. She was licking and rubbing him vigorously with her fist but it was no use, he could feel his prick weakening and shrinking. He pushed her away.

"What's wrong with you?" The girl, annoyed, gathered her shawl, scowling at him.

"Nothing." He began buttoning his trousers.

"I'll keep your shilling, I will. I give you a good blow, sojer."

"Keep it."

"Not my fault your old jerry don't like it."

He shook his head. "Keep it."

"For sixpence, I'll give you another go."

"No."

"Suit yourself." The girl flipped the shilling in the air and caught it. He watched her run back out to the street.

Everything is strangers.

AT THE hay market Canada farmers stood by their carts, wearing tasseled nightcaps, hands in pockets of long woolen coats, pipes jabbed in their mouths. Everything was for sale, the carts and wagons loaded with hay, with firewood, turnips, onions, maple sugar, crocks and bottles of syrup. Cattle, ducks, and chickens. Stone crocks of lard, butter. Barrels of salt pork. Enough food to make you jealous of the world. Sacks of wheat and wheat flour and Indian corn. Sacks of last year's apples.

Fifty-weights of moist black tobacco. Old clothes and furniture. Boots arranged on the pavement as if a company of soldiers were standing in them. A powerful stench of coffee, leaking from somewhere.

The world was composite, various, and got along very well without you. It could sew you up with a couple of stones then drop you into the ocean. It would not remember your name.

THERE WERE horses for sale at the market and at livery stables around the square. Dray horses. Plow horses and pullers. Singles, pairs, teams. A few carriage horses, not many. He liked the little black ones called *Canadiens*, small-ish black cobs with deep chests and shaggy manes.

The manner of buying and selling was no different from what he had observed at the fairs at Scariff. Men trying to get the best of each other, then spitting their palms and slapping hands to seal a bargain.

Something in the loneliness of horses, their garish solitude; something he understood.

Mares and early foals. Saddle mounts, young and old, some quite broken down. Long-legged animals with plenty of snort and clatter, and horses shaggy from winter. Springy little trotters, and cart horses galled from harness, gaunt and dry-skinned, showing too many bones. Ladies' horses and gentlemen's mounts. Nothing so big as an Irish hunter. Horses penned too long on wet ground, with troubled feet. Glossy coats and gorgeous manes, polished bridles. Ponies rough and ragged and cheap as those the gypsies drove out from Chester.

Length of bone was significant when you were trying to judge a horse. Teeth mattered, a horse's life story being in its mouth. The eyes. How they take the halter, walking them out, pacing.

By the end of the morning he had purchased four strong little black animals, *Canadiens,* along with bridles, a leather string line, a couple of sacks of grain to feed, and a saddle.

He asked the liveryman who had sold him his fourth horse, a hardy little black with a cold manner and iron feet, where he might find the road for the states.

"Go out to Windmill Point and take a ferry across the river. If you can walk these beauties to Vermont you'll get a price for them, I suppose," the man said. "They like a black horse down there."

WHILE HE was saddling his best horse, he noticed a boy loitering across the road, watching, with a hungry look.

"Come over here, you."

The boy approached, eyes narrowed.

"Are you willing to work?"

"I am, so."

"I'll pay you a shilling to help me walk these beauties out to Windmill Point."

"Where you taking them, mister?"

"South. What's your name? "

The boy shook his head. Fergus repeated the question in Irish.

"Don't have a name, mister."

"Where are you from, then?"

"I'm out of Ireland."

Fergus looked at him hard.

"I can help you so, mister."

Fergus stepped up, swung a leg over his saddle horse, and looked down at the boy.

"I am very well with the horses." The boy was squinting in the sun.

"Then you may put yourself aboard one, and lead another."

The boy considered the little string. "Does it matter which I ride, mister?"

"Throw a leg over anyone you like."

Taking the lead in his hand, the nameless boy threw himself up lightly on the second-best animal, a clean young mare with a white star on her head. Fergus watched him gather the reins in one hand.

Let him know you're up there.

Don't slump like a plowboy.

They walked the horses through the noisy streets, then out past the fields scattered with huts and shebangs, approaching the point and the wide, breezy river.

In the field beyond the fever sheds, yesterday's trenches had been filled and humped with soil. A pair of workmen were setting new whitewashed crosses every few feet. Knocking them in quickly, using the pans of their spades.

The long ridges of fresh earth looked exactly like the ridges of the lazy-beds where he had planted his potatoes on the slope of Cappaghabaun.

The nameless boy seemed to understand the handling of horses, how calm and steadiness was everything to them, all they wanted of you. He looked a little like Murty Larry, only younger.

Or was it just himself that was older?

A steamer was blaring in, emigrants jammed along her rails. He could hear them screaming with glee.

Joy to the new country.

Her whistle gave a shriek as she bumped the quay.

Concerned that his horses might fluster in the rush, he signaled the boy to stop, then swung down from the saddle. And watched the people spilling onto the quay with their baggage. Hoping to see her figure — small, solitary, quick — in that crowd.

She could have cajoled or bought her way off *Laramie* and out of quarantine. She knew how to get what she wanted.

He did not see her, but the passengers had come off in such an eager panic — all at once, like finches bursting off a bush — that he could not be sure.

He counted a dozen fever cases carried down the iron gangway.

After the last passengers had disembarked, firemen started up the gangway carrying heaves of firewood on their backs in canvas slings, the logs bucked to three-foot lengths, split yellow.

He scanned the faces on the quay, still hoping to see her.

The whistle gave a shout, and at that moment he noticed three bundled corpses, lying on the main deck, by the starboard rail.

Firemen were trudging up and down the iron gangway, boots booming, chanting in their Canadian tongue.

He could just feel the company of his dead.

What to say to them?

Your dead want you to answer for something.

He caught the boy's eye. "Watch over my beauties. Don't let 'em flutter."

Spilling a little feed in front of each animal, he left them munching and crossed the quay. Dodging firemen, he ran up the gangway and stepped onto the wet wooden deck with its litter of orange peels, old blankets, and scraps of newspapers.

Deckhands were coiling lines. The master was nowhere in sight. A pair of mechanics were slushing buckets of grease on the iron machinery that turned the paddle wheel. He could hear wood being slung in the hold below.

The dead were in canvas shrouds sewn up with coarse sailors' thread. He had come aboard to find out if she were among them, but now, standing over them, he had no wish to open any of the shrouds.

Your dead want an answer.

He understood then that he would never lay eyes on her again. She would have nothing more to do with who he was, where he was going, or who he would become. For the rest of his life, whenever he thought of her, he would insist to himself that she was still alive, one among his cohort, an old woman who had kept up with his years and remained in the tribe of the living, but she would have no hand on his destiny. He hardly had a hand on it himself, and just then it seemed to amount to little more than a string of half-broken horses, an instinct to keep moving, and a destination that was hardly more than a phrase to him.

When he stepped back onto the quay he saw the nameless boy had led the horses over to the ferry landing, where they were standing quite easy.

The boy raised his arm, pointing. Looking out, Fergus saw the little steam ferry thrashing its way across from the south shore.

Your dead want an answer and all you have is memory and the road.

"Are you after a good line of work?" he asked the boy.

"What is it, mister?"

"I want a hand, a steady hand, to help me move these beauties. We're going along for the Boston states. Pay of three Yankee dollars per week, grub provided. Are you my man?"

The boy nodded. "I am."

So Fergus spat in his palm, and the nameless boy spat in his, and they slapped their hands to settle the thing.

THE LAW OF
DREAMS

P ETER B EHRENS

A Reader's Guide

A Conversation with Peter Behrens

Andrew Adam Newman, a frequent contributor to *The New York Times* and to National Public Radio's *Studio 360* with Kurt Andersen, speaks with Peter Behrens, author of *The Law of Dreams*.

Andrew Adam Newman: The impetus for *The Law of Dreams* was somewhat personal, right?

Peter Behrens: Yeah, I grew up in a Montreal family with Irish ancestry and always knew that somewhere lurking in the background was the Famine. I don't remember anybody telling me about the Famine, but I always knew about it. I don't remember ever not knowing about it. I imagined Fergus to be my great-great-grandfather of whom I know nothing other than he was an O'Brien—the last name of Fergus—and he came out of County Clare and through Montreal in the 1840s.

When I was a kid I would drive around the city with my grandfather, John Joseph O'Brien, and every once in a while we'd pass the Black Rock, which is the memorial of the Famine graves in Montreal. I don't recall exactly what Granddaddy O'Brien did—he certainly didn't give me a little canned lecture on the Famine and the sufferings of the Irish people. But I think he may have made a sign of the cross—or maybe he just hissed or spat. Somehow I got the message that this was a dark and almost shameful place. A place of quite terrible resonance, which was still kind of radiating its Irish juju 120 years later.

AAN: Can you talk a little about your research for the book?

PB: There's a lot of great historiography that began to appear in the 1980s and 1990s, around the 150th anniversary of the Great Hunger, and that was there for me to dive into. And I went all up and down the Saint Lawrence, where the Famine ships came in. I also went to Ireland a number of times— four fairly serious research trips to Ireland. I'd contacted a number of the writers whose works I'd been reading, who were mostly economists, geographers and historians. A number of them were gracious enough to meet with me and I would interview them and get leads. A lot of the small details that you might think are invented come right out of my notes. The thing about the boy's hair twitching on the ground because there are so many lice in it—that comes from some historical record, from a note I'd made.

AAN: At one point you say someone had "the hunger fur" on his face. I'd never heard of that phenomenon.

PB: Apparently that's one of the symptoms of starvation. You can lose hair on parts of your body and you can start to sprout it on unlikely places like your forehead and cheeks. When I was in Ireland, I also visited the Famine Museum in Strokestown, County Roscommon, which is remarkable. And I spent a lot of time walking.

AAN: Walking?

PB: A couple of trips I dedicated to roaming East Clare. I spent a lot of time just walking the country that I imagined Fergus walked. I was immersing myself, getting to know the ground quite literally—the smells, the quality of its sunlight. On one trip to East Clare I was traveling alone and I had developed a really dire case of the flu. It was November. I actually was pushing the flu to the point where it was almost pneumonia, and I was hiking around boggy country in East Clare, walking up and down these hills and looking at abandoned cabins from the nineteenth century. I was with a raging fever, probably 102 degrees or something and really feeling out of it. But, I also felt that, in a way, my illness gave me more of a sense of the point of view of someone in dire straits in the 1840s. I'm not comparing flu to typhus, but I remember kind of laughing at myself and thinking, "Well, here I am in the midst of a deathly illness, traipsing over the rain-soaked hills of East Clare. I haven't come that far from where this all began."

AAN: When you're doing research that immersive, was the research fleshing out a plot that you had already pretty much worked out?

PB: No, no, no. I never really had a plan for the plot of this book. What I needed the research for was to ground me firmly in a physical and psychological environment, so I was comfortable exploring it with a character. Then it was just sort of a matter of joining him for a journey, knowing the world in fairly close detail, and being patient enough to wait to see what was going to happen next, what Fergus was going to do next. "Okay Fergus, we're walking out of this town of Scariff, and it's cold; where the hell are you going to go now, boy?" And I might be stumped on that for a few weeks or even months. And then suddenly a dray appears and a load of coffins is banging in the back and, okay, let's hop aboard. I went along with Fergus because I had to find out what happened next. I'm not much of a plotter.

AAN: So the research really drove the plot?

PB: I felt the need when writing to develop a close relationship to a tactile, actual world. And also to get some sense of its sort of psychological reality, you know—how the people really see things. Once I was solidly fixed in that world, the passion to relate it on the page sort of came over me, and that's kind of what the book is about. I don't think I've written a very intellectual book. Someone said, "You've written a book about Ireland's smells!" And in some ways I have. The book has a fairly simple plot: It's a journey.

AAN: Does the Famine seem to you like a historical artifact or does it seem like something that's relevant today?

PB: Oh, completely so. When I was trying to figure out the psychological world, I partly went back to the historical research, but I partly drew on what's going on today. I had happened to be in Dublin in 1992 working on quite another story having to do with the contemporary Troubles with a capital "T." I woke up one morning and on the clock radio beside my bed there was a news story that had just broken about this dreadful famine in Ethiopia. Now the story had been happening for a while but you know how these stories break around the world, someone gets a story out with these great pictures and suddenly it's everywhere. Well, it was everywhere in Ireland. Suddenly that afternoon there were kids in the street rattling cans, collecting money for the famine victims. Within the month, the president of Ireland at the time, Mary Robinson, had flown to New York to address the United Nations on the subject of famine.

AAN: I don't recall Americans acting with such immediacy.

PB: Well, it was clear that the Famine—the Great Hunger—was still very much a live wire in the Irish consciousness. And when I began to imagine the psychic world of my lawless children I drew that a lot from what we know happens to kids in places like Africa in this millennium when everything breaks down, either through famine or civil war. When there's no one there to provide any kind of structure or care, lawlessness takes over. The whole notion of the bog boys in the book was inspired by the contemporary accounts I came across. For example, in a monthly police report written by a sergeant in the Royal Irish Constabulatory there was a line, "Lawless children are infest-ing the highways." But I also remember seeing a picture—we've all seen those pictures out of Africa—of eleven-year-old boys toting AK-47s. And you know, that's what happens when everything breaks down.

AAN: Right. Not just that sort of vigilantism, but preadolescents growing up really fast.

PB: Yeah, yeah. So if you want to find psychologically the world of famine that I've sketched in the book, it ain't in Ireland anymore. They've got the lonely, haunted landscape that these people left, but Ireland's a prosperous European country now. The Western Ireland of the 1840s that I wrote about resembles much more Somalia and Eritrea now than it does Ireland now.

AAN: Of course there's a political context for those disasters as there was for Ireland's.

PB: And you know, it's stunning because some people say to me kind of naïvely, "How could the British have allowed this to happen so close to the heartland?" But if you think about it, perhaps Somalia is less remote to us now than Western Ireland was from, say, London in the 1840s. People have asked me, "Did the British cause the Famine?" My short answer is yes. Now, blight—specifically, a fungus—caused the potato crop to fail, but policy and lack of policy turned the failure into demographic disaster for Ireland. Were the responses to disaster inadequate, negligent, even criminally negligent? Yes, I think so.

AAN: Why?

PB: I think a large part of the answer lies in the fact that Ireland in the nineteenth century was a captive nation, governed by a class who did not exactly have the interests of the Irish people nearest and dearest to their hearts.

AAN: But your political take on the Famine isn't really in the book, is it?

PB: I wasn't interested in writing a book about who was to blame for the Famine. I think everything is political and that's as it should be, but my concern was really just to deliver the goods. This is viscerally, sensually, psychologically what the Famine was like. This is what it felt like, to be there. It's not really a book of ideas—the ideas are there, but they're kind of like bones under the surface, moving.

AAN: Writing of course is as much about the choices you don't make as the ones that you do. Can you talk a little bit about the book you did *not* want to write?

PB: The last thing I wanted to do was get all bogus Irishy. For a lot of people who don't know Ireland all that well, the country is swaddled in a kind of mysticism. It's just like with a lot of immigrant groups: We tend to throw the "other" onto where they come from, and it's all the things that we aren't, and the people there are musical and magical and mystical and all that stuff. And I just didn't want to go there. That's not my Ireland. I wanted to be hard and as real as I could and unsentimental.

AAN: Now that you mention it, there's not a fiddle in this book.

PB: Exactly! There's not a fiddle. Nobody step dances. Nobody sits back and tells wild Irish yarns, you know? I think the Irish are a misperceived and misunderstood people—at least in America. The Irish are very hardheaded people.

AAN: "Irish" is also often a sort of prefix for "Catholic." Where's the Catholicism in the book?

PB: The Catholic Church had been repressed in Ireland for most of the seventeenth and eighteenth century. People in Western Ireland kept the Catholic faith but it was laid over a deep pagan tradition and a native Irish tradition. A lot of the physical and psychological shape of puritanical Irish Catholicism was a mid-Victorian development—the institutions, customs, way of thinking. Many of the people in the hills in Munster and Connaught didn't see a priest from one feast day to the next. They'd never had a church—maybe a 'Mass rock' out in a field, but not a church.

AAN: And it's interesting that the sex between men that's happening at Shea's Dragon is sort of distasteful to Fergus but not freighted with all this judgment about whether it's immoral.

PB: There's nothing homophobic about it. He knows the girls are doing what they have to do to survive—he doesn't judge them, but he can't just see himself that way. You'd hand over too much of yourself, as a prostitute; you'd be too vulnerable.

AAN: How did horses come to be so central in the book?

PB: I didn't really realize—until I had some distance from the book and read it through—how equine-obsessed Fergus was. Where did the horses come from? They partly came from some vivid experiences I had observed of horses in Ireland. I know horses pretty well myself because as a young man I worked on cattle ranches. I was a cowboy in an amateurish way and I kind of knew rough horses and rough horsemanship. For Fergus, horses are a way out. Horses are transportation, an escape in some way for him. Also, horses are these independent beings—they don't give a damn, they don't know who you are. It may be your horse, but a horse is not like a dog. You can walk into a stable and the horse doesn't give a damn that you're the owner or somebody else. And Fergus kind of admires that about them, that they're within themselves.

AAN: The book is framed more or less by Fergus being helped onto a horse by someone older at the beginning and, at the end, doing the exact same thing for a younger boy. How early in the process did that closing image occur to you?

PB: Actually, it was fairly late. It seems like that it should have been the architecture of the book from the beginning, but you know, you grope your way through to these things and you try to stay open and finally they suggest themselves.

AAN: This is a narrative that you could presumably pick up right from where you left it. Is that a story that you're interested in?

PB: It seems to be a story that a lot of people are interested in, which I like. It's not the book I'm working on right now. But America in the middle of the nineteenth century is a fascinating world to me. I've had another lifelong historical interest in the Civil War and the western frontier in the Gilded Age. That's later, in the 1870s. But now I'm jumping a few generations and writing about people I imagine as Fergus's descendants during World War II. It's set in northwest Europe and in North America in 1944–45.

AAN: You work a lot as a screenwriter. Is there any interest in a film version of *The Law of Dreams*?

PB: Yes, there has been some interest.

AAN: While there's plenty of action in the book, arguably its real strength is Fergus' private reflection. Could you somehow carry that over to film?

PB: I think I could. I'd like to give it a whirl. Sure, there's a lot of the interior voice you're not going to have access to. On the other hand, some of my favorite films, including almost all the works of my favorite director, Terrence Malick—*The Thin Red Line, Badlands, Days of Heaven*—have these remarkable voiceovers, which are kind of the brain-talk of the characters. And I'm thinking that might be one technique that might be possible. But you also have a camera there to supply all kinds of things that the voice is supplying in the book. I think there's enough going on in this story that, done properly, everything could come through without using any kind of interior voice.

AAN: There was an almost cinematic quality in the book with a few scenes of oil being plied into something. You know, there's Fergus sort of getting anointed with oil by Shea in Liverpool, and there's Molly working oil into the boots in front of the fire, and there's him working the ointment into the horse. Are those moments connected in some way?

PB: Oh, that's interesting, yeah. The salve of life. The sort of sweetness and attention that keeps things from breaking apart. Things can be kind of healed with some sort of attention.

AAN: And always getting rubbed into skin of some sort.

PB: Dry, cracked skin, yeah. I have to say, I hadn't made that connection myself but immediately I see there is a kind of unity of purpose in all that. Some sort of healing is possible if you stop and allow somebody to do it. If it comes from the hand of the other.

AAN: The word "dream" can be used in so many contexts. What's the word's significance for Fergus?

PB: After this horrific event that happens to his family, Fergus is never really sure in the first half of the book whether he's alive or dead. For a long time he's constantly asking himself, "If you were dead, would you feel this?" His testing of himself—his physical sensuality with Luke, and other things, like the plunging in the cold water—is an effort to reassure himself that he is in fact alive. If this is a dream the thing is to keep moving, keep the dream going. And if you are alive, well, you have a responsibility to stay alive, and see what happens. One thing about Fergus, he pays attention. He doesn't know a lot but what he does know he knows down to his bones. He doesn't miss much, that lad.

Questions and Topics for Discussion

1. What do you think the title of the book means?

2. The book is told from Fergus's point of view, except for the prologue, which is told from Farmer Carmichael's. Why do you think the author made that choice?

3. Is Farmer Carmichael a sympathetic character? Does your opinion of him shift depending on the scene you read?

4. Fergus's father, Mícheál (pronounced Mee-haul), tends to be a rolling stone, except when his family's life depends on them moving, in which case he stays put. What is the significance of this, and what does Fergus learn from it?

5. Would you describe Fergus's feelings for Phoebe Carmichael as a "crush" or as something more complicated? What are the symbolic undertones in their repeated ritual of her offering him milk?

6. Why do you think Luke dresses as a boy? Does Fergus think more or less of Luke's powers as a leader after he discovers Luke is female?

7. Fergus has a strong affinity for horses, do you agree? How does he identify with horses? What, if anything, does he learn from them?

8. Different horses appear at meaningful points in the novel—Farmer Carmichael's red horse, the blue horse that Fergus chooses at the railway site (and which kills Muck Muldoon), and the black horses that Fergus buys in Canada at the end. Is it significant that each stage of the book has in it a horse of a different color, so to speak?

9. Molly betrays Fergus in some manner three different times. What are these betrayals, and how does Fergus react to each? Do his reactions make emotional sense to you?

10. Fergus's thoughts are often described in short, one- or two-sentence paragraphs. Is this an effective technique? Does it help shape your impression of the character?

11. The epigraph at the beginning of the book from Thomas McGrath concludes, "May you fare well, compañero; let us journey together joyfully,/ Living on catastrophe, eating pure light." How does this quote capture the book's themes?

12. Fergus often implores himself in the book to keep moving forward. What is the broader significance of his moving forward? What happens to the people in the book who stay put?

13. Fergus would likely be diagnosed with what we now call post-traumatic stress disorder. How would you imagine the events in the book shaping his personality down the line?

14. What impressions of the Famine did you have before reading this novel? How has this book affected those impressions?

15. This novel is based on Peter Behrens's own family history. How and when did your family come to the United States? What do you think the journey was like?

PETER BEHRENS' first novel, *The Law of Dreams*, won Canada's oldest and most prestigious book prize, the Governor General's Literary Award, for fiction. Behrens was a Writing Fellow of the Fine Arts Work Center in Provincetown, Massachusetts, and held a Stegner Fellowship at Stanford University. He is also the author of *Night Driving*, a collection of stories.

Behrens was born in Montreal and lives on the coast of Maine with his wife and son.